THIS DARK WOLF

SOUL BITTEN SHIFTER 1

EVERLY FROST

Flip tables. Flip birds.
Be a wolf.

CHAPTER ONE

*T*he forest is too quiet.

I pause in the act of raising my axe above the splitting block, sensing the shift in the breeze and the sudden silence that has fallen over the clearing beside the cabin.

A shudder threatens to shake me, but I suppress it.

The worst thing I can do is reveal that I've sensed the approach of the three men from within the trees.

Swinging the axe toward the block, I slice neatly through the chunk of firewood resting on top of it. Continuing to act as if nothing's wrong, I leave the blade wedged in the block and throw the cut pieces into the nearby wheelbarrow, each chunk hitting with a soft *thud*. I plant my gloved hands on my hips and take a deep breath to calm myself before I turn back to my task.

My senses expand while I go through the motions of choosing another piece of wood to split.

One of the men is from my pack—his musky scent is as familiar to me as my father's. But the other two men are unknown to me.

New scents.

They reek of ugly intentions.

All three prowl toward me, keeping within the shadows of the forest, their movements stealthy. About a hundred paces away, they spread out from each other, forming an arc, no doubt so it will be easier to catch me if I try to run.

They will assume that I can't sense them, that I will be easy prey, and that I'm not strong enough to fight back.

Unfortunately for me, my father made the rules clear to me from the moment I was old enough to understand them.

I must never reveal the extent of my abilities.

I must act as if I am *not* strong.

I will *never* fight back.

Because if I show my pack how strong I really am... If they ever see me shift into my wolf form... I will become a threat to them. Not just to them, but to every alpha within the Highlands and Lowlands of Oregon.

That's when they'll stop at nothing to kill me.

If I want to stay alive, I'll take whatever crap they throw at me— no matter how many broken bones I suffer or how much they grind my heart into the dirt with their taunts and insults.

I was born different. Unequal. Nobody knows why, but despite having wolf shifter parents, my soul is human, not wolf. That makes me a freak among shifters, a source of scorn, but if they saw my wolf... I'd be dead.

Pretending to take my time positioning another piece of wood on the block, I quickly consider every object around me that I can use to defend myself. Chunks of wood. Axe. Even the wheelbarrow itself. I can make use of the clear ground around the cabin to move around. Running inside is not an option—a door won't keep these men away.

Already, I sense the power radiating from their wolves. Their animals appear in my senses like colors. Around the typical gray that indicates a wolf shifter, each of them blazes gold, which tells me they're all alphas in training. I sense the shape of their human forms—all tall and broad-shouldered with muscular arms and thighs and lean waists.

The two men whose scents I don't recognize must be here for the Conclave. It's an annual meeting when the alphas of the Highland and Lowland packs set aside their differences and gather to discuss matters of mutual importance. Every alpha—past, present, and those in training—is required to attend. It's my pack's turn to host the Conclave this year, which is the only reason my father isn't here right now.

If he were here, these assholes wouldn't dare approach the cabin. Dad might be an outcast now, but he was once the alpha of our Highland pack and has a formidable reputation.

I'm gratified to sense that all three men pause to catch their breath as they climb the last fifty feet to the edge of the clearing around the cabin. The slope sharpens before it plateaus, making it a grueling task to reach my location. I know this, because I've run up it many times.

Dad may have made the rules of my life clear, but that didn't stop him from ensuring I grew up physically fit and strong. Training me like other shifters was out of the question, so instead, he hung a boxing bag in the cabin's back room and taught me every boxing combination he knows. Outside the cabin where other pack members might see me, I split wood, lug water, and run the deserted tracks up and down the mountain. Those same deserted patches of forest are my hunting ground, where I've honed my senses over the years.

The cabin where I live with my father is separated from my pack's main village, which is hidden from humans within the Cascade Range situated east of Portland, Oregon.

The vast Cascade Range is the home of five packs, which we collectively call the Highland packs. The remaining two packs are located in Portland City itself, collectively known as the Lowland packs. There's enough space separating the territories of the Highland packs that we rarely have conflict. The two Lowland packs control territory in the city on opposite sides of the Willamette River. Even with the river separating their territory, they are constantly at each other's throats.

Planting my feet, I allow the axe to fall, splitting another piece of firewood in half, sending a *crack* echoing across the clearing. Leaving the axe in the block, I grip the smaller of the broken pieces in my hand before I turn to the approaching men, feigning surprise at their appearance.

The piece of wood is solid in my hand. I may not be allowed to use my wolf to fight back, but if they threaten me, I won't hesitate to protect myself with all of my human strength and every weapon available to me.

The three men appear at the edge of the clearing simultaneously. They're naked from the waist up, wearing low-slung jeans and boots. Their torsos glisten with sweat in the late afternoon sunlight. Tattoos sprawl across their arms and chests, but the designs are mere outlines—sketches of the full tattoos they'll be given once they become alphas.

The two men standing in the center and to my far right are strangers to me. They smell distinctly similar—brothers, perhaps. I quickly gauge their ages—maybe early twenties like me.

The guy in the middle is the tallest and possibly the oldest. His sandy blond hair is long enough to reach halfway down his neck but is slicked back from his face. His brown eyes are the color of hickory and his gaze rakes up and down my form, narrowing rapidly as he appraises me.

The slightly shorter guy to the far right has darker blond hair and similar brown eyes. His nose is dusted with fine freckles that might look cute except that his lips are turned down in distaste as his gaze drags over me. For a second, a golden blaze breaks through his gray aura, but it's far weaker than the first man's aura. If they're brothers, then he's second-in-line.

The third man—the one standing to my far left—is too well known to me. Dawson Nash is the son of my pack's alpha and one of my constant tormentors. When we were younger, he started in on me with shoves and taunts that quickly became fractured bones and deep bruises as we grew older and he grew stronger.

His brown hair is cut close at the sides, shaved right to his scalp in places that form sweeping lines across the left side, while the top is longer, a wildly scruffy contrast.

We both inherited our mother's startlingly blue eyes.

Every pack has its share of bullies, but I struggle to imagine anyone worse than my half-brother.

My mother abandoned me and my father when I was born and became the new alpha's mate. She has had no part in my life, only tried to see me once, and to my knowledge has never attempted to stop Dawson from hurting me.

Since I turned eighteen and don't have to go to school in the village anymore, I've protected myself from my half-brother by keeping to the mountain slope. The worst Dawson's done to me in the last three years is give me a black eye and bruised ribs.

The look on his face now is dark and wild, his lips pulled back to reveal his teeth.

Damn. He must be here to show the other two shifters how tough he is.

While they take a beat to size me up, Dawson strides straight toward me, calling to the taller blond man at the same time. "Do you see, Cody? She's a freak."

I guess I'm not dressed up enough for them. I'm wearing a navy-checked flannel shirt with the sleeves rolled up. It's untucked and falls past my backside, hiding my curves. My soft leather ankle boots sit below the hem of my jeans. My red hair is piled on top of my head in an untidy bun, a few wisps falling across my shoulders, loosened while I was splitting wood.

Still holding on to the piece of wood, I back quickly toward the splitting block, wrench the axe out of it with my left hand, and circle behind the block. The block isn't big enough to form any real barrier between me and Dawson, but it will disrupt his stride.

"Stay the hell away from me, Dawson," I snarl.

My half-brother laughs as he circles around the block. "Or what, Tessa? You'll tell your daddy I broke the rules?"

He glances back at his friends with a smirk. Dawson is allowed to go wherever he wants within pack territory during the Conclave, but the visiting shifters are supposed to keep to the village. This rule is intended to protect members of the host pack—a rule that my father was relying on to keep me safe tonight.

I heft the axe, holding it securely as I quickly backstep to maintain the distance between us. "Stay back, or I'll slice you open like a piece of firewood," I say.

Dawson misses a step.

It's unusual for me to threaten him. But—*damn it*—if he's here to make a mess of me, then there's a high chance he'll beat me until I'm barely breathing. I promised my father that I wouldn't reveal my strength, but I'm done not fighting back in my human form.

Resuming his prowl toward me, Dawson snarls. "You don't have the strength to challenge me, Tessa. You're weak! A pathetic waste of air."

I pull to a stop beside the wheelbarrow. "Try me, little brother."

His eyes widen. The muscles in his neck cord and his nostrils flare, telling me I've made him truly angry. He made it clear to me when we were younger that he hates the fact that we're related.

His hands dart out. He makes a grab for my head and I picture his intentions a mile off. He plans to knock my head into the pile of wood in the wheelbarrow, kick my knees out from under me, and wrench my hands behind my back before I can scream.

Darting beyond his grasp, I pitch the chunk of wood at his temple, hitting him squarely on his forehead.

He flinches and jerks to the side, gripping his head before he checks the damage.

"Fuck!" His fingers come away coated with blood. "Bitch!"

I don't have time to waste. Snatching up another piece of wood, I aim for his throat, but he dashes to the side and the projectile thuds harmlessly into the ground.

The other two men stride toward me, their animals visible in their sharpening teeth and descending claws, taking on a partial shift. It's hard to predict if they'll fully shift. Only the strongest alphas can maintain a partial shift for more than a minute.

I pitch a piece of wood at each of them, one after the other, as fast as I can. These chunks are heavier than the last, but I'm practiced in chucking wood into the wheelbarrow.

One piece hits the tall blond guy—Cody—in the shoulder. The golden aura around his body suddenly blazes again, much brighter than I was expecting—much stronger than Dawson's aura.

I suppress a new shudder. This guy will be a much more formidable opponent than my half-brother.

The other chunk of wood smacks the younger guy in the ribs. Unlike Cody, his aura weakens with the hit, confirming that his wolf isn't as strong as Cody's.

Both men jolt and curse at me, but they resume their unwavering stride toward me.

Misery rises inside me. I can keep chucking wood at them, but I'm simply delaying the inevitable.

Short of killing them, I can't stop them.

Running away will only trigger their instincts to chase me. They'll shift into their wolf forms, and I can't outrun them as a human.

In the distance, the sun is beginning to set, the horizon flooding with amber light, but it's still another half an hour until the forest will be dark enough that I could hide in it.

I fight my fear and the paralysis that comes with it.

My human side swings between rage and despair.

Do I break the rules I've kept my entire life—or risk death right now?

Raising the axe in front of me, I hold it like a shield as all three men descend on me. "Stay. The hell. Away from me."

To my surprise, Cody pulls to a stop with a growl. His fists are clenched, the muscles in his torso shifting with his indrawn breaths, making the outline of his wolf tattoo ripple across his chest.

His growl is pure animal, the sound an alpha makes when he's establishing dominance. It's directed first at my brother and then at the freckled guy.

"I want her," Cody says.

My heart sinks. For a second, I stupidly thought he was going to back off.

Dawson checks his forehead again, slow and considered, as he studies the blood from the cut I gave him. "If you aren't afraid to draw blood, Cody."

A smile grows on Cody's face. The tip of his right incisor peeks between his lips. "Never."

My half-brother laughs, a low, unsettling sound. "Whatever you want. I won't stand in your way." He arches an eyebrow at the younger guy. "Cameron?"

Cameron shakes his head, grinning. He confirms my theory that he and Cody are brothers when he says, "She's all yours, big brother."

I back away from them. It's unlike Dawson to hand over control of any situation to anyone. If he's willing to let Cody take charge, then Cody must have a lot of power—political or physical.

I've never met any of the other alphas or their intended heirs, but I've heard their names over the years.

Rapidly digging into my memory, I search for any mention of an alpha-in-training named *Cody*.

My blood suddenly runs cold.

Wait... He can't be...

Not *Cody Griffin?*

All packs are supposed to be equal in the hierarchy, but the two Lowland pack alphas are ruthless and feared.

The most ruthless is Tristan Masters, the youngest alpha in our history. He fought and killed his own father a year ago to take his place as alpha of the Western Lowland pack. His territory spans everywhere west of the Willamette River all the way across Portland up to the edge of the Tillamook State Forest. Any wolf who crosses him ends up not only dead, but killed in a way that sends a message to the other packs not to mess with him.

The second most feared alpha is Baxter Griffin. For generations, the Griffin family has ruled the Eastern Lowland territory that stretches east of the river to the base of the Cascades. In contrast to Tristan, he's the oldest alpha and has a large extended family at his back. The Griffins are undefeated, close to gods among shifters.

If Cody is Baxter Griffin's eldest son, then I'm in even more trouble than I thought.

Cody could rip me apart for sport and get away with it.

I continue to backstep away from him, gripping the axe as he prowls toward me. His hickory-brown eyes shift even further, his irises becoming a paler shade of caramel, flecked with gold. The change warns me that his animal is taking over his thoughts and instincts.

A smile grows on his face. He has maintained a partial shift for longer than a minute now, showing his wolf's strength while his physical strength is revealed in the hard muscles extending down his chest, stomach, and thighs.

My senses buzz with the oncoming threat, my feet moving through the grass and leaves, taking me toward the center of the clearing.

I am nothing more than entertainment to Cody Griffin.

My choices now are slim.

If I maim or kill him, his pack will come after me. If I reveal my wolf, *every* pack will come after me.

If I don't fight back, I may as well choose to die.

I flip the axe over so that the back of it will act as a bludgeon, and then I slow my pace, allowing Cody to reach me.

He's already swinging his fist, a blow that will knock me flat and subdue me.

I duck the hit, spin, and aim the iron at the back of his thigh as I stride past.

If I'd landed the blow, it would have knocked him to his knees while breaking his thigh bone, but his reflexes are rapid. He sidesteps and the axe flies wide. Its weight pulls me forward, but I was prepared in case I missed. I spin with the momentum, drop the axe head to the ground, and somersault over it and back to my feet.

I don't have time to check Dawson's response as he watches us, but I sense his confusion. I've never fought like this before, never shown any skill in combat. As far as he's concerned, I've always been an easy target.

I let the axe handle slide through my palm so that I'm gripping the axe head at its base. This way, I can control its weight. I stride toward Cody at the same time.

Using the axe head like a fist, I aim it at Cody's face, allowing the handle to slide smoothly out through my gloved palm. He dodges the hit, and I pull the handle back, flipping it in my hand and swinging it side to side and then forward as he darts left and right and jumps back to avoid the crushing blows aimed at his shoulders, ribs, and stomach.

If I landed the hits, the damage would be catastrophic. The axe head is heavy enough to shatter his bones.

To avoid me, his reflexes have to fire so fast that his expression reveals only his concentration. For a second, I'm satisfied to see that his smirk is long gone, but then his eyes brighten with every attempt I make. I catch a glimpse of his animal in the hungry smile that grows on his face.

He's enjoying this even more than if I'd been easy prey.

I'm now a challenge to be conquered.

I spin to gain speed, letting the axe head slide through my palm as I extend my arm, and this time, he isn't fast enough. The iron smacks his shoulder. He turns in time so that the impact doesn't break his bones, but he roars with pain.

Dawson and Cameron take a step toward us, moving as if they're going to get involved in our fight, but Cody is already retaliating. He throws himself down and forward—a reckless move—to tackle me around my thighs. Lifted off my feet, I raise the axe, preparing to smash it against his exposed spine, but I'm already falling.

He tips me over his back and onto my head.

I don't have time to scream. I manage to turn my shoulder to take the brunt of the fall so I don't break my neck or my wrist.

Get up!

My body takes too long to respond.

Cody's booted foot crashes down onto my axe arm, nearly breaking my bone before I can roll to the side. I whimper when he drops his other knee onto my chest, a knock that makes me wince.

He wrenches the axe from my pinned hand while I thump at his knee with my fist.

"Get off me!" I shout.

My cry strangles short when he leans over me and rests the side of the axe head against my clavicle. It's a casual move, but the handle is turned to the side and the blade is pointed at my throat, positioned a mere inch away.

I keep my axe sharp. It will take a single upward thrust to sever my neck.

Cody leans over me, his chest heaving from the exertion of avoiding my axe, his free hand pressing against my shoulder. His brown eyes are bright, somewhat expectant, as if he thinks I'll find a way out of his hold. As if he's looking forward to it.

A puzzled crease appears in his forehead and his smile fades when I remain frozen beneath him, my chest heaving, panic rising inside me because of the blade resting so close to my throat.

"Tessa Dean." He sounds disappointed. His full lips purse. The light in his eyes fades a little. "Don't stop fighting me."

He leans lower. Slowly. Cautiously. Dropping his cheek to mine, he watches me with every inch he comes closer to touching my face with his, clearly expecting me to fight back at any second. Darting forward the final distance, he nudges the side of my neck with his lips. This close, he smells like a field of grass warmed in the sun, an alluring scent that shouldn't belong to this asshole.

His breath is cool against my skin, a shivery puff of exhaled air.

Then I sense him inhale a deep breath, the air sucking into his chest.

My stomach sinks.

Damn.

I close my eyes, waiting for my unusual scent to register in his senses.

Cody's teeth suddenly sharpen against the skin beneath my right ear. His hand clenches around my shoulder and his claws rake against my skin so sharply that I fight against the scream rising inside me.

"Your scent is..." His growl vibrates through my neck before he draws back, his eyes blazing into mine, his irises becoming even more animalistic.

"Fuck," he whispers.

If I could count the number of times I've heard a shifter tell me that my scent is messed-up...

I smell like a wolf, but not like a wolf.

I have the scent of a human, but not like a human.

My father once explained to me that all shifters will find my scent unsettling and unnerving. It will make them avoid and shun me. But he also warned me that the strongest alphas will be able to distinguish the layers of my scent—the high and low notes. Only the most powerful alphas will be able to detect my true scent.

He told me I didn't have to worry about that, though, because neither my half-brother, Dawson, nor our alpha, Peter Nash, are strong enough to detect my true scent.

But Cody... His reaction tells me I'm in trouble.

He presses the axe head so hard against my clavicle that I'm afraid my bones might snap.

"Tessa Dean." His growl is rough, wild, and reckless. "I can't decide if I want to fuck you or kill you."

He darts forward and brushes his lips across my neck and jaw all the way to my mouth, where I gasp for breath. His chest expands as he inhales even more deeply, drawing my scent in through his lips.

His eyes meet mine and his pupils dilate so fully that his eyes appear completely black in the fading light. A shudder runs through his chest, fierce enough to make me tremble.

Rising up, he pitches the axe into the ground far from my reach.

As he moves, his weight lifts, and I see my chance to get free now that he's abandoned the axe.

Shoving at his knee, I punch his thigh, followed by his shoulder, and aim a third rapid hit at his face, a boxing combination that I've practiced a thousand times—just not lying down. He jolts back and I make it halfway up before he shoves me against the ground again, putting his whole body weight behind his fists as they knock into my shoulders and his knee drops onto my chest again.

My head hits the ground, my chest squeezes, and my vision blurs as I gasp for breath.

His growl washes over me while I try to focus. "Don't fight me now, Tessa," he says. "Or I will hurt you."

His claws catch my hair and rake across my left shoulder, ripping through my shirt from my collar to halfway down my sleeve.

His knee slides to the other side of me, releasing my chest. I inhale as deeply as I can. Now that he's straddling me, I try again to fight my way free with my human strength, but a different power rises inside me.

The pain aching across the back of my head and the sharp sting of the cuts on my shoulder are like a flame to a very short fuse inside me—a fuse that leads to my wolf.

I've heard shifters describe their wolves as energy inside themselves—a separate being with its own needs and wants. Its own personality. A creature that obeys pack law, that can bond with a true mate, and form connections with other wolves.

My wolf has none of that.

She has no soul. Obeys no laws. Has no mind of her own. She will never bond with a true mate.

Nobody had to tell me this. I've known it all my life, deep in my soul, as surely as knowing that my eyes are blue and my hair is the color of blood.

My wolf is pure energy.

Before now, I've pushed her away when I was threatened, smothered her with all my might to make sure she stays hidden. Only my father has seen her—seen *me*—when I shift.

But if I don't use her energy now, I won't escape Cody. I'm done with hiding her. Not when she's strong enough to kill these assholes—even Cody—before he lays another finger on me.

I scream for the first time since the men arrived. Letting out my rage, my cry shrieks around the clearing, growing more fierce as I exhale the sound. My cry tugs at the air, becoming a high-pitched howl.

My vision turns electric blue as my wolf's energy rises to the surface inside me, giving me strength without shifting. The clearing, Cody's silhouette above me, and the trees in the distance—everything becomes brilliant sapphire. The clearing around me is suddenly lit in my vision like it's made of cobalt fire.

My wolf's energy changes my view of the world into heat and power signatures. Dawson and Cameron are pale, insignificant forces compared to the powerful life flowing through the distant trees—their ancient trunks and branches surviving centuries. Cody is bright and strong in my vision. Except that his power signature is made up of confusing swirls of cobalt and crimson, forces at war with each other.

I don't have time to consider the meaning of what I'm seeing.

I need to fight him and escape.

Both Dawson and Cameron flinch as I continue to howl. They drop to the ground, clutching their ears, but my scream only makes Cody more frenzied, only makes the light of his silhouette grow stronger and sharper.

His pupils remain dilated. He continues to focus on my left shoulder and my exposed skin. His jaw shifts and his teeth sharpen to points. My eyes widen with shock when he grips my face with one hand and my shoulder with the other, a possessive move I've seen dominant wolves make with their mates.

He leans across my neck as if he's going to nip me.

Holy damn.

He's not trying to kill me or tear me apart.

He's trying to mark me as his.

I shove Cody hard against his chest, my wolf's strength flooding through me.

Nobody will ever own me.

The strength behind my push finally knocks him off me—so fast that he gains air. He lands with a heavy thud, blinking and shaking his head. He's only down for a second before he leaps upright and charges back toward me.

I roll to my feet, growls growing in my throat, the sensation of energy filling my palms and chest. I retain my human form by choice right now, but my wolf's power flows strong inside me.

Blood drips down my shoulder from the claw wounds he gave me, but the pain is a distant ache now that my wolf's energy has taken over. My hair has come completely loose, falling all of the way to my waist, static making the strands cling to my shape.

Cody launches himself at me.

His right fist knocks into my shoulder, his left swinging toward my face, trying to force me down again, but I twist and absorb each blow.

I retaliate with a punch to his face that sends him sprawling on the grass. I could run, but I have to end this, knock each of the men out so I have a head start and a chance to get away. Already, I'm plotting my course down the other side of the mountain away from the main village.

My boot connects with Cody's side—a hard kick against his ribs as he tries to roll away—before I stomp again, this time at his face.

My foot cracks across his cheek.

"You want to mark me, asshole?" I scream. "Take this and be damned."

Right as I stomp my boot again, preparing to break Cody's jaw, rough hands rip me away from him. I inhale Dawson's musky scent a second before his fist knocks into the side of my face, but my wolf's strength is like armor, preventing concussion.

I spin, drop, and sweep his feet out from under him.

Cameron throws himself at me from the other side, but my hand darts up, wrapping around his neck and squeezing as I use my upward momentum to hurl him backward, flinging him across the clearing. He hits the splitting block and slumps to the ground, unconscious.

I turn back to Dawson just in time to discover he's picked up my axe. I dodge the downward cut he aims at my chest and dart to the side. Shoving both of my hands against his ribs, I knock him to the ground.

Kicking the axe out of his reach as he tries to catch his breath, I drop onto his chest, wrench off my gloves, and wrap my hands around his throat, squeezing tightly. He struggles to free himself, thrashing beneath me and thumping his fists against my sides and chest.

I take the blows without wincing.

I will be bruised. Badly. I'm not immune to damage right now. But my wolf's energy protects me from the pain temporarily.

"How about I break *your* bones, little brother?" I ask, memories of the thousand times he's hurt me rushing through my mind.

Dawson's blue eyes grow wide. He struggles harder. His friends can't help him now. Cameron is unconscious and Cody groans in the dirt a few paces away, clutching his bleeding face. If my scent was controlling his actions before, I'm sure his current pain has driven all thoughts of marking me from his mind.

Dawson's fingernails extend into claws that rake at my clothing, shredding the side of my shirt as he tries to free himself from my grip around his neck. His vocal chords vibrate beneath my hands when he tries to shout, but I squeeze harder, cutting off his sound.

Strength flows through my arms, my vision flickering sapphire again as my wolf's energy courses through me in a new burst. Battle rage is hot inside me, volcanic enough that I don't think about what I'm doing.

"Tessa!" My father's shout breaks through my rage. "No!"

My head shoots up.

I didn't sense his approach—or the approach of the alphas.

My heart sinks as five men and a woman race from the forest into the clearing, followed by their betas. They pull up sharply at the edge of the forest. Every one of them is taller than the average shifter. The men are chiseled, their bare chests tattooed. The woman is dressed in a black leather bodice and tight ebony pants, her blond ponytail drawn high and tight.

The power pouring off them floods my heightened senses, washing across my vision. Despite their strength, none of them matches the cobalt flame of Cody's form that remains bright even while he groans on the grass several paces away.

His focus remains on me despite the pain he must be in. A determined intensity fills his expression. His gaze unsettles me, but I can't worry about him right now.

I have bigger problems.

I've never met any of the seven alphas other than Dawson's

father, Peter Nash, but there's no doubt in my mind I'm looking at them now.

Except... where is the seventh?

The absent alpha isn't my largest concern.

The other alphas won't miss the fact that three alphas-in-training lie wounded or unconscious around the clearing. It's not as if I can hide the fact that I'm squeezing my half-brother's throat, or that I must be responsible for defeating all three of them—despite the fact that I'm supposed to be weak.

My father's fear punches me like a fist as his gaze darts from me to the alphas. "Tessa!"

Dad launches into a sprint toward me, but Dawson's father is faster. Peter Nash races across from the side, cutting Dad off with a punch to his face, forcing my father to veer off course.

My father is strong, as big as any other alpha. His dark brown hair is shaved close to his head—the best haircut I could give him with clippers. The tattoo of his wolf looks outward from his shoulder and chest, one half of its face realistic, while the other half blazes with flames.

Forced aside by his alpha, my father retreats to the side of the clearing, the color bleaching from his cheeks.

He has no power here. He lost everything the day after I was born when Peter Nash accused him of weakness for not killing me at birth. On that day, Peter Nash fought and defeated my father, forcing Dad to retreat to the mountain with me. My mother chose to reject both of us and become Peter's mate.

My father has spent every day since then trying to protect me from this moment.

Now, if he wants to stay alive, he must remain completely silent and not interfere.

"Nobody goes near that bitch!" Peter Nash roars, pointing at me. His brown hair is cut short, but not by necessity. Apparently, he prefers it that way. His neck and chest are thick, the muscles across his shoulders bulging. His biceps and thighs are just as solid. He always reminded me more of a bulldog than a wolf. The tattoo across his left shoulder depicts the skull of a wolf's snarling head, a promise of death to anyone who dares to challenge him. He has worked hard to try to build a reputation as ruthless as Tristan Masters and Baxter Griffin.

Compared to him, I'm like a blade of grass trying to stand in a storm.

He could cave in my skull with a single hit.

I jump to my feet, releasing Dawson, who rolls to the side with a groan. His voice is raspy, his vocal chords damaged, but he manages to laugh, a scratchy sound as he wobbles to his feet. "You're maggot food now, Tessa."

Two of the betas break off from the edge of the clearing, running to Cameron and Cody and dragging them away. Cody struggles against them, his gaze darting from Peter Nash to me. Whatever concussion I gave Cody, it appears to be clearing.

At the same time, Peter Nash hooks a finger at Dawson, sharply indicating that his son should get the hell away from me. My half-brother doesn't hang around, racing after Cody and Cameron to the edge of the clearing.

One of the alphas strides away from the others when the betas drop Cody to the grass. This alpha has the same sandy blond hair as Cody and Cameron, but he's weathered, older. I can only assume he's Cody's father—the notorious Baxter Griffin.

Baxter grabs Cody's shoulders and shakes him roughly before he points at me. My sensitive hearing picks up the derision in his speech. "That freak bitch beat you? You're a fucking disappointment."

He backhands Cody with a strike hard enough to knock his son face-first into the grass. Cody's fists clench and his shoulders tense, but he doesn't retaliate as he rises to his feet, blood dripping from his nose.

Closer to me, Peter Nash demands my attention as the sun finally slips beneath the horizon and darkness begins to fall.

"It's just you and me now, bitch," Peter growls, his thick lips curving into a smile. "I've been waiting for an excuse to kill you."

He and I are left in the middle of the clearing, and now I have a choice to make. Up till this point in the fight, I've only released my wolf's energy to the extent necessary to make myself stronger in my human form.

But Peter's going to kill me anyway.

I'm a dead woman.

I can count what remains of my life in minutes.

I seek my father across the distance. He gives me an urgent shake of his head, but I won't obey him this time.

I'd rather die with my wolf at my side.

With a deep exhale, I release her energy.

Her shape materializes in the dark, a sapphire silhouette that stands beside me—the side of her chest connected to my thigh, as if she's nudging up against me. Her energy pulses like flames around my body, turning the air electric blue, an eerie sight. Her fur appears as pulsing ribbons of light and her eyes are bright, keen, but full of all the power and violence that I need right now.

If I shift fully, I will merge with her shape. I will become a wolf like any other shifter except that my fur will flicker and glow with the same cobalt light that surrounds her silhouette right now.

This is my version of a partial shift. My wolf standing at my side.

The alphas at the edge of the clearing startle, their heads jerking back. Peter Nash takes a quick step away from me, his eyes widening.

"What the fuck?" He recovers quickly, his head lowering, stepping toward me again. "I should have killed you the day I became alpha."

My wolf's energy surges inside me and a reckless smile grows on my face. My shirt hangs off me in tatters, barely concealing my torn bra. Blood drips down my arm. I'm a mess of cuts and blossoming bruises, but I narrow my eyes at Peter Nash, determined to challenge him.

Instead of backing away from him like he expects, I step forward with a snarl. "You call yourself my alpha, but you're nothing to me. Take your best shot, asshole."

Another shock ripples through the watching alphas. I sense their hushed inhales and startled glances. Several of the men lean forward, anticipation growing on their faces, while the woman leans back, her arms folded across her chest. Baxter Griffin watches with keen eyes, his lips pressed together.

Ignoring the watching shifters, I break into a quick stride, closing the distance between Dawson's father and me.

His eyes darken with deadly intent.

I clench my fist, thrumming with my wolf's energy, preparing to take a swipe at him, even if it's the last thing I do.

Oomph! A heavy weight hits me from the side.

I register a large, furred body before the air is knocked from my chest and my feet leave the ground. I barely have time to be shocked—not only from the hit, but from the fact that I somehow missed the approach of this larger-than-average wolf.

Air rushes around me before I hit the ground and roll in a dizzying spin, caught up in his arms, legs, claws, furred limbs—I can't even tell which—as we roll through the grass.

My attacker shifts so fast from man to wolf and back again that I barely catch his animal's scent before I thud onto my back, dazed, my head spinning, the impact jarring through me.

I'm frighteningly stunned and unable to move. His heavy body —in human form now—presses down onto mine so completely that I can't breathe.

Naked—*very* naked—skin presses against my breasts and stomach, heating me where my shirt is torn. As my senses return to me, I try to see who attacked me, but I can't even see his face because he has already bent his head to my ear.

His growl makes me shiver. "Stay the fuck down."

The wild hair falling across his face brushes my cheek, a soft tickle compared to the sharp graze of his stubble across the corner of my lips as he lifts off me.

Released from beneath his weight, my chest expands, and I can finally inhale.

Power.

Pure, devastating, arch-my-back-and-scream *power* pours off this man, making me flush hot from my face all the way down to my toes.

My wolf's vision explodes with cobalt fire before it extinguishes like a burnt fuse and her energy recedes fully. Her silhouette disappears, leaving me completely vulnerable in my human form again.

As my attacker rears up over me, I finally catch a glimpse of him. He can't be older than mid-twenties. Strands of raven black hair fall across his crisp green eyes. They're bright in the emerging moonlight and so darkly rimmed that the contrast is startling. His chin is shadowed with growth that accentuates his strong jaw. As he rises up to his full height, his muscled silhouette reveals that he's tall, leaner than Peter Nash, but bulkier than Dawson or Cody, every muscle in perfect harmony with his movements.

A tattoo of a snarling wolf's head stretches across his left shoulder and chest. The image of a snake slides through the wolf's eye sockets, its body curling down his side and back up again like a noose. The snake's open mouth rises up beside the wolf's head, both creatures baring fangs and teeth. It's a startling image. Like the snake is killing the wolf—an enemy—but also fighting beside it like a protector.

He's also completely naked and doesn't appear to give a fuck about it.

Ignoring his warning to stay down, I rise cautiously to my feet, meeting the fierce gaze of the most beautiful man I've ever seen.

CHAPTER TWO

$\mathcal{H}$e appraises me as I stand, his rapidly narrowing gaze giving me goosebumps that make me icy and hot in rapid flashes.

He told me to stay down, but I'm not his to command.

I lift my chin, defiant, my hair swishing around my hips. I prepare for him to retaliate like any other alpha would—to show me my place with his fists.

I'm surprised when he remains where he is despite the tightness around his eyes and the twitching muscle in his jaw. I don't know who this man is, or what his intentions are, but the power I sense in him tells me he has to be the missing seventh alpha.

His perfectly sculpted chest glistens with sweat, a sheen that indicates he ran up the mountain, taking the slope much faster than the others.

I guess he was late to the party.

Peter Nash remains several paces away, poised where he must have dug in his heels.

His focus is now on the newcomer.

"Tristan Masters." Peter growls. "You finally decided to show up."

Tristan Masters.

I shiver. I can't stop myself from taking an involuntary step back. At the side of the clearing, my father has left his position and moved closer, but not so close that Peter Nash will retaliate. Even without the fearful tension in my father's posture, I know that my situation just became a thousand times more dangerous.

Facing Peter Nash is one thing. Taking on Tristan Masters, the most ruthless of all alphas, is definitely another. If he killed his own father, he won't hesitate to end me.

For some reason, he chose to barrel into me at full speed when I was about to take a swipe at Peter—a wolf I have no respect for and will never obey. Tristan either intended to stop me from doing something stupid—or *he* wants to be the one to destroy me.

Either way, as far as I'm concerned, every alpha in this clearing is my enemy.

Tristan casts a sideways glance at me. My body heats when his assessment lingers on the rips in my shirt, but I refuse to cross my arms to cover myself. It's hard to tell how much I'm flashing everyone right now, but I know I'm bleeding where Dawson's claws caught my skin across my stomach and ribs, along with the cuts across my shoulder from Cody's attempt to mark me.

Tristan swings back to Peter.

Tristan's mouth shapes into a grin that makes my blood run cold. His eyes crinkle at the corners and his incisors peek through his lips. "The welcome party you sent me is lying in a ditch, Peter. I left a few of them alive to crawl home. I hope they weren't your strongest wolves."

My eyes widen as the meaning of Tristan's statement sinks in. Peter must have sent men to kill Tristan on his way here. That seems like a particularly dangerous and reckless thing to do at the time of a Conclave. It would explain why Tristan's late.

Peter's jaw clenches, his eyes narrowing. He takes a heavy step forward, but his voice lowers. "Your days are numbered, Tristan."

Tristan's grin doesn't fade. He taps a suddenly clawed fingernail against his muscular thigh. "All our days are numbered, Peter. Yours more than mine, old man."

Peter hisses through his teeth when Tristan steps into position between him and me. Tristan's stance makes me frown with confusion. In my experience, alphas don't protect. With the exception of my father, alphas possess, intimidate, control, and threaten. What Tristan might intend turns my stomach into knots.

"You will get out of my way," Peter says. "This is a pack matter. It is not your concern."

Tristan inclines his head toward Cody and Cameron where they've retreated to the edge of the forest. "You have trespassers, Peter. Conclave law has been broken. This is a matter for the Conclave to decide."

Before Peter can snarl a response, a man strides from the shadows at the corner of the cabin behind us. He's surprisingly quiet and unobtrusive as he hands Tristan a pair of jeans. Despite his calm demeanor, Peter Nash takes a step away from both of them, as if the newcomer's appearance tips the balance entirely in Tristan's favor.

The newcomer stands as tall as Tristan, just as broad in the shoulders and messily unshaven, but his hair is honey blond, his eyes a deep green like pine leaves. He also wears a tattoo of a wolf across his left shoulder, this one crushing a crimson rose between its teeth, petals dripping like blood down his side.

"Tristan," he says, his voice a low growl as Tristan leans toward him. "Watch your back."

Tristan gives him a brief nod. "Jace, check the perimeter."

"I already did. It's clear," Jace murmurs before he takes up position a few paces behind and to Tristan's right. He has to be Tristan's beta. He must have arrived when Tristan did—and the direction he came from indicates that they ran up the other side of the mountain, the side I was planning to run down once I escaped from Cody and Dawson.

Tristan pulls on his jeans before he raises his voice, speaking to the other alphas. "I am the alpha of the Western Lowlands. I call a Conclave vote on Tessa Dean's fate."

My confusion increases at the fact that Tristan knows my name. My only explanation is that my reputation as a freak extends beyond my pack.

I force myself to remain standing where I am, even though my instincts scream at me to run. I wouldn't get far. I'm now standing within striking distance of two of the most dangerous alphas in the Highland and Lowland—Tristan Masters and Peter Nash—and the third, Baxter Griffin, is already striding toward us.

The friction between the three men makes me shiver. They clearly hate each other.

There's a sudden flurry of movement among the remaining shifters standing at the edge of the clearing. Each alpha pairs off with their beta, widening the space between their small groups as they aggressively walk toward us, their gleaming eyes narrowed as they glare at me.

They take up position in a row on either side of Peter until they stand in a semi-circle with their betas behind them, all facing me while Tristan remains between them and me.

Baxter Griffin's gaze drives daggers into me. He isn't as much of a bulldog as Peter is, but he's certainly not lean. His hair is a darker blond than his son's and peppered with silver. Shifters don't age as quickly as humans, but even so, Baxter's body has taken some knocks. A number of short scars mark his upper arms, mimicking the slash of a clawed hand. He's clearly seen battle—and survived every challenge.

Baxter steps up to Tristan, getting in his face. "That bitch dared to challenge my boys. I vote for death."

I fight the snarl rising in my throat. If I should die for defending myself, then Baxter Griffin should die for pushing his son around.

Peter Nash nods his head in agreement, a gleam in his eyes. "She's an abomination. Her wolf is abnormal. We all saw it. I also vote for death."

At the edge of the clearing, my half-brother waggles his finger at me and mouths, "*Maggot food.*" He may be keeping his statement quiet, but I'm sure I damaged his vocal chords. He won't be able to speak for at least a week. Near to him, Cody remains at the edge of the clearing, leaning up against one of the trees, his focus still intently on me.

I spin back to the alphas, unable to contain my snarls. "You can vote all you want, but one of you has to have the strength to kill me. I won't go down without taking you with me. I promise you that."

The female alpha steps forward, her head held high, her straight, blond ponytail falling across her shoulder in a glossy line. "She's got balls, I'll give her that. But let's be honest about why we're voting to kill her." She casts a cold gaze at the men. "If she knocked down three alphas-in-training, that makes her a threat."

"She's a freak." Peter Nash spits, glaring at me. "I've known it from the moment I caught her scent when she was a baby. Now I've seen her wolf. I should have ended her years ago."

The female alpha shrugs. "Freak. Threat. Whatever you want to call her, Peter. It doesn't change the truth." She considers me with a cold smile. "I also vote for death."

One by one, the alphas speak up, their hard gazes passing across me with varying expressions of disgust, disinterest, and challenge as they announce my fate.

As they vote for me to die, my rage simmers hotter inside me. I've spent my whole life dreading this moment, wondering how many days I have left and how death might come to me. Now it's here and my biggest regret is that my father gave up so much to keep me alive for the last twenty-three years.

I seek him across the distance. He remains at the edge of the clearing. Even though this is his home, he has no more power over this space than I do right now.

He lifts his chin and for a moment, I see again the alpha he must have been before Peter tore him apart. While I picture Peter as something of a bulldog, my father has always been pure wolf. He stands nearly a head taller than any other shifter. The clothing he's wearing right now—flannel shirt and jeans—hides strength that he rarely reveals, certainly never to hurt me. I don't know what my pack was like under his rule, but I like to think it was a damn sight happier than it is now.

He pauses at the edge of the forest, and I can sense the determination thrumming through him. If the alphas vote to kill me, my father is going to do something very stupid to try to save me.

I give him a small shake of my head, silently begging him not to act. It will only lead to his death along with mine.

Finally, Tristan is the only alpha who hasn't voted.

I turn back to the group to find myself the center of Tristan's attention, his disconcerting green eyes fixated on me.

He doesn't seem in any hurry to make a decision, pacing toward me as I stand my ground. His beta—the shifter called Jace who brought Tristan his clothing—is a quiet shadow behind him. They both emanate power, Jace nearly as much as Tristan, which surprises me. Normally, alphas choose betas who are strong but could never challenge them or their chosen alpha-in-training.

Tristan stops so close to me that I struggle not to react to his presence. The power radiating from him is like a golden blaze in my vision. My wolf's energy rattles inside me again, suddenly tugging outward, as if she's going to force me into a full shift. She's never acted without me before and it startles me enough that I lose my emotionless mask, struggling to maintain my indifference in the face of my death.

Tristan leans close, his breathing calm and even. "Stay still," he orders me. "I need to know for sure…"

I frown, even more confused. *Know what?*

His lips part. He darts forward, his mouth nudging my neck, bristles like sandpaper making me gasp and shiver as he inhales deeply.

He freezes, every tense muscle in his chest and arms filling me with dread.

He slowly draws back from me so that I can see his face.

His pupils are dilated just like Cody's.

I brace for Tristan's violent reaction—a fist to my face, his claws and teeth sinking into me—but he remains where he is, a single pace away from me. Other than the brief brush of his lips on my neck, he doesn't touch me.

He blinks—just once—and his eyes clear.

His gaze flicks beyond me. Surprisingly, to my father. It's such a quick appraisal before he returns his attention to me that I'm sure I imagined it.

Tristan returns my cool gaze with a hooded expression, so closed off now that I can't read his intentions. My wolf's energy rises inside me, but my rage is dulled, confused. I'm used to being able to read shifters, my wolf's energy allowing me to sense their emotions. Tristan's thoughts are completely contained, as deliberately controlled as his movements as he turns his back on me and takes up position between me and the other alphas again.

"I want her," he says.

The alphas glance at each other, brows furrowed, heads drawn back, many of them startled.

I give myself a shake. I can't have heard Tristan right.

Peter Nash steps forward with Baxter Griffin close behind him. "You can't have her," Peter snaps. "She dies tonight."

"Only by unanimous vote," Tristan says smoothly. "You voted to kill her—that means you wish to cast her out of your pack. Since you've cast her out, another pack can claim her. I'm staking my claim. I want her in my pack."

Peter sucks in a sharp breath, his nostrils flaring, his teeth gritted. His voice lowers to a dangerous growl. "Are you playing me, Tristan?"

I can't see Tristan's face since his back is to me, but Jace has frozen at the side of the clearing, wide-eyed and even more alert as he studies his alpha. Jace's face suddenly pales, his shoulders tensing. He's poised, on edge as his focus flicks from Tristan to me.

Tristan's answer to Peter is a shrug, but his voice fills with derision. "I thought an alpha as cunning as yourself would see it coming."

Peter spits into the grass. "I may have cast her out, but if you want to claim her, you have to win her from me."

Tristan nods, a slow, deliberate movement. "Then let's fight."

His challenge is like a trigger. The other alphas jolt away from the two men, hurrying to get clear. Baxter Griffin is the slowest to move, snarling at Tristan, but even he picks up his pace, taking himself a safe distance away.

At the same time, Jace advances on me at speed, reaching out as if he's going to haul me out of here. I suddenly feel like the rose trapped within his tattooed wolf's teeth.

"Don't touch me!" I snap, backing away rapidly while he chases after me.

"You don't want to be anywhere near Tristan right now," Jace says, not giving up, his arms outstretched as if he'll herd me like an animal if he has to.

He compels me to move all of the way back to the cabin's porch, driving me up the stairs before pointing to the old wicker chair near the door. "Sit."

Any other shifter would obey an order spoken so forcefully. Jace may be a beta, but he's as commanding as an alpha. But I've never felt compelled to follow pack hierarchy. Without a wolf's soul, I don't have the instincts that force me to recognize the rules that govern other wolves.

I remain standing. "Don't think for a second that you can tell me what to do," I say. "I don't follow pack law."

Jace's gaze rakes over me. "Clearly."

He places himself at the top of the stairs, half-turned so he can keep me in his sights while blocking the way down.

Out in the clearing, the motion-triggered lights on the cabin roof finally flood the space from the front steps to the far edge of the forest.

Tristan removes the jeans he just put on while Peter also strips off his clothing, preparing in case they decide to shift. I shudder at the difference between them. Peter's chest, thighs, and biceps are solid muscle—thick and brutish—while Tristan is leaner but no less muscular. Peter will rely on brute strength and the crushing power of his fists while Tristan... well, I have no idea how Tristan plans to fight.

The fact that he wants to risk anything for me baffles me.

"Why is Tristan doing this?" I ask Jace, my voice quieter now. As Tristan's beta, he must have some idea.

"Fuck knows," Jace murmurs, exhaling heavily as he peers at me across the distance, dark green eyes narrowed as if he's trying to figure me out before he turns back to watch the two alphas. "But whatever power your scent has over him, I don't plan on succumbing to it."

I grin and take a challenging step toward him. "You'd better not get too close to me then."

Despite my bravado, I'm rapidly trying to process what's happening around me and why. My father said that only the strongest alphas would sense my true scent. The golden aura around Jace is not as strong as the blaze around Tristan, but it's close to the strength of Cody's aura, which means my move toward him could be incredibly stupid.

I'm impressed when Jace stands his ground despite the threat of my nearness. He returns his attention to Tristan instead of reacting to my taunt. He doesn't seem as worried about his alpha as I thought he might be—in fact, he seemed more anxious about getting me out of Tristan's way than anything else. It occurs to me that Jace told me to stand clear of *Tristan* before, but he made no mention of Peter.

Out in the clearing, Tristan faces Peter, the two men circling each other as the friction increases. The other alphas lean forward in anticipation, waiting for the first move.

Peter strides forward, taking a hefty swing at Tristan's head.

I gasp at Tristan's instant response.

Tristan shifts from man to wolf so fast that I nearly miss it when I blink. He leaps at Peter and claws Peter's neck as he flies past. Then he shifts back to his human form so fast that he spins and kicks Peter's knees out from under him before Peter can even flinch.

Blood pours down Peter's chest as the older man drops to the ground. Tristan shifts again into a wolf, a dark blur as he leaps onto Peter's back, knocking the older man forward over his knees, face-first into the grass.

I drag in a shocked breath, my eyes widening. Tristan's teeth flash, his wolf's jaws close around the back of Peter's neck, and for a second, I experience a painful sort of hope.

Is Peter dead? Is the alpha who beat my father finally defeated? Did Tristan kill him? Just like that?

Before I can blink again, Tristan shifts back to his human form, reappearing with his hand wrapped around the back of Peter's neck, his knee pressing against Peter's spine. I can't tear my eyes away from Tristan, the way his muscles ripple, every part of his body moving in harmony, strong and completely in control.

I haven't been exposed to my own kind as much as I would have if I'd grown up in the village, but I never imagined any shifter being able to shift so fast back and forth between their wolf and human forms. Shifting quickly into wolf form, sure, but back and forth like that? If I hadn't seen it, I wouldn't have believed it.

Peter twitches, his arms flung out, lying nearly prone on the grass. The way he struggles tells me he's alive and well. Tristan must have missed the vital parts of Peter's neck when he cut him. The only question in my mind is whether Tristan deliberately allowed Peter to live.

Tristan's forceful declaration carries across the distance, making me shiver. *"Tessa Dean is mine."*

CHAPTER THREE

*P*eter's shout is muffled but filled with murderous rage. "Do whatever the fuck you want with her."

Tristan releases the older man and leaps back to his feet without a backward glance. He scoops up his jeans from the ground and pulls them on, hopping from one foot to the other to manage dressing while he walks. Finally clothed, he charges up the porch steps, more threatening than when he first tackled me.

I dart to the side, but he sheds his jeans with practiced ease, shifts, and leaps in front of me in his wolf form, cutting me off halfway across the porch. I skid to a stop as his animal snarls up at me, its teeth bared.

His wolf reaches my waist, a massive, sleek, black-furred beast that makes my own wolf rattle inside me, thudding at the cage of my human body, her energy begging to be released.

I've barely taken a sharp breath—barely blinked—when Tristan looms over me, fully human and stark naked again.

His shifts are too fast for me to follow, too much of a blur, and now I see why Jace told me I shouldn't be anywhere near Tristan right now.

Despite shifting back to his human form, Tristan's eyes are pure animal, his jaw clenched, the shadows casting across his face telling me that he's acting on instinct without rational thought.

My wolf's energy makes the air around me sizzle, but Tristan doesn't appear even slightly fazed.

"Stay away from me," I snarl. My wolf's silhouette appears at my side, her energy forcing its way outside of me. She lifts her head beside me and bares her teeth at him.

"Not an option." Tristan shakes his head, snarling right back at me, fierce before he scoops up his fallen jeans and tugs them on yet again.

"Come with me willingly or I'll make you." He closes the gap, his naked chest bumping into mine even as I backpedal. The power thrumming through him sends my wolf into overdrive, her snarls filling my head and making it hard to think.

I rapidly search for a way out, but there's nothing to save me. No escape. Even Jace is keeping his distance from Tristan right now.

To leave the porch without Tristan means death at the hands of the other alphas, but leaving *with* Tristan… I don't know why he fought for me, but his reasons can't be good. Nobody except my father ever approached me without an ulterior motive. Even my mother, on the one occasion that she came to see me, slapped me in front of the pack to make it clear she is above me.

"Too slow." Tristan barrels into me, anticipating my next move so that he's already right in front of me when I turn to run. Using my own momentum against me, he scoops me up and over his shoulder. *Fucking caveman bullshit.*

My hair cascades down across his thighs and calves as he strides down the stairs with me. My hands form into fists. I'm ready to pummel Tristan's spine and make him put me back on the ground, but I catch sight of the spot where my father was standing.

Empty.

Dad's gone.

Worry floods me. I raise my head, trying to ascertain where Peter and Dawson are—in case they've done something to my father—but Peter still sits in the middle of the clearing where Tristan left him. His beta and Dawson are crouched beside him, glaring at us while Tristan strides down the porch steps with me.

Jace's large form suddenly blocks my view as he follows behind us. I catch sight of a flash of steel as he bends to slip a dagger from his boot, gripping it ready in his hands.

I shudder because Jace's preparation for battle means the fight isn't over.

Tristan's pace is rapid as he rounds the back of the cabin and strides into the forest behind it. It's the direction farthest from the watching alphas. His bare feet hardly make a sound in the fallen foliage that covers the forest floor.

I don't have time to process the fact that I'm leaving my home behind—possibly for the last time. I tell myself I'll have to deal with that later. Right now, my problems just seem to get bigger and bigger.

The moment Tristan took hold of me, my wolf disappeared, gone like a puff of smoke. I seek her energy, but she has deserted me like she did the first time he barreled into me, her fire burning out in the light of his power. I'm human again with human fears and not even an axe or split wood to defend myself.

I also can't ignore my pain.

I knew I was hurt in the fight with Cody, Dawson, and Cameron, but now I feel the full effect of the wounds. I'm bleeding across my stomach, as well as my shoulder. My ribs are bruised, maybe even cracked, and my position on Tristan's shoulder is pressing on my chest.

Agony shoots through me with every step he takes.

As he hurries down the slope between the trees, I can't stop my sudden whimper.

Tristan cuts me off with a snarl. "Do *not* test me, Tessa."

I swallow my sob. He thinks I'm about to give him a tongue-lashing. That I'm still fighting him.

Of course I plan to give him a piece of my mind. I'll fight him too. I don't care how ruthless he is. If he puts me back on my feet, I'll run—despite the pain of my wounds. But we've only gone a hundred paces and I'm already in agony. I'm not sure how much more jostling I can take before I give in to tears. The last thing I want is to show weakness in front of Tristan fucking Masters.

Jace's quiet voice sounds behind us as he follows us. "She's hurting, Tristan."

I squeeze my eyes shut, hating the truth, hating my pain as

Tristan slows to a stop. The air stops whooshing around me and the pain eases. The world ceases spinning for a blissful moment when he finally comes to a complete standstill.

Tristan's arms tighten around me. "Will you run if I set you back on your feet?" he asks, a harsh demand for the truth.

I should lie.

I need to lie.

"No," I say.

Tristan makes a frustrated sound deep in his throat. "Don't lie to me, Tessa. You don't have to like me. You can hate me, but you will *never* fucking lie to me. Now, I'll ask you again: Will you run?"

"What do you think, asshole?" I snarl, thumping my fist against his back. My hand is full of my human strength, but it has no impact on him.

"You'll just have to get through the pain," he says, a cold response as he resumes his quick pace.

"No—" I stop myself before I beg.

Crying is bad. Begging is worse.

"Tristan." Jace's voice carries a warning, but this time, I don't think it's about me. "Cody's coming after her. Baxter's coming after *him*. We need to run."

"Fuck." Tristan exhales, tension thrumming through his shoulders. "Cody got too close to her. Watch my back, Jace. Use full force. Don't underestimate how badly Cody needs to get to Tessa right now."

Jace breaks into a cold grin. His daggers gleam in his hands. "Permission to hurt that fucking family? Gladly."

Tristan doesn't hesitate another second. He breaks into a sprint, and I nearly bite my tongue because the pain is so bad.

I try to exhale the aching, gasping every inhalation. Tristan's arms are like a vise around me as he darts between the trees, taking the slope at a dangerous speed. One misstep and we'll both take a tumble. At this elevation, hitting a tree means a broken back.

Just when I don't think I can take the pain anymore—when a scream works its way up to my lips—Tristan hits his stride and I suddenly feel weightless.

It's like leaping off a cliff and not touching ground.

In those few moments while the pain eases, I sense what Jace warned us about. Cody is following us—I can sense his power signature. Baxter is on the verge of catching up to him, but he's not alone. My half-brother and Peter Nash are with Baxter. Their scents are even stronger now, which means they've shifted—and they're gaining on us because of their wolves' speed. I remember the look in Cody's eyes when he tried to mark me—the dark obsession that seemed to drive him beyond logical thought.

I don't like my chances with Tristan, but I'm dead if Cody and the alphas catch up to us.

Behind us, Jace suddenly spins and drops to the ground, drawing two more blades from his boots. It's difficult to see the details in the dark while we run away from him, but these daggers don't look like normal blades—they are made purely of flattened steel with one gleaming sharp end and one rounded end. Jace is now holding two blades in each hand. They glint in his hands before he lets the two in his right hand fly at the same time.

My jaw drops at the speed and skill of his throw.

One of the blades hits the first wolf that darts around the nearest tree—I recognize Dawson's gray wolf as it yelps and falls. The blade juts from his shoulder when he shifts back to his human form, shouting in pain.

The other blade flies to the right, thudding into the chest of Peter Nash's wolf as he leaps toward Jace. Jace sidesteps smoothly to avoid Peter's flying claws and spins to drive his third blade into Peter's hind thigh.

Tristan doesn't wait for Jace and that's all I see before the trees obstruct my view. It's difficult to make out much at the speed we're moving. It's also getting darker, although my eyes are quickly adjusting to the night. I hold my breath, straining to hear and sense what's happening behind us while my heart beats wildly in my chest and my wolf's energy buzzes inside me.

Finally, I make out Jace's figure, running behind us again, his chest gleaming with sweat, thigh muscles straining, arms pumping. I doubt he'll catch up to us in his human form because Tristan is practically flying now. The power radiating from him hits me in waves, pounding through me. I sense his wolf and his human, working in harmony in a way that I've never sensed in another shifter. He's harnessing his wolf's speed and strength without shifting form, the same way I harness my wolf's energy to make myself stronger.

Except that Tristan definitely has a wolf's soul—a soul I can't relate to. The energy inside him is as foreign to me as an animal in the wild.

He leaps over a fallen tree, holding tightly to me at the same time. I recognize the path he's taking—it's the same one I would have chosen. My pack believes I never leave pack territory, but there's another world a few miles down this side of the mountain range—a small resort at the side of a gorgeous lake where humans come for vacations. It's a safe place for me that isn't dominated by shifters, where I can escape with Dad's blessing and pretend to be human. Blending in among humans is far easier than understanding my own kind. Hell, I have a part-time job in the souvenir shop, selling trinkets. I've even had a few flings with human men that didn't last long because I kept them at arm's length, knowing nothing could ever come of it.

The forest opens up a little more in this part of the mountain range, the trees slightly more sparse down to the dirt road that runs across the slope and finally joins up with the highway that leads into Portland.

A howl behind us makes me jolt, but I'm not sure who made the sound. Two wolves appear in the distance, gaining on Jace—and on us.

These are wolves I've never seen before, but I recognize their scents—Cody and his father, Baxter. Their wolves both have golden fur, one with a white tail and the other with russet-colored fur on its legs.

Jace spins to face them, but it looks like he's out of weapons. He must have used up his remaining blade on Dawson or Peter.

My eyes widen when Jace braces, ready to meet the wolves head on with his human fists.

Why doesn't Jace shift?

The smaller of the two wolves—the one with the white-tipped tail—reaches Jace first. At first, I think it's Cody, but a shiver runs through me as I distinguish the two wolves' scents and realize that the larger wolf with the russet legs is the man who tried to mark me. His golden eyes focus sharply on me across the distance as he races behind his father.

Jace sidesteps Baxter's gnashing teeth and wallops Baxter's head, knocking him across the forest floor into the nearest tree.

Before Jace can spin and throw himself at Cody, Cody's wolf slips past him. I shudder as I realize that Cody wasn't following his father out of subservience. He used his father to distract Jace to get past him.

While Jace and Baxter grapple with each other in the distance, Cody races toward Tristan, gaining on us. His wolf is sleek, beautiful in an aggressive way, his gold-tinged fur catching the moonlight that pours through the tree branches. His russet legs make him appear as if he waded through blood, a savage contrast to his agile appearance.

Tristan is already running as fast as he can in his human form while holding on to me. As fast as he is, there's no way he can outrun Cody's wolf. Not when the power blazing around Cody tells me he's as strong as Tristan—a power I doubt his father recognizes.

I brace for impact as Cody leaps, teeth bared, aiming for the back of Tristan's thigh. It's a move that will bring Tristan down and force him to release me.

At the same time, there's a sudden blur of movement from my right.

A new wolf leaps from the trees, ramming into Cody from the side and knocking him down.

I would recognize my father's scent anywhere. "Dad!"

The two wolves tumble and skid across the forest floor, a tangle of claws and teeth slashing at each other before they separate and leap at each other again, trying to tear each other apart.

I smell my father's blood. He's injured. Cody's claws have already found a mark—a shoulder, maybe his chest. Fear floods through me. I don't know if my father realizes how strong Cody is.

I have to help him.

Pummeling Tristan's back, I struggle against his hold. "Set me down!"

When he doesn't stop running, I thrash with everything I have, my fists thumping against his spine, my feet kicking at his thighs.

My voice rises to a desperate scream. "Let me go! I have to help my father!"

Still, Tristan doesn't let me go. "No!" he roars.

Behind me, my father's wolf yelps. My heart stops, deep fear flooding through me. I lift myself with my stomach muscles, ram my elbow into the back of Tristan's head, and follow up by lifting my knee and crunching it into his face.

With a shout, Tristan veers off course under the impact of my blows. He crashes into the nearest tree, hitting it on the opposite side to where he holds me. The second his arms loosen, I launch myself away from him, landing on my feet, already sprinting toward the fight.

"Dad!"

In the distance, Cody's wolf makes another lunge at my father, but he's rapidly shifting back into his human form at the same time. His fist collides with my father's head, knocking his wolf down.

My father shifts back to his human form, lying naked in the leaves, the scent of his bleeding wounds filling my heart with dread as I try to reach him. He's concussed, but Cody grabs his shoulders, lifting him.

"What is she?" Cody roars at my father. "Tell me what Tessa is!"

My father's eyes are glazed. He gives Cody a bloody grin. "You'll never fucking know."

I'm still twenty paces away. My legs burn on the upward slope, but I'm trained to run up this mountain. Cody's question should confuse me, but it doesn't.

What am I? *Who fucking knows?*

I've nearly reached them, but movement behind Cody makes fear surge inside me. Baxter Griffin appears in his human form, bleeding across his temple and chest and down his naked thighs as he runs.

His fingernails extend into claws as he veers for my father and Cody.

He's closer to them than I am.

Just as Cody lifts my father farther upward, shouting at him again, Baxter rams into them, knocking my father out of Cody's arms.

Dad hits the ground on his back, his fists flying upward,

thumping Baxter's head, knocking into the older man's cheekbone hard enough to shatter an ordinary man's face.

Baxter doesn't slow down.

He drives his claws right through my father's neck, cutting through his throat and impaling him against the ground.

Dad jolts, his shout cut short.

My scream rises, wailing through the trees. My vision turns electric blue, my wolf's energy coursing through me, but the glow around my father's body fades, turning cold before my eyes, and my legs aren't fast enough.

I wasn't fast enough.

My wolf appears at my side, running with my speed, side-by-side while I prepare to fully shift.

All I see is Baxter Griffin's neck.

All I need... is to taste Baxter's blood in my mouth when I rip out his throat and steal the life from his body.

CHAPTER FOUR

I'm only a few paces away from Baxter, but I'm aware of three running human forms around me.

Tristan races toward me from behind.

Cody races toward me from the side.

Jace has appeared from the trees and runs at Cody.

Baxter Griffin simply rises to his feet, his claws dripping with my father's dying blood, waiting for me to reach him.

My body shivers as I start to shift, welcoming the change, needing my wolf's claws and teeth. I taste the change in Baxter's confidence, the smallest fear entering his eyes as I take my final human step—

Oomph! Tristan knocks into me from behind, scooping me into his arms. At the same time, Jace leaps at Cody, putting the force of his momentum into his fist, punching the back of Cody's head and dropping him to the ground. Cody lands hard and slides through the leaves into the nearest tree with a *thud*.

Neither Tristan nor Jace stop.

Tristan swings me around, dragging me up against his body, lifting me off my feet.

"Run!" Jace roars, sprinting past us.

I struggle against Tristan's hold as he hauls me around, unrelenting despite my kicks and thumps. I have to get back to Baxter.

Off to the side, Cody stirs, grabs the tree trunk, and hauls himself back to his feet.

When I scream, Cody's head shoots up, his focus on me across the distance as Tristan hauls me away.

"I will kill you!" I scream back at Baxter. "I will fucking kill you, Baxter Griffin! You and everyone you love. I will rip your sons apart. I will shred your life into pieces."

Tristan wrenches me around and shoves me between him and Jace. He doesn't try to fling me over his shoulder again. Gripping my hand, he barks an order at me. "Run, Tessa!"

There's nothing left for me here. Only the promise of revenge.

I launch into a sprint, my feet flying through the debris covering the forest floor. Tristan remains on my right, while Jace covers my left, the two men staying close. I have no illusions that they're protecting me—they're ready in case I try to get away.

I sense Cody following us, but he's slower this time. He must finally be succumbing to all the hits to his head that he's taken tonight.

A hundred paces away, the trees become more dense, and I consider my chance to escape. I don't need a pack like my father did. Now that he's gone, I have no reason to want to live with my own kind. If I shift, I'm sure I can outrun them all.

The second I think about veering off course, Tristan barges into me, lifting me off my feet again. Before I can fight back, we break through the final line of trees at the bottom of the forest, and the dirt road appears.

A dark gray SUV waits right in front of us.

Tristan swings so that he hits the vehicle with his back, gripping me against his chest and protecting me from the impact. Jace skids to a stop, wrenches open the driver's side door, and slides in. Flipping a set of keys out of his pocket, he starts the ignition.

Tristan opens the passenger door. He doesn't bother ordering me to get in, dropping his hand onto my head so I don't headbutt the side of the vehicle before he pushes me inside.

I immediately slide to the other side of the SUV, ready to wrench open the door and slip out that side, but Tristan slams his door shut and the doors lock just as my hand touches the handle.

"Let me out!" I scream at Tristan before I'm propelled back

against the seat when Jace accelerates. The SUV jumps forward, rapidly picking up speed. I clutch the door handle with one hand and the edge of the seat with the other to stop myself being thrown around as we approach the first bend in the road.

A glance through the back window reveals Cody running from the trees behind us. He skids to a stop in the middle of the dirt road, but he doesn't try to follow. He rises up to his full height, the moonlight casting around his muscular silhouette as he watches us go.

We turn the corner and he disappears from view.

Running away kept my thoughts focused on survival, but now my fears and grief are bashing at my heart.

"I have to get back to my father." My voice catches as I spin to Tristan, who was also momentarily thrown back against his seat. "I have to—"

Tristan slides across the seat, his unsettling green eyes focused and intense as he takes hold of my shoulder in one hand and my face in the other. "Did Cody Griffin mark you?"

I jolt, my movements stiff, unable to escape Tristan's grip. "Fuck you."

His fingers curl around the shredded material still clinging to my shoulder, pulling it apart so he can study my skin. Dim lights along the doors give us enough light to see each other. Even without it, his wolf will allow him to see in the dark.

His thumb skims across the top of my breast above the edge of my bra. I shiver as his palm softens against my neck and face.

He'll see scratches, but no bite mark.

"Good," he says, releasing me.

From the front seat, Jace glances in the rearview mirror at me, then at Tristan, but he doesn't say anything before he focuses on the road again. He maintains our speed along the treacherous road. We'll be lucky if we don't crash.

I want to pull my knees up to my chest, curl up and protect my heart from the loss of my father, but I need my feet planted on the floor to keep myself from slipping around the vehicle. I consider the merits of putting on my seatbelt as Jace continues to take reckless chances driving along the twisting dirt road.

Tristan moves around the back of the vehicle as if the sudden changes in direction don't bother him. He reaches under the seat and pulls a box from it. Lifting the lid, he retrieves a bandage, along with a bottle labeled *disinfectant*. After saturating the bandage with disinfectant, he slides across the seat so close to me that his thigh presses against mine. He raises the makeshift swab toward my bleeding shoulder—the one he just inspected.

I flinch away from him, pressing against the door. "What are you doing?"

"You're bleeding," he whispers, his voice slipping across me like a threat. "You need to stop."

"Why?" I snap. "Because my scent is affecting you?"

His lips rise into a smile while his green eyes harden. His pupils begin to dilate, but he blinks the effect away. "Your scent is the reason you're still alive, Tessa."

I glare back at him. "You want to mark me?"

He shakes his head, a definitive and certain movement. "The woman I mark will be mine forever. I don't expect you to live longer than another year."

His blatant statement makes me run cold, even though the press of his hand against my shoulder and the heat of his thigh against mine suddenly warm my body. "Then… why?"

He leans closer to me and the power I sensed in him before fills my head, making me sway like I'm drunk, an overwhelming sensation. My blood is smeared all over his shoulder from where he held me while he was running, blurring in my vision like a crimson stain.

"Because your power will drive my enemies wild," he whispers.

Rage rushes through me. "Wild enough to *kill me*. I guess that means you want me dead."

Tristan's gaze burns across my face to my lips. His murmur makes me shiver. "Once I'm done with you, there's only one thing any man will want to do with you."

I draw back with a sharp breath, searching Tristan's eyes, not wanting to acknowledge his intentions. That anyone could want to use me that way. I guess he's known as the most ruthless alpha for a reason. Nobody is safe from him.

"You owe me your life now, Tessa," he says, giving me a satisfied smile. "You will do everything I tell you and when the time is right, you will destroy my enemies."

I struggle to breathe.

If I thought for a second there was a chance Tristan might give me my freedom, that hope is gone.

My father is dead. I have nobody to love. Nobody who loves me.

My life is no longer my own.

I'm now Tristan's pawn.

CHAPTER FIVE

*T*he night lights in downtown Portland are more beautiful than I ever imagined, but I can't focus on them. The whole trip takes nearly two hours. After leaving the dirt road, we exit onto the highway and finally enter the eastern side of the city. The tension inside the vehicle rises as we pass through Baxter Griffin's territory. Tristan pulls a gun case out from under the seat, loads two pistols, and hands one of them to Jace before he rests the other in his lap.

I don't breathe easily until we pass across the river, taking the Morrison Bridge into Tristan's territory. As we approach the first buildings after the bridge, two groups of men and women dressed all in black peel away from the sides of the buildings, alert and watching us from among the other passersby on the street.

"Your guards, I presume?" I ask.

"I control every bridge," Tristan replies.

That's when Jace hands his pistol back to Tristan, who returns both weapons to the gun case.

Earlier in the trip, I refused Tristan's offer of help to dress my wounds, snatching the first aid kit from him and cleaning out the cuts across my shoulder and stomach as best I could by myself. But my biggest problem is the wound that isn't bleeding—the blow that I took to my head when Dawson hit me before I subdued him.

By the time the SUV turns into a leafy street filled with immaculate homes, my head is throbbing so badly that I can hardly see straight. I'm not sure where we are. We've left the city itself behind and entered suburbia, but we've also traveled steadily upward so that now I catch glimpses of the city in the distance.

A garage door opens on the right and Jace quickly swerves inside, driving the SUV down into a small parking garage. It contains two other dark gray SUVs, both identical, parked in a row.

The vehicle doors finally unlock, but I'm too exhausted to fight my way free. The garage door has already descended behind us, shutting us inside.

When Jace pulls the SUV into the parking bay beside the other cars, Tristan promptly opens his door and gets out, leaving me in my seat.

I squint through my pain, watching him round the vehicle and stride rapidly toward a tall woman with dark hair and gentle gray eyes who waits nearby. She stands in front of an elevator, which seems odd, since I'm sure this house doesn't have more than two floors, let alone the fact that most homes don't have elevators.

I struggle to move. Along with my aching head, my muscles have cramped up and the cuts across my stomach are sharp and painful. The curtain of my hair falls over my face. It will hide the bruising from the hit I took to my head. I tell myself it's nothing I haven't survived before, but it doesn't make it hurt any less. It doesn't take away my father's death.

I'm not sure if I should prepare myself to fight again, but for now, I'm conserving my energy.

Jace glances at me in the rearview mirror when I don't move. I'm not sure why, but his lips harden into a straight line when his focus shifts to Tristan outside of the vehicle. It's unlikely that he would disagree with Tristan's plans for me.

When Jace exits the vehicle too and strides around to my door, opening it for me, I force myself to slip from my seat. In the past, I could nurse my wounds in private with only my father to see the aftermath of my pain.

Now, I'm struggling to maintain my emotional walls. I take a deep breath and lift my chin, but I don't try to remove the curtain of my hair.

In the distance, the woman is having an animated conversation with Tristan. A fierce crease forms across her forehead, her gray eyes widening and narrowing in turns. My sharp hearing should normally allow me to hear what they're saying, but for some reason, their conversation is blocked from me. I put it down to my exhaustion. I need food, water, and rest, but I count my chances of getting any of those as slim.

"Do I want to know what they're arguing about?" I ask, leaning against the side of the vehicle to keep myself upright, trying to make it look as if I don't care.

"No. You don't." Jace folds his arms. He doesn't elaborate, his gaze passing across the curtain of my hair, but I turn my face away before he can focus on the bruises that must be forming now.

A moment later, Tristan breaks away from the woman and strides back to me, his bare feet quiet on the concrete floor. He stops a full three paces away from me.

His cool gaze rakes over me and I'm grateful for my hair since it will hide the pain in my eyes.

"What now?" I ask, trying to take control of the conversation.

"Helen will take care of you," Tristan says. "Jace will check up on you once a week. When I come back, I expect you to be prepared for whatever I ask."

Jace unfolds his arms, his lips pressing together even harder and a renewed crease forming in his forehead. But still, he doesn't say anything.

"When will you come back?" I ask Tristan.

"Whenever the fuck I want," he snarls. He takes a step toward me, his pupils dilating and this time, the darkness in his eyes doesn't clear so fast.

Without missing a beat, he inclines his head sharply at Jace, who hesitates. He seems to think better of whatever he was going to say, finally responding to Tristan's unspoken command by circling the vehicle. This time, Jace slides into the passenger seat, which I guess means Tristan will be in charge of driving them out of here.

Tristan steps toward me so fast that I flinch back against the SUV, hating my reflexes. All I want is to stand my ground in front of him and there I go, twitching like I'm afraid.

His hand darts out, sliding between the strands of my hair, catching them between his thumb and forefinger before he tucks the strands behind my ear. I have no doubt he just exposed the ugliness of the bruise that's causing the pounding pain in my head. His fingers linger beside my neck, his fist clenching around my crimson locks.

"Don't forget that you're mine now, Tessa."

I bite my lip before I scream at him to get fucked. It did me a fat lot of good screaming at Baxter Griffin earlier. The echo of my threats sounds hollow now. How can I ever hope to take revenge on Baxter for my father's death?

Releasing my hair, Tristan's arms suddenly wrap around my torso and waist, tugging me up against his chest and away from the vehicle. Heat spears through my body, making me gasp as I fight the power rolling off him. The sensation is such a mash of man and wolf that I can't tell whether I'm inhaling Tristan's scent or his wolf's. Whichever it is, it makes me stiffen in his arms, my fight reflexes kicking in again.

As if he senses the danger, he acts quickly. Before I can retaliate, he takes a single step backward, pulls me with him, and deposits me back onto the ground.

He spins away from me before my fist can rise.

Striding toward the driver side door, he settles in behind the wheel and slams the door shut.

I stand my ground when Tristan starts the ignition and backs out in a squeal of tires so fast that the wind across the vehicle catches my hair.

Asshole.

He speeds the SUV toward the garage door, waits for it to open, and then drives out of the building without a backward glance.

I'm left standing in the empty parking space. I judge the distance between where I stand and the garage door, taking a second too long to decide whether or not to run for it.

It slides down again and blocks any escape.

The woman—Helen—hurries toward me. She appears to be in her forties. Her hair is dark ebony and pulled into a high, loose topknot. She's dressed in a soft-looking sweater and tight jeans. Despite wearing barely any makeup, her skin appears flawless.

She's carrying a blanket which—to my surprise—she wraps around my shoulders, drawing me into her side.

"It's okay, sweetheart," she says, her voice unexpectedly soft and warm. "You're safe with me. Let's get you upstairs."

I cast her a horrified glance, attempting to pull away from her.

Is she delusional?

Nowhere that Tristan Masters could leave me can possibly be *safe*. In fact, I should probably be grateful that I encountered Tristan Masters and lived to tell the tale. For now, that is.

As if she reads my mind—now that my hair isn't in the way, I guess the horror on my face is unmissable—she says, "This is a safe-house—a place of refuge. Tristan may control this city, but he doesn't run this house. I do. You have nothing to fear from me or anyone else who lives here."

Damn. It's impossible to doubt the sincerity in her eyes. The blanket is soft and her scent is disarming. I try to sense whether she has power—whether she's human or something else—but I come up blank. I'm not getting any glow from her at all. She draws me toward the elevator, pressing the button for the twentieth floor once we're inside it.

I frown, nearly laugh, but it would be a hysterical sound, so I shut my mouth. This house does *not* have twenty floors.

"Tristan told me what happened to your father," Helen says, making me stiffen. "I'm so sorry, Tessa. Your dad was a good man."

I jolt away from her, clutching the blanket around myself, pulling it with me like a safety net. I haven't fully processed my father's death yet. Haven't allowed myself to cry. Refuse to truly believe that he's gone.

In my mind, he's running through the forest right now.

I choke back a sob. I'm the one who's delusional now.

But if I accept for one small second that my father's gone, I'll break down. I can't do that here. Not yet. I need a safe place to scream. If it takes me hours or days to find that place, then that's how long I'll wait. I'll compartmentalize my grief until then to keep it under control, the same way I compartmentalize pain. The same way my wolf is a mindless energy. It exists. But it has no soul, no heart, and no impact on my life until I let it.

"What the hell do you know about my dad?" I ask.

"I know that—" She stops and takes a small breath, pressing her lips together before she sighs. "What I know isn't important. What's important right now is that we take care of your wounds and get you some food and water."

I'm in desperate need of both and if she's offering, I won't fight her. "What is this place?" I ask, still on edge.

"We call it 'Hidden House.'" She smiles. "It's a safehouse for those in need. It's not like most homes."

Before I can ask her for more information, the elevator door slides open to reveal a warmly lit entrance room with a couple of fabric armchairs in it. A corridor leads off to the right.

"Follow me this way, please," Helen says, waiting for me to exit the elevator before she gestures to the right toward a large room situated off the corridor.

It's also warmly lit, but it's dimmer than the entrance room. The window on the opposite side doesn't have any curtains, so I can see the city lights in the distance, as if we truly did rise twenty floors. The room contains a single medical examination table while the walls are lined with cupboards with opaque doors.

There are only two other objects in the room. One is a wand. The other is a book.

Both float midair in front of the window.

I pull up short. *Wait a minute...*

"You're a witch," I say, peering at Helen's silhouette, hoping to see a spark or hint of a glow that will confirm my suspicion. "You're hiding your power from me." My mind works quickly. "Like you protected your conversation with Tristan from me when we first arrived."

"Yes, sweetheart. I'm a witch." Helen meets my wary gaze with a nod as she glides into the room. "And a damn good one. My magic ensures that the true nature of this entire house and its grounds is hidden from the outside world. Only a trusted few can come and go from here at will."

I narrow my eyes at her with suspicion. Jace drove the SUV straight inside without stopping or asking permission.

My question is scathing. "Tristan Masters is one of those *trusted* few?"

Helen makes a humming sound in the back of her throat. "I understand why you might find that hard to believe, given his reputation and the circumstances under which he brought you here. But, please, sit."

The door closes quietly behind me as soon as I step fully into the room and walk toward the examination table. Helen is already striding toward the book and wand, which float toward her at the same speed so that they meet in the middle. She plucks the wand out of the air but allows the book to continue to float beside her.

I prepare myself for more unexpected occurrences as I clutch the blanket and sink onto the edge of the examination table, intending to perch on it.

Sitting on it is like falling through cotton wool and ending up on the floor.

My stomach lurches, my reflexes trigger, and my hands shoot out to clutch the edge of the table. The blanket falls from my shoulders in the process. I didn't actually move, but it felt like I fell through space.

Helen spins and races back to me, the book flying with her so it ends up floating close by as she leans toward me.

She searches my face, lowering her wand. "I'm sorry, Tessa. Are you okay?"

The room stops spinning, and I can finally feel the solid examination table beneath my backside. "What was that?"

"This table has a number of spells woven into it. They're meant to be undetectable. You shouldn't have felt them. The table amplifies my power and helps me understand your wounds. Sort of like an x-ray machine. I had it calibrated for a—" She bites her lip.

"A shifter?" I ask, sarcasm dripping from my tongue. "Except that I'm not a typical shifter, am I?"

"I'll know more soon," she says. "You shouldn't experience that falling sensation again."

"Great." I eye her warily as she pulls a bottle of water from one of the cupboards and brings it to me.

While I drink the entire bottle, she consults her book, pursing her lips as she flips through it until she settles on a page that appears mostly blank.

She clears her throat as she approaches me and raises her wand. I flinch when she reaches for my face, but my reaction doesn't stop her from sliding her fingers through my hair. Drawing my tresses back, she exposes my face and all the ugliness of the bruises across my temple, neck, and shoulder.

"With your permission, I need to see all of your wounds before I can treat you. Will you remove your shirt, please?"

Reluctantly, I peel off my torn flannel shirt, leaving myself dressed only in my broken bra. Scrunching my dirty shirt in my fists like an object of comfort, I try to ignore Helen's reactions.

She blinks at all of the bruises both old and new spreading across both sides of my torso before she zeros back in on my face. For a second, her eyes go blank, as if she's accessing her power—maybe the power in the table, the book, the wand, or all three.

Refocusing, she busies herself around me, apparently deciding that my head wound needs treating first.

For the next half an hour, she works on my injuries, muttering spells while her wand glides around me and the lamplight makes me increasingly sleepy. When she touches me, her hands are gentle, feather-light, and soothing. Every now and then, she goes to the cupboard and pulls out random-shaped bandages and solutions in bottles that she places or smears on my skin. One of the solutions smells like pineapples. Another like pink candy. She tells me that the bandages are waterproof and won't wash off in the shower.

I suspect that she's using magic to keep me calm and soothe my pain while she works. It's possible that I should fight it, but I don't want to. Feeling numb is a welcome relief.

Helen talks to herself as she works, cataloguing my wounds. When the book tips in my direction, I catch sight of writing forming across the paper... *multiple rib contusions... clavicle intact... fracture in right radius approximately four years old... multiple breaks in metacarpal of both left and right hands...*

Helen is far more clinical in her descriptions of the old fractures in my arms and hands than I was expecting.

"Why are you writing all of that down?" I ask, breaking the silence.

"I don't want to miss anything," she says. "Sometimes the most life-threatening wound is not the visually obvious one."

I can't help my angry laugh. "My most life-threatening characteristic seems to be my scent, since it made one alpha-in-training go off the rails and another decide that I'm worth keeping alive to use against his enemies."

Helen pulls back a little, her voice soft. "One of the reasons Tristan brought you to me is because I can teach you to control your scent."

My eyes widen. "I can control it?"

She nods, her gray eyes softening. "But it will take time and a lot of practice."

I try to hide my surprise, but I'm already working through what it means that Tristan left me with someone who has the skill to teach me to control this thing that could get me killed. I don't for a second believe he left me here for my own good.

The more I think about it, something doesn't add up. My father told me that only the strongest alphas would react to my scent. True to his prediction, only Cody and Tristan responded to me with anything other than abhorrence. So how does Tristan intend to use me against all of the other alphas and shifters—assuming they're the 'enemies' he was referring to?

Helen continues to study me. "I can teach you to both diminish *and* magnify your scent," she says.

And... there it is. Magnifying my impact on other shifters is what Tristan really wants. He told me that when he was done with me, there would only be one thing any male shifter would want from me. I guess sex really is power.

"Then that's why Tristan brought me to this safehouse, isn't it? He wants me to use my scent at will," I say. "Or rather, he will make me use my scent at *his* will."

Helen sighs. "He brought you here to keep you safe, but not only from others."

I snort. "Safe? Don't expect me to believe he cares whether or not I'm safe." Then I scowl at her as I consider what else she said. "What do you mean—not only from others?"

"Until you can control your scent, Tristan can't remain in your presence. This is the only place where you're safe from him."

I glare back at Helen. "Tristan doesn't care whether or not he hurts me."

"Believe what you will." She steps around the table to focus on my back. Sweeping my hair aside, she runs her fingers down my spine, one vertebra at a time. I assume she's now cataloguing all of the wounds I've sustained to my back and spine during my life.

I was sure she'd stop after she tended to my face and arms.

"What are you going to do with all of my medical history?" I ask, my mouth suddenly dry.

"I've already accelerated the healing process for your new wounds. I'm assuming you're now pain-free?"

At my nod, she continues. "Over the next month, I'm going to start the healing process on your old wounds—but this, too, will take time. Mending old breaks always takes longer."

"I don't need your help with those," I snap. "I'm already healed."

She rounds the table again, places both her hands on my shoulders, and pins me in her calm gaze. Somehow, she challenges my assertion with the gentlest of questions. "Are you?"

I try to look away but can't.

The wounds from the past aren't even close to healed. Maybe the bones have knitted back together, but the hurt is raw. All the derision and pain I suffered seems pointless now. I sustained all of these wounds in the pursuit of hiding my wolf.

Now, in the space of an evening, my wolf is exposed. *I'm* exposed. Word will spread and I have no doubt that soon, the entire shifter community will hear about my wolf's strange form and energy.

But the more immediate pain is the chasm that's forming inside my heart because the only person who ever cared about me died tonight while trying to protect me.

"Dad's gone," I whisper, tears burning behind my eyes.

I fight them, refusing to let them form and fall.

"There's nothing I can say to lessen the pain of losing your father, Tessa, but please know that Hidden House is a safe place to feel whatever you need to feel. However long you need to feel it."

"Ha." I bark a sarcastic laugh. "However long that is before Tristan comes back for me."

Helen's eyes gleam. "He won't set foot here until I tell him you've learned control. And I don't have to tell him a damn thing until you're ready." She gives me a sudden and unexpected smile. "Like I said, Tristan doesn't run this house. I do."

I blink at her in surprise. "You'd do that for me?"

She exhales softly, her lips forming a gentle line. "Tristan has good reasons to come for you, Tessa. Reasons he'll have to explain himself. But I will do everything I can to help you while you're here."

"What reasons could possibly explain his intentions toward me?"

Her only answer is the sudden compression of her lips, which indicates she isn't going to elaborate.

Only time will prove whether or not she's telling the truth about keeping me safe.

Helen returns to my back, spending another half an hour working around me. Once she's finished, she places her wand in a holder at her waist. Then she takes a clean shirt from the cupboard and hands it to me.

"I'll find you some new clothes, but this will have to do for now," she says. "Come with me. I'll show you to your room."

Pulling on the soft, gray T-shirt, I follow Helen down the corridor, uncertain what awaits me next.

CHAPTER SIX

*I*nstead of an elevator, I find a set of stairs at the end of the corridor.

"Wait…" I backpedal with a confused frown. "What happened to the elevator?"

Helen gives me a smile. "The elevator is the only way to access the garage, which is the only exit from Hidden House. You won't see it again until it's time to leave. Come on."

She takes a few steps down the stairs before pausing and reaching her hand out for me to follow her.

I eye her warily, my defenses rising again. She said that she controls this house, but I didn't imagine she meant she changes its form at will. *A damn good witch, huh?*

Refusing her hand, I follow her reluctantly, watching my step as we turn the corner at the landing. Another softly-lit room comes into view at the base of the stairs.

"Hidden House has many floors," Helen explains as we descend. "Some floors contain sleeping quarters. Others have workout rooms. There's also a garden on one. The staircase will learn your routines so that a single flight of stairs should lead you to whichever floor you need to access at any given time."

When we reach the bottom of the stairs, she tips her head to the side. "There's a bit of an art to it, though, especially at first. I apologize in advance if you have to climb two flights of stairs a few times until the house becomes accustomed to your needs."

The room we enter at the bottom of the stairs is homely and welcoming. One entire wall is filled floor-to-ceiling with bookshelves full of books. Multiple lounge chairs appear well-used with soft rugs and cushions scattered across them. A wide window on the far side reveals the city lights, indicating that we're still quite high up.

"This floor contains sleeping quarters," Helen says. "Your room is this way."

She waves me along the corridor past numerous closed doors. I attempt to inhale the scents of the women in the rooms we pass by, but my senses are frustratingly silent.

Helen pauses outside a door at the end of the corridor—my new room.

"Your senses will be dampened to maintain the privacy of the women who shelter here," she says. "You won't be able to sense their movements, catch their scents, or detect their supernatural status. The dampening effects will also ensure that your scent is controlled. This is important because many of the women here are extremely powerful and could be affected by you."

Helen knocks softly on the door but doesn't wait for an answer before she pushes it gently open.

I swallow a gasp as I step inside.

The room has no walls.

A forest extends in every direction, filled with the same lush green trees that grow on the mountain where I lived. Soft moonlight filters through the branches onto the floor, which is covered in moss. Even though I can't feel a breeze, the air is fresh, crisp, and carries the scent of new leaves.

A wide clearing directly in front of me contains two beds on either side, about ten feet apart. A closet sits at the far end of each bed, the back of each closet resting against the trunk of an enormous tree. Farther back are two more enormous trees with regular-sized doors carved into their trunks.

A woman in her early twenties sits in a plush armchair at the base of the bed on the right-hand side. Her knees are curled to her chest and her head is tipped back. White-blonde hair the shade of daisy petals falls down her back and cascades over the arm of the chair. Her lips are pursed as if she's sighing into the air, and her brown eyes focus upward while she hugs her knees, remaining perfectly still.

She doesn't react to our arrival, continuing to watch the branches as they sway above her, even though there's no breeze.

Leaving me at the door, Helen kneels in front of the woman, placing her hand lightly on the woman's knee. "Ella, sweetie?"

The blonde woman lowers her head, a slow, unfocused movement, her gaze far away despite the fact that she's looking directly at Helen. She doesn't speak, but the movement of her head seems to be enough for Helen.

"You have a new roommate," Helen says.

Ella's soft brown eyes glide slowly to me. Her gaze, though distant, is unwavering and unsettling.

Her pursed lips part as she inhales. "Wolf," she whispers on her exhale, a mere breath of sound.

"That's right." Helen nods gently. "Tessa is a shifter like you. She needs a forest, so she'll stay here with you for a while. Okay?"

Ella's gaze swivels away from me, returning to the branches. She becomes still again, and Helen rises to her feet, her hand leaving Ella's knee.

Despite Helen's claim that I won't be able to use my senses to scent Ella's supernatural status, I find myself trying to scent the air. For a second, I convince myself that I can sense Ella's wolf shifter status, but it quickly eludes me. Her true scent is as distant and far away as her attention.

"What happened to her?" I ask, keeping my voice low when Helen returns to me.

Helen's lips press into a firm line. "Privacy is paramount here, Tessa. Every woman who shelters in Hidden House is at liberty to tell you as much or as little about herself as she wishes. However, please be cautious with your questions. Even a little knowledge could jeopardize the life of a woman sheltering here—or endanger your own life."

I give Helen a quick nod to let her know I understand. As much as questions burn brightly inside me about Ella—like what pack she's from—Tristan's, surely?—and what broke her so badly—I understand how painful questions can be.

Helen's expression softens as she sweeps her arm toward the bed on the left-hand side of the room, then points to the door in the tree also on the left at the back of the space.

"That's your bed and your bathroom," she says. "The water from the tap in the bathroom is safe to drink. A plate of food will be brought to you shortly. If you're not out of the shower, don't worry. Aida will leave your food on the table at the end of your bed."

"Aida is...?"

"One of my oldest friends and an excellent cook." Helen smiles. "In the meantime, make yourself at home. Come out whenever you want. You're free to explore. The house won't let you go anywhere you shouldn't."

I consider the space around me—the sense of freedom within the trees—not knowing how to feel about my new surroundings. On one hand, I'm trapped here. On the other, this house already feels like the safest place I've experienced since I was born, and I've only been here for a few hours.

Helen pauses at the door. "I don't want you to feel like this home is a prison, Tessa. This building is heavily protected, but it needs to be. Many of these women are thought to be dead. Many of them know things they shouldn't know. Some of them have twists on their power that make them targets—just like you. My only goal is to make sure they're safe. That is my only intention toward you, too."

I fold my hands in front of myself, not sure what to say. The way Tristan brought me here hasn't helped me lower my defenses. I can't suddenly trust this witch, no matter what she says. Time will prove her intentions one way or another.

Helen doesn't seem to require a response. "Goodnight, Tessa."

She leaves me in tranquil silence.

Ella barely stirs in her chair. The rise and fall of her chest is the only movement around me. Everything else is still.

Slipping off my ankle-high boots and placing them beside the bed, I freeze to see the drops of blood dried on the top of them. My own blood.

I need to shower.

Maybe throw up.

Scream. Cry.

Hurrying across to the door in the tree, I wrench it open, half-expecting that I'll find nothing behind it.

I step into a large bathroom, just as tranquil as the forest I left behind. On the opposite wall is a long, mahogany bench with a white porcelain sink. To the right is an alcove with a bath sitting on a bed of pebbles, wood paneling surrounding the pebbles on the floor as well as decorating the wall behind the bath.

On the left, a shower space with an enormous square shower-head is surrounded by earthy-colored tiles. The room is lit with soft lights positioned at intervals along the walls, but moonlight pours through an opening in the ceiling directly above the showerhead.

It's like something out of a magazine.

The moment I step into the room, the bath begins to fill with water. As I veer in the other direction toward the shower, the showerhead turns on. The warm water pouring on either side of me quickly steams up the whole space as I wrench off my borrowed shirt and broken bra and peel off my bloody jeans.

I avoid looking in the mirror as I step under the shower.

The water is gentle, but it drives me to the tiled floor where I curl up, naked except for the waterproof patches covering my wounds.

I finally allow my tears to fall, succumbing to the wrenching sobs. I want to deny that my father is dead. I want to believe that he's coming for me, that tonight never happened.

Flashes return to me as I press against the warm tiling at the bottom of the shower. Baxter Griffin's claws. My father's final shout. Cody Griffin's eyes boring into me. The tilt of his head when he tried to mark me, the power pouring off him when he came after me. Even the *crack* of his father's backhand across his face. All of it is like oxygen to my grief, pulling tears from me for such a long time that my skin is already wrinkled by the time I drag myself out of the shower and over to the bath to immerse myself in the water.

I'm emotionally spent. Empty.

Or I think I am.

As I sink below the surface of the full bath, the memory of the brightest flame suddenly returns to me, fed by the sensation of Tristan's power washing across me, a dizzying wave that burns out every other emotion inside me.

I return to the surface of the water, gasping for air, feeling like flames suddenly rippled from my head to my toes.

The woman I mark will be mine forever, Tristan said.

I hate that *that* statement twists my insides more than his prediction that I won't live longer than another year.

Even if Cody had succeeded in marking me, it wouldn't have made any difference to me. Tristan Masters himself could bite me and it wouldn't mean a damn thing.

I will never bond.

All a mark will do is make it clear to every other shifter that I am claimed.

I will never feel the loyalty that other shifters feel for each other.

When I finally climb out of the bath, I find myself facing the full-length mirror.

My body is an unwanted beat-up sight. Bruises extend across my cheeks, jaw, shoulders, breasts, ribs, hips, and thighs.

Every part of my body should belong to me and not to a man's fists.

My future should belong to me.

Right now, I see my path extending before me with a giant fork in it.

Tristan brought me here for his own purposes. He brought me here to mold me into a woman who will destroy his enemies. I can walk the path he wants me to walk—as his pawn, doing whatever he wants me to do, allowing him to dictate my actions until the day he sends me to an early death.

Or...

I can take whatever I learn here, take whatever he gives me, gain control over my thoughts and my scent, become strong, work within his rules, and then... when the time is right... I'll break away.

I will use everything Tristan gives me to kill Baxter Griffin. On my terms. As a free woman.

If Tristan stands in my way, I'll end him too.

CHAPTER SEVEN

*T*he next morning, I wake to the sound of birds. The soft tweeting breaks through the pain that shoots through every part of my body.

Damn. Whatever magic Helen used on me last night to numb my wounds, it's disappeared, leaving me aching and sore.

Slowly opening my eyes to the early morning sunlight filtering through the tree branches overhead, I assess each part of my body: arms, legs, chest, and face. The worst pain is in my head and my ribs.

Slipping quietly from beneath the blankets, I allow the sunlight to shine across my bare legs and thighs. They are the least bruised, although my multiple falls to the ground yesterday left me with yellowing patches of skin across my thighs.

Focusing beyond myself, I find Ella sitting on the edge of her bed opposite mine. She's dressed in a long, white shirt that reaches her knees while her blonde hair drapes across her right shoulder.

Her left arm is bent at the elbow, her hand raised with fingers splayed. Three brilliantly-colored canaries circle her head and hand, dipping toward her fingertips in turns. She follows their movements with her eyes but doesn't otherwise move.

Each time one dips toward her fingertips, she whispers its color. "Pink... blue... yellow... blue... pink..."

She doesn't seem to notice that I'm awake, but her focus appears sharper, her gaze following the birds' paths as they rise, soar, and dip again.

I could find her repetitive speech irritating, but her voice is soft and melodic. It carries a hum, as if she were once a trained singer and her vocal chords are trying to remember how to sing again.

I also recognize the therapy of making lists, the way simple things can keep fears at bay. I have no doubt the birds are a deliberate part of the environment that Helen has created for Ella. Casting a glance around, I wonder whether there will be special additions for me, but I can't see anything different since last night.

After wrapping myself in a towel last night, I grabbed an oversized T-shirt from the closet and crawled into bed, nursing my new resolutions close to my heart. I have no idea what my path to revenge will involve, but I know where I'm determined it will take me: to Baxter Griffin, ruthless alpha and the man who killed my father.

My heart squeezes inside my chest, but I push my sadness away as hard as I can, locking it up again. I don't need grief. I need anger, the quiet kind that simmers and grows, that will make me single-minded and fearless.

A gentle breeze picks up around me, bringing with it the scent of a new day. Despite my inability to sense anyone around me, it seems that I can still use my human senses to smell and see what's around me. Resolving to move through the pain in my body, I rise to my feet and carefully stretch out my arms.

The sight of a fresh plate of food resting on the small table at the foot of my bed forces me to acknowledge how hungry I am. Aida must have brought it for me. I'm sure there was a different plate of food there last night, but I fell asleep as soon as I crawled into bed.

After filling up on toast, fruit, yogurt, and a glass of orange juice, I test my legs and make my way to the closet to consider my clothing options, hoping for loose jeans and flannel shirts like I'm used to wearing. Not to mention, I won't be able to handle anything tight around my body for at least the next few days.

Opening the closet, I narrow my eyes at the full array of every kind of jeans and every color flannel shirt I could possibly wish for. I suddenly wonder to what extent the contents of this closet are predetermined by Helen or whether the clothing is influenced by my wishes. Last night, I hoped to find a soft, loose shirt and it came immediately to hand.

Deciding to test my theory, I close the closet again, concentrate on the doors, and think hard about little black dresses. Holding my breath, I open the cupboard, but it's still filled with jeans and flannel shirts.

It's definitely for the best. I have absolutely no use for little black dresses.

Ella is still murmuring colors to herself when I emerge from the bathroom fully dressed.

The bruises on my face are worse in the morning light. They're on full display and despite all the wishing in the world, none of the shelves in the bathroom contains makeup I can use to mask them.

I consider whether or not the smart thing to do would be to crawl back into bed and stay there for the next week, but if I accept that Hidden House is a place of comfort, I might never want to leave it.

As I finish tying my hair in a loose ponytail, I mentally prepare myself for exiting the room into the unknown. Helen said I could explore the house as much as I want, but that I won't be able to go anywhere I'm not supposed to go. I intend to test that rule if I possibly can. Even if I'm not ready to leave, I'd like to know whether or not I *can*.

Passing Ella on my way, I notice that the canaries have changed color.

"Purple... green... orange... *wolf*..." Ella whispers as I stride past her.

The last addition to her list registers in my hearing, making me pause midstride.

"Orange... purple... *wolf*..." Ella falls silent, even though the birds continue to dip toward her fingertips. A crease forms in her forehead. She tilts her head to the side. Still focused on the canaries, as if she's speaking to them and not to me, she asks, "Human?"

The inflection at the end of her speech turns her statement into a question.

Am I a wolf? Or am I human?

Honesty seems called for. Ella has done nothing to me. I have no reason to distrust her. "I don't really know," I murmur. "Both? Neither? Nobody could ever explain to me why I was born this way. Not even my dad."

It's a strange sort of relief to speak aloud the difficulty that has plagued me my whole life. When I was younger, I demanded that my father explain to me why I have a human soul—why my wolf has an animal's energy without its soul. He looked me in the eye and told me he didn't know. To this day, I don't know if he was lying to me.

Ella blinks at the birds while I speak.

She's quiet for another moment and it's hard for me to tell whether or not she even understood me.

She resumes her list. "Purple... green..."

I leave her to it and venture into the hallway outside.

A second after I close the door behind me, the door to the room across the corridor opens and a woman steps from inside it. Her long, black hair is piled up on her head and her large, blue-gray eyes are framed with the longest, thickest black lashes I've ever seen. She's wearing knee-high leather boots over tight black pants and a low-cut black T-shirt, the ebony of her clothing making the brightness of her eyes *pop*. The most surprising thing about her is the weapons belt slung around her hips. I count three daggers and two handguns and that's only at the front. The handle of another dagger protrudes at the side of her hip.

The open door reveals a glimpse of night sky beyond her. I blink at her room full of silver spots, glittering like stars, bright, a floor but no walls, before she firmly closes the door behind her.

Unlike Ella, who is quiet and distant, this woman is a picture of confidence and assertiveness.

I'm immediately curious about why she's here since she doesn't look like she needs help of any kind.

"New person," she says, leaning against her closed door with a curious gleam in her eyes, her rose-bud lips pursed as she considers me carefully. "What do I call you?"

I find her directness reassuring. "You can call me 'Tessa Dean.' I'm a wolf shifter."

"Hello, Tessa Dean. I'm Iyana Ballinger." She pronounces her first name 'eye-yah-nah,' running the sounds together so smoothly that it sounds like a melody. At the same time, she casts her gaze across my face and down to the bruises visible on my forearms since I rolled up the sleeves of my shirt. "Someone really fucked you up, Tessa Dean."

Remembering what Helen said about privacy, I decide that the same rules apply to me. I can say as little or as much as I want about my past. Resisting the urge to touch my bruised cheek, I gesture at her weapons. "You look like you can handle anything."

She gives me a wry smile. "I have a habit of biting off more than I can chew. It doesn't always end well for me." She waves her hand over her own face. "This face," she says, "is the result of six months of Helen's magic. When I came here, I was in worse shape than you."

She makes a bubbling sound in the back of her throat—a deceptively light laugh at her own pain—but the cold in her eyes makes me shiver. Somehow, I get the sense that it would take a powerful supernatural to mess with her.

"Has Helen given you the spiel about not asking questions?" she asks.

I nod.

Iyana's smile reveals the tiniest hint of fangs. "Let's make this easy then. Here's what you can know about me: I'm a vampire. Twenty-five years old. I haven't lived with my own kind for the last five years. In fact, I'm one of only a few vampires in Portland. The wolf shifter population tends to keep us away." She stops, considering the ceiling, as if she's thinking about what else she can tell me. She shrugs. "If I told you the rest, I'd have to kill you."

I should have realized she was a vampire from her comment about biting off too much. Also, since her room held no sunlight.

Iyana smirks at my wide eyes. "I've surprised you. You didn't expect me to be a vampire."

I force myself to relax. "Helen said there were many different women here."

"Different." Iyana lets out a heavy sigh. "That's one way to put it. *Broken* might be more accurate." She inclines her head at my room. "How is Ella today?"

"She's listing colors," I answer cautiously, not sure how much I'm supposed to say.

Iyana nods. "Yesterday she was screaming, so listing colors is good."

I blink at the floor as I digest this information. I've been through a lot, but I'm nowhere near close enough to breaking so badly that my memories could consume me like that. My hands shake as I try not to imagine what it would take to hurt a woman so much.

"There's nothing you can do," Iyana says softly. "Helen's the only one who can help her." She clears her throat, and I guess she's trying to lift the heaviness around us. "I'm headed to the gun range. I'll show you around if you want?"

My eyebrows rise. "There's a gun range?"

Iyana grins suddenly, her fangs disappearing up into her gums. She looks pleased that she surprised me again. "Whatever you need, it's here. This morning, *I* need target practice, so I'm hoping Helen won't make me climb three sets of stairs to get to the range this time. Yesterday, I had to walk past the kitchen and the garden first. That woman really wants to shake up my routine."

Iyana inclines her head at the end of the corridor and I fall into step beside her. The idea of climbing *any* stairs today is unwelcome. My shoulders are stiff and the drag of material across my torso is already smarting. I keep my arm movements to a minimum, but at least my legs are mostly functional, allowing me to keep pace with Iyana.

The doors around us remain closed, but when we're halfway down the corridor, one of them opens behind us and steady footfalls approach.

Iyana doesn't look around. "Morning, Danika."

"Fuck mornings," the woman replies.

I study the newcomer from the corner of my eye. She's shorter than Iyana—slightly shorter than me too—with tousled, light brown hair falling to her shoulders, golden highlights soft in the corridor lighting. Her hazel eyes are flecked with gold and rimmed in dark brown. Her jeans are ripped across her left thigh and she's wearing a strappy black singlet top that shows off the intricate tattoo of a bird's wing decorating her entire left shoulder and bicep all the way to her elbow.

I suppress a shudder at the scar that runs through the tattoo from the tip of her shoulder to her forearm. The scar is thick and raised like knotted rope. It must have been a deep cut—possibly deliberately targeted at her tattoo.

At Danika's harsh response, Iyana casts me a warning glance that I interpret to mean *don't say anything.*

Iyana throws a casual question back at Danika as we continue to walk. "Bad night?"

"Are you going to the gun range?" Danika asks, without answering Iyana's question.

"Yup," Iyana replies, popping the 'p' at the end while keeping her focus on the corridor in front of us.

"Good," Danika says. "I have memories to kill."

Danika falls into stride behind us and moments later, we reach the room at the end of the corridor. The full wall of books looks even more inviting in the morning light and the view of the city to the right is pretty as the light glints off the old buildings in the distance.

I'm grateful when we find a set of stairs going down and not up, although I'm not looking forward to coming back up them.

Iyana takes the steps far more quickly than I can in my injured state.

Craning her head around the corner when she reaches the landing, she breaks into another grin. "Hidden House provides! We're at the gun range."

She disappears from view until I round the corner at the landing. The stairs let out directly into a wide entry corridor that sits between two rooms, both with transparent walls. On the left is a weapons room with guns lining the walls and cabinets beneath them. Five firing lanes are situated inside the room to the right.

While I hesitate at the bottom of the stairs, Danika strides straight past me into the weapons room. She picks two different pistols off the wall before sliding open the cabinet drawer beneath them to retrieve two boxes of bullets. I don't know my way around guns to distinguish between them—other than identifying the obvious size and shape differences between a handgun and a rifle—so I have no idea why she picked the ones she did.

Iyana is slower to choose a weapon, appearing to take her time while she casts glances beneath her eyelashes at Danika. I get the sense that she has decided to give Danika a lot of space.

I stay out of the weapons room, leaning against the transparent wall between the entry corridor and the firing lanes, making my stance look nonchalant, even though my body's aching far more than I want to admit right now.

Danika remains single-minded, pushing through the glass door into the firing range without a second glance at me. The door seals behind her, blocking all sound. I can't hear her footsteps as she heads to the middle lane.

Each firing lane is divided by walls at the firing end with a bench sitting between them. The bench provides a place for Danika to set down her weapons and boxes of ammunition. The booths are otherwise open in front and behind.

I turn to Iyana when she pauses at my side carrying only a box of bullets and earmuffs. I guess she already has her weapons of choice sitting at her waist.

"We might want to give Danika a minute," she says, as if this is not an unusual thing.

I jump when the wall I'm leaning against vibrates.

Jolting away from it, I spin to stare at Danika through the glass.

Inside the firing lane, the brown-haired woman stands with her right arm extended, the angle of her body meaning her face is turned slightly away from me. She squeezes the trigger in rapid succession. I freeze when the bullets rip through the exact center of the paper target at the end of the lane. Dead center. So perfect that only a single, widening hole appears in it.

She's a perfect shot.

But it doesn't explain the vibration through the glass.

Within seconds, she must have emptied the entire clip into the target because she slaps the weapon onto the bench in front of her. Snatching up the second handgun, she switches her stance so that her left arm is outstretched.

An *ambidextrous* perfect shot.

Now that her torso is twisted in my direction, I can see that she's screaming. I guess that explains why she didn't bother taking earmuffs with her.

I back away from the wall, wary of whatever magic she controls that's shrieking through the glass between us.

"Don't worry," Iyana whispers. "She's not a banshee or a siren. Her scream can't hurt you." She shrugs. "Other than blowing out your eardrums."

"What is she?" I ask. "I know I'm breaking the privacy rule, but it seems important for my safety that I know."

"Hawk shifter," Iyana says. "As you can see, she has perfect eyesight. She can hit any target. But... like the rest of us... she's a little different than normal. She can shriek in her human form—and at a frequency that can do a lot of damage."

Iyana sighs, pressing her free hand against the wall and spreading her fingers wide. "She's most dangerous when she's upset."

"Who is Danika shooting right now in her mind?" I ask, knowing that that sort of rage can only mean Danika's picturing someone in place of the target.

"Her ex-boyfriend. He taped her mouth shut so she couldn't use her scream to defend herself and then beat her to a pulp. He left her for dead."

"*Fuck*," I whisper, leaning against the glass, feeling the rage and pain vibrating through it. "How did she survive?"

Iyana presses her forehead against the transparent wall, closing her eyes, pensive and subdued. "The same way we all survived. Tristan Masters found her, killed that son of a bitch boyfriend, and brought Danika here. Helen healed her."

I stiffen. I can't keep the shock from my voice. "Tristan saved her?"

Iyana nods. Still facing the firing range, she says, "He saved us all, Tessa. There isn't a woman in this place whom he didn't pull out of some hell and bring here to safety."

Inside the firing range, Danika lowers her weapon, grips the edge of the bench, and leans forward, hanging over the space as if she's trying not to throw up. The air becomes still again, but the silence feels charged as she collects her weapons from the bench and stumbles to the door.

My hands clench and unclench. There's no way Tristan Masters saved these women out of the goodness of his heart. "What was his price?"

Iyana draws away from the wall, casting me a curious glance. Her lips part in puzzlement. "What do you mean?"

"I mean, what does Tristan want in return?"

Her forehead creases. "Nothing, Tessa. He doesn't—"

The glass door hisses as Danika pushes it open and leans against the open doorframe.

"Fuck." Her hands shake as she presses the back of her hand across her forehead, a gun still gripped in it. "He can't die twice, can he?"

Iyana swings away from the wall. "He's dead for good, sweetie."

"For better." Danika picks herself up off the doorframe and wobbles toward me. "I'm sure Iyana has told you what she can about me, but just in case... I'm a hawk shifter. Twenty-four years old. I don't like mornings."

"I'm Tessa," I say. "Wolf shifter. Twenty-three." *My father died last night.*

I fall silent, but Danika gives me a nod of acceptance without asking for more information. My heart opens a little that I can trust these women to understand some things are too painful to talk about.

Danika sways in the direction of the weapons room. It looks like she's struggling to stand up, but even so, she takes care placing the pistols safely back where they belong. Then she drags herself up the stairs.

Iyana exhales slowly as she watches Danika go. "Don't let Danika near your room when Ella's counting canaries. Hawks and canaries are predator and prey."

Now that Danika's gone, I lean against the glass wall, still fighting the pain inside my body.

I accept Iyana's verbal attempt to lighten the intensity of the mood around us and respond just as lightly. "I bet."

Iyana holds the door open for me. "Come on. I can teach you how to handle a gun."

"Who says I don't already know?" I ask, my defenses flying up again.

Iyana's lips rise into a sly smile as she reaches for me and wraps her fingers around my arm. She keeps the door open with her foot. "Honey, if you knew how to shoot a firearm, you would have picked your weapon of choice already."

I swallow a moan as pain shoots through me when her fingers close around my bruised bicep. Leaning more heavily against the glass wall to support myself, I abandon my false bravado.

I desperately want to learn how to handle a gun—I need to learn everything I can from anyone who is willing to teach me—but I shake my head. "Honestly… I don't think I'm up to lifting a weapon today."

Iyana's forehead creases as she studies me. "What do you mean?"

I point to my face with a dry laugh. "*This* is everywhere—shoulders, ribs, hips. I'm having trouble rotating my shoulder. I don't think I have a hope of extending my arms to fire a gun."

Iyana purses her lips, tilting her head to the side. "You're in pain right now?"

My laugh becomes sarcastic. "No, I'm not in any pain at all."

"*Damn.* I thought you looked pale. I assumed it was your normal shade." She carefully removes her hand from my arm as if she's only just now realizing how much she's hurting me. Her shoulders are tense, her grip on the box of bullets in her other hand tight enough to crinkle the cardboard.

"You shouldn't be in pain right now," she says, peering at me, her gaze passing rapidly across my face. "That's not how this works. I need to get you to Helen right away."

I attempt to step away from Iyana but only succeed in sliding along the wall.

I hate the concern in her eyes.

"I can handle pain," I snap. "I don't need your pity."

Iyana's expression hardens. Her lips press into an unhappy line. "This is not pity. If Helen's magic hasn't taken away your pain, then something's wrong. Helen needs to know. Right away."

"I'm fine—"

"Helen!" Iyana raises her voice, as if she expects Helen to materialize out of thin air. "We need you!"

Within seconds, running footfalls precede Helen down the stairs. I'm surprised at how quickly she arrives until I remind myself that this house contains stairways that magically connect floors. Helen is only ever a corridor and a set of stairs away from me. Today, she's dressed in jeans and another soft-looking sweater.

"What's wrong?" she asks, pulling to a stop, her attention dashing across us both.

Iyana is stiff and alert beside me. "Tessa's in pain."

Helen startles. "That's not possible. I used the strongest spell I have."

I attempt to back farther away from both of them but don't make it far before Helen closes the gap, much faster than me in my sluggish state. She grips both of my shoulders in her hands.

This time, I can't stop the moan slipping between my lips when she presses on my bruises. I squeeze my eyes closed, my jaw clenching. "Can everyone *please* stop grabbing me?"

Helen immediately releases me. "This shouldn't be happening. Tessa, can you walk on your own?"

"I can walk fine," I snap, turning myself into a liar when my head swims, and I lose my footing, thumping against the wall behind me before I slide down it onto my backside.

Helen follows me down, kneeling in front of me. "Okay, we'll do this here."

She holds her arm out horizontal to the floor, as if she's reaching for something. A second later, her wand flies down the stairs and across the corridor into her hand. Her fingers close around it and she draws it through the air around my head and torso, keeping the wand parallel with my body.

She moves the wand slowly, as if she's shining light on my body that only she can see.

I watch her carefully, but I'm too exhausted from fighting the pain to push her away. "What are you doing?"

"I'm assessing your body for remnant magic," she says. "If the pain blockers aren't working, then neither is the healing spell."

Moments later, she pulls back, her forehead creased. "I can't detect a shred of magic in your system, Tessa. The spells I used should have lasted an entire week."

"Then... what does this mean?" I ask.

"It means you might be metabolizing magic much faster than anyone I've ever met," Helen replies. "I'll know more once I run some tests, but for now, I'm going to place a basic pain-blocking spell over you so we can get you up the stairs without hurting you."

She mutters under her breath while she waves the wand over me, trailing it across the space in front of my chest and up over my face. Slowly, the ache in my limbs eases, becoming dull and distant, although it's not gone entirely.

Popping her wand into her waistband, Helen pulls one of my arms across her shoulder, gesturing to Iyana to do the same. "Help me carry her, please."

Iyana follows Helen's lead, angling her shoulder under my arm so that the women support me on either side while I clamber to my feet and we proceed toward the stairs.

I pull to a stop when I find myself facing an elevator instead of a staircase. Helen said I wouldn't see the elevator again until I was ready to leave.

Iyana seems equally surprised. "Elevator today, huh?"

Helen's response is gruff. "I'm making an exception. I don't want Tessa tumbling down the stairs and taking us both with her."

Just like yesterday, Helen hits the button for the twentieth floor once we're inside. When the doors open, she and Iyana help me down the corridor to the same room Helen examined me in yesterday.

Once there, they lay me down on the examination table.

Iyana takes herself off to the side of the room out of the way while Helen hovers over me, chewing her lip nervously. "Tessa, I need to do a quick test, but I'm afraid it could hurt you if my theory is wrong."

Tension creeps through me—I'm already in enough pain—but I give her a nod.

With my permission, she mutters under her breath and points her wand at the back of my hand, where I rest my palm on my stomach.

A second later, a golden flame flares across my fingertips, burning hot as it bursts along my skin.

CHAPTER EIGHT

I let out a scream before the flame vanishes.

I blink at my perfectly unharmed hand.

"Did you feel any pain?" Helen asks, her question urgent.

I shake my head. "None at all." My scream was instinctive. A reaction to the pain I thought I would feel.

Helen's eyes are wide as she closely examines my hand, turning it over. "You don't have any burn marks." She steps back, exchanging a look with Iyana before she turns to me. "That test proved my theory that you're highly resistant to magic."

"Okay, like I asked, what does this mean?" I ask.

Helen taps her finger urgently on her wand, the skin around her eyes tight with tension. "Tell me something, Tessa, can you sense what's going on in this House? Where the women are, what their powers are, that sort of thing?"

When I first arrived, Helen told me that my senses would be dampened here. "No," I say. "It's just like you said. I can't use my wolf's senses, just my normal human ones."

The tension around Helen's eyes eases. "Good." She exhales slowly. "And also interesting because it begins to explain to me what kind of magic you're resistant to." She waves her wand gently in the air, gesturing around at the room. As she does so, colors stream from her wand.

"There are many different kinds of magic, but they generally fall into four types," she says.

"The first is light magic. It is the magic of love and strength. A warrior's magic." The colors around her wand begin to take shape, forming into dragons of all colors: crimson, black, and golden. The magnificent creatures dip and soar through the air around us, their powerful wings disturbing the air across my face.

"Then there is dark magic. It comes from draining life. Some know it as sorcery." The dragons crash into a blackened and burned landscape filled with crumbling bones, their bodies smashing into dust that fills the air like snow.

"The third type of magic is elemental magic. It is the power of nature," Helen says, continuing to wave her wand. Green grass sprouts across the barren landscape, a river forms, water rushing over stones, mountains rise up in the background peaked with ice, and bright sunlight streams across the air, brightening the room around us.

"And then there's the magic that sits at the foundation of the world—old magic, which some supernaturals call 'deep magic.'" The perspective of the image shifts again, rising rapidly higher as the sunlight fades and the stars and moon dominate the sky, bright and luminescent.

"This house was formed on a foundation of old magic," Helen says. "It would be a very rare thing if you were immune to old magic. Even creatures of old magic themselves—as rare as they are—are not immune to each other. But you *are* immune to my healing magic, which is light magic. You also resisted the destructive flame I just attempted to burn your hand with. That was dark magic. As for elemental magic, which is commonly controlled by fae creatures, I guess we will have to wait and see."

My voice sticks in my throat. My understanding of magic just expanded, but I still don't understand what this means for me. "Is my resistance a good thing?"

"It is a good thing, but... also a bad thing." Helen grimaces. "It's detrimental because it means whatever pain relief I give you will wear off quickly. It also means your wounds could take longer to heal because my healing spell won't have the intended impact. On the positive side, it means that an enemy who tries to use magic on you will have a very hard time slowing you down."

"What are you saying?"

"I'm saying that brute force can kill you, but magic won't do a damn thing."

My jaw drops. "But..."

Iyana peels herself off the wall. She has been quiet through the conversation, but now she exchanges another look with Helen.

"I was going to leave Hidden House and join Tristan next week," Iyana says, speaking with Helen, the two of them suddenly ignoring me. "But now I think I should stay."

"It's up to you, Iyana."

"Tristan needs me, but... I'll stay for another week. If things look promising, I'll stay longer."

I glare between them. "Enough with the cryptic conversation."

Iyana spins to me. "I'll train you in the mornings. Helen will work with you in the afternoons."

Her statement doesn't explain anything. I narrow my eyes at her. "Train me? In what?"

Iyana grins. "Self-defense. Offense. Weaponry. Whatever you need to learn."

I fire back a response, my pain finally making me cranky, not to mention my pride is suddenly hurting. "I don't need your help."

She arches a perfectly sculpted eyebrow at me. "Your bruises disagree." She strides forward and leans over me, so close that I finally catch a sense of her scent. As elusive as it is, it reminds me of frost on a cold morning.

"Tessa, you have a chance that none of us has," she says. "When I'm done with you, no man will ever fuck with you again."

My eyes widen. She's offering to train me. My father made sure I was fit and knew how to box, along with some basic self-defense. I haven't seen Iyana in action, but judging from her familiarity with the gun range, there's a fair chance I could learn a lot from her.

She promised that no man would ever hurt me again.

I clench my teeth. "If that includes Tristan, then I'm in."

My declaration settles into sudden silence.

Iyana blinks at me for a moment, slowly withdrawing, as if I stung her.

"Tristan?" she asks. "Why would Tristan want to hurt you? He brought you here, didn't he?"

Helen clears her throat loudly enough to make Iyana's attention snap to her.

"Tessa's situation is a little more complicated than normal," Helen says.

The fierce crease in Iyana's forehead deepens. "What am I missing?"

Helen starts to speak, but Iyana suddenly jolts, as if she realized something. Her eyes widen as she stares at my face—at my bruises.

"Fuck," she whispers. Her lips part and her cheeks turn a paler shade of white. "Did *Tristan* hurt you?"

Waiting for me to answer, she reaches out to grip the edge of the examination table, frozen, pinning me with her wide, blue eyes.

At the side, Helen is poised as if she's about to answer for me, but she closes her mouth. After all, she wasn't there, so she doesn't really know.

I bite my lip as I return Iyana's wild gaze. She said that Tristan saved Danika's life and brought her here to safety. He brought all of them here. She clearly believes he's one of the good guys. The anxiety written all over her face tells me it would break her world if the answer were *yes*, that Tristan had hurt me.

"No," I say, truthfully. "Other than manhandling me, Tristan didn't hurt me."

Iyana relaxes her grip on the table. She lets out her breath with a grateful moan. Dragging the back of her hand across her forehead, she says, "Of course he didn't. He wouldn't hurt someone in need."

She squeezes her eyes closed, leaning over the space at the side of the table just like Danika did, as if her whole body hurts. "He wouldn't do that."

Until this moment, I couldn't understand why Iyana is here. She said she was physically messed up six months ago, but she seemed to have it all together. She acts strong. No chinks in her emotional armor. Now I catch a glimpse of extreme vulnerability. Only a severe break in trust could cause an insecurity that deep. Her reaction tells me that if Tristan *had* hurt me, Iyana's ability to trust would have been broken irrevocably. I'm not sure how she'd react if that were the case. I wouldn't want to see it happen.

Iyana sucks in a deep breath before she opens her eyes again. She appears in control again, but her shaking hands say otherwise. "Like I said, you have a real chance, Tessa. I can't teach you everything. I don't *know* everything. But I'll teach you what I can. Now... do you want to learn?"

"I want to learn," I say.

"Good." She spins to Helen, holding her head high. "I need to take a break. Tessa has to heal before I can train her anyway. I'll be in the garden if you need me."

Her boots click across the floor as she strides from the room before Helen has a chance to reply.

The room is silent after she leaves.

I bury my teeth in my bottom lip, studying the magical book that floats in the air at the foot of the examination table. "I take it Tristan reserves his asshole mode for me."

Helen folds her hands in front of her. "Tristan Masters is as ruthless as his reputation makes him out to be. Take every story you've heard about him, triple its brutality, and you might come close to a true assessment of his capacity for violence."

I frown, confused. "Then why does Iyana think he saved her?"

"Because he did."

I let out a bitter laugh. "Without asking anything in return?"

Helen's gray eyes rise to mine. "Tessa, you won't understand Tristan's ability to perceive and neutralize threats—or his unrelenting determination to protect his pack—until you see it for yourself."

Is she trying to tell me that Tristan considers all of these women to be part of his pack? For starters, they aren't all wolf shifters. Secondly, Iyana made it sound like he didn't even know them before he saved them.

Which leaves me even more confused than I was before.

Helen clears her throat and draws her wand again without further elaborating on her statement. "I need to do what I can to help you heal now, Tessa. I'm going to try traditional human medicine this time. Strong pain killers, along with muscle relaxants and sedatives to help you sleep. I'll connect you to an IV drip so we can get the medicine directly into your bloodstream for maximum effect. You'll need to stay in this room for the next few days so I can monitor you."

She isn't really asking me. Not that I would object at this point. I want to escape from this nightmare—this whole mess—and wake up stronger.

After placing her wand firmly on top of the nearest cabinet, Helen busies herself opening drawers and retrieving medical apparatuses.

She's just finished attaching a cannula to the back of my hand when she suddenly jolts, her gaze becomes distant, and a deep crease forms in her forehead, as if she's sensing a disturbance from afar.

"What is it?" I ask.

"We have a visitor. It's nothing to worry about." She presses her hand to my shoulder in a comforting gesture, the contact much lighter than when she touched me before. She doesn't elaborate on the identity of the visitor as she continues to work.

By the time the door opens, Helen has attached an intravenous drip to me and given me a dose of morphine that is making me feel a little too happy.

It's not a bad thing since the sight of Jace would otherwise make my blood boil. In the artificial lights, I'm struck by just how tall and muscular he is, his honey blond hair slicked back, deep green eyes casting across the room and taking everything in, including my current weakened state.

"I wasn't expecting you back so soon, Jace," Helen says, without looking up. "It's only been one night."

Jace steps into the room uninvited but stops far enough away from me that I don't feel threatened. Not immediately anyway.

"I won't stay long," he says. "Tristan wants to know how Tessa's doing." His voice is low, soft, calmer than I remember. He stands in the center of the space between me and the door, a military pose with his hands held behind his back, chin up, head held back.

His calmness only serves to rile me. "You can tell Tristan that his property is doing just fine."

"That's clearly untrue." Jace focuses briefly on the drip bag attached to the IV stand before his keen gaze passes over my bruised face down to the ice that Helen is packing around my ribs.

A crease appears in the center of his forehead. "Why does Tessa need human medicine?"

Helen takes a measured breath as she finishes positioning the final ice pack against my left hip. "We hit a snag. She isn't healing. My spells have no effect on her."

If this news startles Jace, he doesn't show it. "What about her pain levels?"

I glare at him, wanting to drag some kind of reaction out of him. "I'm feeling plenty of pain, thank you." I upset one of the ice packs when I point at the side of my chest. "I'm pretty sure this bruised rib right here is thanks to Tristan's caveman antics. Feel free to pass on my gratitude to him."

"He won't be happy to hear it," Jace replies. He turns to Helen, tilting his head slightly and releasing his hands from behind his back. "I'll return on Friday to see how Tessa's doing."

That's five days away. Five days of freedom from male shifters.

Helen gives Jace a nod, after which he heads to the door.

Pausing with his hand on the doorknob, he asks, "How is Ella today?"

Helen takes a deep breath. When she replies, her speech sounds careful. "Much better than yesterday."

Some of the tension leaves Jace's shoulders. "That's good."

Helen sighs and takes a step toward him, dripping water from the ice pack across the floor as she reaches for him. "Jace—"

"Don't start, Helen." He growls into the silence, half-turning to stop her in her tracks with a firm warning glance. "Ella doesn't need to see me. I'm the last person who can help her."

When the door closes, Helen exclaims, "Damn shifter! He's even more stubborn than Tristan."

She quickly refocuses on me. "I'm going to give you something to help you sleep now, Tessa. Rest is the best thing for your body to heal."

Helen injects a substance into the cannula and I sink into a deep sleep, determined to wake up stronger.

CHAPTER NINE

A crash registers in my hearing.

It's close but sounds far away, the *bang* playing havoc with my senses. I can't open my eyes no matter how hard I fight the pull of sleep. Whatever muscle-relaxing drugs Helen gave me to make me rest, they're powerful, practically paralytic, trying to drag me back into oblivion.

Growls, low and deep, vibrate across the air, holding me in the present. I don't know what time it is or how long I was out of it. It could be hours or days, for all I know.

I recognize Tristan's scent as it washes into my body with every inhale I take. There are so many layers to it that I nearly drown in them. Bitter orange, nutmeg, cedar... and beneath them is an elusive note that I can't identify but reminds me of fire. Inhaling his scent is like running through the forest toward a blazing campfire. It surprises me that I can smell it. I haven't been able to scent anyone since I arrived, but his wolf's energy is at its peak, agitated like a moth batting at a lightbulb. His power buzzes in my senses, sharp and prickly, undeniable as he approaches.

His footfalls are quieter than whispers, barely perceptible, but my instincts are working at a thousand percent, suddenly able to sense everything about him. He stops right beside me. Far too close when I'm vulnerable like this, unable to open my eyes or move.

The air shifts across my face. His breathing is harsh in my hearing. The hitch at the start of every inhale cracks loudly in my ears. I picture the angry line of his mouth, the clench of his jaw, the rapid cast of his gaze across me.

The table's soft surface shifts on either side of my face.

"Wake up," he orders me, as if I can obey him. "Wake up, Tessa."

His voice comes from just above my face. He must be leaning over me, probably having planted one hand on either side of my head.

His breath catches again. Held this time.

One of his hands suddenly lifts, his palm pressing against my chest above my left breast, resting lightly there as I continue to breathe. The heat from his fingers burns through my clothing to my skin. Instead of pressing down like he would if he were trying to hurt or restrain me, his palm rises and falls in time with my breathing.

His soft exhalation reaches me—a sound of... *relief?*

I try hard to picture him resting his palm across my chest, letting his hand rise and fall as he leans over me. There are any number of reasons why he might do that, but one possibility in particular surprises me.

Is he checking that I'm still breathing?

I hear another *crack*. I recognize the sound this time—it's nothing more than the door opening—such a harmless sound that's heightened in my drugged senses.

It's followed by soft footfalls. Helen's comforting perfume fills the room, but it barely blocks the intensity of Tristan's presence.

"Tristan." Helen's voice is low and calm. She sounds cautious, deliberately controlled. "You said you wouldn't come back until Tessa is ready."

Tristan's hand remains pressed on my chest above my heart. "Jace said she isn't healing."

The caution in Helen's voice increases. "You came to check on her?"

Tristan's tone hardens, the same edge I heard in it yesterday, dismissing any possibility that he was worried about me. "I need her healed and ready. You should have told me about the delay."

Helen's voice also hardens. "It's only been two days, Tristan.

She's slept for the last thirty-six hours. We haven't started working on her control yet."

"I can tell," he snaps, his exhalation sharp. Maybe he's trying to expel my scent from his body as hard as I wish I could expel the way his wolf's power curls around my senses. "What about her pain?"

"The human medicine is helping her with that."

Tristan's hand clenches around my shoulder. "Because your magic doesn't work on her."

"Light and dark magic can't touch her." Helen takes an audibly deep breath, lowering her voice as she moves closer. Slowly. As if she's got her hands raised ready—maybe even her wand in case she needs it. The warning tone returns to her voice and I wish I could see what she sees.

"Tristan," she says. "You need to step away from Tessa now."

"Why, Helen?" I imagine the suddenly threatening curl of his lips, a smile before he lashes out.

"Because you've clearly had a bad night." Helen's voice becomes sharp. "And you're not in control right now."

I picture Tristan's dilated pupils and his parted lips as he inhales each breath. His growl—his *wolf's* growl—vibrates all the way through his fingers, brushing against the top side of my breast. Tension builds low in my stomach, a needy pull that draws my wolf's energy from her sleep, but not enough for her to show herself.

"You're going to have to lock me out," Tristan says.

There's a pause. I hear a sudden confusion in Helen's voice. "What do you mean?"

"You need to lock me out of Hidden House. If you don't, I'll be back tomorrow. And the day after. I won't leave without Tessa next time. My ability to control this impulse is diminishing."

Helen sounds suddenly flustered. "But what if we need help? What if something happens and you can't get in? What if we have another situation with Ella? You're the only one who can calm her since Jace refuses to come near her. What if the woman in the dark wakes up? You promised you would be here—"

"That's why I have you!" Tristan snarls. "Do the job I asked you to do, Helen."

Her sharp inhale tells me she's indignant and insulted. *"You* are not the reason I'm here," she snaps. "Each of these women deserves a better life. You know that or you wouldn't have brought them here!"

Tristan's hand leaves my chest so suddenly that the air rushes across the space he leaves behind, a rapid cold that creates a dull ache inside me.

I hear the sound of skin on skin, followed by Helen's gasp.

Did he grab her? What's happening? Damn this human medicine! I fight its pull again now that Tristan's power recedes across the room.

Tristan's fierce growl would make me shudder if I could move.

His speech is slow. Dangerously soft, while every syllable is forced. "Listen to me carefully, Helen. Baxter Griffin killed Tessa's father because his son was coming after Tessa. Cody Griffin *needed* to get to Tessa. That's the effect Tessa has on our wolves. Our wolves will endanger anyone to get to her. I can't let this impulse control me too." The distance between me and his voice increases. "I'm leaving now. As soon as I'm gone, you will lock me out before I hurt someone."

Helen's response is an angry whisper. "Fine. I'll do it."

"Good."

Tristan's retreating footsteps are heavy. The door whispers open, quiet this time, but Helen calls out to him. "You know more about Tessa than you're saying," she says, a deep accusation in her voice. "What are you keeping from me, Tristan?"

"Your magic should give you all the answers you need," he replies, dismissive of her concern.

"My magic tells me her power is nothing I've seen before," Helen says. "Her energy is wolf but not wolf. Her human soul is masking an essence that I can't identify. I can't even define the limits of her power. What do you know that I don't?"

Tristan gives a harsh laugh. "You have your secrets, Helen. I have mine." There's a brief pause and I picture the derisive snarl on Tristan's lips. "What is it that you tell newcomers? A little bit of knowledge can get you killed?"

The door clicks shut and Tristan's scent fades. Not gone entirely. Still filling my chest like a lingering cologne.

I'm left with a mix of fear and confusion. Before he decided to fight for me the other night, Tristan had leaned close and told me he "had to be sure."

But sure of what?

Worse than not knowing the answer to that question is the grief that rises inside me. My scent—the nature of my wolf—drove Cody wild enough that he couldn't let me leave. My father tried to protect me from him, and Cody's father ripped my father's throat apart.

What sort of fucked-up crazy shit is going on inside me?

Whatever it is, I never asked for it and I don't want it.

I don't fucking want it!

A moan rises to my lips.

Shockingly, the sound breaks across the room. Finally, my eyelids flutter open, obeying my internal scream to get up. My fingers twitch and shift across the table, gripping the edge, the muscles in my arms answering my commands.

I roll to the edge of the table but can't keep my balance, falling right off.

Thudding onto the floor, I manage to draw my feet under myself in time to land in a crouch. Several ice packs thump onto the floor around me. A sharp pain in the back of my hand tells me that I've wrenched my IV line around. A second later, the stand topples and crashes to the floor. The nearly empty IV bag makes a wet sound as it slips free of the hook and slaps the floor.

"Tessa!" Helen is poised halfway between the table and the door, clutching her wand.

She hurries toward me, but the door crashes open before she's made it two steps.

Tristan races across the space between us.

I can finally see him now that my eyes are open. He's naked from the waist up. His muscles gleam with dirt and sweat. One leg of his black jeans is slit and tattered. The skin across his left cheekbone is cut, a precise but shallow wound like a knife would make, leaving a crimson line across his face. His raven black hair is slicked to the sides of his neck, damp with sweat, and his crisp green eyes are piercing.

He's a mess of blood, sweat, and bruises.

I blink up at him as he rages toward me, his muscles bunched, biceps tense.

My instincts scream at me to get up.

Get the hell out of his path, Tessa!

He scoops me up just as I scramble to the side. Colliding with my torso, his arms hook beneath mine and he lifts me off my feet. His wolf's growls vibrate from his chest to mine, an overwhelming thrumming that sounds almost like a purr as he hoists me back onto the table into a sitting position. My legs straddle his hips, my thighs pressing against the outside of his muscles, but he doesn't push forward, leaving a gap between our jeans that doesn't exist between our chests.

His right hand slides up my back beneath my shirt, coming to rest over the catch at the back of my bra, gripping the elastic so tightly that it could snap.

His face is inches from mine, his lips parted.

"You woke up," he says, his lips curling into a self-satisfied smile, as if he thinks I obeyed him after all. He told me to wake up when he first came into the room.

Despite his close proximity to me, he's unfocused. Blood oozes from the cut across his cheek and his eyes are dazed.

Someone definitely took a knife to him. *Dear fuck.* I inhale a confusing mix of his sweat and the scent of blood that isn't his. There's a splatter of someone else's blood across his earlobe.

"You had a bad night, huh?" I murmur, trying to calm my breathing and figure out how to extricate myself from his arms without thumping him. He deserves a good wallop right now, but the hitch in his breathing tells me he already has bruised ribs.

"Don't make my night worse, Tessa."

"Worse how?" I whisper, searching his eyes.

"Tell me you're not in pain."

I frown. "I'm not in pain."

His order is harsh, vibrating through me with his increasing growls. "Don't lie to me."

I bite my tongue before I fire back an angry response. After all, he just ordered me to tell him I wasn't in pain.

He either wants me to follow orders or he doesn't.

I arch an eyebrow at him, keeping my voice low. "I'm not in pain, Tristan. These human meds are amazing."

He tips his head at me, his eyes narrowed. "But you whimpered."

I consider the hard line of his lips as he presses them together, along with the clenching muscle in his jaw. I'd moaned seconds before he burst back into the room.

"I heard what you said," I whisper, my voice sticking in my throat, honesty wrenching at my heart. "I was upset because... I killed my father."

His fingers suddenly claw my back and his expression changes so rapidly that it shocks me, gleaming and alert. The deepest rage storms across his face, his eyebrows drawing down, teeth clenching, his incisors appearing and making his voice even deeper.

"No," he says. "You didn't kill your father."

I exhale a frustrated sigh. If he's trying to tell me I'm not responsible for my father's death, then he's turning himself into a liar. "My father died because of me. Because of my fucked-up wolf. I heard you loud and clear, Tristan."

His green eyes storm across my face, his fingers pressing so hard into my back that I arch away from them, which only pushes my breasts harder against his naked chest. My flannel shirt and bra are thin barriers between us. The tension at the base of my stomach increases, a needy ache that urges me to slide my hips forward, but I resist its power.

Forcing my hands between our stomachs and leveraging the gap he left between our hips, I slide my hands up across Tristan's abdominal muscles, curving across the chiseled lines. I rest my palms against his pecs, listening for his quick inhales, aware of the gentle part of his lips. Fighting his power and all of its dizzying effects, I push against him, softly at first and then harder when he doesn't budge.

"You need to let me go now or Helen's going to lose her shit," I murmur.

Behind Tristan, Helen stands with her wand raised. The air crackles in a way that tells me she's ready to separate us using magical force if she has to.

Tristan slides his arms away from me, his fingers trailing down my back, making me shiver before he slowly steps away, taking the scent of sweat and blood with him.

His jaw is tight as he spins to Helen. "Lock me out. Or next time, I won't leave Tessa behind."

The door is already open. He breaks into a run, moving so fast that he slides into the opposite wall in the corridor, cracking it on impact. He doesn't stop. His rapidly disappearing footfalls sound down the corridor.

I listen to every beat, hearing Tristan's movements, his running feet, pumping arms, his inhales and exhales, until they finally, suddenly stop and I know he's gone. All the magic in the world can't seem to dampen his impact on me. For better or for worse.

Helen lets out her breath.

"Okay, then." Her shoulders finally relax and her wand lowers. She clears her throat. She's still collecting herself as she strides toward me. "Are you okay, Tessa?"

At my nod, she says, "I want to check you over before you attempt to stand on your own."

Raising her wand again, she quickly runs it across the air in front of me. Her eyebrows rise a little, but the tension disappears from around her mouth. "Good news. Your body is healing itself far more rapidly than I expected. The bruising around your ribs has settled, so has the swelling in your face. Most of the visible bruising is gone too. How long does it normally take you to heal a broken bone?"

"About a week for a bad break," I say, answering her factually-spoken question with a matter-of-fact response.

"You heal far more rapidly than most shifters then."

"It's how I've taken so many beatings," I say, staring back at her.

It's how I'll take many more. I have no illusions that my future is filled with peace.

Helen's jaw clenches. "Not anymore, Tessa. Not on my watch."

I'm starting to believe she means it. That she genuinely wants to help me.

I break the charged silence by swiveling to the window to confirm that it's the middle of the night. "I'm starving and I really need to pee," I say.

Helen pulls away. "Of course. Let me get this off you."

She quickly removes the cannula, releasing me from the fallen medical apparatus on the floor beside the table.

One thing I'm *not* is sleepy.

"Is there any chance Iyana is up and about?" I ask. I'm hoping that her vampire behavior will follow the cliché and she mostly sleeps during the day.

Helen smiles. "She keeps erratic hours. She should wake up any time now."

"Good, because I don't feel like sleeping."

I feel like training. I've wasted enough time already. I plan to make the most of every moment from now until Tristan comes back for me.

I shake off the remnant power that reminds me of him.

It doesn't matter how much Helen tries to protect me, my future will contain more battles. But I'm determined that the next fight will be on my terms.

CHAPTER TEN

$\mathcal{T}$he 9mm pistol feels foreign in my hands, a cold weapon for cold kills.

Iyana shuffles around me while I stand at the bench at the top of the firing lane. She instructs me about my stance and posture, shifting my arms and feet until I'm in the position she thinks is best. Her hands are cool, but not as cold as I was expecting a vampire's touch to feel.

"Knowing how to safely hold your weapon is just as important as knowing how to hit your target," she says.

We have the whole place to ourselves. It's still early morning, but even so, Iyana told Helen not to allow anyone else onto the gun range this morning. I guess she's worried I might not stick to my lane.

"If you're moving around a space carrying your handgun, hold it close to your chest like this," Iyana says, continuing to demonstrate. "You need to be ready to fire at any moment, but you also need to maintain control of your firearm at all times. A trained killer will also be trained to disarm you."

With a final look at me, she says, "Okay, you're good. Take your first shot when you're ready."

She places a pair of earmuffs over my ears. Apparently, I'll move on to silenced weapons eventually, but for now, I need to protect my ears.

I breathe out quietly, trying to center myself while Iyana steps back and pulls on her own earmuffs.

Taking aim—or at least what I'm hoping is a good aim—I squeeze the trigger like Iyana showed me.

The first bullet tears through the paper target at the end of the firing lane, leaving a ragged rip in the right-hand edge.

I'm way off target.

Adjusting my aim, I try again, this time tearing through the left-hand side of the target.

I empty the remaining fourteen rounds into the target before I lower the weapon, the corners of my mouth turning down as I survey my handiwork. It's not so much "target practice" as the slaughter of every edge of the target, leaving the center frustratingly untouched.

I can feel Iyana's disappointment burning across my back. I guess she hoped I'd be a quick study.

Placing the empty weapon carefully on the bench, I remove my earmuffs.

"Shake it off," she says. "It's your first day. Let's keep at it for a while and then we'll head upstairs to the gym."

Twenty minutes later after making zero progress despite all of Iyana's instructions, I bite my lip in defeat. I even managed to hit the targets in the neighboring lanes several times.

"That's okay," she says. "You just need practice."

She's far more gentle with my feelings than I was expecting her to be.

"Let's try again tomorrow." She inclines her head toward the door.

After showing me how to clean the pistol, she leads me back up the stairs. A single flight up, the corridor opens into a gym with a boxing ring at the closest end, weights on one side, and punching bags on the other. At the far end is an open area with wrestling mats leaning up against the wall.

Before she can say anything, I point to the boxing bags, needing to redeem myself.

She arches an eyebrow at me, as if she didn't expect the bags to be my first choice.

When I go to choose a pair of boxing gloves from the ones

hanging on the wall, I'm not surprised to find a pair in my size. Hidden House constantly adjusts itself to my needs. I strap my hands while Iyana leans against the wall. She's already smiling, since it's clear I know what I'm doing this time.

Taking up position and finding my balance, I jab the bag a few times to get a feel for its weight and density before I lay into it with a rapid combination of punches, dodging around the bag while it swings before I pound into it again.

Damn, it feels good to hit something knowing it won't hit me back.

After keeping up a series of rapid combinations while I dance around the bag, I'm sweating through my shirt by the time I step back to find Iyana smiling at me. Tomorrow, I'm going to dig around in my closet for better workout clothes—hopefully a gym shirt and shorts to train in.

"That's good, but can you kick?" Iyana asks.

I smirk, take a step back, and wallop the bag with my foot—high and fast where a man's face would be.

"Okay," she says, her smile broadening into a grin. "Now that I know what you've got, be prepared to work harder than you've ever worked before."

By late morning, we've progressed to the mats and Iyana has tested my reflexes and identified weaknesses she wants me to work on. I'm not upset that she finds chinks in my combat skills—I'll never be invincible, but I can't let any man beat me again. I have to be stronger and faster than anyone else.

Iyana hands me a towel and a bottle of water when we're finished. "Tomorrow, I'll start you on some different styles of martial arts. We'll see what you take to."

Turning to leave the gym, I find two women standing in the doorway whom I haven't met before. They're nearly identical—both have tawny brown hair with golden highlights and sage green eyes, and their cheeks blush peach. They stand shorter than Iyana and I both, petite, wearing flowing skirts and loose sweaters—but I spy the shape of gym shorts and straps of gym tops under their clothing. One of the women clutches a pack of cards in her hand, while the other leans against the door.

They're blocking the exit but don't appear to have any intention of getting out of the way anytime soon.

Iyana doesn't seem fazed by their behavior. "Morning, Lydia." She greets the one leaning against the doorway first, then inclines her head at the one holding the pack of cards. "Luna."

"It's afternoon," Lydia says, rising from her lean.

Iyana grins at her, still appearing unconcerned by the fact that the women continue to block the exit. "It is. But in an hour, will it still be the afternoon?" she asks.

Lydia grins back. "Yes." She folds her hands in front of herself, but a flash of uncertainty fills her face, her grin fading before it reasserts. She nods firmly. "It will still be the afternoon."

Iyana smiles in a way that makes me think this is some kind of game they play—or maybe therapy. "That's great, Lydia."

The other woman—Luna—interrupts the conversation by flicking a card off the top of the pack. The square of paper flies up into the air until it stops and floats above our heads. I make out the image of a human heart speared with a dagger as the card spins slowly around and around.

A trail of white light curls across the air between the card and Luna's upheld hand. She doesn't speak, turning to Lydia instead.

Lydia focuses on me, her sage eyes gleaming for a moment, revealing a small flash of power. "My sister says that your true enemy is the one whose face you can't see."

"O-kay." Iyana jumps in between me and the twins with unexpected speed. "Enough future gazing for now, my dears. Tessa and I need to get cleaned up and have some lunch."

The twins shrug and step around us as they head for the wrestling area we just vacated. I sense Luna's gaze burning my back as she turns in my direction while I stride away down the corridor.

Iyana urges me toward the stairs. "So the official spiel about the twins is this: Luna and Lydia. Card mages. Twins, obviously. Twenty-one years old. But you also need to know that they struggle with space and time. They won't understand that they're in your way, and they sometimes wander down the hallway eating breakfast in the middle of the night. Luna can access her sister's power as well as her own, so she's twice as powerful as an ordinary card mage, but she can't communicate on her own. Lydia needs to speak for both of them."

I study the walls as we walk. The surface ripples through a

rainbow of colors before settling on pale blue, a calming color. It seems to know what I need right now.

We climb the stairs to the library at the beginning of the sleeping quarters.

"Meet me back here after a shower," Iyana says. "We'll head down to the garden for lunch."

"I thought we were supposed to eat in our rooms," I say.

Iyana's eyebrows rise. "You can eat wherever you want, but the garden is where we mostly gather for meals."

"Okay, sure. See you soon."

Returning to my room, I find Ella fast asleep, curled up on the end of her bed, her feet toward her pillow. Her blonde hair falls over the edge. Her locks are so long that the white-gold strands touch the floor.

I tiptoe past her to the bathroom, where I wash off my sweat and check my bruises before donning a fresh pair of jeans and a flannel shirt and then braiding my hair.

I find Iyana sitting at one of the plush couches in the entrance room, flipping through a book. She's dressed in black pants and a lilac T-shirt. Several books are scattered on the coffee table in front of her.

My stomach growls loudly when I arrive and she jumps up right away.

"I'm starving!" she says. "Let's go."

Walking beside a hungry vampire might not be my best move. I risk a laugh. "Should I be worried?"

"Nope," she says, popping the 'p' like she sometimes does. "You're safe with me."

This time, the downward stairs let out into a shaded garden. Directly on the left as we enter, a waterfall flows down one entire wall. Trees and flower bushes circle the space, which gives off a tranquil vibe. Wooden tables and chairs are scattered around a courtyard in the middle of the garden. Women sit around the tables, some in groups, some alone. I'm not surprised to see them since Helen said that many women shelter here. Given her rule about respecting privacy, I'm also not surprised when they don't jump to their feet to introduce themselves. A few raise their heads to give me small smiles, but nobody stares at me. The house prevents me from sensing what they are and it's not obvious from their appearances. We could all be human women out for lunch at a garden restaurant.

Seconds before Iyana steps onto the courtyard, the lighting changes. The blue sky disappears to be replaced with a night sky. The trees light up along their branches with silver fairy lights, glittering and pretty, giving the entire space a silver glow.

Iyana pauses on the bottom step, flushing slightly. "I hope you don't mind eternal night when you're around me. I don't do well in sunlight."

None of the women complain, let alone flinch. One of the women—a petite brunette—gives a happy sigh as she gazes up at the glittering tree branch above her. I think I spy a pointed ear beneath her thick hair, but I'm not sure.

Entering the courtyard, I follow Iyana to an empty table at the back. "We could be out in the open right now, not inside a building."

Iyana smiles as she sits down. "We are outside. This house is constantly transforming itself. Don't worry, you'll get used to it."

"I'm not sure I want to," I say. "I don't want to take it for granted."

A new presence appears beside me and I look up into the kindly face of an older woman with deep brown hair and pale blue eyes, dressed in a black dress.

"What would you like to eat, dear?" she asks.

"You must be Aida?" I ask.

She folds her hands in front of herself with a quiet nod.

"Uh, I would kill for a steak," I say.

"Coming right up." She smiles as she turns to Iyana. "The usual for you, Iyana?"

"Yes, please, Aida," Iyana responds.

Aida gives Iyana a nod and then disappears. I stare at the empty space she leaves behind.

I'm assuming Iyana means blood, and I'm not sure to what extent my human soul will be comfortable watching her drink it, but I push away my reservations.

It won't be real blood. Most likely. Probably.

Iyana watches me squirm with a growing smile. "Don't worry. I don't drink blood."

"Oh. Okay. You mean you abstain?"

"No. I mean I don't need to drink blood." She stares at the bright branches above us. "I have a slightly unusual craving that doesn't involve human blood, but it makes other vampires uncomfortable around me."

I'm amazed when Aida reappears seconds later with a plate laden with a thick steak and roasted vegetables, including hot chips for me.

She places a small shot glass of silver liquid in front of Iyana.

Moaning with delight when I take my first mouthful of food, I pause long enough to watch Iyana drink her silver liquid all in one go before licking her lips. The liquid slides right out of the glass and not a drop remains clinging to the sides.

"What was that?" I ask, with a quizzical glance at the pristinely empty glass.

"My unusual craving," she says, tipping the glass. "Mercury."

My eyes widen. "But that's toxic."

"To you, yes." She gives me a contented smile. "If I can't get a hold of mercury, I can get away with zinc or cadmium. Lots of human vitamins contain zinc. But I need a sip of mercury at least once a month."

"Why would that make other vampires uncomfortable?"

She raises her eyebrows. "It's poisonous to them too. It doesn't kill them, but it makes them very sick. Some hunters used to include it in potions when they went vampire hunting."

She sighs happily as she leans back in her chair and gazes up at the stars, leaving me to inhale my food at speed. Finally, only a small sliver of steak remains on my plate and I'm not sure if I can fit in another mouthful. "How does Helen do all of this?"

"You mean how is any witch powerful enough to create and sustain a place like Hidden House?" Iyana asks.

I murmur a 'yes' around the last mouthful, which I decide is worth consuming even if I have a stomachache later.

Iyana gives me a satisfied smile. She looks like she's ready to fall asleep and I remember that if she's been up since midnight, it's probably her bedtime now. "Helen's responsible for setting all of the spells that make the house function the way it does, but she has a secret source of power that keeps the spells operating so she isn't drained."

"What source?"

Iyana rolls her eyes at me, a lazy motion before she gives a soft laugh. "What part of *secret* source isn't clear?"

I snort. "You seem to know every other secret."

She leans forward, suddenly more alert. "I'm not actually sure," she says. "I can only guess from what I've pieced together over the last seven months."

"Which is…?"

She exhales. A crease forms in her forehead. "I believe there's a woman who sought shelter here long before anyone else. She's so powerful that she remains in a deep sleep—hidden somewhere inside the house." Iyana lowers her voice. "Which could be why Helen nearly freaked out the other day when she thought you might be able to break through the house's old magic and sense the women living here and what their powers might be."

I frown. "So Helen keeps a woman here and siphons off her power while she sleeps? But that's not right—"

Iyana interrupts me. "No, I don't think it's like that. I think this woman willingly offered up her power in exchange for a safe place to retreat from the world."

Iyana falls silent while I chew my lip. I've known pain, but it's hard to imagine agony so great that I would welcome the darkness of sleep.

Wait…

"The woman in the dark," I whisper. "Last night, Helen talked about someone she calls *the woman in the dark*. She was worried about what would happen if the woman woke up and Tristan wasn't here."

Iyana nods. "I'm not sure I'd want to be here when a woman that powerful wakes up." She suddenly narrows her eyes at me. "Why wouldn't Tristan be here?"

Footfalls on the stairs interrupt us. Looking up, I discover that all of the other women have left already, their tables cleared and clean.

Helen appears on the stairs and makes her way to my side. Her hair is loose and she sweeps it to the side, the glossy, dark waves falling across one shoulder.

Iyana immediately yawns and stretches. "Looks like it's bedtime for me, then."

Helen gives her a smile before she says, "Tessa, it's time for your first lesson."

CHAPTER ELEVEN

$\mathcal{T}$he space transforms around me as soon as Iyana disappears up the stairs.

I gasp as the tables and chairs whoosh backward and disappear into the trees, which suddenly shoot new branches at an astounding rate, sprouting new leaves until the broad, lush branches form a thick canopy directly overhead.

The ground brims with flowers and vines of all kinds. It's still the middle of the day, but the moonlight above us softens, somehow whiter, appearing more like starlight.

Helen gestures to the two oversized plush cushions that appear in the middle of the grassy, moonlit clearing. "Take a seat, Tessa."

I hesitate while she sits and crosses her legs, her hair cascading down her back. A trailing silver vine meanders across her right foot, sprouting silver flowers that bloom before my eyes. They blossom and turn toward Helen's body, snuggling against the cushion on which she sits.

She lifts her hand off her knee to gesture at the empty cushion opposite her.

I pick a path through the flowers spreading across the court-yard, miraculously succeeding in leaving them all intact, before I lower myself carefully onto the cushion and fold my legs under me.

A light breeze touches my face, carrying a scent that is both wild and free, as if it has swept off ice-capped mountains, through flower fields, and among blossoms before it reached me.

A sense of space fills me despite the closeness of the trees and the blossoms flowering around me. Magic thrums through every leaf and flower—even the ground I'm sitting on.

This is not a place to eat meals anymore. It's filled with magic that both exhilarates and frightens me with its intensity.

My wolf's energy rises inside me, but it's a calm, tentative surge. I've kept her energy quiet ever since I arrived here, needing to keep her hidden and safe, not wanting to expose her—not wanting to expose *myself*.

Vines sprout around my legs, slipping across the space between my feet and the grassy ground. A silver flower blossoms right beside my hand, its center dusted with gleaming specks of light.

I've never seen anything like it.

The moment that the flower brushes against my fingers, my wolf's energy rises, her form flickering into sight at my side.

She's joined to me like always, this time at my shoulder, her body curving around me. She nudges her head against my chest and brushes the bottom of my chin, her energy buzzing across my jaw and chest.

Opposite me, a smile touches Helen's lips when my wolf appears.

"The most important thing you need to learn is that your scent isn't a smell," she says, startling me with this revelation. "Your scent is your *power*."

My wolf's gaze turns to Helen, as transfixed as I am.

"My power?" I ask.

"That's why the fiercest alphas can detect it. They recognize your strength. As long as you're splashing it around, they are drawn to it and—like all dominant creatures—they need to control it. To leave you uncontrolled is to diminish their own power. Do you understand?"

I remember Cody's declaration after he inhaled my scent. He said he couldn't decide whether he wanted to fuck me or kill me— dominate or destroy.

"I'm a threat," I say.

She nods. "A significant one."

"So to control my scent, I have to control my power," I say, drawing conclusions from what Helen said.

She smiles. "I believe you've spent your whole life pushing your wolf away, denying your power, because that's how you had to survive. It's time to really get to know your wolf, Tessa. You have to understand your power before you can control it."

Fear is cold inside me. I've never hated my wolf's energy, but her unusual nature has caused me constant pain, both physical and emotional.

"I don't know how," I whisper. Reaching out to run my hand through my wolf's insubstantial form beside me, my fingers float right through her shape. "She's energy inside me. Even like this, I can't touch her unless I merge with her. And then I'm still me, just in another form. She has no thoughts except for mine, no heart except for mine."

Helen leans forward with a soft smile. "Then you need to get to know *yourself*, Tessa. You need to understand your own fears, strengths—your capacity for love, hate, indifference, happiness, grief, and all the emotions in between."

I stare at Helen, helpless. "How?"

She settles back onto her cushion. "Let's talk."

While my wolf lowers her head to the flowers, nudging them and tapping her paws on the new ones that blossom in front of her, Helen asks me questions.

She starts with my first memories of the cabin where I grew up and the things I remember about my father in my early years. She touches on my first meeting with my mother when I was school age and required to walk down the mountain to the main village for the first time.

I fall silent at that point.

My wolf's hackles rise at memories I want to forget.

My mother was waiting at the school gate. That was the first time I saw her and her new mate—Peter Nash. My mother stood tall, her red hair a different shade to mine, more orange, like a sunset. Her eyes, startlingly blue, were cold in the early morning light.

She strode up to me, stared down at my six-year-old self, and smacked me across the face so hard that I fell onto the pebbled path. I remember the clatter of my pencils as they scattered across the stones, the crack of her boots as she walked past me, driving her heels into the pencils and snapping them in half before she strode away without a backward glance.

"She hated me," I say. "I ruined her life."

The first two years of school were bad. Then my half-brother Dawson was old enough to attend and things got even worse.

I wince and veer away from the memories, but Helen forces me to refocus on them. "Tessa, the broken bones you sustained tell a story you might not want to remember, but—"

"You're going to tell me that my pain made me stronger." I give her a cold glare. All that *what doesn't kill you makes you stronger* bullshit.

"No, actually, I was going to say that it's not the physical pain that does the most damage. It's the psychological harm of being made powerless—*despite* the strength flowing through your body."

"Then what do I do about it?" I snap, my defenses in full swing.

"Let her out, Tessa."

"What?"

"Your wolf. Stop constraining her. I sense the power inside you trying to free itself. Let your wolf out the way you must have wanted to let her out when you first experienced your mother's hatred. When Dawson broke your arm the first time. Until you know your full strength, you won't understand how to mask your scent."

"I can't..." I edge away from Helen, scooting back across the cushion. "I can't let myself feel that angry."

"Nothing bad will happen," Helen says. "I promise."

I give a sarcastic laugh. "You say that now."

"Look around you, Tessa. This garden is full of magic and beauty—"

"I'll destroy it."

"You won't. The magic here is stronger than that. The most peaceful things are often more resilient than you can imagine."

Demonstrating just how destructive I can be, I slam my fist down onto the nearest silver flower, my wolf's energy crackling through my hand.

The blossom tears apart beneath my blow. "See?"

Helen only smiles. "Take another look, Tessa."

I lift my hand. Silver dust from the broken flowers coats the back of my fingertips, but I'm shocked when the flower reforms, quietly knitting itself back together. A second and third flower form on the vine on either side of it.

It's such a beautiful reaction to my violence that it takes my breath away.

Before I can respond, a shadow passes across me, casting me into cold darkness.

Looking up, I find that the space around me has transformed.

It's early morning and the sunlight should be warm, but my hands are clammy, my bottom lip chewed so badly from nerves, it's cut and bleeding.

I stand again at the school gate, the brown brick pillars rising on either side of the wrought-iron entrance. My mother stands in front of the gate, her sunset hair glowing like a halo. She should have been my angel, my source of love and kindness.

Peter Nash looms beside her, a giant to me, his wolf skull tattoo making me shudder.

Mom casts a cold glare at me across the distance, her head held at a haughty height. I stop on the path, gripping my backpack, my palms sweating so much that my fingers slip as I try to adjust the straps.

I feel her hatred deep in the core of my soul—a hatred I never expected to be so intense. It stops me in my tracks, rips at my stomach, makes my heart burn.

My older self screams at her in my defense: *For fuck's sake. You're my mother. I was only six years old.*

She strides toward me and I remember... in that moment... my wolf's energy questing inside me, asking to be released. I could sense every watching eye on me. The other kids. Several teachers in the background. Peter Nash's cruel smile as he watches his mate descend on me. My mother's shadow looming over me—so large because I was a tiny girl. Her hand rising...

Not this time.

Not again.

My wolf's energy bursts out of me, taking shape at my side, but this time, I merge with her, shifting fully.

The world around me turns into cobalt fire and I'm astounded at the paleness of my mother's power, how insignificant it is compared to Tristan's, even Cody's, certainly nothing compared to my father's.

I take on my wolf's shape, welcome my wolf's claws and teeth, snarl with her vocal chords, and leap with her strength.

My mother screams, tries to shift into her wolf form, but I'm faster.

I knock her down.

My claws rake across her chest, and I sink my teeth into her neck. But I don't rip out her throat, pausing as her blood fills my mouth.

This is an illusion.

I never did this. I have never conquered my fear of remaining unloved and unwanted by everyone but my father.

As I release my screaming mother, my surroundings change again. Her screams become a sigh on the breeze as the garden reappears.

Only my full shift actually happened.

I'm still in wolf form, the silver flowers and vines forming a carpet beneath my paws. Snarling, I lower my head, my wolf's rage flowing through me as I take a threatening step toward Helen. Her silhouette burns bright cobalt in my vision, her power so intense that it lights the space around us in a myriad of sparkles. Her power is as intense as Tristan's, threatening to burn out my wolf's power like his did.

"Tessa," she says, quiet and unafraid, meeting my wolf's eyes. "Let her out."

I'm confused. My wolf is already out. This is as *out* as she gets.

Helen rises slowly to her feet. "You're holding her back, Tessa. Stop caging her!"

I take a startled step back, but my rage rises, my snarls deepen. A thought rises inside my mind, as if my wolf's energy somehow finds its own voice: *What does this witch know of me?*

Nothing.

Not a fucking thing.

I scream inside my mind, a sound that takes the form of a fierce growl, my wolf's snarls shivering across the air.

A burst of energy flows through me as I prepare to leap forward, but a tearing sensation fills me, ripping through my heart and mind.

My wolf leaps ahead of me, detaching from my body as she leaves the ground and leaps toward Helen.

I scream in shock.

She's separate from me!

I'm left crouching in my human form in the middle of the vines while my wolf slashes at Helen with her claws and teeth, a wild creature somehow existing outside of me.

At the same time, my vision splits.

I can see the scene in front of me—Helen's magic bursting around her body to protect herself as my wolf attacks—while I can also see what my wolf sees: a closer version of Helen's magic swirling around them both.

I'm seeing through my wolf's eyes as well as my own, even though my body remains behind her. It makes my head spin and the contents of my stomach threaten to return to me.

My wolf rips through Helen's magic, but the animal's teeth pass through her arm, not leaving a mark.

I'm filled with both relief and horror at the scene in front of me. Without me, my wolf has no substance. No form. She can't do any damage, even though she's outside of me.

It doesn't stop her.

She tries again, leaping and attempting to savage Helen's thigh, but my wolf's teeth pass right through Helen's body.

Shuddering, I smother another scream rising inside me.

I drop to the ground and squeeze my eyes shut.

Even with my eyes closed, I can still see what my wolf sees.

Helen stops fighting back, allowing her magic to recede, standing very still instead.

My head spins and the contents of my stomach rise as I struggle to maintain my sense of space and time—of where I am. Of *what* I am.

My mind tells me that with my eyes closed, my vision should be dark, but the scene in front of me tips and whirls, shifting with every savage movement my wolf makes, my ears filling with her snarls.

"Stop!" I cry, clutching my head, pressing my hands to my ears. "Come back!"

My wolf whimpers in response to my command, backing slowly away from Helen. She is so proud that she doesn't stop snarling, her lips drawn back from her teeth until she backs into me.

Her energy merges with me again, her form melds into mine, and my vision returns to normal when I dare to open my eyes.

I tip to the side, drawing my knees to my chest, curling up in the carpet of silver vines as I struggle to breathe. "What just happened?"

Helen's quiet footsteps approach.

She kneels beside me, her comforting scent surrounding me again. Her hand is warm, firm, on my arm. "You did what no shifter should be able to do," she says.

My breathing is rapid. Panicked. "I could see with her eyes."

"Then she can scout for you, Tessa."

My gaze flies upward. "What did you say?"

"I said this is a good thing." Helen's smile is gentle. "Your wolf has enormous capacity, Tessa. She's part of you but can separate from you. Tell me: Did you feel weaker when she was away from you? As if she took your strength with her?"

I shake my head. "I felt the same. Just as strong as when she's with me."

"Then her ability to separate could be a huge advantage in a fight. She can scout ahead or keep watch at your back. You just need to control what you see without it messing with your head."

I exhale, my breathing finally slowing. "Did you know that I could do this?"

Helen shakes her head. "I wasn't sure, but I sensed your power bashing around inside you—tied to you but also trying to escape."

"I think I need some time to process this," I whisper.

"Take all the time you need, but remember this: You controlled her. She attacked because you were angry. She stopped when you needed her to stop. She has no mind other than yours."

Helen presses her palm against my chest above the location of my heart. "When you really understand your power in your heart, then you'll control your wolf's energy completely and you won't be afraid of her anymore. That's when you'll also control your scent."

Helen helps me to my feet, but I can't quite meet her eyes.

I bite my lip as guilt rises inside me. "I'm sorry that she—I mean *I*—attacked you."

She waves away my concern. "You'd be the exception if you hadn't. Every woman who shelters here has learned to distrust everyone around her in order to survive. I don't judge anyone for that."

Helen supports me as we walk to the stairs, leaving the quiet garden behind. Even two days ago, I never would have accepted her help. Now I hold on to her without shame, feeling like a barrier has been lowered between us.

My wolf attacked her and she stood firm, facing my rage without flinching. Any woman who can do that deserves my respect.

CHAPTER TWELVE

*F*or the next two months, I remain single-minded. Each afternoon, I spend hours with Helen, learning how to separate from my wolf and to control my power. Each morning, Iyana trains me in weaponry first and then combat after that. My shooting aim improves marginally, but nowhere near as quickly as my ability to take on new combat techniques. At our gym sessions, Iyana introduces me to the art of Muay Thai, and I don't look back, learning to extend my boxing skills and make more effective use of my elbows, knees, and shins. Every part of my body becomes a weapon, not just my fists and feet.

I'm not the only woman in the house who makes progress.

Ella ventures out of our room and starts spending her mornings in the garden, making her way back up to our room before everyone comes to the garden for lunch. We often meet in the library and walk silently along the corridor back to our room together—me to have a shower, her to crawl into her bed and sleep away all of the sensory input from her morning spent outside.

Over the course of the first month, several women leave the house, including the woman with the pointed ears. Before she goes, Helen places a glamour over her ears to hide her true appearance from the world and protect her.

Jace is a regular but quiet visitor each week, but he only ever visits the gun range, observing me from a distance before disappearing again. It frustrates me that he always turns up first thing in the morning, watches me scowl my way through a shooting session in which I inevitably miss the target about a thousand times, and then he leaves before we head upstairs to the gym.

He has no idea of the progress I'm making in the combat ring.

I tell myself that's a good thing. Jace reports back to Tristan. If they don't know about my progress, then they'll underestimate my skills.

Even so, my pride smarts every time I sense his gaze burning my back. I can feel his judgement cutting into my self-esteem through the soundproofed wall as he watches me fail at target practice time and time again.

Danika, the hawk shifter, often joins Iyana and me in the mornings. And then at lunchtime too. She doesn't talk much about her past, but when she shows me her room, my jaw drops. She sleeps on the edge of a cliff, where she can shift into her hawk form and soar across the sky whenever she wants to.

As far as the gun range goes, I envy Danika's ability to hit the target every time, no matter what type of gun she's using. At one point, she takes pity on me and tries to tell me that it helps to hate my target, to imagine it represents the person I despise most in the world.

I try imagining that the target is Baxter Griffin in the moment that he ripped out my father's throat. Then I try to imagine it's Cody. And lastly, Tristan. Even with all of my anger, my bullets continue to chew up the edges of the target day after day, never hitting the center.

Finally, at the end of my second month at Hidden House, I place my empty weapon onto the bench in front of me, remove my earmuffs, and plant my hands on my hips, staring at the untouched target.

If Danika or one of the other women were here, I would keep my earmuffs on for safety reasons, but Iyana and I have the place to ourselves.

Iyana stands a little behind me and I can already hear what she's going to say: *Shake it off; you'll do better tomorrow.*

We both know I won't.

It's time to admit that guns aren't my thing. "It's like I'm primed to hit everything other than what I'm aiming for," I say.

As I turn to give Iyana the news that I'm giving up, the door in the glass wall behind us opens.

I freeze as Jace enters.

He was so quiet this morning that I wasn't aware of his presence. More surprisingly, this is the first time he's come anywhere close to me since my first days at Hidden House.

Iyana shifts a little closer to me as he approaches, a protective gesture that he doesn't miss—causing him to stop short. She was originally going to leave Hidden House after my first week. Instead, she's stayed two months.

Jace folds his arms across his chest as he stops several paces away from us. He's wearing his usual low-slung jeans, but today, a black T-shirt conceals his wolf tattoo.

I frown at the ugly bruise stretching across his cheek. It's faded, maybe a week old. My own bruises are long healed, even if the memories of that night will remain with me forever.

"Maybe you should try throwing knives," Jace says.

I glare at him, unimpressed by his condescension. "Very funny."

"I'm not trying to insult you," he says, his tone serious. "I can't shoot a gun to save my life, but I can hit a guy's eye with a knife from twenty feet away. While he's running in a zigzag, no less."

Jace takes a step toward me, but I stand my ground.

"We're shifters," he says. "We need instinctive weapons. Guns are as cold as vampires. No offense, Iyana. Knives are visceral—up close and bloody. That's how shifters fight."

Uncertain, I cast a questioning glance at Iyana. So far, we haven't started working with blades, but Jace's claims resonate with what Helen has been teaching me about my wolf—she is part of me at a deep, instinctive level. My power follows the most basic instincts—claw, tooth, life, lust, and death. There is no threat here in the gun range. My target is always at a distance, removed from me and made of paper, even if I try to imagine it's someone I hate.

"I'm willing to try it," I say, beating back my own misgivings.

"It's completely up to you, Tessa." Iyana tips her head in acquiescence. "But blades aren't my forte. I can fight with them, but I'm no good at throwing them. Jace will have to show you." She gives him a pointed and cold look, pinning him with her icy blue-gray eyes. "If he's willing."

Jace pauses before he inclines his head in agreement. The length of his pause tells me he thought he could throw his suggestion out there and move on. He clearly wasn't counting on having to teach me.

"Let's head up to the gym for this," Iyana says, seeming to take his silence for agreement. "You'll need a solid target."

Jace steps well clear of us as we pass by. On the night my father died, Jace told me that whatever power my scent had over Tristan, Jace didn't plan on succumbing to it. I warned him that he'd better not get too close to me. I'm still not sure if Jace is a powerful enough shifter to detect the high and low notes of my scent like Tristan can, but I don't want to find out.

I can't help smirking, though, as I wonder how he's going to show me how to throw a knife without touching me to check my footing or the position of my arms. Maybe he'll demonstrate from a distance.

But then I wonder... What if my scent has no impact on him because I have it under control now?

On the way up the stairs, I suddenly realize that I'm in a dangerous position.

In the last two months, Helen has taught me how to control my wolf more thoroughly than I ever thought possible. She has taught me how to diminish my scent, as well as accentuate it, controlling it at will. She helped me see that the cobalt fire that fills my vision when I harness my wolf's energy is the color of my fear, that I can control my fear and tame it. Helen has taught me to turn my wolf into a quiet predator, scouting through the garden, relaying every-thing my wolf sees—everything *I* see—back to my human form.

Helen also promised that she wouldn't tell Tristan that I was ready until I asked her to.

I'm not ready to leave Hidden House yet.

Soon. Just... not yet.

Now, Jace might find out that I'm a whole lot more ready than Helen has been reporting to Tristan.

A sense of trepidation fills me by the time we reach the gym.

The only way I can avoid being discovered is if I keep my distance from Jace and make sure he doesn't suspect I'm in control already.

Reaching the gym, we find the room magically rearranged. The boxing ring has been replaced with an open area with large, wooden targets standing in a row. A large rack holding a myriad of different-shaped knives sits at the front of the space nearest to the door.

The card mage twins meet us in the doorway as we arrive. They're disgruntled and sweaty, wearing their gym clothing.

"We *were* using the boxing ring," Lydia says, gesturing to the now-empty space. "Until it disappeared and the room rearranged itself."

I suck in an apologetic breath. "Sorry, ladies."

Lydia rolls her eyes. "Well, I guess it's time for our *mid-morning* snack anyway," she says, winking at me.

"Are you sure it's not afternoon?" I ask, with a completely straight face, testing her ability to tell the time.

She rolls her eyes at me. Over the last two months, the twins have become much more cognizant of time and space, so much that they'll sometimes remind me when I'm late for something.

"I'm certain," she says.

Beside her, Luna is fixated on Jace, her sage green eyes widening and her cheeks filling with color. I've learned that Luna's blush is not a sign of embarrassment, rather that she's accessing her power.

Lydia notices too, startles, and gives Luna's arm a firm tug toward the corridor, but Luna refuses to budge. She pulls her playing cards from her pocket, a deep crease of concentration forming in her forehead. I catch the startling image of a weeping wolf on the card she holds.

Jace returns Luna's stare with a calmness I wasn't expecting. "Don't worry," he says to her, a hint of bitterness tugging at his lips. "I know what you're going to tell me."

Just when Luna moves as if she's going to throw the card into the air, Lydia grabs her sister's hand, covering the cards and stopping her.

"Not today, dearest," she whispers to her sister. "It won't end well."

Luna's eyes soften as her luminous gaze passes across Jace to her sister.

Lydia gives a long, low sigh at the silent conversation she has with her sister. "I know," she says. "But no good can come of it."

This time, Luna doesn't fight her sister's wishes.

"We'll be on our way." Lydia slips her arm through Luna's and guides her away.

I exhale, suddenly realizing that I was holding my breath, uncertain what Luna might say.

The pause in the doorway has forced us to stand much closer together than I want us to be. As soon as Iyana strides away from Jace and me to take up position on the right-hand side of the room —a safe distance from the knife targets—I hurry away from him as quickly as I can.

I stop in front of the knife rack, keeping Jace in the corner of my vision, satisfied when he stays at a distance. Studying the knives, I consider my options, uncertain which blade to choose, but not because I'm uncomfortable. Already, I'm feeling more at home around these weapons. The difficulty is that there are so many to choose from.

I pick up the blade sitting directly to my right, gripping it and getting a sense of its weight and balance. It has a basic black handle and a sharp point while the edge itself isn't sharp.

"Those are good to start with," Jace says, lifting his voice so I can hear him across the space. "You're less likely to hurt yourself while you learn."

I stop myself before I huff. *Hurt myself. Right.*

He points at a spot near the knife rack about six feet from the first target. "Stand there. Right foot a little forward. Back straight. And relax."

I glare at him. His barked orders aren't exactly conducive to relaxation.

"Hold the knife by the handle, blade to the sky. You're going to try for a full rotation when you throw it," he says.

Taking a deep breath and attempting to relax, I follow his instructions and pitch the blade as hard as I can at the target. It bounces off the wood and flies wide, clattering and sliding across the floor.

Oops...

I'm grateful Iyana is standing well away from its trajectory.

"Not so hard!" Jace shouts. "You want to use medium force, not everything you've got. Here…"

He strides toward me, veers toward the knife rack to pluck another knife off it, and then barges straight toward me.

I back away from him like a startled cat, needing to keep my distance. My arms fly up into a defensive position as I move, taking on a combative pose. "Stay back!"

He pulls up short, his eyes widening at my stance. His arms rise away from his sides before he bends slowly to put the knife on the floor and back away from it.

"It's okay," he says, lowering his voice as he backsteps. "I'm not going to hurt you."

Damn. He thinks I'm afraid of him.

"That's not…" I lick my suddenly dry lips. "Just keep your distance. Okay?"

"Sure." He nods before inclining his blond head at the knife on the ground. "Try that one. This time, use moderate force."

I wait for him to return to his original position before I stride to the knife, scoop it up, and resume my stance six feet away from the target.

"Relax," he calls, much more gently this time. "Hold the handle with your thumb on top. Point the blade at the sky. Remember: moderate force, not full force."

I follow his instructions, bending my arm at the elbow, and let the knife fly.

It makes a satisfying *thud* as it hits the target and sticks.

I break into a grin and let out a whoop. It's not exactly a bullseye, but it's much closer than I ever got with a gun.

"Yes!" Iyana calls from the side, grinning from ear to ear.

"Not bad," Jace says, striding toward me again. "Better than guns, right?"

"Much better." I smile back at him.

For a second, I forget that I need to keep my distance.

I also forget how fast he is.

He closes the gap between us in a blink. His hand whips out to grip my wrist in a suddenly aggressive move.

What the hell—?

I retaliate on instinct, twisting, dropping my weight, and flipping him onto his back. He hits the ground but is already rolling back to his feet and coming right back at me.

Iyana runs toward us, but she pulls up short at the warning look I give her a split second before Jace tries to grab me again.

Blocking his attempts, I hit back, landing quick, sharp blows on his face and shoulders before dropping him right back to the ground.

He jumps up again, barreling into me with full force and wrenching me off my feet. It's the same move Cody used on me, but I know how to deal with it this time. Before he can hoist me over his shoulder, I ram my right knee into his chest, forcing him to double over. He drops me to the ground, where I use our downward momentum to flip him over me once again.

He lands with a heavy thud, gripping his side and, this time, he remains where he lies, chest heaving, staring up at the ceiling.

I loom over him, elbows bent and hands up, prepared in case he tries to grab me again.

"Stay down," I order him.

"Fuck," he says, still staring upward, his deeper-than-green eyes cast into shadow when he runs the back of his hand across his forehead. "I knew you couldn't be afraid of me."

Very slowly, he twists to the side and rises to his feet, squaring his shoulders, reminding me that he's a powerful shifter with an angry wolf concealed inside.

He exhales…

And inhales. Deeply.

I step back, but it's too late.

He knows I'm in control.

CHAPTER THIRTEEN

$\mathcal{I}$ watch Jace carefully, unsure if I've got my power as under control as I think I do. I'm wary of the telltale dilation of his pupils that will mean he's about to lose his shit.

Nothing happens.

He exhibits no signs of uncontrollable rage, desire, or any other emotion. Except a hint of betrayal in his suddenly rough voice.

"You didn't want me to find out," he says, shaking his head at me, his eyes holding an accusation I can't deny. "Helen said you were months away from being ready, but you've got everything under control already."

I clench my fists, screaming internally. "Don't blame Helen. She's only trying to protect me." I keep my voice low and calm. I'm determined not to beg him to keep my secret. "You can't tell Tristan. Not yet."

A muscle clenches in Jace's jaw. He narrows his eyes at me, his expression cold. I should be wary of his rising anger. After all, he's Tristan's right-hand-man.

"What do you want from me, Tessa?" He snarls. "Do you want me to lie to Tristan? Is that it?"

"Don't tell him, Jace. I need more time."

Jace runs his hand through his honey blond hair as he presses his lips together. He shakes his head, glares at the floor, then turns his glare on me. "Tristan and I have always been honest with each other," he says. "Even when we don't like what the other has to say. Now you're asking me to lie to him. He hates liars."

"Then he'll hate me more than he already does," I snap. "It's not like he plans to keep me alive."

Jace's glower intensifies. I expect him to have a comeback—I *need* him to have a comeback, because otherwise his silence confirms my belief.

To Tristan, I am expendable.

Jace spins on his heel without another word.

My heart sinks.

"I'm dead once I leave this house, Jace," I say, my lips twisting. "I can start counting down my days."

He pulls to a stop five paces away, his shoulders tense, fists clenching.

"Give me another month. Just one." I take a step toward him, trying not to hold my breath when he doesn't pull away. "I have a home here. With people who care what happens to me. The second you tell Tristan that I'm in control, he'll rip it all away from me."

Jace is silent. His fingers slowly uncurl, relaxing, and I have no idea whether or not that's a good sign.

"Please," I whisper, hating that I'm begging when I promised myself I wouldn't. "Just another month."

He sighs. Half-turns. "I'm sorry, Tessa."

My heart sinks. "Fuck you," I whisper.

I have no choice but to watch him walk away.

Iyana hurries to my side as soon as he leaves, reaching out for me. "Tessa, what's going on?"

Despite all the time I've spent training with her, I haven't told Iyana about the impact of my power on other wolf shifters or about Tristan's intentions for me. I want to tell her, but the memory of her reaction when she thought Tristan might have hurt me is still raw in my mind. I can't break her beliefs.

I stick to what I can tell her. "Tristan's coming back for me. That's all."

She grabs my arm when I attempt to turn away. "You told Jace that you'll be dead once you leave this house," she says, trying to force me to look her in the eye. "Why?"

I avoid her gaze. "Tristan has plans for me. That's all you need to know."

"Tessa—"

"I have to find Helen." I pull away from Iyana, hurrying for the door.

Racing down the corridor, I hope that the staircase will lead me wherever Helen is currently located.

I enter the garden to find her meditating like she often does.

Normally, I would take a seat on the cushion opposite her before I speak. I'd focus on my own breathing and allow my wolf to separate from my body, taking advantage of the silence to practice controlling my wolf and my power.

Today, I'm too agitated, striding toward her with heavy foot-steps. "Helen, I—"

"Calm," she says without opening her eyes. "Remember what I taught you."

I take a breath instead of arguing with her. One of the most important things I need to do is remain in control no matter what's going on around me, to let it all wash off me without losing my cool.

Over the last two months, Helen has been teaching me how to control my anger and defensiveness. Those emotions are still a big part of me, but she's trained me so that I can use them as weapons. Or at least she's attempted to.

Sinking onto the pillow, I breathe deeply, focusing only on my breathing and the soft breeze around me before I allow my wolf to separate from me.

Released from the confines of my body, my wolf pads away through the trees, calm again.

I close my eyes and take in everything she sees and smells—the slightly damp earth, the new violet tinge to the silver vines trailing along the lush tree branches, and the quiet call of a distant bird—a hawk. The bird's call sounds a lot like Danika's voice when she speaks.

Helen and I and my wolf stay like that for nearly half an hour until finally, Helen draws me out of my calm when she exhales a deep sigh.

Opening my eyes, I recognize the regret in her expression, the way her hands turn across her knees, palms up.

My wolf continues to explore around us, but I've learned how to put her sensory input to the side while I focus on what's in front of me.

"Tristan knows that you're in control now," Helen says, her voice soft. "In my last message I sent with Jace, I told Tristan that you weren't ready. He knows I lied to him."

I lower my gaze. "I'm sorry, Helen. I never wanted to create conflict between you and Tristan."

"Hush. You didn't ask me to do this. I offered. Besides, he's still locked out. He can rage all he likes right now."

Her smile remains gentle.

I close my eyes and take deep breaths. "I won't survive once I leave this house. Tristan will throw me into situations I don't want to be in. He doesn't care if he gets me killed."

Helen lowers her gaze, studying her hands. "You're stronger than that, Tessa," she says, finally meeting my gaze. "You've trained harder than any other woman who's ever set foot in this place. You've conquered your wolf and tamed your energy. You've grown strong in your body and your mind. And… you shouldn't underestimate your value to Tristan."

Frustration burns hot in my chest, but I calm myself again. "I'm a chess piece to him."

Helen tips her head, her dark hair floating at her side. She's wearing a dress today with flowing sleeves that flutter around her wrists. "Not an ordinary piece, Tessa. You're the queen on the board."

My eyes widen. I don't know much about chess, but the queen is the most powerful piece—and her end can have significant consequences.

"Right now, you're waiting at the back of the army," Helen says. "But Tristan plans to put you into play. After that, your choices are your own."

Her statement makes me shiver.

"I expect Tristan will come for you tomorrow," Helen says. "In the meantime, take the afternoon off. Prepare yourself emotionally and mentally."

I pick at my nails, feeling nervous enough that my wolf raises her head from the flower she was inspecting.

"Deep breaths, Tessa," Helen says gently. "You can do this."

I give her a nod, slowing every movement down to maintain my calm. I remind myself: "I have everything I need."

Drawing my wolf back to myself, I stand and take the stairs more calmly than I thought I would in the face of Tristan coming back for me.

Instead of returning to my room, I spend the next few hours until lunchtime exploring Hidden House like I promised myself I would one day but thought I had more time to do.

Opening my mind to possibilities, I ascend the stairs and find myself stepping out onto a glittering mountain, rockfaces soaring up on either side of me and only a narrow pass in between. In the distance, a sliver of clear sky beckons to me.

A cool breeze whistles through the mountain, but the wind is at my back, urging me to take the steps to the cliff's edge, where the sky opens up and the rockface plummets, a smooth face that's so high up, all I see is clouds beneath me.

I smile into the wispy white. "Love the metaphor, Helen," I say, imagining she can hear me right now.

I'm about to walk a narrow path, boxed in on both sides with only one way forward with an inevitable fall at the end of it. But who knows what's hidden beneath the clouds? The possibilities are endless. I just have to trust that I'll have the courage to find out.

Turning and taking the narrow pass back to the stairs, I finally venture down to the garden for lunch.

I'm nervous about what I'll say to Iyana—and how I'll bring myself to say goodbye to her and Danika.

By the time I reach the garden, the trees have receded since my meeting with Helen, opening up the courtyard, which is filled with tables and chairs. The night sky above me tells me Iyana is already here, since otherwise, the midday sunlight would spear through the overhead branches.

I spy Iyana and Danika sitting at the far table nearest to the tree at the back. They gesture to me. I sense their quiet mood and catch the glances they throw each other as I approach.

I stop at the side of the table. "You want to know what's going on?" I ask.

Iyana leans forward, gripping her empty shot glass. Her long, black hair shines where it lies across her shoulder.

She doesn't bother with small talk, launching right into it. "We've only seen one side of Tristan—the rescuer. Fuck, I hardly even remember the night he brought me here. I was barely alive." She stares down at her glass, her eyes filling with sudden tears, but she blinks them away. "All I remember is that he sat with me the whole night, holding my hand while Helen worked over me..."

I find my seat, my movements heavy. I've never seen Iyana cry. Other than my first day here, she has been a pillar of strength in my life.

"My former employer sent me into Tristan's territory for a job that turned out to be a death trap," she says. "Tristan was a protector when I needed one. But I get the very strong indication that your relationship with him is different."

I fold my hands over each other in my lap, where my friends can't see me wring them. Iyana and Danika know a version of Tristan that I have never met or experienced. It's like we could be talking about two completely different people. "My relationship with Tristan is complicated."

Danika persists. "Trust me, we understand complicated. You don't have to give us details, but we need to know if Tristan is the man we think he is." She reaches across the table, her hazel eyes filled with concern. Her tousled light brown hair is longer than when I first arrived and brighter than the first day we met, the golden highlights catching the moonlight. "You're our friend, Tessa. The prickliest, most defensive friend we've ever had—and that's saying something—but you must know by now that we care and worry about you."

My eyes suddenly fill with tears. I try to blink them away like Iyana did, but Danika's declaration has stunned me. My relationships with these women means more to me than I've told them. Theirs are the only friendships I've experienced. Along with Iyana and Danika, Helen has cared for me, and even Ella is my quiet friend, giving me strength with her silence when we walk together each day from the library back to our room. I didn't know what friendship looked or felt like until I came here.

My voice sticks in my throat, but I take a deep breath and remind myself to be calm. "You already know that I'm resistant to light magic and dark magic. Well... there are other aspects of my power that Tristan thinks he can use against the other alphas to destroy his enemies. On the night I came here, he fought to save my life, but he also made it very clear that I belong to him now."

I start at the beginning and tell them everything—about my father, about my half-brother, Dawson, about Cody Griffin, and then the way Tristan brought me here. Iyana and Danika listen quietly. By the end, we're nearly the only ones left in the garden. A few other women and Helen remain, finishing their lunch on the other side of the courtyard.

Iyana leans back in her chair, casting a questioning glance at Danika. "The ownership thing is alpha shifter bullshit, right?" she asks. "Vampires don't have that culture—it's more *kill each other to rise to the top* where I come from. So you're going to need to explain it to me."

Danika tips her head in the affirmative. "Pretty much. The alpha needs to assert dominance. But..." She leans back in her chair. "I don't think we'll know until we get out there whether this is a case of pure domination or whether there's more to it."

I give them a confused frown. "We?"

Iyana breaks into a grin. "We're coming with you."

"What?"

They both lean forward, big grins on their faces. "You're not leaving the house alone."

"But I have no idea what I'm walking into," I splutter. "I can't let you endanger yourselves."

Iyana scoffs. "I was going to join Tristan when you first arrived. I don't have anywhere else to go, and I figured he could use my help."

"I'm ready to leave, too," Danika adds. "I'm getting itchy wings."

My eyes are leaking already. "That's... I'm..."

"Don't cry on me, Tessa," Iyana says, nudging my foot with hers.

I jump up and hug her, knocking over her shot glass as my arms close around her. Danika launches herself across the table and joins the hug. I don't care that it's awkward and we bump elbows. I need these women to know how much I appreciate their support.

"Thank you," I whisper, closing my eyes and accepting their friendship.

A sudden crash at the side of the garden makes us leap apart and spin toward the sound.

Helen stands half out of her seat, gasping and clutching her chest. Her plate lies shattered at her feet. She must have knocked it off the table when she stood up.

"Helen!" I shout. My wolf leaps away from my body, separating and racing to her side, reaching her before I do.

The other women remaining in the garden crowd toward her, but my wolf keeps them away with soft growls, herding them back. It can't hurt them, but they stand clear, allowing me through.

I slide to a stop at Helen's side with Iyana and Danika close behind me. "Helen! What's wrong?"

She grips my shoulder, her fingers biting into my arms. "Tristan just broke the lock. He's already here."

CHAPTER FOURTEEN

I stare at Helen in shock. "How did he break into the house?"

Helen's face is pale, her dark hair fallen loose from her topknot and the collar of her shirt ruffled, as if the force of the magical break blew through her body.

She leans close to me and all of the sounds around us stop. I suddenly realize that she's shielding our conversation.

"Remember what I told you about old magic being able to affect old magic?" Her hands shake around my arms and her voice is a hoarse whisper. "Tristan is stronger than you can imagine, Tessa. I think you've sensed his power. Even this house can't control him."

She releases one of my arms to brush my hair back from my face. "You might be the only one who can truly match him. But he's not here because of you. Not yet..."

My ears pop as she leans back again before I can respond or ask her what she means. Whatever shield she placed around our conversation is gone in an instant and our exchange is no longer private.

"Tristan needs help." Helen tries to stand fully but stumbles against the table. I tighten my hold on her while Iyana rounds the table to support Helen's other side. "I need to get to the medical wing right away."

Iyana's eyes are round. "Tristan must be bringing somebody wounded. Help me get Helen upstairs."

Nobody new has come to the house since I arrived, even though a handful of women have left. If Tristan's broken through the lock to bring someone who needs help, it must be urgent.

Danika leans forward across the table to me. "I'll make sure everyone stays safely in their rooms, and I'll check on Ella to make sure she's okay. You stay with Helen and help her in any way she needs."

As the room empties around us, I assist Helen to stand.

"I'll be fine," she insists. "My magic just got a shock. I'll be okay soon."

"Deep breaths," I whisper to her as I continue to support her on one side while Iyana holds her other.

Together, we shuffle our way across the floor and up the stairs.

I haven't been back to the medical wing since I healed after the fight with Cody and Dawson. I shake off the memories while I help Helen into the first room on the right.

She's standing straighter by the time we get there, regaining the color in her cheeks.

"I'm okay now," she says, taking her first unsupported step since her shock in the garden. She turns to Iyana and tells her to go help Danika with the other women.

"Make sure they're all calm," Helen says.

Iyana gives Helen a nod, but she casts me an uncertain look as she passes me. I take my own deep breaths and fight the impulse to squeeze myself as far into the back corner as I can before Tristan arrives.

Remember, Tessa: Calm. Control.

I remind myself that I'm not the same woman Tristan left here two months ago.

Helen casts me a questioning look, similar to Iyana's, but I give her a firm nod. "I'll stay with you. What do you need me to do?"

"Come stand by my side. Remember who you are and what you're capable of," Helen says, calling her book to her side. The book flies up into the air, floating on the opposite side of me as I join her at the foot of the medical examination table.

"As soon as I know what we're dealing with, I'll ask for your help," she says.

"Okay," I reply. "I'll be ready."

Seconds later, running footfalls thud in my hearing.

Despite the dulling power of Hidden House, Tristan's presence is like a dizzying burst of light in my senses. Closing my eyes and daring to expand my senses, pushing against the spells within the house, I make out Jace's presence, as well as two female shifters I've never met.

"Helen!" Tristan's roar is like a smack across my head, his power pouring ahead of him and flooding my senses. I rush to pull back my power—to stop sensing so much around me—before I'm overwhelmed.

He bursts into the room, carrying a girl whose hair is so covered in blood, I can't make out what color it is as it falls over his arms. She's unconscious, her eyes closed and her left arm hanging loosely. Her face and body are covered in slashes that stop the breath in my lungs—cuts from a dagger or from claws, I can't tell which. She's smaller than an adult. She might only be fourteen, possibly even younger.

Jace runs in close behind Tristan carrying an even younger girl. Her left arm is held at an awkward angle against her chest while Jace holds her so he doesn't hurt her. She's awake, sobbing against his chest, the sound of her cries wrenching at my heart. She's wearing ragged jeans and a T-shirt with a rainbow printed on it. She can't be more than nine years old.

What kind of monster would hurt these kids?

My wolf's energy rises inside me—far from calm—and it takes all of my concentration to calm my anger.

Helen gasps as soon as the men enter, her hand flying over her mouth. Her gaze shoots from the teenager to the younger girl. "Carly! Becca!" Her teeth clench. "What happened?"

Tristan races to the examination table, laying Carly onto it while Jace retreats to the side of the room with Becca.

"Baxter fucking Griffin happened," Tristan says. "She's been stabbed in her chest, back, and thighs. He clawed her face. She was trying to defend her little sister."

Tristan presses the back of his hand against his forehead, his fist clenched, as he backs away from the examination table. "I didn't get there in time." His voice is raw, exposed, more vulnerable than I've ever heard him sound as he sucks in air. "I couldn't fucking... get to her... Not fast enough..."

He reaches out to steady himself against the table at the side of the room, his chest heaving, lips drawn back, teeth gritted. He's naked from the waist up. Bare-footed. The top button of his jeans isn't done up, telling me he shifted and didn't have time to dress properly after. He's dripping sweat, beads of liquid slipping down the side of his face and the center of his chest.

A thin line of blood cuts across his chest from his shoulder to his hip. It's a claw mark, not deep enough to do any damage but clearly intended to gut him. He must have got out of the way just in time.

"Tell me you can save her, Helen," he says, a demand.

Helen doesn't reply. Her book zips closer to her side, pages flipping rapidly. She's already whispering spells as she works over Carly at a frenzied pace. I watch in awe as spells pour from her mouth and she layers her magic, one spell over another, across Carly's chest—her vital organs—followed by Carly's head and face.

Despite Helen's efforts, Carly's breathing becomes more shallow with every passing second and the furrow in Helen's brow grows more intense, a fierce but desperate intensity in the speed of her spells.

I want to help, but there's nothing I can do to heal Carly's wounds.

It's all up to Helen.

Which seems to be making Tristan even more agitated.

His growled demand cuts across the space between them. "Helen!" he shouts when she doesn't answer him. "Promise me you can save her!"

Still, Helen doesn't respond, but I suddenly realize how I can help her. I need to play interference between her and Tristan so she can concentrate on her work without the distraction of his fear.

I round the table and position myself so that I'm standing between Tristan and the examination table, becoming a visual obstruction. "Helen's doing everything she can, Tristan. You have to trust her."

"*Trust.*" He spits the word. His fierce green eyes focus on me for the first time since he arrived, a deliberate move, as if he's been consciously blocking my presence until this moment. Somehow, no matter the circumstances in which we see each other, his gaze always feels sharp, as if he's trying to scrape back my defenses and tear at the heart of me.

With a snarl, his focus rakes up and down me, all the way from my ruby red hair, down my usual flannel shirt and jeans, to my booted feet, and back up again. "I can't trust someone who lied to me."

I relax my hands at my sides, restraining my wolf's energy, which is rising inside me, ready to be released if I need it. "Then trust that she had good reasons for protecting me."

Tristan closes the gap between us so fast that I fight to catch my breath.

"Helen protected you at the expense of others," he says, his accusation burning deep in his eyes and in the angry downward pull at the corners of his lips.

I tip my chin, verbalizing a belief I've only just acquired. "My life is worth just as much as theirs."

He snarls, leaning close. Whispers, "Not to me, it isn't."

Oh.

I press my lips together. Slowly. I try not to react to his harsh statement, even though it feels like he cut through my fragile self-belief before it was even fully formed.

He's agitated, maybe even hurting, but it doesn't excuse his choice to hurt me right now.

The old me would try to escape at this point, retaliate with force, compartmentalize my hurt, and take myself off somewhere to harden my heart. But the new me...

Pain has a meaning in my life and it has to be faced head on.

I breathe it out, the slowest exhale, expelling it as gently as I can, giving my heart the care it needs. From myself. I don't need care from him.

Tristan is silent, standing so close to me that every inhale he makes threatens to bump his chest against mine. If I were to try to strip back his defenses as badly as he seems to be trying to strip back mine, I might imagine he already regrets what he said.

It hits me with striking clarity that despite his claim that I'm worth nothing to him, the real source of his anger is that I wasn't there when the girls were attacked. Sure, he would rather lose *me* than *them*, but he needed me.

He *needs* me.

My lips are dry—a condition that would have made me feel even more vulnerable before—but I pull my bottom lip between my teeth to moisten them before I sway toward him.

His gaze drags from my lips to my eyes before I close the scant gap between us. I dare to brush his jaw with my lips, grazing my skin with his sandpaper growth, my position forcing my upper body to press against his.

His shoulders tense, arms twitching as if they're going to rise around me, but he otherwise remains still.

He said my life wasn't worth as much to him as the girls' lives, but…

"Now who's lying?" I whisper.

I draw back, cast my own challenging glance at him, and glide to the side before he can react.

Helen continues to work behind us, but the other little girl is still distraught and her cries continue to tug at my heart.

Jace has nowhere to sit, so he leans against the wall, his breathing only now beginning to slow after his rush to get here, sweat dripping down his face. Unlike Tristan, he's not bare-chested and I'm guessing he didn't shift—the same way he avoided shifting during the fight with Baxter and Cody on the night I came here.

He holds Becca against his chest. Her weeping is a little quieter now, her eyes wide and scared as she watches Helen. If the other girl is her sister, then Becca will be afraid for her.

I have to assume Becca's wounds aren't life-threatening because Jace hasn't drawn Helen's attention to her, but the pitch of her soft sobs tells me she's in pain.

I wish there was something I could do for her while Helen is busy.

Jace watches me closely as I approach, his focus flicking between Tristan and me. "Tessa?"

I break eye contact with Jace, focusing on Becca.

She whimpers and I sense her wolf, cowering and frightened

inside her. My wolf's energy flickers inside my mind, asking to be released. I'm not convinced that's a good idea yet, so I hold my wolf's energy back, cautious for now.

I reach out to Becca, brushing the hair from her clammy forehead.

"Hi, sweetheart," I whisper. "I'm Tessa. You're safe now."

Her eyes come to rest on me, soft cries releasing from her lips.

"I'm going to look after you," I say. "Where do you hurt, sweetheart?"

"M-My arm."

I run my gaze along her left arm from her wrist to her elbow. Deep, red bruises mark her forearm directly below her elbow as well as around her wrist. The dirty partial print of a boot forms a third, shocking bruise across the middle of her arm. Someone took hold of her, dragged her down, and then stepped on her arm.

Tristan said that Baxter Griffin attacked the girls, but I'm suddenly flashing back to memories I'd rather forget.

My voice hardens as I glance at Jace.

"Who did this to her?"

I already suspect the answer, but I don't want to believe it's possible. It's the same maneuver Dawson used to use on me.

My hands start to shake and I can't stop the motion. Dealing with the pain when it happened was traumatic, but seeing it now inflicted on someone else brings back fears I've pushed away for years. "Did my brother do this to her?"

Jace gives me a stern nod. "It was Dawson Nash."

"How is that possible? Dawson lives in the Highlands."

Why would my brother be anywhere near here? He shouldn't be in the city. He should be far behind me back in the Cascade Range.

I gasp a mouthful of air and squeeze my eyes closed, pushing away my questions. I need to restrain my power or Tristan will react to it.

We have enough problems already.

Jace remains silent, his focus shifting to a spot behind me, and I sense Tristan move closer.

"Your former alpha, Peter Nash, has pledged an alliance with Baxter Griffin," Tristan says. "He sent his son to the Eastern Lowlands to join forces with Baxter against me. The other alphas will soon join him. Since my father died, they've been trying to claim my territory."

I thought I'd left Dawson behind...

Taking a deep breath, I begin reciting lists, the same way Ella does, whispering them beneath my breath. *"Blue treasure... Pink ocean... Yellow forest... Violet sunset..."*

My breathing returns to normal.

I open my eyes.

I'm aware of Tristan's gaze burning my back, the slightly unsettled crease in his forehead when I glance his way, but he doesn't say anything about my list reciting.

I can't do anything about Dawson right now. I focus on Becca. Focus on what I *can* do.

"Give her to me," I say to Jace, hooking my arms beneath Becca without waiting for him to agree.

His lips purse. He looks ready to say 'no,' but he surprises me by shifting her carefully into my arms. She's heavy, but I'm ready for her weight. I sink slowly to the floor with her, curling my legs under her body and releasing my wolf at the same time.

Becca doesn't try to fight me, turning her eyes up to mine.

My wolf's energy emerges slowly.

My wolf raises her head at my side before curling her body around Becca, her energy passing right through the girl as my wolf takes up position as close to my chest as she can. My animal stands with her head lowered to Becca's chest, her gentle eyes meeting the girl's.

"You'll be okay," I whisper to them both, telling myself that too.

Becca is fixated on my wolf, her sobs slowly subsiding and her breathing becoming more regular. As far as I can tell, her injuries are bruising and shock—and fear for her sister. All I can do is ease her emotional turmoil as best I can.

We stay like that for another ten minutes while Becca's eyelids lower, open again as she fights my wolf's calming energy, then lower again.

"Everything will be okay," I whisper to her.

Beside me, plastered up against the wall, Jace stares down at us with an unsettled expression that matches Tristan's. The way I'm sitting, I'm blocking him from moving away. He has just enough space between my legs and the wall to slip free.

Tristan takes himself off to the other side of the room until, finally, Helen falls silent.

She's stopped speaking spells.

My focus wrenches to her where she stands gripping the edge of the examination table, her wand abandoned on it.

She's pale, trying to catch her breath, but she raises her head with a smile. "Carly's going to be okay." She pulls away from the table. "I need to help Becca now."

Using my wolf's energy to give me a surge of strength, I rise to my feet holding the resting girl before I remember that there's nowhere to place her. Carly's taking up all the space on the examination table. When I stood up, my wolf remained standing at my thigh. I'm not willing to separate from her and reveal my skills to Tristan or Jace yet.

Determined not to fail Becca, I carry her toward Helen, who works over her quickly, humming spells under her breath, the pages of her book flipping over every now and then until she finishes.

"Well done, Tessa," Helen whispers to me before she draws back and turns to Jace. "Jace, you can take Becca now. Her arm is healed and she had no other wounds. She's sleeping. As is Carly."

With another mutter beneath her breath, Helen spells a chair to appear beside the examination table. Jace wraps his arms around Becca and transports her there, carefully laying her with her head on the armrest and her now-healed arm against her side.

I'm aware of Tristan's gaze, the same prickly heat that would strip back my defenses, making my breath catch on every inhale.

"I can't leave the girls," Helen says to him. "So we're going to have to have this conversation here. Tell me what happened."

Harsh growls leave Tristan's lips. "Baxter Griffin stepped right into the heart of my territory. He sent his men to the north to distract me while he and Dawson Nash attacked Carly and Becca when they were walking home from school. That's how brazen Baxter's become." He casts a hard glance at me. "They know that if they can't hurt me, then they can hurt my pack. I can't be in two places at once."

He pulls away from the wall. "I need Tessa," he says. "Not in a month. Not soon. *Now*."

Helen's lips press together in an angry line, her response sharp. "Tessa isn't ready."

Tristan's lips pull back into a snarl. "I'm looking right at her, Helen. Her wolf is under control. Like fuck she isn't ready."

Helen's wand smacks the back of her own hand with a *crack*. I've never seen her angry and it alarms me.

"Tessa's *not* ready, Tristan. She's far more vulnerable than she appears."

I cringe at Helen's description of me. *Vulnerable* may be accurate, but it isn't the descriptor I would have preferred.

"I can see that too," Tristan says, glancing at me.

I bite my lip. As hard as I try to remain in control, I couldn't hide my reaction to Becca's wounds, or my list counting. Tristan doesn't seem to have missed anything since he arrived.

He shakes his head, a slow, dangerous movement. "We're headed for war, Helen. Baxter Griffin is determined to destroy me. I don't have any heirs or an alpha-in-training. He's taking out all of my possible successors." He gestures at the girl on the table. "Carly was my next option. If I step aside—or if I die—Baxter will slaughter every member of my pack. I won't let that happen. I will fight him. I have no choice but to go to war."

"War is not the way, Tristan," Helen says. "A war between wolf shifters is bad enough, but conflict in this city will draw in other supernaturals—bounty hunters, assassins. Humans will get caught up in it too. Their law enforcement isn't equipped to deal with a war between supernaturals. The streets will turn to blood. I won't let you put Tessa in the middle of that." Helen's expression is sharp, and my heart hurts that she's fighting so hard for me. "Find another way."

"Tessa *is* the other way," he says, leaning against the bench. "The last possible hope for my pack."

"Can you guarantee that she won't be killed?" Helen asks.

Tristan exhales. He gives it a lot more thought than I was expecting him to. His gaze lowers to my wolf, who remains at my side. "I can't."

"Then I won't let her leave."

The corners of Tristan's mouth rise into a smile while his eyes are hard, the same dangerously threatening expression he turned on Peter Nash before he fought him. "I'm not *asking*, Helen."

Helen taps the tip of her wand against the back of her hand. "I don't take orders from you, Tristan."

I draw in a sharp breath. "Stop. Both of you." I exhale slowly. "I'll go with Tristan."

Helen takes a quick step toward me. "Tessa, no—"

I hurry to her side, taking her free hand in mine. "Baxter Griffin killed my father. Dawson Nash has tormented me since we were kids. I can't stand by while they continue to hurt others."

I spin to Tristan. "I'm not doing this for you." I point to the sleeping girls. "I'm doing this for them."

"I don't give a fuck who you're doing it for, Tessa," he snarls. "As long as you follow orders."

I allow a small smile to rise onto my lips. "I'm coming with you, Tristan, but that doesn't mean I'll follow your rules."

His eyes narrow, but it's a confident look. "We'll see."

There seems very little more to say than, "I'll go get my things. I'll be in the garden in half an hour."

I stride from the room with my heart in my throat.

I'm not sure if I just handed myself to the devil or took my first step on my path to revenge against Baxter Griffin.

Perhaps both.

CHAPTER FIFTEEN

$\mathcal{O}$n my way to my room, I find Iyana and Danika in the library.

They hurry toward me.

"It's time," I say. "I'm leaving tonight. In half an hour."

"Then we need to pack quickly," Danika says.

My forehead creases with worry. "You're sure about coming with me?"

"Deadly certain," Iyana replies. "I might need a moment to source some vials of mercury from Helen, but I'll make sure to bring enough for another year. Where should we meet you?"

"In the garden," I say.

Danika squeezes my shoulder. "Fuck alpha shifters, yes?"

"Fuck 'em," I say.

I hurry to my room but slow myself before I barge in. I don't want to upset Ella.

As soon as I open the door, her humming calms me.

"Blue treasure... pink ocean... orange grass..." She stops as soon as I step into the room. "*Domination.*"

I hold my breath for a moment, hoping that my emotions haven't upset her rhythm.

Her brown eyes widen. She pauses where she sits on the edge of her armchair, crushing a silver flower in her fist, spreading glittering dust over the floor. Her head is tilted to the side, a string of flowers in her hair. One of them drops to the moss at our feet when she shivers.

I've suspected for a while now that Ella has strong empathic tendencies. She demonstrated them to me on my first morning here when she asked if I was wolf or human. Her empathy would make exposure to violence even more devastating for her. It also means I have to regulate my emotions around her or I can negatively affect her with my mood.

I focus on breathing normally, regaining my calm. "Orange grass," I say, keeping my voice low, a lull that matches the sighing breeze in the trees around us. "Blue treasure, pink ocean, violet sunrise—"

"Yellow forest, blue treasure..." She exhales. The tension leaves her shoulders. She curls up in her chair, pulls her knees to her chest, and closes her eyes, humming to herself again.

The corners of my lips twitch upward into a smile.

She's the sweetest woman I've ever met. Even when she breaks down, her tears only highlight the honeyed flecks in her eyes and the paleness of her hair. Over time, I've figured out that she's the same age as me—twenty-three. I feel like she's the sister I never had.

Leaving her is hard.

Without thinking, I lean over and plant a kiss on her cheek.

Realizing it could distress her, I pull back, ready to calm her down again, but she relaxes against the seat.

"Cobalt treasure." She exhales before her breathing deepens. She's fast asleep within minutes.

I choose to believe that she means my wolf's energy, that she's trying to tell me she knows I'm her friend and that I don't have to be afraid.

"Sleep well, sweetheart," I murmur. "I will come back one day. I promise."

Quickly pulling clothes from my closet, I fold them into a bag I find in the bottom of the closet. It makes me wonder if there's a bag hiding in every woman's closet, waiting like a promise of a new life. In my case, it's a promise of life-threatening danger, but as I pack my things, I discover that I'm ready for it.

I'm ready to go back out into the world.

I raid my bathroom for toiletries since I'm not sure what the amenities will be like where I'm going, check my reflection in the mirror, and retie my hair, and then I exit my room and stride down the corridor, meeting Danika halfway along.

She's carrying a duffel bag that's bulging as fully as mine. She's wearing her favorite ripped jeans with black calf-height boots and a sleeveless V-neck T-shirt, and her hair is tied up. Unlike me, she's comfortable showing off her curves.

I tug at the base of my loose flannel shirt. "Ready?"

"Iyana's just gone to collect a case of mercury vials," she says. "She'll meet us in the garden."

Iyana's waiting for us when we get there, her arms folded across her chest. She's wearing tight black jeans, knee-high black boots, a low-cut blue-gray T-shirt that brings out the color of her eyes, along with a victorious grin.

A silver hard case sits on the floor beside her along with a full-to-the-brim duffel bag. The hard case has a handle and wheels. I'm guessing that's because its contents are much heavier than water.

Mercury mission accomplished.

Danika and I join her and await the men.

As the breeze washes over me, carrying the faint scent of silver flowers, I feel a pang in my heart. Damn, I'm going to miss this place. Being here among the trees and vines is like touching something bright and pure. It's a stark contrast to the darkness I'm about to encounter outside these walls.

I sense the house about to shift moments before the staircase rearranges itself, walls and steps detaching and reassembling before my eyes, changing color and substance and forming the shape of the elevator I haven't seen for months.

The doors slide open and Tristan and Jace step out of the elevator with Helen behind them.

Tristan pulls up short while Jace finds a spot at the side. Tristan is wary as he greets us. "Iyana. Danika. I'm glad to see you looking well." He taps his thigh with his fingers as the women return his greeting. "What's going on?"

"We're all coming with you," I say.

He doesn't look as disgruntled as I thought he might. A

surprising smile crosses his face. "Good." He inclines his head at the elevator. "Let's go."

I pick up my bag, Iyana and Danika do the same, and we all squeeze into the elevator together.

After we exit into the parking garage, Helen hugs each of us in turn. Silence falls around each of the other two women as she hugs Iyana and Danika, allowing Helen to speak privately with them.

Whatever she says to them is for their ears only. I'm not the only one venturing back into the world for the first time in months.

When it's my turn, Helen pulls me close. "Remember to guard your heart and protect yourself, Tessa. Be calm. Stay in control. If you need to come back, look for the house on the hill. The doors will always be open to you."

"Thank you, Helen. For everything you've done for us."

She hugs me a moment longer before she draws back and plants a kiss on my cheek. "Stay alive, Tessa."

Just as we turn away, she stops Tristan and silence falls around them as she speaks with him. She seems to have a lot to say, and for once, he seems willing to listen, head bowed slightly as she speaks rapidly.

I turn away from them, following Jace to the SUV parked on the other side of the garage. He opens the trunk and we pile our duffel bags into the back. When Jace picks up Iyana's hard case, he nearly topples over.

"What the hell have you got in here?" he asks.

Iyana arches an eyebrow at him. "Shoes," she says before she rounds the vehicle and slides in to the back seat on the left side.

Jace climbs into the driver's seat, I sit in the middle of the back seat with Iyana and Danika on either side, and we wait quietly for Tristan.

He's subdued when he returns, merely giving Jace a quick nod before Jace turns the ignition.

The garage door rises. The vehicle pulls out.

I leave Hidden House behind.

CHAPTER SIXTEEN

$\mathcal{T}$he moment we leave the garage, my ears *pop* and my senses flood with sights and sound.

Iyana, Danika, and I gasp in unison.

Danika grips the edge of her seat beside me while Iyana suddenly sits up straight.

They both turn to me. "Do you feel that?"

My eyes widen at the golden glow around Danika's body, the power I can finally sense in her. Spinning to Iyana, I can also see her power glowing around her body, an icy white that matches the hints of frosty scent I got from her while we were inside the house.

When we moan in unison, Tristan and Jace both cast startled glances back at us—Jace in the rearview mirror, Tristan by twisting in the front passenger seat.

I can't help the laugh bubbling up inside me. "The house isn't dulling our senses anymore."

"Oh, that's practically orgasmic." Iyana laughs, only making the startled crease in Tristan's forehead deepen.

"I've missed this." She waves at the passing buildings and then the people walking along the footpath as we exit onto a busier road. "All of this."

Danika murmurs her agreement, but I fall silent.

Now that my senses aren't dulled, everything around me is suddenly too vibrant. Too bright. Controlling my power was so much easier inside the house. I'm struggling against my wolf's energy right now, a dangerous need to explore the world around me. At the same time, I want to retreat from it all. There are too many people, too many unknowns. Even on the mountain, I was secluded from the public, left alone a lot of the time.

It feels like mere minutes that we drive through the streets of Portland into the heart of the city west of the river. We reach another building, this one tall, situated on a corner. It's made of white stone with multiple levels rising upward, while large arches decorate it at street level. Craning my neck, I make out the structure of a clock at the top of the building before we turn the corner. It looks like a clock tower. An old one but well-cared for.

We turn directly off the street toward the garage door to the left at the base of the building, and Jace drives down into a basement garage. I'm grateful for the sudden silence—not a silence of sound, but a silence of energy—as we pull away from the humans going about their business out on the street.

I lean toward Tristan as the SUV pulls to a stop beside ten other dark gray SUVs. "Do you control this building?"

"Control?" Tristan says with a sharp backward glance. "I *own* this building. Along with others."

"Oh." It wasn't the answer I expected. "This is where your pack lives then?"

As I speak, Jace jumps out, rounding the back of the vehicle and opening the trunk. Danika and Iyana also slide out, leaving me sitting in the middle seat, caught in Tristan's gaze.

"Yes, this is our home." He clears his throat, lowering his voice with apparent effort. "I'll show you everything tomorrow. I need to get cleaned up now."

There's a smudge of blood on his cheek and shadows in his eyes. He nearly lost a member of his pack today. He seems more tired than anything now. When I look closer, I can see the dark rings under his eyes and signs of exhaustion in the tension around his mouth.

"Of course," I murmur. "Answers can wait."

He's still turned in my direction, paused. His lips part, but whatever he was going to say is lost in the *bang* as the trunk shuts.

I shake off our quiet interaction—the quietest we've had—as I slip from my seat out onto the concreted area to find Iyana and Danika waiting for me.

Tristan shuts his door and strides past us. "Come with me. We'll get you settled with the others."

Our boots tap a beat as we follow Tristan to the elevator at the side of the garage and once again cram inside it. This time, I'm standing closest to Tristan, close enough to see that he still hasn't done up the top button of his jeans.

I remind myself that he has a wolf's soul. He's comfortable being naked. In fact, he's probably more relaxed naked than clothed, whereas my human self finds the idea of walking around nude in front of random people incredibly uncomfortable.

Quickly refocusing upward, I'm caught in his lazy smile, surprised by how relaxed he looks now that we're inside the building, although I have no idea what I've done to make him appear so pleased.

"Unknown to humans, my pack occupies most of this building," he says, causing Iyana and Danika to focus on him while Jace watches the rising floor numbers above the door. "The first three floors are leased to humans who have no idea that we live here. You'll stay on the seventh floor with the single female pack members. The eighth floor is for the single males. They have designated apartments, but don't expect them to keep to them."

A flush creeps through my cheeks. Along with being comfortable in their naked skin, shifters like to mingle.

Tristan continues. "The ninth and tenth floors are for families. The eleventh floor is a gym, which you're welcome to use whenever you want."

The last statement makes Iyana smile. "We will, thank you."

The elevator dings and the doors open at the seventh floor. Jace holds the elevator open for us.

Danika is the first to step into an entrance room that looks as homely and well-loved as the library back at Hidden House. The sound of female voices filters across the space as I move forward after Iyana steps out.

The female shifters in the distance don't sound unhappy, even if there's an edge of tension in the pitch of their speech, indicating a state of concern that's natural if they're worried about Carly and Becca.

In contrast, my tension increases. My senses are nearly billowing out of my control and I'm not sure how I'll contain my wolf's energy when I'm surrounded by so many supernaturals without the dulling power of Hidden House. Above all, I have to make sure I'm calm and in control, but right now, I feel anything but relaxed.

Before I can take another step, Jace turns to face me so that his big body blocks the exit, stopping me in my tracks.

Tristan's arms snake around me from behind, holding me where I stand in the elevator.

"Not you, Tessa," he whispers into my ear. In the same move, he deftly swipes a card across the scanner below the elevator buttons and presses the button for the twelfth floor.

Jace tips his head apologetically at me as he backsteps out of the elevator, making an obstacle of himself between me and my friends.

Iyana tries to leap around him, her face flushing with alarm just as the doors close. "Wait a second—!"

I freeze, my back pressed against Tristan's chest, his left arm a firm restraint around my waist. My first instinct is to ram my elbow into his ribs and force him to release me, but I need to pick my battles.

He has plans for me.

I need to know what they are so I can find a way through them and keep myself alive. Fighting him every second will only lead to exhaustion. It won't help me when the time comes that I really have to fight for my life.

On top of that... a quiet relief rises inside me. Now that the elevator doors have closed, the immediate flood of sensory input from the female shifters disappears, leaving me in control again.

Tristan seems surprised that I've remained in the circle of his arms. I turn my head slightly, catching the crease in his forehead as he studies me while I wait patiently for him to let me go.

He doesn't.

I turn to face the elevator doors again, my heart sinking a little as I take a guess as to the real reason why he's holding on to me.

I suspect that it's not to restrain me.

"You need to be sure," I say quietly, still facing the elevator doors. "Jace told you I'm in control of my power, but the problem is… if I'm *really* in control of it… that means *I* could be in control. Not *you*. And you might not even know."

I tip my head back against his chest, meeting the hard planes of his upper body. I sense the wildness of his wolf, so foreign to me, and its questing to understand my wolf's energy. Our wolves may as well be different species.

"That's what you need, isn't it?" I ask when he remains silent. "For me to manipulate your enemies? But that also means that you have to fight me. Every step of the way. To make sure I'm not also manipulating you. You need to make sure that you're still… *you*."

He neither confirms nor denies my theory, spinning me roughly as the elevator doors open. The movement is so quick that I barely catch sight of the penthouse suite beyond the elevator doors before I'm facing him again.

A dizzying whirl of furniture passes me by—lounge chairs, tables, desk, a tiled kitchen farther back, and another door that might lead to a bedroom.

Tristan propels me backward through the doors, gripping my waist with one arm, my wrist with his other hand like some sort of dangerous dance. Releasing my waist, he scoops up my duffel bag from the floor and brings it with us, dropping it beside me.

He pulls me to a stop several paces into the room, still holding me close. I settle against his chest, inhaling his subdued power.

My feet sink into plush carpet, the kind I'll probably love walking on barefoot. Ceiling-to-floor paintings of a forest cover the wall on either side of the elevator, reminding me of my bedroom in Hidden House. What I can see so far of the color scheme around me is relaxing, comfortable. Maybe even cozy.

For a perilous second, Tristan's head tips to mine, aiming slightly left toward my neck.

I read the challenge in the darkness of his eyes, the shadow across his lips. He wants to inhale my scent the same way he did on the night we met. He needs to test my control and test his resistance. He wants to challenge me to overpower him.

He lets me go just as suddenly as he took hold of me, releasing me without lowering his face to mine after all.

"I'm going to clean up," he says. "There's food in the fridge. Help yourself to anything you want."

He strides away from me, leaving me with a sense of confusion.

At some point, I'm sure he's going to have to test my ability to control my scent and my power, but apparently, not right now. As he walks away to the enormous-looking bedroom on the right, he reminds me of the first night I saw him, every muscle of his human body in perfect harmony with his wolf as he prowls into the next room.

Through the windows on the left, the sun is setting and the city lights are starting to shine like gems. Tristan flips the lights on as he leaves the room, illuminating the living area around me as well as the bedroom he's entering. Through the open door, I can see a mammoth bed covered in tangled sheets, the door to a bathroom on the left, and discarded clothes on the floor. The living area is neat and tidy, but his bedroom is messy.

Moments later, the shower turns on.

Left in relative silence, I slip off my boots and place them neatly beside the elevator before I test the *down* button. Of course, nothing happens. The scanner below the button indicates I need the security key to make the elevator work.

I take in the positives. The carpet is amazing. I can sink my toes into it. The view—also amazing. Threat to personal safety? Seems low right now, but I guess I'll wait and see.

Placing my duffel bag on the large leather lounge that looks like the best candidate for my bed, I cross to the kitchen to verify Tristan's claim that it contains food.

It does. Along with half a bottle of red wine, a quarter of a mud cake, and a packet of strawberries. There's even ice cream in the freezer, although the whole tub is untouched.

I'm confused. This is not the food of a bachelor. I'm suddenly a little worried that a woman is going to appear from some corner of the penthouse and ask me what the hell I'm doing here.

When nobody does, I forage around in the kitchen cupboards for a wine glass and pour myself a glass, the first alcohol I've touched in months, but I think a drink is called for. I take a chance and pour Tristan one too. I also cut two pieces of cake—one for me and one for him—before I grab a cushion from the lounge and find a spot on the floor beside the windows to curl up with my glass of wine and my slice of cake.

Watching the cars pass by below, I raise my focus to the horizon and imagine that I can see Hidden House from here.

I sense Tristan's arrival in the lounge room before he speaks.

His presence is once again overwhelming. But at least my senses aren't going haywire from all the sensory input that I would experience around other shifters.

"It looks peaceful from up here, doesn't it?" Tristan asks, lowering himself onto the arm of the nearest lounge chair. He stretches out his legs. He's once again naked from the waist up, wearing a clean pair of jeans. Droplets of water follow the chiseled lines of his muscular chest to his waist.

He seems even calmer than before and I wonder if being in his home environment relaxes him as much as being at Hidden House relaxed me.

"You're trying to warn me that it's not peaceful at all," I say.

Tristan points. "Two blocks over that way is where Baxter and Dawson attacked. Right outside the library. In broad daylight. They dragged the girls into a van. Made sure the humans didn't see anything."

I chew on my lip as I process the violence of the attack. "How did you know it was happening?"

Tristan taps his thigh, the first sign of tension. "I have guards posted around the city. They call me if something's wrong—but I don't have enough pack members to cover every block." His gaze lowers to mine. "In this case, I sensed Carly's fear."

I'm surprised. "You sensed she was in trouble?"

"I'm her alpha. I know when anyone in my pack is in danger. But knowing and acting are two different things. I was all the way north near the Fremont Bridge. I couldn't get back here fast enough."

The muscle in his jaw tenses. A shadow passes across his face, as if he's reliving the moment when he sensed the danger—the girls' pain and fear—and he couldn't reach them in time. I'm familiar with that panic. I felt it when my father was killed.

"Is that what happened when Iyana and Danika were in trouble? You sensed it?"

Tristan sucks in a sharp breath. "The only good thing my father taught me is that anyone can be pack." His focus becomes distant. "Everyone on this side of the river is part of my pack—the humans included. I look after my pack. If they're in trouble, I help them."

His eyes gleam with a menacing light. "If they step out of line and hurt someone, I take care of it."

"You're an alpha to all." I try to read Tristan's thoughts, to understand his plan for me. "How am I supposed to help you?"

"Tonight, you're staying up here," he says. "I'm giving you one night to get your bearings and get used to being out in the world again. Tomorrow, I'll show you my city. After that... you're coming out with me."

I perk up. "On patrol?" I'd love to test out my new skills.

He shrugs. "Something like that."

Before I can ask him exactly what he means, he seems to shake off his thoughts, lifts off the lounge, and strides away to the elevator as if he's going to leave.

I jump to my feet, nearly sloshing wine across the carpet. "Wait, where are you going?"

He casts me a backward glance. "Out. You can sleep in my bed. I won't be back tonight."

"But I cut you a piece of cake."

It's possibly the most idiotic thing I could say to this dangerous man.

I bite my lip, wishing I could swallow it back.

He pauses in the act of swiping his security card, half-turning back to me with a wary expression, his gaze flicking to the glass of wine and the plate waiting on the far kitchen table.

He scowls before turning away again.

I blush. Of course he doesn't want any fucking cake.

He swipes his security card, the elevator doors open, and he disappears inside it, bare feet and all.

"Um... but..."

The elevator doors close and I'm left talking to an empty room.

The penthouse is silent around me.

"Okay, then. He's gone." I place the wine glass down on the

nearest coffee table more forcefully than necessary and begin to prowl, my wolf's energy rising to meet my agitation.

First he separated me from Iyana and Danika and then he left me here. I have to find a way out of here somehow. I stomp to the elevator door and thump on the button multiple times, even though I'm sure it won't get me anywhere.

Placing my hands on my hips, I survey the rest of the penthouse.

Maybe this is some sort of test.

There has to be a spare security card somewhere.

I blast through the kitchen first, churning through the obvious places like the drawers that inevitably accumulate a bunch of crap. Fruit bowl. Side of the cabinet where keys might hang.

Making my way into the bedroom, I inhale the scent of male shifter like a punch to my head.

Holy fuck.

I make it three steps before my senses go wild, too overwhelmed by Tristan's lingering power to think straight. Judging by the tousled sheets and wayward pillows, Tristan is a light sleeper *and* hates making his bed.

His presence in this room is overpowering.

As if I could sleep in his bed at all, let alone tonight. I can't even step foot in his room to find a damn security card.

It'll be a shame when I need to shower or use the bathroom since the only bathroom I see is the one I need to access by crossing his bedroom. I'll just have to run for it when that happens, but that's a problem for future Tessa.

Assuming defeat, I rush out of his room and stomp toward the far window again, forcing myself to accept that I'm stuck here tonight.

Unless...

My wolf's energy shivers inside me at my sudden thought.

I've never had a reason to try to send her through solid objects before, but I know she can do it. After all, she's pure energy. She curled herself around the little girl, Becca, and calmed her. I'm sure my wolf can travel through inanimate objects too.

The biggest challenge will be whether or not I can make sure my wolf's energy isn't seen since she glows cobalt blue, but I've been practicing a skill that I'm keen to test. I didn't tell Helen about it because I wasn't sure what she would think.

Grabbing another cushion like I would in the garden at Hidden House, I flick off the light, allow my night vision to adjust, and then I place the cushion on the floor beside the window.

I sit cross-legged facing the city lights, close my eyes, and allow my wolf's energy to rise and separate from me, taking in the world from her point of view.

She pads to the glass, turning back to me for a second, and her lips curl in a snarl of delight. *My* delight.

She backsteps through the glass, her color changing to pure raven black, the same as the darkness of the night sky. I can't stop the smile growing on my lips while my eyes are closed. I'm not sure what Helen would think about my ability to drain the light from my wolf's energy.

It's time to test how far into the shadows I can go.

She is my dark wolf now.

CHAPTER SEVENTEEN

ity sounds billow across my wolf's hearing, blowing through my own senses. Car horns, people speaking, walking by.

At my command, my wolf disintegrates into specks of dark light that swirl for a second before her energy plummets to the footpath far below.

The drop is dizzying, leaving my stomach behind me as I fully integrate with her energy.

She is me and I am her.

I may as well not be in Tristan's penthouse anymore, but here, on the street, my paws padding across the wet pavement as I quickly back away from the streetlights and into the shadows at the side of the building to assess which way I should go. It must have rained at some point this evening, although I don't remember the sound—maybe a quick rain shower while we were in the elevator.

I'm facing a wide open square that takes up the whole block opposite the Tower. White pillars are situated along each side and the courtyard is paved with red stones. It's far too exposed for my wolf to go that way.

I'm about to turn away from it when I catch the elusive fiery notes of Tristan's scent. He appears on the corner at my left, stops by a man who gives him a quick nod—a guard maybe? Definitely another wolf, judging by the musky smell of him—before Tristan crosses the street toward the square.

I follow Tristan's line of sight to where Jace waits, leaning against one of the pillars.

A streetcar approaches on my right, and I lose sight of Tristan for a few seconds. Once the streetcar passes, I follow his scent across the street, keeping away from the light cast by the tall, gray lampposts. There are far too many passersby here for my comfort, but I'm counting on my darkness to make me blend in to the night, to become a mere dark spot in their human vision. As long as I stay out of the light, they shouldn't be able to see me.

Finding shelter behind one of the pillars at the side of the square, I'm only ten paces away from Tristan and Jace and feeling very pleased that they haven't sensed me.

Helen taught me to conceal my power well.

I ignore the other input around me and focus only on them, listening for their conversation. Now that I'm experiencing the world solely from my wolf's point of view, all of the sensory input is much easier to distinguish and process.

Jace pulls away from the pillar he was leaning against. "Where's Tessa?" he asks, as if he expected to see me.

Tristan pulls to a stop. "Safe and sound on the twelfth floor back at the tower."

Jace shakes his head at Tristan, his lips drawing back in a snarl. "You're a fucking coward, Tristan."

Tristan narrows his eyes with a growl. "I can't be near her tonight, Jace. She's too—" He snaps his mouth shut. His jaw clenches. He casts an angry glance around the courtyard without continuing.

Jace barrels into him, bumping shoulders like he would if he were in wolf form. "Too what, Tristan?"

"She's too fucking beautiful." Tristan shoves Jace away. "Too fucking vulnerable to be around an asshole like me tonight."

I freeze at his descriptions of me, wary of how brutally honest he seems right now. At the same time, an unexpected heat builds in my chest, a shiver of warmth but also confusion, as I don't know what to make of what he said about me.

"So you left her all alone?" Jace paces around Tristan, circling him like an alpha would circle prey. "Without her friends?"

Tristan barely reacts to Jace's circling. "Helen told me Tessa wouldn't be able to handle a crowd of wolves tonight. She needs time to adjust to the outside world after the protected environment at the house."

"That had better be true." Jace stops circling and gives Tristan a disappointed growl. "You're a real fucker around her."

Tristan's composure changes, his head lowering, eyes narrowed, facing Jace's accusation head on. "I can't let her get close to me. You know that."

Jace presses his lips together before he suddenly darts in and grips Tristan's shoulders, a more human move. "You can't push every woman away your whole life. You've got years before the three-headed wolf gets you—"

"He's already here, Jace."

Jace freezes, his hands clamping around Tristan's shoulders. "Already? It's too soon."

"I can sense him," Tristan says, holding Jace's gaze, his expression like stone. "The three-headed beast is coming for me the same way he came for my dad."

"Fuck." Jace lowers his hands, his shoulders slumping, more beta than alpha now. "Tristan... you know I can't help you..."

Tristan's jaw clenches. "But Tessa can. She's strong enough. She might be the only one who is."

Jace's head flies up. "*She's* your answer to this? Fuck, Tristan. *This* is the reason you want her?"

"If I make sure she doesn't get close to me, she'll be able to kill the three-headed wolf for good," Tristan replies, his voice a low growl. "She'll be the end of him. Once and for all. Then everyone will be safe."

Jace runs his hand through his hair. "Be careful, Tristan. You're playing with wildfire that could get out of your control."

Tristan suddenly grins, reckless, his green eyes gleaming. "I'm not trying to control the fire, Jace. I just want to light it and watch it burn."

Jace gives a heavy exhale, a troubled crease forming in his forehead. "If the wolf is coming for you, then we need to deal with

Baxter Griffin sooner rather than later. We need to make sure the pack is safe from the threat of the other alphas."

"One enemy at a time," Tristan says.

His head suddenly snaps to the right. "There's trouble under the bridge."

He breaks into a run and Jace follows, both men so fast and agile that the human passersby barely register their sprinting forms before they're gone.

I race after them, slower than they are as I attempt to keep to the shadows between streetlights, following the trail of their scents, my thoughts in turmoil.

Who or what is the three-headed wolf? And why is he coming for Tristan?

More importantly, why does Tristan think I can stop him?

Racing after Tristan and Jace, I follow them much farther than my wolf's energy has ever traveled from my human form, all the way toward the river.

I sense the disturbance ahead when we're still a block away. I blank out the sounds of vehicles traveling across the bridge above us to isolate the growls and snarls from the grassy area ahead that sits in the shadows under the bridge.

Five wolves are fighting in the darkness. I don't know any members of Tristan's pack yet, so I can't tell who is a friend and who is an enemy. I can't help them anyway—other than calming Becca, I haven't ever impacted anything with my wolf's energy. I can only observe.

Tristan and Jace split up as they race toward the fight, charging at the wolves from either side. Jace's fists are already forming. He uses his momentum to ram into the dark gray wolf on the far right just as it's about to leap at a smaller russet-colored wolf. The dark gray wolf yelps and rolls, transforming back into his human form seconds before Jace hauls him up and lands a cracking punch against the man's broad face.

The man darts to the side to avoid another punch, shouting, "It's Tristan and Jace! Time to scatter!"

Tristan remains in his human form, leaping onto a second dark gray wolf on the other side of the fight before it can escape. He charges into it, lifts it off the ground, and throws it back down into the earth. It yelps and I sense its fear seconds before Tristan drops his full weight onto the wolf's body, his knee landing on its spine.

There's a sickening *crack*.

The wolf's scream is cut short as Tristan grabs its head and breaks its neck with an efficiency that makes my world spin.

Helen warned me about Tristan's capacity for violence, but the way he killed so quietly, without even a roar of effort, makes my wolf's heart beat cold and quick.

Tristan hauls up the body and throws it at the man with the broad face, who froze at the death howl of his comrade. The body hits the man in the chest and he loses his footing, scrambling to get back to his feet, dragging the body with him. The third attacking wolf yelps and darts out of reach, shifting into the form of a smaller man who races away with the broad-faced man, carrying the slain wolf between them.

Within seconds, the sound of doors slam and a vehicle speeds away in the dark.

Jace races to Tristan's side.

"You let them leave," Jace says.

"I want to send a message. I won't be so merciful next time." Tristan strides over to the two shifters who remain in the shadows, helping them to their feet and checking over their wounds.

One of them is a woman with auburn hair—she was the russet wolf. She quickly turns and reaches for her discarded clothing, but nobody seems to mind—least of all her—that she's giving everyone an eyeful of her naked body.

"That's the second time they've tried to get past us here tonight, Tristan," she says, pulling on a black T-shirt and jeans. "I know we're stretched, but we need reinforcements. Those fuckers love this bridge."

Tristan exchanges a look with Jace before he turns back to the woman. "Do you have any problem with vampires, Bridget?" Tristan asks.

She doesn't appear to turn a hair. "Nope. As long as the vampire's on my side, I don't have any problem at all." Her face suddenly lights up with anticipation. "Wait! Is Iyana here?"

Tristan grins. "She is."

The woman tips her head back with a *whoop*. "Best news all day.

I'd love to have her help."

"Then I'll have reinforcements for you tomorrow night," Tristan says. "Can you hold out here tonight?"

"Yeah," she says, still catching her breath, checking her partner's response. He's a tall man, wiry, who appears slightly older. He has also hurried to dress.

He nods. "They shouldn't attack again now that one of them is dead."

Jace studies the bridge for a moment. "I'll stay here just in case."

Tristan also considers the bridge and the parking lot nearby.

"That felt too easy," he says, a crease suddenly forming in his forehead. "What if—?"

His focus suddenly snaps to Jace. Even in the dim light, I see the blood leave Tristan's face. "It could be a diversion like the one this afternoon."

Jace grips Tristan's shoulders, steadying his alpha, giving Tristan the same look that Helen gives me before she tells me to take a deep breath. "Do you sense anyone in trouble?"

Tristan's gaze becomes distant. "No. But I can't sense Tessa's wolf. She's invisible to me. Not like that first night." He's suddenly agitated. "Fuck! I never should have let her out of my sight tonight. I need to make sure she's okay."

"There's no way Baxter Griffin could know where she is," Jace hurries to say.

Tristan pulls away from him, already launching into a sprint, his arms and legs pumping as he runs back along the street.

Jace yells after him. "If you can't sense her, then neither can he! Nobody can." He lowers his voice. "Fuck, I hope I'm right."

I pull back into the shadows so that Tristan doesn't see me as he races past. He won't be able to sense my presence with his power, but he could still see me with his human eyes.

I'm shocked at the focus and determination on his face as he runs past. I remind myself that I'm important for his plans. He doesn't care about me. He can't afford to lose control of me.

And I can't afford to lose control of myself right now.

I need to return to my human body as fast as I can.

I tell myself that even when I'm separated from my wolf's energy, I'm still strong. I still have my power. She's one part of me, but not all of me. If Tristan returns to the penthouse before she does, then I can keep her outside until she can rejoin me when he won't see her.

I'm not ready for him to discover that I can separate from her.

Tristan is a running blur ahead of me on the street now. The rain starts to fall and suddenly, all the smells of the city overwhelm me. Tristan's scent becomes harder to detect.

No! I need his scent to find my way back to the penthouse.

I squint in the rain, panic rising inside me before I recognize the square up ahead.

Relief fills me, but it's suddenly ripped away from me as if my heart's on a hook and someone just yanked it out of my chest.

An energy I've never felt before hauls me to the left, nearly lifting me off my feet, pulling me savagely off course.

I slide to a stop inside the dark entrance of an alley, scrambling to find my feet and struggling to get my bearings.

The energy uncurls from around me just as quickly as it took hold. Released, I raise my head, peering down the alley.

My panic increases for too many reasons. I need to get back to the penthouse and now my chances of reaching it before Tristan are even slimmer.

What's worse is the wrenching power that dragged me off course. My wolf's energy is insubstantial. I can be seen, but nothing should be able to take hold of me.

What sort of being would have the power to stop me?

I shiver inside the alley's entrance, ready to run as soon as my damn legs begin obeying instructions again.

I freeze as a form takes shape in the darkness several paces away from me. A bright swirl of white light rises and grows between the alley walls. The light stretches out, rippling, streams of energy morphing into a shape that nails me to the spot.

A large, ivory wolf snarls at me from within the darkness, its teeth glowing, sharp and deadly. It's twice as big as me, but its body is just as insubstantial. Electrifying. Terrifying.

It's pure energy.

It's just like me.

The white wolf lowers his head, his eyes glowing crimson red. "Hello, little one," he says.

CHAPTER EIGHTEEN

*M*y hackles rise, growls growing in the back of my throat. "What the fuck are you?"

The white wolf snarls, giving me a threatening growl as he prowls toward me, pushing me toward the entrance of the alley.

"I am the same as you," he says, tipping his head at me. "But I see the confusion in your eyes, little one. I wonder if you know what you are?"

I glance around me, wary of the streetlight directly behind me and the humans walking past, worried about being seen by them. My human heart is also beating hard inside my chest all the way back in Tristan's penthouse because he's only minutes away from reaching me.

The white wolf laughs. "Are you worried that the humans can see you? Don't be. Only other supernaturals can see you."

"Then *you* should be worried," I snap. "There are shifters everywhere around here. Powerful ones."

"Shifters." The wolf pulls back its lips in a derisive snarl. "They are pitiful shadows of true wolves. They are nothing compared to me." He casts a gaze over me that feels like acid tearing through my fur down to the skin beneath. "And now, it seems, I should say that they are pitiful shadows compared to *you*."

He takes another step toward me, but this time, I stand my ground.

"Who are you?" I ask.

"That's a better question." He has the most expressive mouth. Now, his snarl is a smile. "I have three names, but they all mean the same thing in the end."

"Three names," I murmur, shuddering. Tristan mentioned a three-headed wolf. He said he could sense him coming for him. I look for shadows around the white wolf's head that might indicate he has more than one head, but I don't see anything. Maybe the three heads aren't literal. It could be a reference to this wolf's three names.

I lower my snout with a threatening snarl. "Where is your human body?"

The white wolf smiles again. "My human form is surprised but delighted to discover that you exist, little one. I thought I was alone."

He takes another step toward me, ending up so close to me that the tip of his nose could touch mine. He has no scent. Nothing at all. But the fiery glow in his eyes suddenly feels scorching.

"Tell me: Where have you been all this time?" His growl deepens and the crimson light in his eyes increases, a deep flame that burns hot. "Tell me who was hiding you from me so I can end them."

"Nobody was hiding me," I snap.

I've completely lost Tristan's scent now. I'm running out of time. Have already run out of time to make it back to the penthouse before him.

The white wolf laughs. "Oh, little one. Someone was hiding you from me. Even if you didn't know they were doing it. It must have been somewhere that my power couldn't reach. A place blessed by old magic, perhaps. To hide you from me all your life is quite a feat."

His laughter turns into a snarl. "I will find out who kept you from me and I will end them."

His attention suddenly shifts to the sky. Above us, the storm clouds part briefly, revealing a clear night sky.

He stares up at the stars for the fleeting moment that they are visible and takes a deep breath, sighing the air out as if he were expelling his anger. "Now that we've finally met, the future has shifted. Some paths have closed and others have opened. We will see where these new paths lead us, little one, on our journey together."

I shiver, my hackles rising again. He claims that someone was hiding me from him for my whole life. He can't mean Helen because I was only staying with her for the last two months. Before that, I was in the mountains with my father. There's no way my father was hiding me from this creature... unless he was.

I shudder as I remember how many times my father told me not to reveal my wolf's energy. That it would get me killed. That the other alphas would see me as a threat and do everything they could to kill me. As a consequence of his warnings, I rarely accessed my wolf's energy, only releasing my power for short bursts at a time, never as long as I have tonight.

Tonight is the first time I have separated from my wolf outside of the protected environment provided by Hidden House.

What if the other alphas weren't the only threat my father was protecting me from?

What if I alerted this creature to my presence by releasing my wolf tonight for the first time in the outside world?

"We do *not* have a path together," I say, raising my head, snarling at the white wolf. "Nobody was hiding me. And you will stay away from me. Whoever the hell you are."

He leans in, his nostrils flaring as he inhales. The air tugs around me, the smallest pull, a gentler version of the wrench that hauled me into this alleyway. "There's no stopping the future, little one," he whispers. "I sensed your energy for the first time tonight, but you won't be able to hide from me again."

He backs up, a delighted snarl revealing his sharp teeth. "I have to go now, but I will see you again soon."

He backs away from me into the darkness, his form disintegrating into swirls that fade into the night. I'm left with a bright spot in my vision, as if I stared into a light for too long.

I try to blink it away.

I don't have time to process what just happened.

Back in the penthouse, I can hear the whir of the elevator rising. Tristan is twenty seconds away from reaching my human form.

It's time to return all of my senses to my human body.

Opening my eyes in the penthouse again, I stare through the window at the square below me, seeking the spot in the distance where my wolf's energy is hiding in the shadows.

I make a sudden, determined decision.

I want her back with me.

Now.

Gritting my teeth, I pull on her with all of my will and determination. I sense her disintegrate, just like the white wolf's form did before he disappeared. My wolf's dark energy rushes into the air and toward me, a black spot, a blur in the night. If the white wolf's claim is correct, then the humans won't see her. As for supernaturals, most won't look high enough. Even if they do, she'll pass by too fast for them to figure out what she is.

Her energy rushes toward me and I brace for impact.

The elevator's doors are opening.

My wolf's dark blur of energy is a silent arrow. She pours through the window glass and hits my heart, knocking me onto my back in an awkward heap, my crossed legs tangled beneath me on the floor.

I fall back just as Tristan runs into the room.

"Tessa!" He charges toward me, shifting into his wolf form so fast that I gasp at the speed of it, let alone how easily he slips his human clothing. His jeans are still airborne as he lands in his wolf form, looming over the top of me.

He's large enough that his paws can rest easily on either side of me, his body covering mine, while his head is lowered and alert, swinging to assess the space around us. His teeth are bared, his growls aimed at anyone who might be about to attack.

If I weren't aware of the events that led him to this moment, I'd thump him for scaring the crap out of me. I should probably act as if I don't have any clue what's gotten into him—scream at him, maybe—but I'm not good at pretending.

Tristan's wolf is the same color as his hair—raven black—its fur seeming to suck the light out of the room, unnervingly similar to my wolf's power. Her energy has only just returned to my body, but already, she rattles inside me, begging me to shift fully and find out what it would be like to look eye to eye with Tristan's wolf.

I try to find my voice, finding it more difficult than I expected since I was using my wolf's energy to speak in growls and snarls moments ago. Come to think of it, speaking in wolf was easier than using my human vocal chords. Now my human voice feels harsh inside my throat.

"If this is your idea of standing guard over me, it's not necessary," I say.

Tristan's wolf snarls down at me, turning his full fury on me.

Okay, well, I wondered what it would be like to look eye to eye with his wolf. It's an unsettling experience. His wolf's eyes are as crisply green as his human eyes, rimmed just as darkly, but they're flecked with amber, a startling combination.

The white wolf is a distant threat to me now. I can't worry about him when the real threat is right in front of me.

I hate how foreign Tristan's animal feels to me. If I were like any other shifter, I would be able to read his body language right now—I'd instinctively know whether he were angry or worried, and I'd know how to respond according to pack law.

Tristan's nostrils flare. His animal pulls in my scent just like the white wolf did, but it has a different effect on me. Rather than a physical wrench, my response is more subtle. A tightening low in my stomach, a sudden ache in my chest, a hitch in my breathing that I fight to straighten out before Tristan notices.

"Tristan?" I wait for any sign that he understands me. "There's nobody else here. I'm safe." I wish I could come up with an excuse for falling backward, but any explanation I give will have to be a lie. "Everything's fine."

I blink and he shifts back into his human form. His fists rest on either side of my head as he holds himself above me, his face level with mine. He's completely naked, but I keep my focus on his eyes and chest and... *nope*. Not looking lower.

He wears a fierce crease in his forehead. I try to read his human emotions, but they're fleeting and concealed quickly.

"Good," he says.

It looks like he's about to roll to the side—his muscles bunch in that direction and I take advantage of his movement to awkwardly straighten out my legs—but he pauses, returning to me slowly.

Suddenly, his presence feels more dangerous than before.

The corners of his mouth turn down. "I couldn't sense you before, but now I'm drowning."

I purse my lips, not sure what he's talking about. Unless... I'm not in control right now.

My eyes widen as I do a quick check. My wolf blasted back into me seconds before Tristan raced into the room. I just encountered the white wolf. All of my power was exposed during my conversation with the ivory animal. Then I used my power to pull my wolf back to myself and now...

I'm not in control.

That means Tristan isn't, either.

He gives his head a small shake, but he can't hide the dilation of his pupils.

Oh... no...

His fists whiten on the floor on either side of my face, where he clenches them so hard, they lose blood. He's breathing faster than he should be, but he closes his eyes and slows it down, breathing deeper.

As if that's going to help.

He lets out a growl that tells me he just inhaled a chestful of my power. If what he's feeling is anything like what I felt when I tried to enter his bedroom, then he's currently experiencing a dizzying punch to the head. Maybe repeated punches. Increasing with force with every breath.

My anger rises and it isn't helping me control my power. With rage comes a terrible sort of desperation. I've only been out of Hidden House for a few hours and I'm already back to where I started.

Was it all for nothing?

"Helen warned you." I snarl, my own breathing increasing as I watch Tristan struggle with the effects of my scent—even more than he did on the night we first met. He blinked away my power then. Right now, he's sucking in more of it with every inhale, his chest expanding in dangerous increments. I'm suddenly drawn to the tattoo across his shoulder and chest—the snake killing the wolf while fighting beside it. As if he *chooses* to welcome his demons into his life.

I prepare for a fight with him. At least I know I have the skills to beat nearly anyone now. Whether I can beat a butt-naked, out-of-control Tristan remains to be seen.

I lower my voice, angry with him. "Helen told you I wasn't ready, Tristan."

Tristan opens his eyes. I'm shocked to see his pupils are fully dilated, but he doesn't shake his head or show any signs of fighting the effect anymore.

"Would you ever be ready?" he asks, his voice much more controlled than I was expecting.

I glare back at him. This was a hiccup. If it weren't for the white wolf—whoever he is—I'm sure I'd be completely in control right now. It was a combination of that animal's appearance and my rush to get back before Tristan returned that threw me off-balance.

"You took me unawares. This will never happen again." I tip my chin as best I can while lying on the floor. With a concerted effort, I slow my own breathing, trying to transport my mind back to the garden in Hidden House, already feeling much calmer.

"My fault then," he murmurs. "I'll remember not to surprise you in future."

His pupils are no less dilated, even though I'm sure I'm getting myself under control now. His balance shifts to the right as he raises his left hand off the floor to stroke the strands of my hair that have fallen across my cheek, light brushes that make me shiver. My stomach muscles suddenly clench, along with my inner thigh muscles. An intense toe-curling sensation builds, surprising me.

"Tessa," he murmurs. "There's a more important question."

"What is it?" I whisper when he falls silent.

"Why are we fighting this?" he asks, searching my eyes.

My lips part slowly.

"I'm not going to hurt your body," he says. "I will never lay a hand on you in a way that will harm you. I'm not going to mark you or try to claim you. I can give you everything you want and nothing that you don't want. At least for a time. All you have to do is ask."

I lick my dry lips. My wolf's energy has stopped beating inside me and now she unfurls, more like a cat than anything else, luxuriating in Tristan's low, growled promises.

But my human mind is confused. "What would I ask for, Tristan?"

Tristan dips his head, his lips nudging the edge of my jaw, soft brushes like the way he stroked my hair.

"Everything you want," he whispers, slowly brushing the corner of my lips with his.

My wolf's energy is in tune with my body. The slow burn that began in my stomach ignites at my center, my tension building. But my power and my body are at odds with my human heart.

"How can I ask for anything except my freedom?" I whisper.

Tristan freezes. "I can't let you leave."

"Then you can't give me everything I want." I want to scorch him with my glare, raking it across his extraordinary eyes, the fullness of his lips, his jaw, even his broad shoulders, and most especially the image of his wolf dying by snake bite.

"Get off me," I snarl.

A hint of surprise passes across his face. I guess I'm not so fucking vulnerable after all.

He immediately rolls to the side, gliding to his feet, as agile as his wolf as he scoops up his jeans, but this time, he doesn't stride to the elevator, veering toward his bedroom instead. I thought he'd leave and return to Jace, but it seems he's determined to stay. I guess Tristan did say to Jace that he shouldn't have left me alone in the first place.

I rise to my feet, as quiet as my dark wolf, not quite calm and not quite in control, but right now, I'd give anything to fight him.

Tristan pauses with his back to me, a perfect sculpture of a man, the muscles across his shoulders and back rippling as he rolls his shoulders and stretches his neck side to side as if he were easing out his own tension.

Without fully turning—without bothering to put on his jeans—he casts a challenging smile back at me before he inclines his head toward his bedroom. "The offer stands, Tessa."

He told me I could sleep in his room tonight.

Now he means with him in it.

"No fucking chance," I snap.

I'm dazzled by his broadening smile. He seems infuriatingly

pleased with my rebuke. He casts his jeans aside as he enters his room and leaves the door wide open, stalking into the bathroom and leaving that door open too.

He leaves me with an ache I can't ease and a set of elevator doors that I can't open.

CHAPTER NINETEEN

I sleep fitfully on the couch. I miss the forest sounds of my bedroom at Hidden House. I also miss Ella's humming. Being so far away from Hidden House gives rise to heartache.

I'm vengefully satisfied to hear Tristan tossing and turning as much as I am. Finally, the glow of sunrise hits the horizon and I have an excuse to abandon my attempts to sleep. Rubbing my eyes, I slip my legs over the edge of the couch and sigh out my frustration.

Breakfast can wait. I need to beat the crap out of a boxing bag.

The only way that's going to happen is if I steal Tristan's security card.

I narrow my eyes at his bedroom in the distance before I lower my feet to the carpet floor, drawing my wolf's energy awake and harnessing it to creep across the floor.

Quiet mice have nothing on me right now.

I pause at the door, listening to his deep breathing.

I smile because he's finally asleep.

Prowling one silent step at a time, I enter the bedroom, only to sway like I'm drunk at the concentration of power that confronts me. The white wolf said that shifters are a shadow compared to us, but I'm sure Tristan is in a different league.

If Tristan and I were allies, I would tell him about the white wolf. I could ask Tristan about the three-headed wolf that he's worried about. Hell, if we were allies, I would help him fight the three-headed beast. As much as I want to rage against Tristan for caging me, I don't have any reason to hate his pack or wish them harm.

My shoulders slump as I remember Carly and Becca and the way Becca curled into me, seeking my help. I didn't feel a connection with her like Tristan must feel—a sense of being pack—but I felt protective of her. I wanted to help.

Even though I struggle to push away Tristan's power, the sight of the security card on his bedside table drives me onward.

Tristan is asleep on his stomach, lying across his bed at an angle, the white bedsheets curled around his hips leaving his upper body bare along with his calves and feet. One of his arms rests under a pillow thrown to the left, while his head rests on the corner of another pillow, which is also caught around his other arm.

I smother a self-righteous giggle.

Any woman who dares to sleep in a bed with Tristan Masters had better be prepared to be jostled in her sleep.

Fixing that thought in my mind, I make it all the way to the bedside table and reach delicately for the security card. Holding my breath, I slowly curl my fingers around it and lift it off the surface without scraping it against the table.

I continue to hold my breath all the way to the bedroom door as I backstep toward it and creep across to the elevator.

Now, the tricky part is going to be if the elevator dings when it arrives. I can't remember if it did that last night...

I suck air across my teeth.

It's a risk I'm prepared to take.

Swiping the card, I press the *down* button and prepare to move quickly.

The doors open with a *swoosh*, I dart inside, and they close again.

Yes!

Oh, the small wins.

I press the button for the eleventh floor, preparing for the freedom of punching the lights out of a boxing bag when the elevator doors open right back up again.

Tristan glares at me.

His hair is tousled. He has dark rings under his eyes. He's wearing jeans that he must have pulled on in a hurry because his zipper isn't done up, let alone the top button. He leans against the opening doors, arm raised in a way that accentuates the muscles across his stomach and biceps.

I smother an inward sigh, unimpressed at how quickly he woke up and came after me.

Arching an eyebrow at him, I point to the buttons where the eleventh floor is already lit up. "I'm going to the gym."

"Then I'm coming with you." He prowls into the back of the elevator, keeping to the other side of it.

Despite looking like he had the worst night ever, he smells like the best night ever, a combination of bitter orange and cedar that brings to mind tumbling through warm grass beneath a summer sun. There's a sleepy sort of relaxed movement to his upper body as he leans against the side of the elevator. The steel doors are reflective enough for me to catch sight of myself—hair unbrushed, my clothes crinkled. Also—dammit—one button of my flannel shirt has popped open.

The ride is fast, only one floor. As soon as the doors open, I shoot out of the elevator to quickly assess the layout of the gym in front of me. A combat ring sits in the middle. Treadmills and weightlifting equipment are located nearest to the windows on the left, while on the right-hand side, right at the back, are the objects of my desire. Two boxing bags hanging side by side.

I'm sure it will be too much to hope that there are gloves in my size, but I head for the bags anyway, noting the sign that indicates a bathroom is located around the corner behind them. I'll be able to wash up in there first.

Tristan breaks off from me, taking up position at the windows, his hands held loosely at his sides and his back to me while I head straight for the bathroom. I use the facilities quickly, fix my shirt, then splash my face with water and dry it with paper towel. I use my fingers to comb through my hair before fishing out a hair tie from my pocket and tying my hair up into a topknot.

I'm scruffy, but it will have to do.

I pause when I emerge. Tristan has remained at the far windows, but I'm surprised to find two women sparring in the combat ring despite the early hour. They must have arrived while I was in the bathroom. One of them is the auburn-haired woman from the bridge last night—Bridget. She and the other woman stop what they're doing and I'm surprised by the sudden aggression in their stares. Bridget apparently doesn't have a problem with vampires, but she definitely seems to have a problem with me.

My scent can't be putting her off because—other than the hiccup last night—I have that under control. I shouldn't be detectible, either. Although the absence of a scent could be just as unsettling.

Ignoring them, I reach for the pair of gloves that looks to be my closest fit and quickly strap my hands. I jab the bag to get a feel for it before I ease into a rhythm. It's difficult to concentrate when every five minutes, I expect to hear Iyana's voice calling out some instruction or words of encouragement, and instead all I hear are the two women sparring behind me.

Until I don't.

I pause at the silence behind me, my senses expanding and then filling with confusion.

They're creeping up on me. As if they intend to jump me—

One of them aims a fist at the back of my head while the other drops and prepares to sweep my legs out from under me. Success would see me face-plant hard against the bag.

I duck the hit to my head and drop at the same rate as the woman who is about to perform the leg sweep. My gloved fist smacks into her stomach—which she left wide open.

Now that I can see them, I identify Bridget as the one who tried to hit my head. She regains her balance and takes another shot at me, but this time, I'm ready and facing her.

I duck, anticipate her step to the left, and take a swipe at her, knocking her to the side. Grabbing her arm before she can fall, I flip her onto her back and press my foot to her chest. Not hard enough to hurt her.

"Stay down!" I shout at her.

The other woman tries to grab me from behind, but I fling myself into her, using her body to brace as I rapidly climb the boxing bag with my feet and kick off it. Backflipping to land behind the woman, my glove connects with her lower back and she stumbles away from me, banging into the bag.

She attempts to regain her balance while Bridget recovers, both women quickly prowling toward me again. I back into the clear space at the front of the room, eyeing them warily.

What is this behavior? Are they trying to establish dominance? Pack hierarchy?

If so, it's no wonder Helen told Tristan to keep me apart from the pack last night.

Too much sensory input, my ass.

Helen knew—*Tristan* knew—they'd come after me.

I was always an outcast among my own pack, my status determined right from the start—from the moment my mother slapped me, to be exact. From that moment on, every other wolf was above me.

Now, I'm a grown wolf who has entered a new pack. I guess the women need to know where they stand.

I'm aware of Tristan pacing at the side of the room, more twitchy than I've ever seen him. He's agitated, shoulders hunched, stepping toward me and then back, as if he's having a mental war with himself.

He can't get involved.

If he comes to my assistance, I won't gain any respect at all. I don't know much about pack law, but I do know *that*.

So far, I haven't needed my wolf's energy, but I'm prepared to access it if I have to.

Just as the two women force me out into the open, a group of five women emerge from the elevator. The behavior of the first two is like a trigger. The newcomers immediately drop their gym bags and begin to circle me.

Great.

"Prepare for a walloping," Bridget says with a nasty grin.

I should be calm, but I'm not. The past is my enemy. I've trained with Iyana for months, but the real fight is in my head. My last battle, which I was also forced into, ended with my father's death. His voice was always a constant reminder inside my head. *Hide your wolf. Don't show your strength.*

Now, for the first time since he died, my wolf is my friend.

As quickly as I can, I pull at the straps keeping my gloves on and pitch the gloves over the top of the women's heads into the combat ring, as if I'm chucking split wood.

Keeping watch on the seven women as they circle me, I rapidly unstrap my hands. They seem content to wait as I prepare for the fight. I guess they figure that the delay gives them more time to psych me out.

They have no fucking idea how many times I've faced down pain and hurt and dealt with it.

I breathe deeply. I'd love to release my wolf, but that's a secret I won't reveal until I need to.

One of the women suddenly breaks from the others and leaps at me, her fist raised. I drop, avoiding the punch, and land a hit to her stomach, hearing the breath leave her body before I spin and kick the legs out from the next woman coming at me. Rising to my feet, I respond to the rapid punches of the third woman by blocking and hitting back with a quick combination that busts up her nose.

Blood streams down her face. She gives a howl, but I feel no regret.

Spinning to the next woman, I put all of my strength into a kick that connects with her chest and sends her flying backward. My wolf's energy rises inside me, a response to the violence around me, making me stronger and faster.

Exchanging rapid blows with another woman—a blonde—I duck and dodge to evade an attack by a woman behind me at the same time, aware of yet another elevator full of shifters emerging into the room—some male this time.

The women in the new group immediately run to join the fight against me.

Oh, for fuck's—

I stop defending and start attacking, ripping one woman off her feet as she runs toward me, smacking her with my fist and using her own momentum against her to knock her out cold. I duck through an assault from three others to target a fourth woman, flipping her off her feet and kicking her spine.

She screams, but again, I feel no regret.

They picked this fight, not me.

I kick, hit, punch, swing, and flip my way through the rest of the attacking women, until only Bridget is left standing.

She's ranked the highest. I see that now. The others were following her lead. She's not Tristan's beta, but she must be some sort of delta.

My chest heaves and sweat drips down my face, but I haven't sustained a single wound from the altercation.

She was cocky in the beginning, but now she's wary, eyeing the eleven women groaning on the ground around us as I prowl toward her.

"Come on," I say, my voice rising. "This is what you wanted, isn't it? To make sure I know my place? Well, I know my place. It's right beside Tristan. Not lower than him. Certainly not fucking lower than you."

Her gaze flicks to Tristan.

It's the first time she's checked his response to our fight.

He looks like he might kill her if I don't, his fists clenched, his lips drawn back in a snarl, his focus lined up with hers.

Her eyes widen and the blood drains from her face.

If she were in wolf form, she'd tuck her tail between her legs right now. I guess there are many pack laws I still don't know about, but it looks like she broke one of them by engaging me in a fight.

She drops her gaze from mine and backs away from me.

Her body language is probably an acknowledgment of my status, but my human side is wary of another challenge. If I don't end this now, the shifters in Tristan's pack could keep coming at me.

Spinning away from Bridget, I discover that a crowd has grown at the entrance to the gym, both men and women, even some older teens. The women I beat slowly stumble to their feet and also back away from me, clutching their ribs, arms, even heads, but I know I didn't do them any serious damage.

"Who else?" I scream at the crowd, my wolf's energy rising inside me so that my scream turns into a shrieking howl. "Who else wants a piece of me?"

In the background, I finally see Iyana and Danika trying to push through the men and women gathered in the opening, but the shifters won't budge, blocking their way.

Iyana looks like she's ready to bite the next wolf who keeps her from me. Her fangs are fully descended while Danika keeps reaching for her hip as if she's expecting to find a pistol with a handy silencer on it.

I wait in the silence that ensues.

"Come on!" I scream. "No men? Are you all fucking cowards? *Fight me!*"

Tristan flinches, suddenly more subdued, and I'm not sure why my challenge had that effect on him.

"You either challenge me now or you challenge me never!" I scream, my gaze raking over the crowd. Waiting for someone to answer my call.

"Really?" I ask when the silence continues. "Nobody else?"

"Nobody is stupid enough," says a quiet male voice at the side of the room.

Jace steps out of the crowd, approaching me cautiously, warily. I put him on his backside at Hidden House and I guess he remembers it.

He looks like he got dressed in a hurry. He was probably out patrolling the city for most of the night—might have only had a few hours of sleep before he came up here to the gym. I can only imagine how quickly the news must have spread that a fight was going on to bring all of these shifters up here to see it.

Jace steps to my side, placing himself carefully where I can see him, as if he's wary of my wrath. He turns to the pack. "Tessa Dean is the daughter of Andreas Dean, former alpha of the Middle Highlands pack. You've heard the stories—the rumors."

Murmurs grow among the onlookers, but they hush when Jace says, "They're all true. Tessa's wolf is unique but formidable. Two months ago, Tessa fought Dawson Nash, Cameron Griffin, *and* Cody Griffin at the Conclave. She challenged her alpha, Peter Nash. But as a consequence of defending herself, she lost her father. He was one of the last true alphas. A friend of this pack. We feel his loss deeply." Jace gives me a careful nod. "Tessa is part of our pack now. You will welcome her and treat her with the same respect with which you treat each other."

Some of my rage evaporates with Jace's firm and clear speech, but my underlying distrust remains. I was within their presence for two seconds and these shifters turned on me.

Nothing has changed. I'm a target and that's what I'll remain.

Jace continues to eye me warily, cautiously, before he turns toward Tristan.

I hold my breath, waiting for Tristan to respond, waiting to see if he'll reinforce Jace's statements and make sure the message is clear—that I'm safe among the pack.

Tristan's gaze flicks from me to Bridget and back again. The muscle in his jaw clenches and I sense his inner turmoil again—about *what*, I'm not sure.

He strides across the room, but everything freezes when he passes behind me and walks straight to Bridget.

Ignoring me, he grips her shoulders and murmurs something to her.

Shock passes through me.

He has disregarded me in favor of my attacker.

A quick check of Jace's reaction reveals that he has also frozen, his shoulders suddenly tense. Jace's gaze flicks to me and I can't stand the apology in his eyes.

Fuck this. I can't stay here in this room a second longer.

Taking a quick breath, trying to control the rising tide of hurt and anger inside me, I turn away from Tristan and Jace and stride toward the elevator, my fists still clenched.

The crowd parts immediately to let me through, every shifter backing away from me in a hurry, casting quick glances from me to Tristan.

I don't look back, snarling at them as I pass by.

Now that the crowd moves out of the way, Iyana races toward me, wrapping her arms around my shoulders and pulling me away from the watchful shifters. Danika holds the elevator door open for me, gesturing for us to hurry inside it. There's no direct sunlight in this room or I imagine their roles would be reversed.

As soon as Iyana and I enter, Danika lets the doors close, thumps the button for the seventh floor, and throws her arms around me. Iyana follows, their arms tangling in a group hug that makes it hard for me to suppress my misery.

"Oh, sweetie," Iyana says, stroking my hair as I drop my head to her shoulder. "That was seriously fucked-up pack bullshit."

My eyes are burning with tears. The fight was bad enough, but Tristan consoling Bridget at the end has now sent a message to his pack that rips away my worth: They can attack me and he will side with them.

They are his pack and I am not.

I can beat them, knock them down, but I will never be one of them.

Danika rubs my back and I can't stop my tears from flowing.

"Fuck mornings," I say.

CHAPTER TWENTY

The corridor is deserted as Iyana and Danika help me to their room. I'm a shivering, shaking mess by the time we reach it.

The aftermath of my fight with the women is worse than all of the times Dawson took his shit out on me, and I don't understand why it's affecting me so much right now. It's not like I'm physically wounded.

My teeth chatter as Iyana pushes the door open to their room at the end of the corridor. "This is where they put us."

It's a corner room with windows on two sides—both covered with block-out blinds that Iyana has taped to the window frames around the edges to keep the sunlight out. Separate beds sit along each far wall, and a small bathroom is located off to the left. I remember Tristan saying that the seventh floor is for the single women, some of whom I'm assuming are currently upstairs—the ones I put on their butts.

Iyana firmly closes the door but mutters unhappily that there's no lock.

I stumble inside the room while Danika keeps hold of me.

"Are you hurt, sweetie?" she asks, guiding me to the nearest bed and helping me sit. "We can get ice if you need it."

I shake my head, pressing my lips together, unable to speak.

Iyana crosses to the bed and kneels in front of me, looking me over with alarm when I start to rock back and forth, curling over my knees.

"Are you sure you're not hurt?" she asks.

"She must be in shock," Danika says, leaning across the gap between beds to snatch the blanket off the other bed and wrap it around my shoulders, rubbing my back and holding me close. "She let her guard down and they attacked her. I've seen it happen. It's worse than when you expect an attack."

With my arms now wrapped up in the blanket, I can't swipe at my tears, hating the continuing burn at the back of my eyes. I wasn't prepared for someone to try to hurt me. Despite the conflict with Tristan, I thought I would be safe among his pack at least. Hell, last night I was eating cake.

All of my rage has evaporated and left me vulnerable. Having friends who care about me is only making it worse, giving me a safe place to fall apart.

Except that it's not so safe after all.

Tristan's presence suddenly floods my senses again. His footsteps thud in my hearing, rapid beats approaching along the corridor.

My heart lurches. Iyana's head snaps up. At the same time, Danika's arms clench tighter around me.

"I'll tell him to fuck off," Iyana says, rising to her feet and storming across the room, throwing open the door before closing it firmly behind her.

I sense Tristan pull to a stop. I count the beats of silence while I imagine Iyana is casting death stares at him if he comes a step closer.

When he finally speaks, he's a lot quieter than I was expecting. "I need to speak with Tessa."

"Fuck off, Tristan," Iyana snaps, true to her promise. Her footsteps are quiet, and I picture her muscling up to Tristan, who is practically twice her size. "You and your pack have done enough damage for today."

I was expecting an aggressive response from Tristan, but he remains subdued. "Nothing like that will happen again. Can you please make sure Tessa knows that?"

Iyana pauses now too. But she rallies quickly. "It had better not happen again. Or we're out of here, and from what I hear, you need our help."

"I do." There's another pause. "Does Tessa need anything?"

"She needs to be left alone." I picture Iyana holding her head higher. "And she's staying with us from now on."

"Okay," he says. "I'll have Jace move you to the family floor upstairs. There's more room there."

Now I picture Iyana unfurling her fists, maybe tipping her head to the side. If she's surprised, she doesn't sound it. "Good."

I sense Tristan turn swiftly on his heel and stride away.

Iyana returns to the room, closes the door behind her, and presses back against it. Her eyes are wide, her lips pursed. She looks shell-shocked. "What just happened?" she asks.

I drag air into my chest. "He hasn't left."

My senses are going haywire because Tristan's presence is like a burning flame, a scorching spot nearby, burning brighter than normal. So fiercely bright that I must be feverish. His footsteps stop at the end of the corridor and pause. I sense his inner turmoil like a growing wildfire about to rage out of control and then…

"You need to step away from the door, Iyana," I manage, still gasping for breath, trying to fight the clawing sensation inside my heart and chest. No matter how hard I try to hold myself together —no matter how firmly Danika hugs me—my insides are coming apart.

I fight the moan that threatens to slip between my lips.

I'm stronger than this.

I'm stronger—

My groan releases, a painful, wrenching sound.

A second later, the door flies open.

Iyana steps clear just in time.

Tristan looms in the doorway. His shoulders are hunched. He's partially shifted, his eyes nearly full wolf, his animal dominating the room with its presence.

"No." He growls at Iyana, his voice barely human.

She stands her ground, edging between him and me. "Get out of here, Tristan…" She flounders. "Or Tristan's wolf. Or whomever I'm speaking to right now. Get out, or I swear I will grow a taste for wolf blood."

"No." He growls again. "She needs me."

"Tristan's wolf," Iyana addresses him while her fangs descend and her lips draw back. "Tessa needs you like she needs a claw in her back."

Tristan's response is low and dangerous, simple statements that make me run cold. "Her wolf is breaking. I can sense it. You can't help her. I want to walk away, but I can't. She's my responsibility." He glares at Iyana. "She needs me."

On the bed, I drag my knees up to my chest. This pain has to be a consequence of more than the aftermath of a fight. It's a deep, tearing sensation, as if I'm about to lose a part of myself and I'm afraid of what will happen when I do.

Iyana casts a quick glance at Danika, who chomps down on her lip. "I hate to admit it, but Tristan's right. This is more than shock. Tessa wasn't hurt in the fight—not that I saw—but she's in physical pain. I'm not sure what's causing it or what we can do..."

"Her wolf needs my wolf," Tristan snaps, apparently impatient with the conversation already. "If you don't want her to break, then you will let me pass."

Iyana's fists clench. With a groan of frustration and defeat, she finally steps out of Tristan's path, but she jabs her finger at him, her fangs clearly visible. "If you hurt Tessa, things are going to get very messy between us, *wolf*."

Tristan stops when he's level with her, his eyes narrowed, but he suddenly reaches into his pocket and flips her a card that looks like a security card. "Do not come near the twelfth floor for twenty-four hours. After that, you're free to come and go."

Iyana stares at the security card before she snatches it from him. "Fine." Her gaze darts to me. "Please, make sure Tessa's okay."

Tristan ignores her plea, scooping me up blanket and all, one arm under my legs, the other supporting my back, keeping me as curled up as possible as he pulls me against his chest and strides from the room with me.

Giving in to my increasing pain, I allow my head to rest against his chest as he carries me to the elevator, but I tug at the blanket, making sure it covers me and forms a barrier between us.

It's infuriating that he suddenly seems to have spare security cards everywhere, pulling another one from his jeans pocket to trigger the elevator to take us up to the twelfth floor.

When the blanket slips a little as he bends to scan his card, I grab at the material to pull it tight again.

"Stop that." He growls at me as he straightens and adjusts his hold on me. "You're not helping yourself."

I can't even scowl at him. Right now, I'm simply desperate not to throw up all over him.

I'm both suffocating and tearing apart. The blanket is my final defense, keeping all of my pieces together.

The elevator doors open into his penthouse and he launches into action. I freeze in shock when he rolls me onto the couch and rips the blanket away from me.

I've barely registered that the blanket's gone when he hauls me up by the front of my shirt so fast that he rips the buttons off it, tearing my shirt open, exposing my bra. His arms whip around my waist, sliding against my naked ribs as he yanks me up against him.

"What the fuck are you doing?" I scream at him, my fists flying out, punching into his shoulders milliseconds before my chest can collide with his.

My defensive maneuver barely has an impact on him.

"You need skin on skin," he snarls, his voice throaty, his big hands unrelenting where he grips my waist.

I'm still processing the ease with which he nearly undressed me, still coming to terms with his strength. I thought fighting Cody Griffin was terrifying. I thought the white wolf was intimidating.

But if Tristan hadn't chosen to stop right now, I wouldn't have a chance.

Fuck.

My forearms press against his chest, my arms bent at the elbows, the only barrier between us. I seek my wolf's strength, but she's writhing inside me. She's hurting. And the worst part is that where my arms press against Tristan's chest... I'm receiving the smallest relief from the pain.

His wolf's power—*his* power—promises to be the drug that will ease my pain. But if it means embracing him—worse, stripping off —I'll have to make myself completely vulnerable to him to get it.

"I won't hurt you," he says, his voice thick. "But you need to give in to this."

I tip my head back, my hair falling heavily to my waist. I search for any hint in his eyes that he sees me as anything other than a means to an end.

I don't find it.

"No!" I thump him and he releases me, his arms dropping to his sides.

I crumple to the floor, unable to stay upright without his support, one arm outstretched to ward him off as I gasp my speech. "Stay... the fuck... away from me..."

"Tessa, you need my help. You need my body. Nobody else can help you right now."

I find strength enough to reply with a sharp tongue. "Oh, because you're so strong? I need big, strong Tristan to help me, is that it?"

"You need an alpha! And right now I'm the only one you've got."

I back into the coffee table, bumping my calves against it before I veer to the side. "I don't need *anything* from you, Tristan Masters. Least of all a bodice-ripping."

He shakes his head at me, dangerously slow as he follows me at a prowl. "You have no idea what you did this morning. You asserted dominance over the strongest women in my pack. Do you understand what that means?"

"No, because I don't understand your rules or your laws or your fucking aggressive pack behavior."

"Aggressive?" His head jerks back as he stops short. "You haven't seen the beginning of my *aggression*, Tessa."

I shiver, because I think I *have* seen the edges of his aggression, not least in the way he ripped off my buttons just now, but especially in the terrifyingly efficient way in which he did it. Helen warned me that I should take every story I've heard about Tristan, triple its brutality, and I might approach a true assessment of his capacity for violence.

I shiver uncontrollably as I realize that, in the last twenty-four hours since we left Hidden House, he has concealed and subdued his true nature.

Recklessly, despite the threat of violence, I lash out anyway. "If that's true, then why do you care to help me at all?"

"Because I won't be my father." He doesn't shout, but if anything, the low pitch of his growl scares me more than a roar would have. "I won't be like him."

For a terrifying second, I glimpse the depth of violence in Tristan's eyes, held in check only by sheer will.

I lower my voice. "Then stay away from me—"

Pain shoots up through my chest all the way into my neck and shoulders. I double over, dropping to my knees, desperately keeping one arm outstretched, as if that will ward him off.

I can't stop my sobs. My right hand sinks into the carpet, clawing it, trying to find relief.

I *need* relief from the pain.

"It's my fault your wolf is tearing herself to shreds." He blocks out the light with his big body as he stands over me, merciless. "I need you to understand, the last time there was a fight like the one this morning, my father killed the loser. He encouraged fights and then he took his revenge on the one who failed. We lost good wolves to his bloodlust. I needed to make sure Bridget knew I wasn't going to kill her. I can't lose her. I can't lose another member of my pack—"

"You walked right past me." I tip my head back with a snarl. It *is* his fault that I'm hurting. The pain started the moment he walked past me to console Bridget. "You rejected me!"

"I only needed a minute, Tessa." He tilts his head at me, teeth gritted, the corners of his mouth turned down. "Half a fucking minute to make sure she knew she was safe. You left before I could get to you. You couldn't wait half a minute so I didn't lose her—"

"But you were willing to lose *me*!" I scream. "You were willing to shame me in front of your pack."

My accusation falls into the silence between us. Helen told me that Tristan has an unparalleled ability to perceive and neutralize threats and an unrelenting determination to protect his pack.

It's his loyalty to his pack that leaves me screaming now.

"I am nothing more than a possession to you." I moan, lowering my left arm to clutch my stomach, tangling my hand in my open shirt. "I'm not a member of your pack. I'm a means to an end—

whatever fucking end that actually is. The only reason you want to help me now is because you can't afford to lose me."

He's blank, ruthless.

"Yes," he says.

I can't stop my scream. The clawing in my stomach and chest is like daggers suddenly ripping up through me. I dip toward the floor, nearly buckling beneath the pain.

Tristan drops to the carpet in front of me. One of his hands grips my shoulder, the other my waist, pulling me upright, forcing me to look up. "You say you don't understand pack law—and maybe *you* don't—but your wolf does," he says. "I rejected you, and now she's tearing herself apart because she fought for dominance— she won it—but she was cast aside anyway. She knows what has to happen next."

"And what..." I gasp, tears falling down my cheeks. "Is that?"

"We either fight or I mark you as my mate."

Everything freezes.

I reel as his emotionless statement hits me, but he grips me tightly, relentless in his determination to keep hold of me.

"When you dominated the strongest women in my pack, you asserted yourself as the alpha female," he says.

Pain and shock have become a state of being to the point where I'm turning numb. I can barely feel my feet or my hands, my arms sliding to my sides as he pulls me farther upright into a kneeling position like him.

"Bridget had no idea how strong you are when she challenged you or she never would have done it," he says. "Her instinct was to show you your place. Knock you down and be done with it. She had no idea you'd retaliate like you did. No fucking idea that you're strong enough to challenge *me*. I want to kill her for putting me in this position."

Tristan's declaration bounces back and forth inside my mind, a painful beat. *The alpha female... the alpha... fuck...*

"That's not possible..."

"The problem is that you're not my mate," Tristan snarls. "If you were my mate, you would rule at my side. We would be equal part- ners. But instead, our wolves are now in a power struggle. Yours is tearing herself apart with breathtaking violence, while mine is slowly burning up. If I could walk away from this—if I could be the good guy—I would."

Tristan's grip on me tightens, his palms dragging across my skin, tingling, making me shiver, as he slowly pulls me forward, my chest to his.

"We either fight each other to see who can assert dominance over the other—and restore their wolf's position of power," he says, husky now. "Or we play a different game of dominance in the bedroom. I know which one I prefer. It's your choice, Tessa."

I can't breathe. Last night, he'd nudged the corner of my lips, made my toes curl and fierce heat grow between my legs, and told me that he would give me everything I wanted and nothing that I didn't.

But that's not how it will be today. Today will be about control and submission.

"I want another option." My eyes are leaking, tears dripping all the way down my cheek, falling from my jaw onto his bare arm. They leave shiny rivers across his muscles. "Give me a third option."

"Those are the only two options I'm prepared to accept," he says. "Make your choice."

CHAPTER TWENTY-ONE

he only two options he's prepared to accept? That means there must be a third or even fourth option he isn't telling me...

"You're lying to me!" I scream at Tristan as the pain billows inside me. "There has to be another way. *Please.*"

He jolts, the fire in his eyes increasing, and it makes me wonder what his wolf is going through right now.

"There is," he whispers, his teeth gritted as he answers my question with reluctance. "It's called *melding.* It's an ancient way to resolve the issue of dominance. My pack knows about it because knowledge was passed down through my father, but not so many wolves know about it anymore." He levels his gaze with mine, a hitch in his voice giving the hint of pain he's keeping hidden. "It's dangerous, Tessa. The chances of surviving are extremely low."

My teary eyes meet his. "Why?"

"Because it involves experiencing each other's darkness." The shadows in his eyes grow. "If we can't control the darkness and emerge from it, our minds will be lost forever. Our bodies will succumb to the pain and die."

"I'm dying anyway." I moan. "What do we have to do? Tell me."

"You have to trust me."

I narrow my eyes at him. "I *don't* trust you."

"Then we're back to the first two options."

"No! One of us will die if we fight and the other option is..." I shake my head, groaning. "I won't do that."

His voice lowers, but it's not soft, all sharp edges. "Why are you so afraid of fucking?" He pauses and considers me with more caution than I was expecting. "Did someone hurt you?"

He's assuming the worst. I meet the dangerous glint in his eyes, the sharp contradictions. He *resents* me. But if someone hurt me, he would end them.

"I'm not worried about sex," I say, hating the whimper in my voice. "I can't let anyone mark me."

"Why not?"

It's impossible to find a lie when the pain inside me is as relentless as his questions. "Because I can't bond. I will never have a true mate."

"Why would that determine whether or not you choose to be marked?" Tristan's forehead creases. "A mark is a sign of belonging. It means standing side-by-side. The bond between true mates rarely happens anyway. I know only a few wolves who have found their true mate."

"But it will *never* happen for me. I don't want a constant reminder of what I can never have."

Tristan draws back a little but doesn't let me go. He is grim as his gaze rakes my face. I imagine he's searching for any sign that I'll choose a different path.

"Then we have no choice." Lowering his gaze, he stares at the shiny rivers of tears trailing across his arm. His jaw clenches. "The first step is trust. Real trust. You have to do what I say and have faith that I won't hurt you."

"And how is this dangerous for you?" I'm scathing. "Since I'm the one who has to blindly trust you."

His jaw tightens. "Because I have to accept your trust and not break it. Believe me, Tessa, that will be difficult for me."

He waits while I grit my teeth. I'm not going to survive this pain much longer. I'm already reduced to whines and whimpers. It's only going to get worse.

"Fine," I say, squeezing my eyes closed.

This time, he approaches me slowly, sliding his left hand around my upper right ribs, anchoring me. "From this moment, we have to stay in contact at all times," he whispers. "Breaking apart will break our trust."

Slipping his right hand beneath my shirt, he wraps his fingers around my shoulder before pushing the material off it, sliding my left sleeve as far as possible down my arm before drawing me up against his chest so he can remove my shirt completely.

He works one-handed, keeping firm control of me with his left hand around my ribcage.

I don't fight the contact this time, turning my head into the crook of his neck and allowing my chest to rest against his as I extend my arms to allow him to slip my shirt over my wrists, finding moments of relief in the connection.

He told me I needed skin-on-skin contact and—*damn him to hell and back*—he was right.

He draws me to my feet and undoes the top button of my jeans —still without removing his left hand from my ribs. The soothing warmth from his stationary hand spreads across my stomach, filtering lower to my pelvis, and higher across my breasts. I press forward, needing the brief brushes of his chest against mine, swaying when he pushes my jeans across my backside and tugs them down to my ankles, one leg at a time, kneeling so he can reach my calves and feet.

All of this, he does without removing his left hand. If I could curl my entire body into that part of my ribs where his palm and fingers press, I would.

He leaves my underwear in place before he rises slowly from kneeling, his right hand trailing a tantalizing line up my bare calf and thighs.

He stops rising when his head is in line with my pelvis.

His hand curls around my thigh, his thumb nudging the top of the gap between my legs, making me gasp when he lightly brushes my center. A single stroke before he draws his thumb back, gripping my thigh in the crease at the top of my leg.

Pursing his lips, an inch from my body, he blows softly across the space between my legs, a light caress.

I nearly scream.

Pleasure and power rampage all the way through me from my center to my heart at that light touch of air.

"That's what you're missing out on," he says with a smile, the relentless glint returning to his eyes as he rises to his feet, undoes his jeans, and removes them one-handed.

Before I can register that he's completely naked, he steps up to me, shifts his left hand to flatten against my back, and bends at the knee, drawing my legs around him as he rises again.

I tense and nearly jump out of his arms, which clench around me.

"Trust," he reminds me.

It's so much harder to trust him than I ever thought possible.

He carries me toward his bedroom, but my arms fly out on either side when we reach the door, gripping the doorframe. "No," I say. "You're not taking me in there."

He exhales, but he doesn't push. If he did, he could break my arms. "Why not?"

"Your bedroom smells like you," I snarl.

He studies my face. Since I'm gripping him around his waist with my legs and balancing against the doorframe, pressing hard against it and keeping myself in position, he is able to let go of my backside—but only with his right hand. His left remains against my back, a constant anchor.

He brushes the hair away from my eyes.

I'm not sure what he sees that makes him suddenly smile, but it mingles with a snarl. He said his wolf was burning up. I haven't seen much evidence of that up to this point other than the glint in his eyes, but now I perceive the rapid rise and fall of his chest, the tension around his mouth despite the rising corners, as if he's welcoming the pain, finally letting it in.

He dips his lips to my neck, nudging the curve across my shoulder. "You know my scent as well as I know yours. You're more wolf than you think, Tessa."

His lips trail back up across the soft skin beneath my ear, along my jawline, his hand cupping the back of my head and tangling in my hair. Soft growls slip from his lips, but they're low, ragged, a startling mix of pain and desire.

He said this would be hard for him.

He draws back a few inches before he suddenly dips his mouth to mine, but he pauses without making contact.

My grip on the doorframe falters as I inhale his exhales.

Every breath he takes is filled with the power I sensed in him at the moment we met. The kind that could make me forget that I can't bond.

He rasps, "*Trust.*"

I release the doorframe and adjust my balance so I don't fall backward, my stomach muscles clenching. The anchor of his left hand doesn't let me fall in the time it takes me to lean forward into his chest again.

Carrying me to his bed, he slowly lowers me onto it, descending with me so that our torsos are never far from each other. My pain levels have eased since we started, but it feels like a reprieve that won't last.

Staying in contact with me, he eases me across and up the bed until my head rests on one of the pillows before his left hand slips around my body to my front and he turns me so that I'm facing away from him.

He lines up his chest with my back, his hips with mine, the front of his thighs against the backs of mine, even the bend of our knees as best as possible given our different heights.

His left arm slides up my chest between my breasts while he presses in behind me, spooning me.

"Where is your heart?" he asks, his mouth pressed to the back of my neck.

The fingers of his left hand splay as he speaks, curving across my breast. I pull his hand over the top of my breast to the location of my heart, fighting the fierce pleasure that ripples through me at his touch, while embracing the same easing of pain that washes through me.

"Now we need to breathe together," he says. "Our bodies and our wolves need to fall into the same rhythm. Breathing and heartbeats. We need to be in sync."

I shiver. His voice catches on nearly every word. His inhalations are more rapid than mine, harsh growls that tell me he's in pain.

I grip his hand tightly over my heart, press my back against his chest and match my breathing to his. Rapid. Ragged. But just a little bit slower.

His fingers claw a little, fingernails pressing into my skin, and

I'm suddenly terrified. I thought that trusting him meant letting him undress me and lie nearly naked with him in his bed.

I was so wrong.

If he shifts—partially or fully—his claws will impale my heart and kill me.

This is worse than fighting him. At least then, I'd have a chance. Lying like this, I'm just waiting for him to kill me if he loses control.

My breathing is suddenly as rapid as his.

"Yellow forest…" I whisper. "Blue treasure… pink ocean… violet sunrise…"

I remind myself of what Helen said to me when I left Hidden House. *Remember to guard your heart and protect yourself, Tessa. Be calm. Stay in control.*

"Silver flowers… silver vines… silver trees…"

My breathing begins to slow as I breathe out the lists, aware of Tristan's focus, his quiet behind me, the way his head rests against my shoulder, a heavy weight that tells me my lists are relaxing him too.

I dare to slide my fingers between Tristan's where he rests his palm against my heart so that our hands are splayed together, my palm over his, pressing his hand even closer to my chest where his claws will drive right through.

If I'm going to die, I'm going to make sure it's quick.

White wolf… Dark wolf… Cobalt wolf… Tristan.

My breathing is deep now. Calm. I listen carefully, sensing Tristan's breathing, discovering that it matches up with mine.

He exhales against the back of my neck, a slow release of air that sends shivers down my spine, the tension finally easing out of his arms, torso, and legs.

Concentrating on my breathing has taken my focus away from the clawing pain inside me. Now that we're breathing in time with each other, the pain eases fully, a release like a tide racing out of my body.

He said we would experience each other's darkness but all I feel now is calm. Peace. Maybe trusting each other was the hardest part…

My senses suddenly scream at me and I can't stop myself from tensing up again.

A new wave of pain washes through me and... *oh, damn...*

It burns.

I gasp, my breathing becoming wild as the sensation of flames rushes through me, spreading through my body, making me shiver and sweat. At the same time, Tristan groans behind me, a sound of pure agony. His fingers splay against my chest, stretching and clawing again, more dangerous than before.

"What's happening?" I gasp, trying to understand this new pain.

"Our wolves," he groans. "They're experiencing each other's pain now. The darkness will follow. My wolf is tearing itself up like yours was. But now yours—" He writhes behind me, all the hard planes of his chest and thighs pressing up against me. His fingernails drag through the top of my bra, cutting through the padding, scratching across my chest.

He moans against the back of my neck. "Your wolf will feel what I feel when I'm near you."

He said his wolf was slowly burning up.

But there is so much about *burning up* that he didn't tell me.

It's a different kind of ripping apart—not self-destruction from hurt and rejection, but two desires raging against each other. My senses fill with darkness and the recognition of a threat greater than any I've encountered before. I struggle against its pull, even though my mind screams at me that the darkness Tristan perceives is *me*.

I am the threat.

But on the other side of the battle is a wildfire, a burn that spreads through me and it doesn't want me to fight the darkness. No, it *wants* the darkness. To become part of the darkness. To lose myself in it.

I pull air into my chest. Close my eyes. Let the heat wash through me in waves. Let the seductive pull of the dark drag me down.

Gripping Tristan's hand, I twist, scissor my legs, shove his upper shoulder to push him onto his back, and straddle him, while somehow managing to keep his palm pressed against my heart.

On top of him now, I rest on his hips, ignoring the fact that he's naked and that for the first time, he's in too much pain to over-power me.

His breathing is shallow, his gaze unfocused, his stomach muscles clenched. The pain that was ripping me apart is destroying him. My own inner darkness, forged from rejection and pain is tearing him apart.

The fire rising inside me whispers to me to take whatever I want from him while he's vulnerable. Take my pleasure from his body. Take control of his pack. Take his life. Succumb to the dark, know that I am stronger than anyone else, and do whatever I wish.

His biceps tense as he reaches up with his free hand to push my hair back—to see half of my face, the other half hidden behind the remaining curtain of my hair.

"Your eyes," he says. "They show me everything I don't want to see about myself."

Gripping his hand, keeping it pressed against my heart—the only anchor I have—I lean close to him, balance myself on my fist beside his head on the pillow and fight the desire that rages through me, the overwhelming sensation of my heated skin against his. "What do you see now?"

"You're going to kill me," he says.

The rising fire inside me tells me to do it.

Do it now. Claim your freedom.

I shake my head, denying the burn.

It feels like power, but it's just another form of destruction. Right now, Tristan is feeling what I was feeling, all my rejection and hurt. He warned me that our minds could be lost in each other's darkness. If I give in to the impulses to dominate him, I'll only be killing myself.

Slowly lowering my torso to his chest, I trap his hand between us and dip my head to his shoulder, turning my ear to listen to his heartbeat. It's thready. Dangerously weak. Despite the power that thrums through me, I sense my own heartbeat slowing with every passing second. My heart is giving out.

The power I thought I felt is an illusion.

We're both dying, drowning in pain and darkness, while our minds deceive us.

I refuse to accept that this is the end of me.

Sliding my right arm up along Tristan's chest and neck without lifting my head, I brush my fingers across his jaw and into his hair, holding on to his head, the same way he's holding on to mine.

"Breathe with me," I say, my voice muffled against his chest. We got into sync once, we can do it again. "Breathe in... breathe out..."

For a moment I think he's going to push back—the same way I wanted to lash out—but he shudders and relaxes beneath me.

For the next ten minutes, we do nothing but lie together and breathe. Our chests rise and fall in unison, deep or shallow, but always in the same rhythm, the same speed.

Slowly, my head begins to clear. The burn recedes a little, but with every space it leaves behind, my former destruction fills it until I sense both sides of us pushing at each other in equal measures. A final struggle—my destruction and his fire—testing each other's resolve, as if we're both part of each other, fighting the same battle now.

His breath hitches, just the slightest, and I squeeze his hand tighter, press his palm as hard as I can against my heart, urging him to fight the pain *with* me. To survive *with* me.

Until finally... *finally*... the pain recedes, draining out of me.

I sense the moment he becomes himself again—it's the same instant that I become myself again.

Deep relief fills me, but I don't move. I stay right where I am, plastered against him.

His breathing is deep. Even. "We're equals now, Tessa," he whispers, his voice ragged. "Our wolves understand each other. We're melded. Neither one of us can dominate the other."

He keeps referring to 'my wolf' because that's what he knows—a wolf that has its own needs and wants.

But she isn't 'my wolf.' She's me.

I understand him. At least the part of him that sees my darkness.

I don't get up. Understanding him means knowing, instinctively, that this is where I need to stay.

"Sleep now," I say to him.

His deep breathing tells me he's already drifting off.

Seconds later, I sink into oblivion.

CHAPTER TWENTY-TWO

I'm cramped and stiff when I wake. My arms and legs ache like I ran a marathon and my fingers are numb where I hold Tristan's hand squished between our bodies. He lies beneath me and me on top of him in exactly the same position that we fell asleep. The shade of light in the room tells me it's early morning, but that would mean we slept for nearly twenty-four hours straight. It could be the case, judging by how hungry I feel.

Carefully tipping my head back without lifting my body from his, I check Tristan to see if he's awake.

He's fast asleep. His free hand rests on my upper back while his arm remains curled around me.

Neither of us has moved.

If he's normally a restless sleeper, he wasn't last night.

I find myself matching my breathing with his again, finding it scarily easy.

Our relationship has changed. Yet again. When I first laid eyes on him, he was an aggressor in my life. Then he was my captor. Then he placed me with Helen and gave me a strange sort of freedom. Then he was my captor again.

Now, his presence is as strong as it was before, his power all-encompassing, but it's a constant simmering burn in my senses instead of an overwhelming wave like it was before.

I'm controlling my reaction to him for the first time since I met him. How much I soak in is up to me and, for a moment, I soak it all in. His body beneath mine, every muscle, the tilt of his head, the growth across his jaw, the lips that are more relaxed in sleep than I've ever seen them. Not snarling or growling.

His breathing doesn't change, but he opens his eyes, his gaze just as fierce, just as crisply green. More than two day's growth shadows his jaw now and it makes him look wilder than yesterday. His fingers curl into the strands of my hair, brushing my scalp in a way that relaxes me, making me sigh out my next breath.

A faint smile touches his lips. "Good morning, Tessa."

"Tristan."

With a groan, he drags his trapped hand upward, taking my arm with him so that I stretch above my head. The movement serves to plaster my breasts against his chest. His smile grows, his eyelids lowering.

If I didn't know better, I'd say he looks contented.

Testing his resolve to keep a hold of my hand, I tug, gratified when he slowly opens his fist. Drawing my hands down his arms and chest, I arch my back like a cat, stretching out my spine before rising to a sitting position to roll my shoulders and stretch out my neck, swaying side to side to ease the cramps in my back and shoulders.

A quick assessment tells me that my bra is a little torn, but my underwear is otherwise intact.

Tristan observes me with a lazy smile, one arm still resting above his head, the other at his side. "Fuck, I wish you'd chosen option two."

I laugh, and it feels easy. The longer I stay in his presence, the more I feel an intoxicating liberation, a freedom with my body and mind. "Keep wishing."

My laughter dies when he twists and rolls me onto my back beneath him, his hips pressing into my thighs. It's a quick move, like his wolf wanted to pounce, but he keeps his animal in check, handling me lightly.

A smile plays around his mouth as he lowers his head to nudge my jaw before trailing soft nudges down my chest between my breasts and across my stomach. I can't call them kisses, they're more like brushes, but the second he reaches my pelvis, he strokes his flat palms all the way from my bent knees to the crease at the top of my legs, stopping before he touches any part of my body that would ease the sudden ache inside me.

I fight the impulse to reach down, pull him back to me, and urge his lips to mine, not sure if he'll come back on his own.

His smile grows as he continues on his downward path without a word and slides off the bed, immediately turning his back on me and prowling to the closet to throw it open.

I take a second to get up, studying Tristan with a different view. From the outside, he and his wolf are in constant unity, but I've seen the messy turmoil within. Somehow, it makes his ability to control every second of his body's movement even more impressive.

It's hard not to admire the chiseled lines of his back, all the way down to his backside and thighs, but I tell myself to get up before I do something reckless, like inviting him back to his bed. We've just reached a tenuous truce. Nothing is worth risking that.

The open door leading out to the living area reveals the dawn light shining through the far windows. It's hard to believe that we slept all that time.

Without asking his permission—I don't feel like I need to—I stalk to the bathroom, close the door, and turn on the shower. It's been nearly two days since I felt the soothing sensation of water. Stripping off, I step under the spray and close my eyes.

My sense of Tristan's power isn't overwhelming like it was before—an overpowering force that was a threat to me—but it's heady if I dwell on it. I sense him moving about in his room and then the kitchen. I'm suddenly sorry to wash his scent off my body, but *damn*, it's nice to shower.

Quickly washing my hair, I leave the bathroom wrapped in a towel to find a fluffy bathrobe laid out on the bed. I pull it on while the scent of coffee wafts through the open door, tugging me like a rope.

When I enter the room, Tristan stands at the far window opposite the kitchen table. He's dressed in a new pair of jeans. He has assumed the same pose he took up yesterday morning at the gym. I wasn't sure what he was doing then, but today, I understand that he's checking the status of everyone in his pack.

I shiver at the realization that I can sense his intentions more quickly than my own.

"The pack was unhappy about my absence, but there were no attacks last night," he says without turning, the tension in his shoulders easing.

A phone rests on the table. It's still lit up as if he checked it only seconds ago. Before the screen goes blank, I see a string of notifications. All missed calls from Jace.

I suddenly realize how challenging it must be for Tristan to close his eyes at night, not knowing if he'll be woken to the distant cries for help from his pack. I guess that's the reason for the dark rings under his eyes and his twisted bedsheets.

"You were worried," I say.

He pauses, rolling his shoulders. "Not until I woke up. It's the first night in a long time that I've slept through until dawn."

"A day and a night," I murmur. "We slept a long time."

I consider the cup of coffee resting on the kitchen table. Assuming it's for me, I nurse it in my hands. "What happens now, Tristan?"

He turns and gives me a slow smile. "I've never had an equal."

I roll my eyes at him. "Arrogant asshole."

Approaching the table, he leans on his elbows, the muscles in his shoulders and biceps bunching. "When I took you to Hidden House, I considered you a threat," he says. "I'm sure you felt the same way about me. In fact, I made sure you considered me your enemy."

I acknowledge his statement with a nod. "We aren't a danger to each other anymore."

His eyes meet mine. "Actually, Tessa. You're a significant threat to me." He rises from his lean on the table. His incisors peek between his lips. "As I am to you. That hasn't changed."

My heart thrums in my chest, but I accept the truth in his statement without allowing my defenses to rise.

He rounds the table, but he stops and folds his arms across his chest before he reaches me. "However, you're more of a threat to my enemies," Tristan says. "Until I experienced your wolf, I didn't fully comprehend just how badly you want revenge on Baxter Griffin and your half-brother, Dawson. Peter Nash too. Your family hurt you, but I thought I'd have to force you to help me. Now I realize that you want to destroy them more than I do."

Tristan is a mere pace from me. His statements draw out memories I'd rather forget, but it's easier to face them today. The coffee is warm in my hands, comforting, and Tristan's presence is—remarkably—soothing. "What do you propose?"

"Baxter Griffin is hosting a celebration for his son, Cameron's, birthday in a week. Their security will be vulnerable because of all the people coming and going. We can strike at the heart of them."

"We'd go into their territory?" I ask. "Is that wise?"

He grins and I'm mesmerized by the way he makes a smile look threatening. "Short of luring each of them here, it's the best opportunity we'll get."

Taking Baxter Griffin out was never going to be easy. Striking in his territory is exactly the sort of inflammatory act that will beg his pack to retaliate. "We can't fail or they'll retaliate with force."

"Then at least we'll have a fight that ends this feud once and for all," Tristan says. "Right now, they're picking us off one by one. Random, unpredictable attacks that demoralize my pack."

I'm quiet. "You could have killed Peter Nash on the night you took me. Why didn't you?"

"With five other alphas and their betas standing nearby waiting for a reason to kill me?" he asks. "I'm ruthless. But I'm not a fool."

He leans forward, switching back to the problem at hand. "You have to decide if you're in or you're out, Tessa. I can show you my city today. Then I can give you all the tools you need to end everyone who's ever wronged you. I'll give you the means and the opportunity. It's up to you whether you carry through."

"You're going to light the fire and watch it burn," I say, raising my eyes to his.

Tristan's forehead creases and I remember that I was an eavesdropper on his conversation with Jace two nights ago when Tristan first mentioned the three-headed wolf.

Revenge is a fire I want to burn, but I also need to test how much control I really have over my future now.

"What if I don't accept your proposal?" I ask.

He tips his head, eyeing me. "Then it gets complicated."

"How so?" I place my coffee cup on the table and close the gap, challenging the space between us. "You said we're equals now. Explain to me why I can't walk out of here right now."

His eyes darken. "What we did yesterday hasn't been achieved in hundreds of years, Tessa. We bonded at a higher level—"

I jolt away from him. "That's impossible. I can't bond."

"I'm not talking about being true mates." His voice remains low, but his hands rise. "I'm talking about a connection even purer than that. Your wolf and my wolf stepped into the heart of the other. We experienced each other's darkness. It's nearly impossible to survive that kind of darkness that hungers for death."

A growing storm fills his eyes as he speaks and I sense his inner turmoil.

"You didn't care if you survived," I whisper, my eyes widening with the surprising realization. "You're living on the edge of death and you would have welcomed your own end. You say you're not reckless, but I'm not so sure about that, Tristan. That's what makes you so dangerous. You're unpredictable."

His lips press together, his expression hardening, but his green eyes gleam like emeralds. "Do you see, Tessa? You can sense my emotions now. Mates can communicate by speaking into each other's minds, but you and I don't need to use words."

"You mean you can read my thoughts?" I ask, suddenly anxious that he knows about my encounter with the white wolf—and about my ability to separate from my wolf.

"No, I can't read your thoughts. It's more primal and instinctive than that." He steps forward with a rapidity that takes my breath away, but I'm just as fast, anticipating the reach of his arms as I twist away from him. It's difficult to move agilely in the thick bathrobe, but I manage it. He predicts my evasion and steps into the space I'm aiming for. Except that I sense he's going to do that, so I step in the opposite direction. For a few seconds, we chase each other along the table, each predicting the other's moves.

We could do this all day, neither one of us achieving our goal.

My head spins as I come to a deliberate stop beside the table.

He also stops. Smiles at me. Then he inches forward, testing my resolve to keep him at a distance.

I remain where I am, allowing him to approach.

He takes it slow as he slides his arms around my waist outside of the robe, pulling my hips against his, before lifting me onto the edge of the table with ease, guiding my legs to either side of his hips.

"I understand your strongest emotions," he says. "I can anticipate your impulses, your wants, and your needs. But your thoughts —the things you choose to keep secret—are hidden from me. You can choose to hide your emotions from me too, if you wish. But I can sense the emotions you don't cage. For example…" He dips his lips to the corner of my mouth, a tingling contact. "I know that if I kiss you right now, you won't push me away."

He tugs at the sash keeping my bathrobe in place, allowing the strip of material to fall to the floor. My breath catches when his palm presses against the exposed skin at the base of my stomach.

He leans forward and presses another kiss to the other corner of my mouth.

"I love that you let me win just now," he whispers.

I allow myself to smile, brushing his cheek with mine. I was the one who chose to stop dancing around the table.

He said that our strongest emotions will be plain to each other. I read the desire in his eyes, but I keep my own in check. With difficulty.

Damn, it would be so much easier to give in.

"We can embrace the connection between us," I say, assessing our situation. "Or we can use it against each other. Both options carry risks."

He gives me a single acknowledging nod.

Since the fight yesterday, Tristan has allowed me to choose our path. I suddenly understand what a leap of faith that is for him. He gave me the choice yesterday to decide how to resolve the power struggle between us. Now he's allowing me to choose our future.

It takes me by surprise to realize I have more power than I thought I did.

I turn my mouth to his, catching his lips. A brief contact. It's nearly too much. I thought the lightest touch would give me some sort of closure, but now I don't think any contact with his body will ever be enough.

The growth across his jaw makes my lips tingle before I force myself to pull back, drawing on every bit of will inside me not to return to his lips and give in to the desire to explore his mouth.

"I accept your proposal." I curl my fingers around the back of his neck. "Show me your city. Give me what I need to kill the shifters who hurt me. I'll stay for as long as it takes to end them."

Removing my hand from his neck and placing both my palms on his chest, I push him firmly but slowly away from me. "But remember that I belong to me. Once I'm done here, I'm leaving."

I wait for his response, wondering if he will raise the subject of the three-headed wolf—if he will finally reveal to me that he wants me to stay and kill it.

He simply gives me a nod. "I accept your terms."

CHAPTER TWENTY-THREE

*R*eaching an agreement puts us in a position of an alliance, a situation that is so unexpected that I'm trying not to be thrown by it. After eating a quick breakfast of toast and fruit, I've only just finished getting dressed in the bathroom when the elevator whirs.

I hurry out to find Tristan alert where he stands at the window, but he relaxes when Iyana and Danika appear.

Iyana looks like she's prepared for war, wearing her leather boots over tight black pants and a black shirt, her outfit complete with a weapons belt sporting daggers and—I'm surprised to see— her handguns.

Both women head right for me, Iyana skirting around the pool of sunlight pouring through the window while Danika strides right through it.

I meet them halfway, accepting their hugs, pulling Iyana safely to the far side of the living area, which is darker.

Neither of my friends appears well rested.

"We were worried about you," Danika says, squeezing me hard and making my eyes burn with tears.

Iyana kisses my cheek and whispers, "Do I need to kill him for you?"

I pull them both tighter, a group hug that I don't want to end.

"You're the best friends I could ever hope for. But no, you can rest assured, Tristan doesn't need killing today."

"Good." Iyana breathes out a sigh of relief. "Because I'd hate to kill the man who saved my life."

She's come a long way from the woman who nearly crumbled at the possibility that Tristan wasn't the good guy she thought he was. When we finally break apart, Tristan stands with his arms folded across his chest, looking every bit the alpha. I bite my lip to hide my smile that he's chosen to locate himself directly in the sunlight. He's wise not to underestimate Iyana.

Or Danika, for that matter.

Our hug revealed that she's carrying a pistol at her hip beneath her long tank top, which shows off the tattoo of a hawk's wing that covers her left shoulder and bicep.

"Tessa and I are heading out to see our territory today," Tristan says. "You're welcome to come with us."

Our territory? My eyes narrow, but I let it pass.

Iyana huffs at him. "You know I can't come out into the sunlight."

Tristan shrugs. "Then Tessa can take you out tonight when she goes on patrol. She'll need backup."

Iyana's scowl fades. "I'll be there."

Danika is more relaxed. "I'll watch over you both today. I've been dying to take to the sky. I'm assuming I don't need to be worried about other airborne shifters."

"As long as you stay directly above us, you'll be safe," Tristan says. "Remember not to fly above the forests. They belong to witches, who won't take kindly to your presence."

"Noted," she says.

"Then let's go." Tristan strides straight for Iyana and swipes the security card right out of her hand as he passes by.

"Hey!" she objects, her jaw dropping at how fast he moved. "We need that."

"You don't," he says to Iyana, passing the card to me. "Tessa's staying with you from now on, so you have no need to come to my floor. But she needs a way to see me if there's an emergency." He pauses. "Unless, of course, you were planning on coming up here to visit me, Iyana?"

Iyana grins madly and her blue-gray eyes *pop* with her smile. "You wish, wolf man."

Tristan strides onward to the elevator and I'm left holding a security pass that I would have killed for yesterday. I quickly deposit it into my pocket, grab my duffel bag, and join the others in the elevator.

To my surprise, Tristan presses the button for the roof. "You don't need a pass to access the roof, so you can head on up there anytime you need," he says to Danika.

Her hazel eyes are bright with anticipation. As soon as we exit the elevator into a small room with a transparent door, she begins stripping off, dropping her clothing into a pile in the corner.

Tristan averts his eyes and holds open the door for her. She runs through it, sprints right up to the edge of the building, and leaps off it.

My breath catches, my heart leaping into my throat when she jumps. She transforms mid-leap and I let out my held breath. Her hawk is a gorgeous honey color with bronze-tipped feathers and a massive wingspan. She soars into the wind and upward, circling the building. Her eyesight will allow her to spot us from up high and follow us.

Back in the elevator, Iyana tells me that she and Danika are living on the tenth floor now—she asked Jace to move them yesterday. When the doors open at the tenth floor, she takes my bag with her. "See you tonight, Tessa." She gestures quickly before the doors close. "Seventh door on the right."

Alone again, Tristan leans against the other side of the elevator, seemingly prepared to continue in silence. When Danika and Iyana arrived, he told them we were heading out to see *our* territory today. Not his territory. I see my opportunity to ask him about it now that we're alone.

"*Our* territory?" I ask.

He stiffens but relaxes as his gaze passes from my topknot to my boots, lingering on my curves. "A slip of the tongue."

I 'hmm' lightly, sensing that I have to accept his answer for now. He said that we can sense each other's strongest emotions, but not the feelings we cage. Right now, he's a blank slate.

When we reach the garage, Tristan is all business. "Don't worry about encountering humans," he says. "The floors that are leased to businesses have their own elevators. The security pass I gave you will also allow you to come and go from this building."

Jace waits for us at the side of the garage, next to the door with the exit sign above it. He appears as badly rested as Iyana and Danika. Unlike them, he doesn't relax when he sees us, the tension remaining in his shoulders and narrowed eyes.

"Tristan." He growls. "What the hell? You were unreachable for twenty-four hours. The pack nearly lost their shit."

Tristan grips Jace's shoulders, facing off with him, and I'm once again reminded of how much like an alpha Jace is, how equally matched both men are. Except that Tristan is reining in his wrath for once.

"Thank you for keeping them calm. I know it can't have been easy." He is unyielding. "But it was important."

Jace's fierce glare transfers to me, his scowl deepening before his expression suddenly clears and his eyes widen. He steps back quickly, shaking Tristan off. "What. The. Fuck?"

I'm not entirely sure what looks different about me today that has startled Jace so much. Maybe I should have taken more than a quick glance at myself in the mirror. I know I feel different, the most in control, the calmest, I've felt in my life.

Jace's focus flicks rapidly from me to Tristan, back and forth, until he squeezes his eyes shut, shakes his head like an angry wolf, and backs away until he bumps into the wall. The *thud* he makes when he hits the wall is so fierce that I wince.

"You're breathing in unison," Jace growls without opening his eyes. "You're reflecting each other's emotions. Fuck, it's making my head spin."

I consider Jace warily. Danika and Iyana aren't wolf shifters, so that must be why they didn't react the way Jace is.

Tristan is unmoved by Jace's reaction. "Tessa and I resolved our differences."

"By tempting death," Jace snarls, fists clenching as he opens his eyes. He jabs the wall at his side, an angry *tap-tap*. "Nobody survives The Melding. You could have died."

"It was the only way," Tristan says, still calm, but his chin is raised, his focus narrowing.

Jace launches himself off the wall, a threatening tower of muscle, his head lowered, eyes shifting to his wolf's, claws extending. "Because fucking each other would have been a chore?"

Tristan retaliates, fast and aggressive. He launches himself forward, grabs Jace's swinging fist, twists, and wrenches Jace's arm behind his back. Forcing Jace to his knees, Tristan drops the weight of his knee onto Jace's spine, making him curl forward, completely submissive. "Do *not* disrespect us, Jace. We're melded and that's the end of it."

Jace thumps his free fist against the concrete. "You're determined to kill yourself before your time! You forget there are wolves you're going to leave behind."

Tristan exhales into the ensuing silence before he releases Jace and steps back. I steer clear of both men, knowing this is something Tristan needs to deal with himself.

He waits for Jace to rise to his feet before he levels his gaze with Jace's. "I'm showing Tessa around the city today. I need you to watch everything here. Can you do that? Or do we have a problem?"

The muscle in Jace's jaw clenches, but he gives a firm nod. "I can do that."

Tristan spins on his heel, strides to the exit, and holds it open for me. Jace squares his shoulders, his expression blank as I pass him by. I want to reassure him, but I'm not sure how. Anything I say will sound trite.

But that doesn't mean I shouldn't question Tristan about his choice to spend the day with me instead of with his pack.

As soon as we exit the building onto the busy street outside, I reach for Tristan's arm and level my gaze with his. "Should you be with your pack right now?"

"I'm right where I need to be," he replies, breaking my gaze to survey the sidewalk and the oncoming traffic. He ignores the traffic lights and the crosswalk to our left, drawing me across the road when the traffic eases. "My pack will be fine. Sometimes they don't appreciate what's best for them."

I tug him to a stop beside one of the white pillars at the side of the square. "Jace is worried about you. I don't know what it's like to have a pack that cares for me, but don't underestimate his loyalty to you."

Tristan's glare is fiercer than I was expecting, his eyebrows drawing down. I sense his inner turmoil, his darkness, before he closes himself off. Even though we're connected now, we can't sense each other's innermost thoughts or the parts of ourselves that we choose to keep secret. For some reason, my comment has ignited a conflict inside him that is deep enough that he's put up a wall.

"Tristan?"

"That's close enough, Tessa," he says.

I sigh. He means I've got as close to him as he's going to let me.

"There are some things you don't want to know about me." He raises his gaze from my hand on his arm to my eyes. His own are partially shifted, so suddenly aggressive that I carefully uncurl my fingers.

If he'd looked at me like this yesterday, I would have thought he was about to end me. Today… the faintest sense of anticipation rises inside me. Tristan's aggression is a weapon that I can use.

"Okay," I murmur, reminding myself that I'm here for a purpose: to end Baxter Griffin, Peter Nash, and my half-brother. If I take out Cody Griffin at the same time, all the better. "Show me your city."

We spend most of the morning and early afternoon walking the streets. Tristan takes me to the northernmost bridge first, pointing out all of the weak spots, explaining how difficult it is to protect the border of his territory because of the ease with which vehicles can pass across the bridges. We walk along the wide tree-lined park beside the river, all the way to the South Waterfront before we head farther west, then up through Goose Hill toward the Northwest District.

Tristan tells me that his pack used to be so large that they once lived in both Southwest Portland and up through Cedar Mill, but he had to pull everyone in a year ago because they didn't have the numbers to defend the bridges anymore.

"My pack would be safer farther west," he says. "But then we'd leave the bridges vulnerable and Baxter would take control of them. After that, it would only be a matter of time before he backed me into a corner."

"How many wolves are in your pack now?" I ask.

"We used to be a pack of a thousand wolves," he says. "Now I have one hundred."

One thousand wolves is a lot. One hundred is not. The Highland packs have around five hundred wolves each and Baxter Griffin has close to a thousand. Tristan is severely outnumbered.

Every now and then, I glance upward, knowing that Danika is following high above us, even if I can't see her. I also keep alert for any sign of the white wolf. I haven't been outside the tower since I saw him, but I'm wary of another surprise encounter—especially when I'm with Tristan. I don't have any hard and fast answers about whether or not the white wolf is the three-headed wolf that Tristan said is coming for him, but for now, that's my best theory.

I also don't know how the white wolf is connected to me. It's a question that burns at the back of my mind, but I have to put it aside. Right now, all of my energy and attention needs to be focused on where I stand with Tristan.

We grab some food along the way before we stop at the edge of Forest Park. The lush forest calls to me, begging me to explore its secret places. I rise onto the balls of my feet, itching to run, but Tristan takes hold of my arm.

"The forests are out of bounds," he says, disappointing me. "The most powerful coven was led by a witch named Mother Serena. She and her entire coven were wiped out several years ago. I don't know who or what took them down, but the other covens are still fighting over her territory. Once they resolve their issues, I'll be able to negotiate with the winner to access the forest again. Until then, we can't run or shelter in the forests. We don't want to get caught up in their war."

I should be tired, but I'm buzzing by the time we return to the clock tower and reenter the elevator.

"I want to patrol the central bridge for the next few nights," I say. "It's the quickest route from the Eastern Lowland to your home here. I know my half-brother. He's lazy. If he's going to attack again, he'll enter via that bridge."

"If you're ready," Tristan says.

I sense his uncertainty. When I was confronted with Dawson's violent treatment of Carly and Becca after Tristan brought them to

Hidden House, I nearly had a panic attack. It hasn't even been a week since then, but a lot has changed. "I'm certain."

Tristan leans against the other side of the elevator. "I need you to come with me to the pack meeting this evening when I let everyone know what's going on. Iyana and Danika will show you where that is." The corner of his mouth rises into a fleeting smile. "It could be better if you're wearing something a little more intimidating when you get there."

I cast a quick glance at my jeans and flannel shirt. "This is all I have."

Tristan shrugs, as if it doesn't matter.

The doors open to the tenth floor and I step outside.

Tristan gives me a formal nod before the elevator closes again.

I stare at the doors, resisting the urge to use the security card in my pocket already. Freedom is an unfamiliar feeling after the last two months of not-quite-captivity.

Spinning on my heel, I find myself being quietly observed by a little girl, who doesn't appear much older than two years. She's holding the hand of a well-loved cloth doll, smudged with floor dust, that looks like it's been dragged alongside her a few too many times. She has vivid, brown eyes and dark brown hair.

There are no adults in sight.

"Hello," I say, thrown by the little girl's bright and curious stare. "Where do you live?"

This floor feels vast. I sight down the corridor to all of the doors that must lead into apartments.

She points toward an open door three doors down on the left and then lifts her arms up to me, as if she expects me to carry her there. "Up."

After learning how to flip grown men onto their backs in a fight, she weighs nearly nothing as I prop her on my hip. She promptly sticks the doll's arm in her mouth and sucks on it. I catch a flash of growing incisors before we reach the open door.

I pause when I sense several female shifters inside, their voices wafting out to me before I can knock.

"Why can't she stay somewhere else?" a woman with a mature voice says. "She's not even a normal shifter."

My hand freezes inches away from the open door. It doesn't

take a genius to figure out they're talking about me. They won't realize that I'm here. My scent is so much under my control that even Tristan can't scent me and they're likely to be so engrossed in their conversation that they won't be listening for intruders.

"She's not like us," another woman says. This one sounds sour, unhappy. "I heard she doesn't even have a wolf. I don't understand why Tristan brought her here. Her pack wanted to kill her. He should have let them."

Ouch. I tell myself to let it roll off me.

A third woman speaks up. At the sound of her younger voice, the little girl's eyes brighten, so I can only assume she's the girl's mother. "Did you hear what she did yesterday morning?" the young woman asks. "She beat the absolute shit out of Bridget—"

"Yes, and we all know what *had* to happen after that." The sour woman snaps. There's a clunk that sounds like she thumps a glass down on a table. "Jace isn't telling us anything, but Tristan was with that…" She splutters. "*Woman…* for a full twenty-four hours before they were seen again this morning."

The younger lady responds with a laugh. "Well, maybe Tessa is an almighty good fuck."

"Watch your language, Jemimah!" The first woman—the oldest—sounds overly shocked, but her voice carries a smothered laugh.

The sour woman makes a disgusted sound, but the young woman asserts, "I don't care if Tessa Dean doesn't have a real wolf. She's strong. And fuck knows we need all the strength we can get."

I bite my lip and back away from the door, sliding the little girl to the floor at the same time. She clings to my hair and I discover that she's chewing on it. Attempting to extricate myself and finally succeeding, I push the damp strands behind my ear and straighten, only to find myself staring at a twenty-something female with dark brown hair the same color as the little girl's.

She must be Jemimah.

"I didn't know you were there," she says, her eyes wide. "I didn't sense you."

I shrug. "One of my strengths." I step away from her, not wanting to get caught up in any conflict, especially when the sour woman speaks up behind her.

"She's not even a real wolf at our door." The sour woman snarls.

I don't bother glancing back to see what she looks like. Ignoring them, I proceed to the seventh door on the right like Iyana instructed me, welcoming the darkness inside the apartment that tells me Iyana is sleeping, fighting the darkness creeping back into my heart.

CHAPTER TWENTY-FOUR

"Something intimidating, huh?" Iyana asks, pulling yet another flannel shirt out of my duffel bag.

We've eaten and showered. It's nearly time to go to the pack meeting, and now Iyana is attempting to find me something to wear. She scrunches the shirt in her hands. "Your wardrobe needs serious help, Tessa."

I give a nonchalant shrug. "I like to be comfortable."

"You don't like showing off your figure." Iyana gives me a pointed stare, daring me to contradict her. She's already dressed in her usual tight black pants and tight low-cut shirt, her black hair piled on top of her head and red lipstick making her eyes appear bright.

I pick at my fingernails while I perch at the end of the couch. "I'm still a target," I say. "Nothing will change that. Curves make things worse."

Iyana slips onto the couch next to me, wrapping her arm around me. "I get it."

She rests her chin on my shoulder and raises her eyes to mine. "But maybe it's time for you to look like the badass that you are."

I chew my lip. "Do you have something I can borrow?"

She grins. "I might. Come with me."

Half an hour later, I hardly recognize myself. I'm wearing a strapless leather bodice that hugs my ribs and pushes up my breasts. It's cut down the middle to my sternum, revealing the inner curves of my breasts while a belt sits around my waist, making my waist look smaller than it is. I'm wearing a tight leather skirt beneath the bodice that extends down to my mid-thigh and has a serious slit up the left leg. My usual boots look a whole lot sexier combined with this outfit.

"Holy hell, you're a double D cup," Iyana announces, grinning at me like she's going to burst. "Here, you need this."

She hands me a thigh holster for a small dagger and helps me tie the weapon around my left thigh, where it will be visible.

"How do you feel?" she asks.

I test my movements. The bodice is incredibly supportive and the skirt allows me to move in every way that I might need during a fight. "It feels good."

"Then you're wearing it out on patrol tonight," she says with a wink.

Danika rushes into the apartment just then, glowing, her hair windswept. "Damn, it feels good to fly again. But I know! I'm late!"

Iyana gives her the eye. "And you need to shower."

Danika hurries past. "I'll only be a minute." She misses a step, breaking into a smile. "You look good, Tessa."

True to her word, Danika emerges a few minutes later, dressed in similarly intimidating black jeans—distressed at the knees—and a black tank top that shows off her wing tattoo, scar and all. She scrapes her hair back into a tight ponytail and holsters several pistols in a belt around her hips. Then she grabs a duffel bag and stuffs some spare clothing in it, along with a rifle. "We can carry our weapons in here while we walk through the streets," she says.

"Are we ready?" Iyana asks.

"Ready." I take a deep breath, sensing the shifters milling outside in the hall waiting for the elevator.

We file from the room into the corridor.

It falls silent.

A woman with pinched lips glares at me from the side, holding the hand of a boy who looks about five years old. She must be the sour one. I consider the other women, all of varying ages, all with children. None of the children appear older than fourteen. None of the women appear to have mates with them.

I take a moment to assess their reactions, accepting the way they clear the corridor ahead of us, standing aside so we can pass.

When we reach the elevator, the shifters who were about to get into it also stand aside so we can walk right in. They don't attempt to join us.

I let out my breath as the doors close.

"They're not going to treat me as anything other than a threat," I say, leaning against the back of the elevator as I turn to Iyana and Danika. "You could have walked out of here days ago, escaped from all this shit."

"Not on your life," Iyana says.

Danika smiles. "We're here for you, Tessa."

"This might sound stupid," Iyana continues, "but we're your pack now. Tristan says that anyone can be pack. Well, that's us. We need each other."

I shake my head at her, fighting the tears that fill my eyes. "You're going to make my mascara run, aren't you?"

"Making you smile is my favorite pastime, Tessa," Iyana says.

We exit the elevator at the sixth floor and enter a conference room to find it nearly full already. I scan the crowd for the women I beat yesterday, finding them sitting together with Bridget at the back of the room. Only a couple of them glance my way. The others quickly look to Bridget, who fixes her focus on a spot at the front of the room.

Tristan stands at the far window, but he turns the moment I step into the room, a move that isn't lost on the shifters. Iyana and Danika follow me closely as I stride to the front of the room, where Jace waits.

Jace has taken up a military pose. Like Bridget, his focus is firmly fixed anywhere but on me.

Tristan seems surprisingly relaxed, considering the growing friction in the room. He takes a moment to look me up and down, a smile growing on his face as he approaches me while Iyana and Danika stay with Jace at the side.

Leaning in, Tristan murmurs, "Now they really want to kill you."

I arch back, tipping my head. *"That's* why you're smiling? That's not a good thing."

"Wait and see."

His smile vanishes as he turns to the crowd, giving a low growl that hushes them. We wait in silence for the remaining families to enter and take their seats.

"This is going to be quick," Tristan says, the corners of his mouth turning down as he levels his gaze on them all. "The rumors stop. Right fucking now."

If the room was silent before, now it's deathly quiet.

"Bridget broke the rules yesterday. She challenged Tessa without my permission. She's lucky Tessa didn't kill her. In fact, you're all lucky to be alive." Tristan's voice rises. "I have rules for a fucking good reason. Your pack was nearly destroyed."

He pauses, scanning them, before he announces. "Tessa and I have melded."

Gasps and murmurs fill the crowd before they quickly fall silent again.

"Tessa Dean is now a lone alpha, allied to the Western Lowlands," Tristan continues. "She's here as my guest. She will fight beside us, protecting our border. You will treat her with the same respect that you would treat any visiting alpha. Do *not* challenge her. Do not look sideways at her. Do not displease her. Or I will kill you for dishonoring me. Do you understand?"

They're all silent.

Tristan roars into the silence. *"Do you fucking understand?"*

His shout is like a trigger. The entire congregation breaks into a roar in the affirmative and, surprisingly, the tension breaks.

Tristan grins at them and they all grin back.

I'm not sure how his speech broke the friction, but the danger of conflict instantly disappears.

"Now," Tristan says. "Let's fight to live another fucking day. Get the fuck out of my sight."

I return to Iyana and Danika and we wait while the shifters mill about and take their time leaving. I don't want to get pulled into the crowd, so I stand clear of them all. The other females leave quickly, but I'm surprised when Bridget approaches us.

I glance at Tristan, who has remained at the center front of the room, to gauge his response to her approach. He seems calm but watches us closely.

She stops at a respectful distance away from me, her hands folded in front of her. "If you're going out to the bridges, I'd like to help."

There are any number of reasons why she could be offering assistance. Sabotage is the most likely. She could be planning to undermine me, either in a fight or to spy on me and report back my failings to the others. Worse, she could get me killed.

"Do you have Tristan's permission?" I ask.

She nods. "I asked him before you arrived."

Still, I narrow my eyes at Bridget. To my left, Tristan watches me and I consider what he's feeling. It's somewhat of a shock to me to realize that he wouldn't deliberately put me in danger right now. If he said *yes* to her, then he thinks it's safe for her to come out with us tonight.

As my resolve softens, Iyana nudges me. "Second chances," she murmurs. "That's a thing your human soul probably believes in, right?"

Hmm. "Not always. Some acts are unforgivable."

It also means I'll have to keep my wolf hidden. I won't be able to let her run free, which I was looking forward to doing under the cover of darkness, since Iyana and Danika both know I can separate from her.

I spin to Bridget. "Don't slow us down."

She stands straighter. "I won't."

Before I can turn to the door, Tristan catches my eye again. I stride back over to him, aware of the way Bridget and the other shifters watch us with alternating expressions of surprise and quiet observation. It's starting to unsettle me.

Tristan doesn't touch me, but he lowers his voice and bends his head, his cheek very close to mine. "You're struggling with my pack's emotions."

I can't stop my wry smile. "Just a little. Why did they cheer when you shouted at them?"

"Because their greatest fear is that I've changed—primarily that you've weakened me." He pulls back so I can see his eyes, always fierce.

I allow myself to smile. "You showed them that you're still the same aggressive asshole they're used to dealing with."

The corners of his mouth turn down into the snarl that I'm used to seeing and I relax a little. Odd that I feel more at ease when he's irritable and aggressive than when he's being considerate.

"And the way they're looking at us now?" I ask.

"Because they can see us predicting each other's moves and emotions. Even our breathing is visibly in sync when we're standing this close to each other. Jace saw it this morning. They're coming to terms with what that means for them."

A glance at his chest tells me he's right. We're breathing in unison without any conscious thought—at least not on my part.

He lowers his cheek to mine again. It's not a possessive move. A gentle brush. "Be safe out there."

Even with melding, Tristan Masters treating me gently and telling me to be safe is as unexpected as me suddenly developing a wolf's soul. "If by 'safe,' you mean be aggressive and kill things, then sure, we'll be safe."

I pull back, giving him a bright smile that makes him pause, his focus shifting quickly from my lips to my eyes before he relaxes. He folds his arms over his chest. "Jace and I will patrol the neighboring bridges. We won't be far if you need us."

I give him a confident smirk, hoping I'm not about to bite off more than I can chew. "We'll be fine."

Turning on my heel, I stride back to my pack.

My pack.

I give them a firm nod, a sense of anticipation rising inside me as we head out on our first patrol together. "Let's go."

CHAPTER TWENTY-FIVE

*T*he air is moist, the threat of rain imminent, when we reach the bridge. We find a spot in the shadows of the enormous parking lot beneath it to plan our defense.

We concealed our weapons in the duffel bag on the way here so that we wouldn't raise the alarm among the humans. Now, I retrieve the dagger Iyana gave me and slide it into the holster at my thigh.

Once we've taken all but Danika's rifle and her spare clothing from the duffel bag, Danika shifts into her hawk in the shadows, takes hold of the bag in her talons, and flies it up to the top of the nearest building. She'll leave it there until she's ready to take up a sniper position on the rooftop and cover us with firepower.

Beside me, Iyana checks the daggers and pistols on her hip holster, readying herself. I only have the single dagger, but I'm planning on using my strength and my power tonight.

While I know that Danika can hit any target with a gun and that Iyana can take down any opponent in a fist fight, Bridget's skills are unknown to me. I've seen her grapple with her enemy in wolf form, but she didn't overcome me with her combat skills yesterday.

"What is your strength?" I ask her bluntly before we leave the shadows under the bridge.

"I'm here to learn," she says, awkwardly keeping her distance.

"I'm a good defender. I can take a punch. I'm not too shabby with a blade. But I'm not as fast or as strong as you."

It's an honest answer that puts me more at ease. "Okay, then. Stay out of danger tonight. Only get involved if you feel confident about the situation you're getting into. Whatever you do, don't get in our way. Iyana, Danika, and I will train in the gym before we come out on patrol each day. You can join us if you like."

She nods. "I'd like that, thank you."

"Okay, let's find our positions."

Tristan pointed out the biggest challenge about defending the bridges today: Baxter Griffin can send whole convoys of his pack straight into the heart of Tristan's territory within seconds. Worse, it's difficult to scan for supernaturals in vehicles, so we need to be on high alert.

On top of that, we need to avoid being seen by humans. I'm already regretting my choice of clothing, since I'd blend in more easily in jeans.

After considering our options, we take up position in the shadows at the side of the building opposite the parking lot, deciding to remain as close as possible to the exit ramp. The parking lot extends across at ground level under both the exit and entrance ramps onto the bridge, which means we'll have plenty of room if there's a fight.

As the hours pass, we switch positions, alternating between the building to the left of the exit ramp and the second, smaller parking lot across the street, keeping to the shadows as much as possible.

I relax a little when the human population disappears and the stream of oncoming vehicles thins out as the night goes on.

Close to midnight, when the place is mostly deserted other than a sprinkling of parked cars, my senses prickle.

In the distance, Danika's hawk swoops sharply toward an SUV speeding across the bridge.

Her hawk rises before it swoops again, scraping the top of the vehicle with her talons before rising into the air again. Whoever is in that vehicle will know they've been spotted.

We want them to know. They'll be more likely to turn back if they think they're going to meet resistance.

Her job done, Danika soars up and back toward the location

where the duffel bag is hidden. She'll dress and take up position in her human form as fast as she can. I need her to remain at a distance and cover us with sniper power as soon as possible.

Iyana steadies her own weapon, quietly settling into a crouched position beside me, her pistol resting on her forearm as she waits for the vehicle to come close enough to take her shot.

"I'll fire a warning shot to the left of the front passenger," she whispers. "We don't want the vehicle to crash and draw attention, but we want them to know we're serious."

"Do it," I say, watching the vehicle approach, counting the seconds before it's near enough for Iyana to shoot.

I make out two men in the front and more in the back. The two in the front are strangers, but one of the passengers in the back makes my blood boil. It's difficult to catch any scent from inside a speeding vehicle, but my keen eyesight picks my half-brother out of the shadows in the back seat.

Iyana's silenced weapon whispers as she fires.

The windscreen cracks on the front passenger side. I can't see exactly where the bullet hits, but the passenger ducks. The driver wrenches the wheel and the vehicle swerves before it rights again.

If they're smart, they'll take a quick left and immediately use the exit ramp to return the way they came.

Instead, the vehicle squeals into the parking lot and halts on the far side. I don't bother with a sigh of disappointment that they chose to fight. Dawson was never smart.

"Stay here unless it's safe to join us," I say to Bridget. A quick glance upward confirms that Danika is in position on the corner of the building above us. "Danika will cover this position."

Bridget jumps to her feet. "But—"

I'm already running toward the vehicle with Iyana beside me. She's holstered her gun in favor of a dagger. In the distance, five shifters, including my brother, jump out of the SUV. They immediately split up, drawing us in opposite directions, one group heading for the street on the left, the other for the street one block over. Danika could pick them off one by one right now, but she won't fire unless our lives are threatened.

Our goal—unlike them—is not to waste life, but to deter them from invading Tristan's territory again.

"You take the group on the left," I shout to Iyana. "Dawson is mine!"

Iyana races off to the left, running so fast that she's a blur. She catches the nearest man, throwing herself through the air and knocking him down before she spins and throws her dagger into the shoulder of the next man. Within seconds, she's engaged in a fist fight with both of them.

I veer right, my wolf's power surging through me, increasing my speed as I race to cut Dawson and the other two wolf shifters off. I catch the nearest man, who shouts, wide-eyed, and tries to dodge me. His cry chokes into silence when my boot connects with his throat, sending him sprawling onto the pavement.

I can't afford to stop. Racing after the second shifter, I grab his arm just as he spins toward me, a pistol aimed right at my chest.

My reflexes kick. Pushing his arm up just in time, the bullet flies wide of my head, but it nicks the tip of my ear, sending shockwaves through me.

In the distance, I hear a hawk's screech of frustration. Danika can't take a shot while I'm this close to my attacker and we're moving around so fast. She also can't use her hawk's scream to help me, even in her human form, or she'll hurt me along with my attacker.

Fear fuels my defenses as I grip the man's wrist, step, spin, and flip him onto his back. The pistol slides from his hand into mine at the same time. He's at close range, but I've never hit a damn target with a gun in my life.

In the second that I hesitate, the first shifter charges at me.

I spin and kick. His own momentum increases the *thud* as he meets my foot and stumbles backward. At the same time, I throw the pistol wide, slip my dagger free from the holster around my thigh, and drop to ram it into the shoulder of the man on the ground. Wrenching the blade out, I spin again and throw it into the thigh of the shifter I kicked.

Two blows to the head and they're both sprawled unconscious on the pavement. I retrieve my dagger before I search for Dawson.

The distraction has given him enough time to run across the parking lot. His legs are a dark blur in black jeans, but his chest is bare, his brown hair flying where it's cut longer on top.

I give chase, darting after him, pushing myself to go faster as I try to catch up. I don't know what he plans to do, but I can't let him get anywhere near the clock tower.

Bullets hit the pavement right in front of him. Danika fires warning shots that force Dawson to pull up sharp, leap backward, and swerve off-course. He veers to the left, away from the street he was headed for, and races alongside the building opposite the parking lot. If he rounds the corner, he'll be out of Danika's sights.

But avoiding her bullets slowed him down. The delay is all I need to catch up with him.

I hurtle the rest of the way across the street and ram into him, using all of my strength to knock him against the brick wall at the side of the building and bring him to a complete halt. The impact shudders through me, contact with his body that I don't welcome. I follow up with a punch, but he recovers fast enough to duck and I nearly hit my fist into the bricks before I pull the punch.

I evade the retaliatory blow he aims for my stomach.

For the next thirty seconds, we trade quick blows as he tries to get past me, but I continue to force him up against the wall, blocking each attempt to escape. I sacrifice my defenses to keep him there—taking a punch on my chin and another across my temple.

By the time he slumps against the wall, I'm bleeding down the side of my face, but he's in worse condition, blood dripping from his split cheek and his eye closing up.

He slides down the wall and I follow him, gripping his shoulder with one hand while I bend my knee and rest it against his chest, pinning him in place. "Why are you here, Dawson? What's Baxter's plan?" I demand to know.

Dawson stares at me, his good eye narrowing. He spits blood onto my chest and watches it drip when I don't wipe it away. One corner of his mouth rises into a cruel grin. "You look more like yourself with a bit of blood on you, Tessa."

I snarl. "Are you here to beat up more young women?"

He laughs, spitting more blood as he speaks. "Giving those bitches what they deserved was nowhere near as satisfying as feeling your bones pop beneath my hands."

My stomach turns. He fractured my bones too many times and always with fanatical intensity.

My jaw clenches. "Those days are over."

He pushes his chest against my hold. I watch for any sign he's going to strike out, but his arms remain at his sides. "Those days will never be over, Tessa. You won't be safe for long."

My fists snap out, raining blows on Dawson's face and torso. He manages to evade one of the hits, but the others land—one on his cheek, one across his temple, a third across his ribs before he attempts to fight back.

His fist catches me on my shoulder before I strike him across the head hard enough to daze him.

But what really makes me sick is that he seems to be enjoying it.

"Hell, big sister." He laughs. "Your pathetic father taught you how to take a punch, but someone else has taught you how to fight. I'm going to love breaking you again."

"Tell me what you're doing here! What is your plan?"

He laughs, coughs, and clutches his ribs. "I'm here to borrow a book from the library."

There's a library two blocks from the tower where the pack lives. It's where he and Baxter attacked the two girls.

Rage burns hot inside me. "The only reason I'm letting you live tonight is so you can take a message back to Baxter Griffin. Whatever he plans, he will fail. The next wolves he sends across the bridge will die."

"Baxter doesn't give a fuck!" Dawson shouts, revealing the first sign of real emotion—anger—that he's shown tonight. "He wants to tear Tristan's world apart, one piece at a time, one pack member at a time. The more he hurts Tristan, the better. He doesn't care about conquering territory. He wants to destroy Tristan."

I narrow my eyes at my half-brother. The packs have always been at odds with each other, but if Baxter's only goal were to gain territory and power, he would attack in one swift strike, not take out Tristan's pack, one member at a time, leaving them battered and broken.

"It's personal," I whisper, the realization making me shudder. Tristan told me that *I* hated Baxter Griffin more than he did, which could mean... whatever the feud between them is... *Baxter* is the one who feels wronged.

I grip Dawson's shoulders tightly, demanding that he answer me. "What did Tristan do?"

Dawson's good eye brightens. His grin grows wider, but he remains silent.

He won't tell me.

Releasing Dawson with disgust, I prepare to haul him back to his vehicle, but he grabs me, demanding my attention. "Has Tristan told you about his mother?"

I pause, my forehead creasing.

Tristan has never mentioned his mother and he's barely spoken about his father—other than telling me he was determined not to be like him. I saw Tristan's inner darkness when we melded, but I didn't see his memories. I don't know anything about his family history other than the fact he killed his father a year ago.

Taking advantage of my loosening grip, Dawson edges to the left of the wall, drawing my attention with him. "I heard that Tristan killed her, just like he killed his father. He hurts everyone close to him. Does that include you, Tessa? Are you close to him?"

I'm done with this treacherous conversation.

I release a growl, ready to knock Dawson out when it suddenly hits me...

Everything around us is so quiet.

Dawson grins at me as he observes me freeze.

He leans forward to whisper, "I've done what I came to do, Tessa."

I jump away from him, looking up for the first time since I caught him against the wall. I sight along the building and then spin to the parking lot across the street behind me where the SUV first pulled in. I've had my back to it all this time.

A glistening wall shimmers around us, curving up and around our position. It's far enough away, and high enough up, that it didn't shimmer at the edge of my vision and catch my attention. Inside the glimmering cage, I hear only the expected sounds: a breeze that carries the hint of rain, the quiet hum of a sleeping city, the distant lap of water at the edge of the river.

I hear Dawson's breathing.

But outside the cage, the parking lot is in turmoil.

Two enormous men, both dressed in full body black clothing and masks, stride through the wolf shifters who lie either unconscious on the ground or are too wounded to get up.

The first man is built like my former alpha, Peter Nash. He isn't carrying a weapon, but his body bulges with muscle—thick chest, enormous biceps, muscled thighs. He walks straight at Bridget, who must have joined the fight at some stage.

Warning bullets pluck at the pavement at the enormous man's feet—the same pattern Danika used to force Dawson off-course. She's trying to ward him off, but her next bullets won't be warnings.

Iyana steps into the enormous man's path, pulling out her gun, but he bats her away. His big fist knocks into her chest so hard that she flies backward, lands heavily on her side, and doesn't get up.

With breathtaking speed, the man grabs Bridget's arm—the one she's using to throw a punch at him—and then her neck, lifting her off her feet. Her mouth is open. She's trying to scream—might have screamed already, but I can't hear her. Her legs kick, her free arm hits at her captor, but he doesn't let go.

The man behind him appears slim in comparison but is as bulky as Tristan. He carries a wooden shotgun with an impossibly crooked barrel, so warped, he couldn't possibly fire bullets from it. It would explode in his face. Surely.

With his firearm outstretched in his left hand, perfectly balanced despite its length, he aims high as he pulls the trigger.

Light flashes around the shotgun's chamber. A glowing bullet shoots from the barrel. I spin, my hair flying, trying to follow the bullet's trajectory to the roof of the building, where Danika is hiding.

The glowing bullet hits the edge of the building. At the same time, lightning shimmers in the sky above, striking directly downward to the spot where the bullet hit, as if the bullet is a lightning rod.

The rooftop lights up.

Danika's rising silhouette is sharply visible in the explosion. She leaps from the roof, shifting midair into her hawk, beating her wings furiously as she tries to escape.

The man pulls the trigger again.

The second bullet narrowly misses her outstretched wings as she banks left. Lightning spears from the sky and hits the air right where she was flying a split second ago.

That shotgun is not an ordinary gun.

These men are not ordinary men.

On the ground, the first man is gripping Bridget so hard, he's going to break her neck.

"No!" My scream sounds empty inside the shimmering cage.

All of it has happened within the space of a few seconds, so fast that I'm screaming at myself to move, to get out there, to fight them.

"You won't get out of this cage, Tessa!" Dawson shouts as he races past me, spinning to face me before he slips backward through the shimmering wall.

He gives me a final smirk. "Have fun watching your friends die."

I step toward the magical shield. Something or someone made this cage and it wasn't Dawson. Magic thrums through it, a magic that reminds me of electricity, sharp and biting like the lightning the second man is conjuring.

Helen told me that I repel magic.

It's time to test the extent of my abilities.

With a scream, I run straight at the glistening wall.

I punch right through it, sending shards of glittering wall spraying through the air before they disappear.

The remaining magic is like cobwebs sticking to my skin, but I shake off the feeling with a scream of rage.

In the distance, the man with the warped gun jolts and spins in my direction. Only a few paces away from me, Dawson loses his footing, stumbles, and shouts. "Fuck! That's not supposed to happen." He takes off, sprinting away from me, heading across the parking lot.

Suddenly, all of the sensory input I was missing floods in.

Magic crackles around the man with the gun. Even his weapon has an aura of power around it. It's definitely not a normal shotgun, and he has to be some kind of warlock.

The enormous man holding Bridget glows icy blue, but he

doesn't carry any weapon that indicates what kind of supernatural he is.

I don't care what they are. Bridget's retaliation is weak now.

She's dying.

On the ground nearby, Iyana hasn't risen to her feet, and I can't see Danika in the sky—can only pray that they're both alive.

I launch into a run. I can't let the enormous man kill Bridget, but I won't reach him in time with my human speed.

Without thinking, I release my wolf.

She leaps ahead of me, speeding across the distance toward the enormous man. She is dark again, her energy more inky than Tristan's wolf.

She reaches the man in seconds.

Leaping at his chest, her energy rages through him. I feel the rush of air before she hits him, then the clawing, raking, tearing sensation as she passes through his body. She is not a calm force this time, but a destructive one.

Landing easily on the other side, she finds her feet and spins back to him.

He roars with pain, drops Bridget, and jolts away from my wolf, clutching at his chest where she clawed through his body. I never imagined that my wolf could hurt someone. I thought she would distract him long enough for me to reach them, but her energy was sharp like real claws. If I could see his face beneath his mask, I'm sure it would be twisted with pain.

I'm only five paces away from ramming into him when the warlock with the shotgun turns his weapon toward me.

Thunder rumbles above us as he pulls the trigger. The chamber sparks, I sense the lightning gather in the air all around me, and there's no time—none at all—to dodge.

Lightning spears through me.

The white hot bullet hits my chest.

CHAPTER TWENTY-SIX

*P*ain explodes through my torso.

The impact throws me back onto the pavement where my head hits, the blow stunning me. Light bursts around me as I fall, sparks leaving my body, lightning running off me in liquid streams. It pools around my arms, hands, and fingertips as I lie with my head turned to one side, trying to understand why I'm not dead.

I repel magic.

But *damn*, that hurt.

A shadow looms over me and once again, I scream at myself to move.

The warlock with the gun tilts his head, looking down at me, his weapon lowered. I can't see anything beneath his face mask, not what he looks like, or read anything from his expression.

All he says is, "Fuck."

My chest feels like it's on fire. I might repel magic, but the physical impact has knocked the air out of me. I manage to roll to the side as the pools of liquid lightning disappear into the ground.

I push myself up just in time to see the warlock run to the enormous man and grab his arm.

They both glance back at me a second before they disappear.

I blink at the spot where they were located a second ago.

Across the parking lot, two wounded shifters pull their unconscious comrades into the SUV while Dawson shouts at them to hurry up. Another second later, the doors slam and the vehicle squeals out of the parking lot toward the bridge.

I drag myself to my feet, stumble, and drop back to the ground while my wolf whines, her head lowered to Bridget several paces away. Beside my wolf, Iyana is finally recovering, gripping her chest, her face pale.

"Tessa!" she calls, her voice weak.

Wings flap above us and Danika's hawk plummets to the ground, her feathers singed. She's gripping the duffel bag, collapsing onto it before she shifts back to her human form, smoke rising from her back.

Bridget doesn't move.

My heart wrenches as I drag myself the last few feet to her side.

Ice particles cover her arm where the enormous man held her, extending all the way from her wrist to her shoulder. The icy burn also spreads around her neck and halfway up her left cheek.

Her lips are blue, but when I lean over her, the faintest breath warms my cheek.

I told Tristan we wouldn't need backup. I told him we'd be fine. I allowed Bridget to come with us. I regret every one of those decisions.

Bridget was my responsibility. Tristan entrusted a member of his pack to me—albeit one I had an issue with—and now she's hurt.

We're all hurt.

My wolf whines again, lowering her nose to Bridget's cheek, but the contact doesn't make any difference to the ice burn. My wolf may be able to tear at the senses of someone she passes through, but she can't heal a dying shifter.

Danika drops to her knees beside me, her golden brown hair burned at the ends, smudges of soot smeared across the backs of her hands and her cheeks.

She shakes as she reaches for me. "What do you need, Tessa?"

"Can you fly to Tristan? He needs to take Bridget to Helen. She's the only one who can help her. I don't know what sort of supernatural that man was, but—"

"Ice jotunn," Iyana says, dragging herself upright on the opposite side of Bridget. "He was an ice jotunn." She pronounces the creature's species as 'yuh-tun.'

My eyes widen. "An ice giant?"

"Not actually giants, but yeah, they're big guys. And rare. I didn't know any still existed." She rubs her heart. "One icy punch to my heart and he knocked me out cold."

Danika takes hold of my shoulder, trying to turn me toward her. "Tristan's on his way already. That's where I went. To get help. But, Tessa…" She gestures. "You're hurt too."

I shake my head, refusing to look at my chest. "I'm fine."

"You're not fine." Her voice is gentle, compelling me to check the damage to my chest.

A single glance, and I wish I hadn't. Part of the bodice is melted away, burned and curling at the edges. My left breast is only just covered by the strapless bra beneath it. My skin is split and bleeding across the location of my heart—a three-inch-wide wound, although it's shallow—while a dark bruise is developing around the impact area and across my left shoulder. "I'm going to be okay."

I sense Tristan's approach, his power streaming ahead of him.

My wolf shivers and I suddenly realize that she's exposed. I wrench her back into my body so fast that she disintegrates before my eyes, leaving behind only a black spot in my vision. Her energy passes across the air in a blink and blends with my human form again. The bright blaze she leaves behind is tinged with cobalt blue light—the color of my fear. She reminds me exactly of the way the white wolf disappeared in front of me the other night.

"Tessa!" Tristan's roar breaks across the distance. He's bare-chested, jeans unbuttoned. He probably shifted into his wolf form to run all the way here, and then dressed on the run a block back.

I was expecting to see Jace too, but he's nowhere in sight.

I'm not caging my emotions and they must be exposed and wounded, buffeting Tristan in waves. The same way his emotions are hitting me hard.

He's angry.

So angry, I don't need melding to read his mind. Neither, it seems, do Danika and Iyana, who both brace, tensing up as Tristan sprints toward us.

"You should both get out of the way," I murmur to them. "I can handle this."

They shake their heads, but I grimace. "Please. This is my responsibility."

They slowly rise to their feet, leaving me beside Bridget, but they don't go far, standing protectively behind me, Iyana paler than normal and Danika singed and smeared with soot.

"What the fuck happened?" Tristan shouts as he drops to his knees, sliding the last inches to stop at Bridget's other side, despite ripping up the knees of his jeans in the process.

"Two men. An ice jotunn and a warlock," I say, waiting for Tristan to look at me. "The ice giant got Bridget." *While Dawson distracted me.*

Tristan leans over Bridget, pressing his hand to her heart, searching her face. He rejected me the other day so that he wouldn't lose her, so she wouldn't run, to keep her in his pack. He risked fighting me for this woman.

He still hasn't looked at me. I'd like to believe it's because he's busy assessing her wounds, but it's more than that. I feel it in the anger he isn't hiding.

I failed him.

"She needs Helen's help." I grit my teeth and bury my own emotions, determined that Tristan won't sense my regret or pain— or my shock.

"This is on me," I say, my voice flat. "It was my job to keep her safe."

Tristan scoops Bridget into his arms, the ice burn across her arm a sickening sight as he gathers her up against his chest. "Jace has gone to get the SUV. He'll meet me halfway."

Tristan is gone before I can reply, carrying Bridget away as fast as he carried me on the first night we met, his powerful legs pumping.

I remain kneeling where I am.

The sky finally opens up above us, and it starts to rain.

Turning my face up, I welcome the water dripping across my face and hair, down my chest and back.

Iyana and Danika hover at my side. "We should get back to the tower," Danika says.

I shake my head. "I need some space."

Back home, I would have run through the mountain forest, let my feelings wash away in the wind. Here, I'm surrounded by walls. Buildings, damn elevators, walls everywhere.

I meet their worried eyes. "I'll be okay, but I can't go back to the tower right now."

"Then we'll stay with you," Iyana says.

"No." I give her another firm shake of my head. "Please. I'll be fine. I'll see you back there soon."

I spin on my heel and take off across the parking lot before they can try to talk me out of it. Behind the parking lot is the long park that extends along the edge of the river. I head straight for it at a sprint, my boots squelching in the wet grass when I reach it and veer left.

Sunrise is still at least an hour away and the night is now at its darkest. I release my wolf, confident that humans can't see her, and send her to scout ahead of me.

Rain splatters my face and chest. Trees line the side of the park closest to the river, giving me the illusion of being back on the mountain. My cut stings, a physical pain that I focus on to distract myself from my deep sense of failure.

I never saw it coming. Dawson's distraction. Those two supernaturals. Helen said that a war between shifters would draw in other supernaturals—bounty hunters, assassins, and the like. It looks like it already has—and they're aligning themselves with Baxter Griffin. She didn't want Tristan to put me in the middle of it, but here I am. Right in the middle of it.

Finally slowing, I stop near the edge of the river beside a tall tree. My wolf returns to my side. The city lights glow behind me and across the river while fat raindrops fall from the branches above me onto my head.

"Little one," a voice growls behind me.

I spin to the white wolf, my wolf also whirling as his powerful energy latches on to her, forcing her to remain where she is.

He appears several paces from me, materializing out of the dark, his teeth glowing white, his eyes fiery red. Unlike the last time he took hold of my wolf, he doesn't release her immediately, his energy remaining curled around her chest.

His burning gaze takes in my human form, from my dripping

red hair to my muddy boots. He snarls. "Your human form explains much to me."

My wolf whines, turning her head to me. He's gripping her chest too tightly—I feel the pressure as if he's squeezing my human body too.

I grit my teeth and slow my speech, growling each word. "Let. Me. Go."

The white wolf tips his head at me, the blaze in his eyes becoming cold. "You're mine, but you continue to elude me. I'll let you go when I'm ready."

"Yours?" I spit. "Everyone seems to think that I belong to them. They claim me and then they reject me. Over and over."

"Tell me how you manage to hide from me, and I'll let you go," he says.

"I haven't been hiding from you—"

"Oh, but you have been. I can't sense you unless your wolf takes separate form. And then you are a burst of energy that ripples across my senses, demanding that I come find you."

I start to speak and then stop. The first time he found me—claimed to have been made aware of my existence for the first time—was the first night I released my wolf outside of Hidden House. I haven't released her again until tonight.

I choose my response carefully. "You can only sense my wolf when she takes this form?"

He begins to pace, his big paws leaving no marks on the muddy ground, no pawprints.

"Tell me why!" he shouts.

I suddenly remember Helen asking Tristan for answers about me. She told him that my power was nothing she'd seen before. That my energy is wolf, but not wolf. And, most importantly, she said my human soul is masking an essence she couldn't identify.

I allow myself to smile, refusing to give away the pain the white wolf is causing me as his grip tightens. "My human soul protects me from you."

He jumps forward, baring his teeth at me. "Your human soul is a shell. A cage. You will only know your true power when you rid yourself of it. When you recognize it as the vessel that it is."

"No." I stand my ground. "My human soul is more than that."

Straining at his hold on my wolf, we both edge forward. "My human soul makes me who I am."

His lips draw back. He gnashes his teeth at me. "You are too much like your mother."

I jolt, feeling as if he slapped me. The insult burns. I push my damp hair away from my face, glaring back at him. "I'm nothing like her."

I would never reject my daughter or slap her down in front of others. I would never allow her to be hurt.

The white wolf squeezes so hard around my wolf's ribs that my breathing becomes rapid and shallow.

"You." He advances on me. "Are exactly like her."

Burning anger rises inside me. I want to strike out at the white wolf, but he's like my wolf—insubstantial. I can only assume his form will claw through me and the pain will all be mine.

I have to get free. I scream against his hold on me, my wolf writhing within his grip. My human body drags at my wolf's energy, trying to pull her back to me. As soon as I do that, he won't be able to stop me from escaping.

In a desperate move, I snatch the dagger from the holster around my thigh. Even though I know it's futile, I leap forward with a scream, the dagger gripped in both of my hands.

The wolf's burning eyes widen, the dagger's blade reflecting his sudden fear as the steel descends toward his head.

In the next instant, he's gone, leaving behind nothing more than a bright spot in my vision.

My dagger sails through air.

The pain around my chest disappears.

I land on the ground at a crouch, stopping the dagger before it would lodge into the earth. Taking no chances, I call my wolf back into my body and close my eyes with relief once she's safe again.

My relief is short-lived. Too soon, my inner turmoil returns.

When I couldn't control my power, I was vulnerable to the strongest alphas. My power drove them wild—can still drive them wild if I let it. But now that I have control, so much control that I can release my wolf from my body, the white wolf can find me.

He told me that he has three names. If he's the three-headed wolf that Tristan is worried about, then getting to me would be his first step to getting to Tristan.

I haven't told Tristan about him. Tristan doesn't know about my ability to release my wolf, either. Suddenly, that feels like a mistake.

I grip my stomach, my breathing shaky again.

The three-headed wolf is coming for Tristan.

Baxter Griffin is coming for Tristan.

An ice jotunn and a warlock with a fucking shotgun for a wand are coming for Tristan.

And I'm caught between them all.

CHAPTER TWENTY-SEVEN

*T*he sun is on the verge of rising when I reach the clock tower again. I didn't bring much with me on patrol, but my past self was forward-thinking enough to pop my security pass into the hidden pocket inside my skirt's waistband.

Letting myself back into the building, I scan the parking garage for Tristan's usual SUV. Its parking space is empty, which means he's still at Hidden House.

My heart wrenches suddenly because I miss its safety and its occupants. I've only been gone for a few days, but it feels like a lifetime ago. I miss Ella's humming. I miss reminding the card mage twins, Luna and Lydia, about the time of day. I miss Helen most of all and the comfort of her advice, her ability to help me keep everything in perspective.

I shudder as I remember Luna's prediction that my real enemy is the one whose face I can't see. I'm not certain yet, but she could have meant the white wolf, who must have a human form somewhere. He said his human form was delighted to discover my existence. If he is as in control of his power as he appears, then he won't have any scent, no way to detect him.

I remind myself that I'm lucky to have Iyana and Danika and that they'll be worried about me right now.

Taking the elevator upstairs, I pause when I step into the small living area in the entrance. Jemimah sits on the couch under the window staring out at the night sky as she bounces her little girl on her lap.

I attempt to tiptoe past them, but she spots me.

The dark rings under Jemimah's eyes shout exhaustion.

I should probably be tired too, but after sleeping through an entire day and night, I'm doing okay.

The little girl jumps off her mom's lap and runs to me as soon as she sees me. She lifts her arms up to me. "Up. Up."

Since her mom doesn't look like she wants to stab me, I bend and prop the child on my hip. She promptly starts gnawing on my hair again.

"Sorry. She's teething," Jemimah says, rubbing at her eyes. "Teething shifter babies are not fun."

The little girl makes chomping noises at my ear and I think she might be chewing my hair right off.

Meh. It'll grow back.

"Do you have anyone who can help you?" I ask.

Jemimah sighs. "The other ladies try to help out, but, you know, they're struggling to get enough sleep too. All of our mates are…" She presses her lips together, leans forward over her knees, and quickly looks away before she swipes at her leaking eyes.

I take a hesitant step toward her, wary of making an unintentional mistake. "Are you okay?"

"I miss him," she says, nodding and wiping at her eyes. It's a losing battle as the tears continue to fall. "Even if he wasn't my true mate. Our pack number is too small to have any hope of finding a true mate anymore." She shrugs, her voice wobbly. "Unless you look outside of the pack like Jace did. But what happened to Ella was…"

She shudders visibly, her tears falling, and now she doesn't try to wipe them away. "I don't blame Tristan for not acting faster. How can you kill someone you're supposed to love? But I wish he'd ended his father sooner. Our mates would still be alive if he had."

Taking a deep, shuddery breath, she drops her head into her hands before she wipes her face again. "I'm sorry. I have no filter when I'm sleep-deprived. I shouldn't have said any of that."

"It's okay," I murmur, not sure how to process all of the fragmented pieces of information she just gave me.

She said that Jace looked outside of the pack for a mate—and she implied that Ella was that mate. I'd suspected from comments Helen made that there was a connection between them, but I don't know what that has to do with Tristan killing his father...? Or why other shifters died because Tristan didn't kill his father sooner? Tristan himself told me that his father would encourage fights and then kill the loser, but I assumed that only happened once or twice.

A glance at the little girl tells me that—surprisingly—chewing on my hair has sent her to sleep. She drools on my shoulder, her lips parted enough that it only takes a gentle sweep to extract the remaining strands of my hair before I hand her back to her mother.

Jemimah swallows visibly. "You do know that we hate you because you're strong enough, right?"

My forehead creases in confusion. "Strong enough for what?"

"To be with Tristan." The corners of Jemimah's mouth turn down. "Nobody else is."

I'm not sure what to think of this revelation. I'm not *with* Tristan. As for being strong...

I sigh and leave Jemimah with her daughter, then tiptoe down the corridor, aware of the other moms who need their sleep as I slip quietly into my apartment.

I find Danika crashed on the couch, where she was probably waiting up for me. She looks a lot better now that she has showered and washed off the soot. I do a quick visual check for wounds, but she appears okay, her breathing deep and peaceful.

Retrieving the blanket from her bed, I rest it over her before I check on Iyana, who is also crashed out on her bed. A wide bruise is visible across the top of her chest above the V of her nightshirt, and the intensity of the bruise makes me reluctant to leave her alone in case she needs me.

Pulling a blanket from the bed in the third room—a bed I've never slept in and doesn't feel like mine—I make a place for myself on the floor beside Iyana's bed. I'm still wearing my damaged clothing and it's not made for sleeping in, but now that I'm back, I don't feel like I can leave Iyana alone.

I failed one woman tonight. I won't fail another.

I toss and turn for the next half an hour, struggling to work through everything that happened in the night. Every time I close my eyes, I hear the crackle of the warlock's shotgun, see again the flash as the chamber lit up, sense the magic hitting me and streaming off me onto the ground. I hear, over and over, the white wolf telling me I'm just like my mother. Feel his magic pull closer and closer around my chest until I'm gasping for breath—

"Tessa." Iyana groans, making me shoot upright.

"What is it?" I ask, urgently leaning across her. "Are you okay?"

"No, I'm not okay." She moans, throwing her hand over her eyes. "You're keeping me awake."

"You're hurt," I say. "I won't leave you alone."

"I'm a vampire, sweetie," she says, snorting a little. "I've sucked down a dose of mercury. This bruise is nothing I haven't dealt with before. I'll be right as night after a solid sleep." She removes her hand from her eyes and gives me a pointed stare. "Assuming I can get to sleep."

All of the tension drains out of me.

She's definitely okay. I lean across and give her a hug.

She smiles against my cheek. "Love you, Tessa. Now go get some sleep."

"Love you, too." I scramble up and drag the blanket with me, but I stop when I reach my bedroom door.

The tightness in my chest remains. I thought it was the memory of the white wolf's power, but now I'm not so sure.

Closing my eyes as I grip the doorframe, I try to take a deep breath and can't. My chest squeezes. My inhale catches.

I try again.

Fail again.

My breaths come faster and now I'm on the verge of panic.

I can't breathe and I don't understand what's wrong. I'm about to call out to Iyana for help when I sense my wolf's power inside me. I'm shocked to find her quietly writhing in pain. It's the same clawing pain I felt moments before Tristan and I melded...

I gasp. "*Tristan.*"

I spin on my heel and hurry from the apartment, latching the door behind me as quietly as I can, even though my hands are shaking. Jemimah isn't sitting in the entrance room anymore and the elevator arrives nearly immediately.

I swipe my security card across the scanner and bump the button for the twelfth floor before I slide down the wall of the elevator, attempting to keep myself upright by hanging on to the handrail at the side.

The doors blur as they open and I crawl through the gap, wheezing and gasping for breath, the world spinning as I try to get enough oxygen.

In the distance, Tristan grips the edge of the kitchen table, leaning back from it, a roar growing in his throat. He thumps the surface with his fist, cracking it. His muscles bunch seconds before he upturns the table, flipping it halfway across the room. It slides to a stop, dangerously close to the windows.

I freeze where I grip the elevator's doorframe.

Tristan's rage washes over me, a thousand times more intense than the anger I sensed pouring off him when he saw Bridget. It's his pure rage without walls or boundaries that's squeezing my chest now.

He jolts upright as he becomes aware of my presence.

Remaining where he is, his voice is a menacing growl. "Get out of here, Tessa. You can't be around me right now."

His warning contains raw truth.

I have two choices. I can crawl back into the elevator and try to gasp enough oxygen to breathe until he calms down—at which time I hope I'll be okay.

Or I can follow my instincts.

I launch myself to my feet, race toward him, and throw myself across the distance, wrapping my arms and legs around him as I knock into him.

He braces as we connect, his arms flying around me, scooping me up so we don't fall and tumble across the kitchen tiles.

My chest presses to his. My legs wrap around his waist. I arch against him to make sure our chests connect as much as physically possible as we come to a complete stop.

Oh, sweet oxygen.

I inhale my first full breath of air since I returned to the tower.

My chest expands and my head clears. But now I'm breathing in Tristan's rage and all its sharp edges, and it *hurts*.

His arms clamp around me, his shoulders tense. One hand grips the back of my head like a vise, preventing me from looking up at him. "You can't be here right now, Tessa. I'll destroy you."

I push against his hand, my wolf's energy giving me the strength to raise my head and meet the darkness in his eyes. I lace my hands behind his naked back, flexing my palms against his muscles, and lock my ankles around his waist.

"I'm strong enough," I murmur, edging forward to press my lips to his, inhaling the same back-arching power I felt when we first met.

Our mouths have barely touched when he pulls me away from him, quick, aggressive, holding my head an inch from his. He lashes out with a snarl. "You're too vulnerable. Too fragile."

Two months ago, I would have retaliated against his assessment of my strength. I would have tried to prove to him just how fragile I am *not*.

Tonight, I have greater perspective. The kind of rage he's experiencing is sourced from pain. The deepest pain. It has to be more than Bridget's injury. And it's making him lash out with an intensity that he already regrets.

"What happened?" I ask quietly.

"The past happened," he says through gritted teeth. "A past and a future I can't escape."

"Your father," I whisper.

His grip becomes excruciatingly tight on my scalp, but he leans forward, closing the gap nearly completely between us. "Deceiver. Coward. Killer. That was my father."

I press myself as close to Tristan as I can, my muscles straining with the effort, but I refuse to let go. "You aren't him."

He growls, low and soft. "He destroyed everyone who cared about him."

Tristan's anger washes across me in waves that push and pull at me. I'm buffeted in the storm of his rage, but I refuse to let go.

"How can the child of a monster not become a monster?" he asks.

I level my gaze with his. "You aren't him."

Tristan's green eyes are half-animal, darkly rimmed. Strands of his raven black hair fall across his eyes. The first rays of sunlight break across the horizon and shine through the windows, high-lighting the curve of his lips.

I brace, using the strength in my thighs to remain where I am as I remove one of my hands from his back and reach up behind his hand—the one pressed to the back of my head that is keeping me at a distance.

Slowly and carefully, I slide my fingers over the back of his, taking control of his hand so I can lean forward again.

My lips press to his fully for the first time, fitting to the curve of his mouth. He inhales sharply as I explore the shape of his lips, traveling the upper and lower curves.

The taste of his mouth is intoxicating. I moan against his lips, nudging at them, wanting to feel more.

The muscles in his arms flex across my back, the hand with which he holds my head gripping me painfully.

"Tessa," he says. "Leave while you still can."

He's giving me another choice.

For a long time, I didn't think I had any choices with Tristan, but he has always given me options. Live or die. Fight him or fuck him. Leave or stay.

"I'm staying."

His forehead creases, his eyes narrow, a moment of distrust. His grip on my head changes, pulling me closer, pausing while his gaze scorches mine.

My heartbeat is rapid inside my chest, my wolf's energy rising to the surface, but I focus on maintaining my calm, determined not to taint this moment by losing control of my power.

His lips nudge mine, a testing pressure, before he pulls back to assess my reaction. The brief contact is tantalizing, the insistent question in his eyes unrelenting. I sway toward him as close as I can without kissing him, waiting for him to make his own decision.

With a throaty snarl, he swoops toward me and demands full access to my mouth. His lips push mine apart, his tongue grazing across my tongue. Scorching need bursts through me, both mine and the need he has kept under control since... *Damn...* His emotions tell me that he's kept his need for me under control since the night he first laid eyes on me.

I respond by releasing his hand and running mine up his back into his hair, holding him as firmly as he's holding me.

He breaks the contact as suddenly as he started it, casting a withering glance at the flipped table, which is of no use to us, before he strides with me to his bedroom.

His scent envelops me as soon as we enter, a relentless mix of fury and desire as he carries me to the bed.

"I want you naked," he says, his lips meeting mine in a blistering kiss that ignites the ache in my center.

Every move he makes is intense as he presses me back onto the bed, my hips raised above its edge while my legs remain curved around his hips where he stands at the bed's edge.

He unzips my skirt with fierce efficiency before unfurling my legs from around his waist, pulling my skirt off, and pitching it off to the side. Flipping me onto my stomach, he unzips the back of my bodice all the way down so that it falls away from me. With another quick movement, he unclasps my bra, leaving me only in my underpants.

His palms graze my stomach as he bends over me, his chest pressed against my back as he slides his hands beneath my ribs. Pulling me back into a standing position, his hands slide up my stomach and ribs to cup my breasts. At the same time, his mouth nudges the side of my neck, tasting the skin at the curve between my shoulder and neck and working his way up to my ear, tugging my sensitive earlobe between his lips.

Moans leave my mouth and I brace against the edge of the bed as his hands explore my breasts, hips, and the curve of my pelvis. He turns me in his arms to face him, trailing kisses down my neck, across my collarbone, nudging my breasts on his way to my underpants before he pulls them off and down to my ankles.

His hands are firm around my hips as he guides me to sit on the edge of the bed before drawing my legs apart and tasting the skin across my inner thigh, one side and then the other, before his warm mouth closes over my center.

I moan, gripping his shoulders as intense pleasure rides me. It's a mix of release and growing need as his tongue curves and licks across my most sensitive folds.

The pleasure builds so fast that I cry out in protest when he stops right when I'm on the brink of climaxing. I dig my fingernails into his shoulders, growling my unhappiness deep in my throat.

He wears a self-satisfied smile as he rises to his feet between my legs, ridding himself of his jeans before he pushes me back onto the bed. It's the same smile he gave me when I woke up at Hidden House after he commanded it. But this time, his smile carries an edge of anger that hasn't diminished despite the attention he's giving my body.

He warned me that he would destroy me, but destruction works both ways. I have the power to destroy him too.

Standing over me, he takes in my entire form from my red hair spread across his bed, the stray, crimson strands resting across my breasts, to my waist and thighs. It's a lingering appraisal before the animal returns to his eyes. Taking both of my hips in his hands and positioning himself, he pulls me closer to the edge of the bed.

"You are fucking beautiful," he says, thrusting inside me.

My body is completely ready—he made sure of it. I arch up off the bed, crying out as intense pleasure rocks me. He withdraws slowly, testing my responses before thrusting again, an act that feels like being claimed, a deep marking.

My own darkness and recklessness rise to the surface as he rides me. I match him, meeting every thrust, fisting the sheets and using them to brace, demanding more from him. Arching and lifting my hips off the bed, I push myself against him, taking control of our movements, curving my own hips up even further, drawing him deeper inside me.

With a groan, he leans down close, planting both hands on either side of my head, his mouth demanding access to my lips again, the taste on his tongue a heady mix of his scent and mine.

He grips my torso, sliding his arms beneath me and wrenching me upward, his movements wild as I meet every thrust with my own relentless need. If I could tell him what I wanted, I would, but all of my focus is set on taking his anger and turning it into the flames that will feed my own desire, in matching his darkness with my own.

"Fuck, Tessa!" He grips my backside as I use every muscle in my body to push against him, needing release, wanting to take it all from him.

He drops me back onto the bed, crashing deep inside me at the same time.

I scream as I orgasm, powerful heat rushing through me, tearing me apart wave after wave. My whole world rips and it feels like my foundations shift. It's more than pleasure. It's darkness and need, hope and violence. As I match the fury in Tristan's final thrusts before he crashes with me, my wolf's energy rises to the surface, seeking, trying to reach beyond me.

I'm searching for the true mate bond I can't attain. Will never attain.

With furious determination, I push the threatening heartache from my mind, refusing to allow it to define this moment. I have to accept who I am, that I can share my body and heart with Tristan, even if there will never be a soul connection between us.

Tristan remains poised above me, his fists on either side of my head, his chest rising and falling, rapid breaths that match how fast I'm breathing. He searches my eyes, demanding but not furious anymore, before he dips his head to nudge my lips with his, another brief testing pressure.

I arch to follow his lips, demanding that he kiss me fully, enjoying the taste of his mouth before I drop my head back onto the bed and wait for him to respond.

He makes a pleased sound in the back of his throat, his lips relaxed, a satisfied smile growing on his lips again.

The bedsheets are strewn around us. I'm still gripping a section of them in my fist and I slowly release it, sighing with remnant pleasure as he withdraws his body from mine.

I'm prepared for him to leave the bed, but he stays where he is, dipping his head to my thighs and nudging them, one after the other, with his lips, stroking kisses up to my lower stomach.

His tongue swirls across my skin, along my ribcage, across my breasts, pausing at the bruise I sustained tonight. The cut has closed already, but the wound will take another day to disappear. He whispers kisses around its edges before he continues over to my shoulder, down my right arm, all the way to my fingers, where he turns my palm over and sucks on the inside of my forefinger. I gasp and shiver as he works his way back up my arm and across my collarbone to my other shoulder.

It's a careful, methodical process that makes my wolf's energy purr, contentment lulling me into submission as I accept his attention.

His lips ease across my neck, his hands brushing across my body. I don't think anything of it when he folds one hand around my left shoulder and presses the palm of his other hand against my jaw on the same side.

I watch him lazily as his incisors descend and he lowers his mouth to my shoulder, preparing to nip.

My eyes fly wide. "No!"

His only reaction to my sudden tension is to pause and level his gaze with mine. "My instincts tell me this is right, Tessa."

My breathing is suddenly out of my control, but it's because of misery not panic. He's forcing me to face the fact that I'm losing something I never had.

"You said that the woman you mark will be yours forever," I say. "How can I be yours forever when I won't live longer than another year?"

He doesn't deny my question, but his response is equally unequivocal. "My forever only lasts as long as I'm alive. My forever will be shorter than yours. But for the time I have left, I want you by my side."

He's telling me he doesn't expect to live beyond the next few months. I've never wanted to say *yes* more badly in my life. My lips part, my body more alive even than when my wolf runs free.

Tristan's thumb strokes my shoulder, his other hand soft and compelling against my jaw. "You withstood my worst, Tessa. Hell, you invited it." His voice is thick, his calm receding, a new anger growing in his shifting eyes, becoming more animal as he speaks.

"There's no such thing as normal bonding for creatures like you and me because our true nature is to rip apart anything that binds us," he says. "We refuse to be caged. You have fought me every step of the way. You would rather tear yourself apart than give in to the idea that I have any control over you."

His grip tightens on my shoulder, demanding that I agree. "I will never find an equal like you. You're the one I want."

I guard my thoughts, making sure he doesn't have a window into my inner turmoil. My response could break us. I will never agree to be marked, but I don't want my refusal to be interpreted as rejection.

I breathe carefully in the silence between us as he waits patiently for my answer. His body still rests between my legs. Slowly, I bring my knees up beside his hips and curl my legs around his backside. Equally slowly, cautiously, I brace my left palm against the side of his chest and my right hand against his left shoulder.

He tips his head, wary of my intentions just as my muscles flex and I use my strength to roll us over in a quick maneuver, reversing our position so that he's beneath me.

With rapid movements, I grab his jaw and his shoulder like he was gripping mine and lower my mouth, as if I'm going to mark *him* instead.

Tristan jolts, his eyes flying wide. His hands whip around my wrists, stopping me, a growl in his throat warning me not to proceed.

I take a breath, pause for a beat as his muscles flex against mine, a challenge of strength that either of us could win.

Satisfied with his reaction, my lips curve into a smile as I hover dangerously close enough to nip his shoulder. "We refuse to be caged," I say. "Just like we refuse to be marked. That doesn't mean I won't stay at your side, Tristan."

My tongue darts between my lips, pressing to the chiseled muscle at the top of his arm, tasting the skin without leaving a mark.

He watches me carefully, his hands still clamped around my wrists, ready to take back control. "What are you saying?"

"I'm saying I don't need a fucking mark to dictate my loyalty or my trust."

Slowly unfurling his fingers from around my wrists—an act of trust—he lowers his arms, one coming to rest above his head while the other grazes down my side.

I rebalance myself as I trail kisses down his arm all the way to his palm, drawing his forefinger into my mouth as I sit up, strad-dling him. He's already hard again and it's the most natural act for me to draw him inside me.

I bury my moans against his hand and lose myself to our rhythm as we begin again.

CHAPTER TWENTY-EIGHT

$\mathcal{F}$or the next four nights, I relocate myself to Tristan's penthouse. I spend my afternoons in the gym with Iyana and Danika, my evenings on patrol, and my midnight hours in Tristan's bed.

Iyana and Danika don't ask me for any information that I don't offer, although they tell me they're here for me if I need to talk. They still respect Helen's rules about not asking questions, and I realize that I do, too.

Tristan has so many secrets, so much history that I don't know, but I won't ask because I know how painful and destructive it is to drag up the past.

My focus is now on the future.

On the afternoon of the third day, Tristan calls me, Jace, Iyana, and Danika to the meeting room to discuss the plan of attack on Baxter Griffin.

When we arrive, he's gathered a handful of chairs together in a loose circle and is sitting with his elbows on his knees, his chin resting on his clasped hands. He's dressed in jeans and a perfectly fitted tank. It's only been a few hours since I left his bed and his gaze heats me all the way to my toes.

Jace has been evasive since the night Bridget was hurt, only approaching me once, yesterday, to tell me that Bridget is recovering well at Hidden House. He's the last to arrive, dressed in jeans and a bicep-hugging T-shirt that hides his tattoo. He waits for me to choose my seat next to Tristan before he picks his own chair opposite us. Danika and Iyana split up on either side of Jace.

"Tessa and I are going alone," Tristan says, startling me.

Iyana and Danika both shoot me a no-fucking-way look before they turn to Tristan in unison.

"Not happening. You need backup," Iyana says.

"Going alone is the best way to get yourselves killed," Danika asserts.

Tristan turns to me, seeking my opinion next, but I'm slower to give it. He hasn't spoken to me about specifics, but I sense it's been churning away in his mind for days, just like it's started weighing on mine.

"We saw firsthand the kind of allies Baxter has now," I say. "We're not only talking about my old alpha, Peter Nash, and his son, Dawson. The supernaturals we encountered the other night might only be the beginning."

I lean toward my friends, predicting their objections. Iyana will tell me she can take care of herself. Danika will insist she won't be spotted in the sky.

"They will sense you and strike you down," I say. "Even you, Danika. There are only so many times you can outfly lightning. Whereas..." I take a deep breath before I continue. "Tristan and I won't try to hide. Isn't that right?"

I turn to him for confirmation. It's a guess on my part, based on what he's told me in the past: that he would give me the tools to destroy my enemies and that it would be up to me whether or not I used them. He also told me—on the first night we met—that my scent would drive them wild.

I've put two and two together and formed a picture that is breathtakingly dangerous and could go horribly wrong. It's the destruction that Tristan originally planned for his enemies. What I don't know is whether or not our relationship has now changed how he perceives the future.

"We're going to walk in the front door," Tristan says, confirming my suspicion.

Jace's chair scrapes loudly as he pushes it back, nearly knocking it over, his eyebrows drawn down. Without a word, he prowls to the far window, a silent objection.

Iyana hooks her thumb in his direction. "I'm with Jace."

I reach out, briefly placing my hand on Tristan's knee as he moves to go after Jace. "May I?"

Tristan gives me a stiff nod.

Quietly crossing the room, I'm aware of the silence behind us as I draw level with Jace and consider the rain beating against the window. It's a perfect day for Iyana to go outside, not a ray of sunlight to be seen.

"You're walking blindly to your death," he says, his voice low.

I continue to focus on the window, even though Jace's fierce gaze burns into me. "Don't count me out so quickly, Jace."

"You don't know whose bed you're keeping warm."

I meet Jace's eyes, deep green, reminding me of the forest on the mountain. "Then enlighten me."

Jace is tense. He presses his palm against the window, but he answers my request with a question. "Has Tristan told you what happened to Ella?"

I shake my head. "No. Will you?"

Jace returns his stare to the window, following the raindrops zigzagging down the glass.

I bite my lip, my mouth dry. "She's your true mate. Isn't she?"

Jace flinches. "Was. Until she was broken." He squeezes his eyes shut, a rare sign of pain. "That's why I don't shift anymore. I can handle the pain of our broken bond if I don't shift."

His response is more open, more honest than I was expecting, an unexpected trust.

Carefully, I ask, "How do you break a true mate bo—"

His warning growl cuts me off. "Only with extended violence. The kind of violence that only a few supernaturals are capable of inflicting." He grabs my shoulder, his gaze level with mine, his voice low. "The three-headed wolf is coming for Tristan. When he gets here, you'll witness firsthand the kind of violence that broke a beautiful, strong-willed woman like Ella."

The pain behind his eyes is almost too much. I remember the way he told Helen that the last thing Ella needed was to see him. I remember Ella's long, blonde hair and empathetic brown eyes, her ability to perceive my moods, her instant understanding that I was both wolf and human. I remember how broken she is. But I also recall the white wolf and the surprising moment of fear in his eyes when I leaped at him with my dagger.

"No," I whisper. "I'll kill him before he hurts anyone."

The muscle in Jace's jaw clenches. "I hope you're strong enough to do that, Tessa." His gaze flickers beyond me, pausing on Tristan. "I believe Tristan is gambling our future on you being strong enough."

His grip on my shoulder eases to a firm squeeze. "Stay safe."

With a formal nod, he turns on his heel and exits the room, leaving me to return to Tristan's side.

"We're going alone," I say.

Iyana and Danika exchange a glance, but they don't renew their protests.

On the morning of the birthday party, I wake alone to find two boxes sitting side-by-side at the end of Tristan's bed.

One is a large, ebony box tied with an ivory ribbon. It's well-wrapped, a beautiful glossy box, the kind that comes from an expensive shop.

The other is a smaller box lined with red velvet and wrapped in a violet ribbon.

I take hold of the black box first, tucking my legs under my backside before I open it. Inside, the contents of the box are hidden by fine, black tissue paper. Brushing the paper aside, I pull out a dress made of silky, black material. The skirt consists of layers of transparent tulle that will fall to my ankles with a long slit up the leg for ease of movement, but the bodice consists of two wide, slanted straps that confuse the hell out of me.

I turn it this way and that, trying to figure out how the straps are supposed to cover my breasts until I spy the card in the bottom of the box. It contains a picture of a model wearing the dress and it's suddenly clear how it's supposed to be put on.

The dress is one-shouldered. The wide straps are connected at the top of my right shoulder and cross from that shoulder to my left hip at the waistband. Each strap will cover one of my breasts—but barely. A whole stretch of flesh and cleavage will be exposed between and around the straps.

Quickly slipping the lid off the second box, I push aside the crimson tissue paper that covers its contents.

A laugh bursts out of me.

I take hold of the top of a strapless black bodysuit. The bodice and thong consist of ribbons and lacy whorls that will push up my breasts, circle my waist, and cover my groin with a small triangle but otherwise leave me bare.

I've never worn anything like it in my life.

"Fuck," I whisper.

Tristan told me he'd give me the tools.

Now I need to decide how far I'm willing to go to end this deadly feud between the packs and avenge my father's death.

CHAPTER TWENTY-NINE

*T*he city lights twinkle through the window of the SUV as we pass across the bridge into Baxter Griffin's territory. The first time I crossed the Eastern Lowlands, we kept to the north and passed as quickly as possible into Tristan's territory. Now, we're heading right into the heart of a place where we are not welcome.

Tristan sits behind the steering wheel. A pistol rests in his lap, but we're otherwise unarmed. He's dressed in a perfectly tailored black suit and tie, his raven hair slicked back. He's clean shaven, making him look far more civilized than I know him to be.

I cross my right leg over my left, the tulle skirt falling to either side. I'm slowly adjusting to the black heels I'm wearing. I spent half of the afternoon practicing walking in them and the other half getting dressed. Danika helped with my hair—a half up-do with waves flowing down my back and shoulders. I hardly recognized myself once I put on makeup, my lips scarlet red, my lashes dark, my blue eyes appearing sultry.

Finally ready, I'd sauntered into the living area to find Tristan dressed and ready, standing at the opposite window—his customary position. He'd appraised my reflection in the glass for a heated moment before he turned and tipped his head in the direction of the elevator, his emotions blank as stone.

When I leaned toward him, wanting to close the gap, he pulled back. "You can't have my scent on you," he said.

He hasn't touched me since he left his bed this morning. His emotional walls are up, but I sense his inner struggle. He may have put the boxes on the bed, but I suspect he hoped I'd rip the clothing to shreds.

It takes a mere half an hour to travel through the city and into a forested area in Portland's southeast where the houses are sparse. We enter a winding road that takes us higher until we reach the entrance to a private road with security guards stationed at it. A scan of the perimeter tells me that armed shifters are stationed at intervals all along the fence line, together with security cameras.

Ours isn't the only vehicle lining up waiting admittance. The SUV in front of us pulls up beside the security guard at the gate, who leans in to take a slip of parchment that is presumably an invitation while another three guards check over the vehicle before they allow it through.

Baxter Griffin isn't taking any chances tonight.

Tristan presses the button to wind down his window, grips the wheel with one hand, and slides the pistol down beside the door before we drive forward to pull up beside the guard at the gate.

Revealing his incisors, Tristan smiles at the security guard, speaking before the guard can say anything. "Tell Cody that Tristan Masters is here to see him."

The guard jolts, gives a shout, and suddenly, about a million guns are pointed in our direction.

It isn't lost on me that Tristan requested Cody and not his father. Slowly lifting my hands so they're visible through the windscreen, I carefully reach for the door handle and push the door open.

Holding my hands high, I slip from the vehicle, angling for full visibility by the security camera at the top of the gate, gratified to see it follow my movements. I tip my head back and wait as the tense seconds stretch out.

All it will take is a trigger-happy shifter and I'm a dead woman.

The security guard whom Tristan greeted points his weapon directly at Tristan's head while the seconds tick by.

His two-way radio finally crackles. "Escort them in."

The radio distorts the speaker's voice, but it sounds like it was Cody himself who responded.

The guard gestures at me. "Back in the vehicle. No sudden movements."

Carefully and slowly, I slide back into the passenger seat and close the door while Tristan drives the vehicle forward at a crawl, slow enough that a dozen security guards can jog at the side of the vehicle.

A minute down the private road, we finally arrive at a sprawling building, multiple levels high, a mansion with a grand entrance all lit up.

Tristan slips the pistol beneath his seat after he brings the vehicle to a stop. He raises his hands like I did and we both wait inside the vehicle, hands visible while the security guards usher the guests on the stairs into the house.

Baxter Griffin and Cody Griffin stride down the front stairs, both dressed in black suits and ties. I focus on calming my breathing and remaining in control. The last time I saw these men, they stood over my father's body.

Because of the way we're facing, I'm closest to them.

Cody looks different as he stops at the base of the steps only five paces away. His sandy blond hair is cut short now—it was slicked back and halfway down his neck the last time I saw him—and his upper body and thighs appear larger, as if he's spent that last two months working out. It could be the cut of his suit, but there's a finely chiseled edge to his silhouette that wasn't there before.

In contrast, his father appears more weathered, his hair more gray, his mouth set in a cold line, his brown eyes turning hard as he focuses on me.

"Get them out and search them," he orders.

The security guards on either side of us open our doors. Tristan exits and steps to the side of the vehicle, where Baxter and Cody can see him. He promptly submits to a thorough pat down.

I take my time slipping my feet to the ground. An appraisal of Cody tells me he hasn't glanced at Tristan once, his focus intent on me. Angling my legs so that the split in my skirt does its work by falling away from the curves of my left leg all the way up to my thigh, I slide from my seat.

Finding my feet, I appraise Cody quietly from beneath my lashes, my lips parting, and now my confusion is genuine. The first time I saw him, he glowed with power. Now, he's more controlled, but his control feels dangerous, the same way I am more of a threat now that my power is held tightly within my grasp.

When the security guard reaches out to pat me down, I lean away from him. "Oh, honey," I say to him. "It takes stronger hands than yours to handle me."

The guard growls a denial, but Cody is already crossing the distance under his father's sharp eye.

"Step aside," he says to the guard. "I'll check her."

I sense Tristan watching us as closely as Baxter is, although Tristan's emotions are so walled off that I'm getting barely anything from him.

Cody reaches for me without pause, his hands gripping my waist and ribs in a firm hold, his face tipped to mine. Up close, his eyes appear more animal, his hickory brown irises flecked with gold. He speaks my name with a rumbling growl. "Tessa."

"Cody." I inhale his scent. Like his appearance, it's changed too, now with layers it didn't have before, but I don't know what the change means. I remember when I first saw him through my wolf's power, the glow around him was a confusing mix of cobalt and crimson, forces at war with each other. Now I sense that one of those forces has since won the battle.

I bite my lip, uncertainty settling in before I remember I'm supposed to be playing a part. Recovering quickly, I tip my head back to whisper, "Just so you know, I like it gentle."

The corner of his mouth tugs up, his focus shifting from my lips back to my eyes. "Prepare to be disappointed."

His hands slide up beneath my breasts, pressing firmly, his thumbs grazing across the naked skin between the bodice straps before traveling around my breasts to my shoulders.

I tip my neck side to side to give him access as his palms rise up and around to the back of my head. He slides his fingers into my hair, cupping the back of my head, pulling me up against him. He inhales as deeply as I did when he first approached, drawing my scent into his chest.

He won't sense anything now. My scent is long gone, my power an undetectable threat.

His eyes narrow as he pulls back, a hint of confusion that he hides quickly as he continues patting down my back and across my backside.

My lack of extensive underwear will be obvious to him.

He releases me from close proximity with his body and lowers himself to squeeze down my right leg all the way to my ankle before switching to my left leg, flipping the tulle out of the way to travel all the way from my naked calf up to the top of my naked thigh.

Wrapping both of his big hands around the top of my leg, he stops, holds me there, and turns his focus on Tristan, checking Tristan's reaction.

I prepare myself for Tristan's wrath, but he returns Cody's challenging gaze with a nonchalant stare so convincing that even I would believe it if I weren't so attuned to his feelings.

He wants to fucking kill Cody right now.

Not getting a rise out of Tristan, Cody lifts himself, his palms returning to my chest and resting across my breasts, a light and swift touch, before his focus shifts to my left shoulder.

His thumb strokes across the spot where he tried to mark me that night—where I also refused Tristan's mark.

Now I understand why Tristan chose a one-shouldered dress. The fact that I haven't been claimed is plain for all to see.

Cody steps back, his expression shuttered. "She's clean."

At his announcement, Baxter storms down the stairs. "What the fuck are you doing here, Tristan?"

Tristan keeps his arms extended at his sides. "I'm here to negotiate the terms of a truce."

"Truce?" Baxter shouts. "We'll never have a fucking truce—"

"Dad." Cody's quiet growl makes Baxter pause. "We should hear what Tristan has to say."

Baxter glares at his son, but Cody doesn't back down. "This dispute is getting out of control. We've lost ten shifters in the last week alone. We should consider what Tristan is willing to offer."

"Nothing could ever be enough," Baxter spits, but he returns his son's firm stare, becoming more subdued by the second.

The last time I saw these two men interact, Baxter walloped Cody over the head, smacking him down the same way my mother did to me, but now the tension between them feels different. The power between them has shifted, but I'm not sure exactly when or how.

I'm suddenly aware of a woman hovering in the doorway at the top of the stairs, but I don't get a good look at her. Her long, blonde hair and jewelry catch the light before she withdraws into the shadows.

"Fine," Baxter says between gritted teeth. "Be our guests. The party ends at midnight. Then we'll talk." He muscles up to Tristan, who remains impassive. "If you cause even a hint of trouble or ruin this night for my family in any way, I'll have you gunned down like the animal that you are, do you understand?"

Tristan doesn't blink. "I understand."

The second that Baxter backs off, Tristan's focus zeroes in on me again. He prepares to return to my side, but Cody steps between us.

"Tessa will come with me as collateral," Cody says. "To ensure good behavior."

Tristan tenses but remains where he is.

Cody offers me his arm like a perfect gentleman, but the tension around his mouth and eyes increases. "This way, Tessa."

CHAPTER THIRTY

$\mathcal{P}$ushing away the nerves invading my stomach as we ascend the stairs, I glance at Cody from beneath my lashes.

I'm intensely aware of Tristan watching us go.

"Taking me as collateral implies that I can't defend myself," I say to Cody. "I'm a little offended. What makes you think I'm not the greater threat?"

"I know you are." Cody's growled response is more genuine than I was expecting. His gold-flecked eyes gleam in the lights as we step inside the door. "I'm not a fool, Tessa. I may have walked a foolish path once, but I leaped off it when I witnessed its deadly consequences."

We enter a room with the same grandeur as the exterior: marbled floor, golden pendant lights hanging from the ceiling, and waiting to take my coat is a butler, who arches his eyebrow at me when it's clear I have neither a coat nor a bag to hand over.

The woman I glimpsed before is gone.

Music floods in from both sides of the house—a thumping beat from the door to the right and classical music from the door to the left.

Cody steers me toward the room with the classical music. "I'm sorry about your father."

I should play disdain, hide my true feelings, but I can't. My reaction is instinctive. I flinch away from Cody, snarls rising to my throat, hot rage shooting through me. "*You...* have no right to speak of him."

Cody lets me put distance between us, but despite my warning, he continues. "Your father was a good alpha. A good man. I don't know if he realized the extent of the bad blood between my father and Tristan when he got between them that night. He was trying to protect you and for that, I'm sorry."

I take another step away from Cody, a hot mess of confusion and anger rising inside me. "You're saying your father was coming after *Tristan* that night. He wasn't coming after me."

"My father doesn't give a fuck about you, Tessa," Cody says bluntly. "But he should. He's lost perspective. If he could see beyond his need for vengeance, he'd realize he's made an enemy of you." Cody's smile is cold, but his speech carries an element of respect I was not expecting. "You're an enemy nobody can afford to have."

Cody casts his burning stare at the door as Tristan steps through it, but he speaks to me. "Tristan was smart when he took you that night. He's a lot smarter than anyone realizes." Cody's focus shifts to my bare shoulder again. "You should consider the fact that he knew your father would die trying to protect you."

I shudder as the memories of the events before Tristan fought for me flood back. There was an instant when I thought I imagined an unspoken communication pass between Tristan and my father. If Tristan knew my father would die, then my father knew it too.

My breathing is too rapid. I look to Tristan where he remains just inside the front door. His emotions are still walled, preventing me from sensing what he's feeling, but mine are leaking all over the place. The clench in his jaw tells me I'm like a wailing storm to him right now.

I thought I knew the rules of the game we would play tonight—a game of innuendo, seduction, and lies that would lead to me ripping out Baxter Griffin's throat like he ripped out my father's—but Cody has snatched the foundations out from under me with his honesty after I've barely set foot through the door.

I take a deep breath, close my eyes, and hold it, exhaling my tension. *Pink ocean... orange grass... violet sunrise... yellow forest...*

It's been nearly a week since I needed to recite lists, but it calms me now. I remind myself that I'm not fragile or vulnerable. I'm strong enough.

My goal hasn't changed.

Baxter Griffin killed my father. He invaded Tristan's territory and attacked innocent shifters. I'm here to end him.

I open my eyes and reach for Cody's arm. "Well, then, now that we understand each other, let's pretend to be friends. You can get me a drink, we can make small talk, maybe flirt a little, and enjoy your brother's birthday party like civilized people."

Cody takes my hand, his palm closing over mine as he draws me back to his side. His smile tells me he'll play the charade, but his statement makes me shiver. "I'm sure we can be convincing."

A bar is situated to the far right of the room while circular tables set out with sparkling glassware are scattered throughout the space. Pendant lights across the ceiling give a soft glow. The room is filled with shifters, who all appear completely comfortable in their suits and dresses.

I bite the inside of my mouth and hold my head high when they stop in the middle of their conversations, casting sharp glances at us.

Cody narrows his eyes at them.

"Carry on," he says, an edge of command in his voice. He's acting more like an alpha than an alpha-in-training and it makes me wary. Baxter Griffin might still be calling the shots, but every pack transitions at some point. Cody might be preparing to take the reins.

The guests' conversations restart, although the stares continue, growing more intense when I sense Tristan enter the room behind us. He doesn't come after me, heading directly to the bar instead.

"Where's your brother?" I ask Cody as he leads me across the room, winding between tables. "I should wish him a happy birthday." It sounds like I'm trying to be polite, but I need to know where all members of Baxter's family are located.

Cody tips his head in the other direction. "Where the real fun is."

I guess he means the side of the house with the thumping music.

"And what of my half-brother?" I ask, not seeing Dawson in the crowd.

"He returned to his father in the Highlands." Cody gives me a sudden, cold smile. "He needed to lick his wounds."

Damn. As much as I'm glad I had an impact on Dawson, I wanted to deal with him tonight, too. I even hoped my old alpha, Peter Nash, might be here.

Cody leads me through the throng to a table on the far side of the room. "You should meet my mother."

The woman I glimpsed earlier rises from her seat. She's wearing an elegant mermaid dress with a silver overlay that trails behind her when she moves out from behind the table. She was conversing with another woman about the same age—maybe late thirties, although it's hard to tell since shifters age slowly once they hit their thirties—but it looks like a fake conversation.

Her attention is all on me.

She sips her drink as we approach her, her tight grip around the stem giving away her increasing tension.

"Mom," Cody says. "I'd like to introduce Tessa Dean." He turns from her to me. "Tessa, this is my mother, Charlotte."

She's shorter than me, petite, her blonde hair perfectly straight and cut to her shoulders. She casts me an overly bright smile. "Tessa. It's lovely to meet you. Finally."

This is the part where she says, *I've heard a lot about you.*

Instead, she says, "I hear you're a formidable opponent."

Her lips press together, her shoulders are tense, and her chest rises and falls a little too rapidly. I could interpret her body language in different ways, but the haunted look in her eyes gives her away.

She's fucking afraid of me—despite being surrounded by her pack and with her son standing at my side.

If her husband has lost perspective, Charlotte seems to have a crystal clear view of my strength.

Baxter appears at her side just then, angling between us, a defensive move, his lips pulled back as he snarls at me. I guess he disagrees with his son's decision to introduce me to Charlotte.

I expect Baxter to grab his mate and haul her out of there, but she's the one gripping his arm, raising her eyes to his as a silent communication passes between them, after which she turns to me.

"I look forward to speaking with you more later, Tessa," she says, her gaze flicking past me to Tristan. "Now, if you'll excuse me..."

Baxter takes her arm, waiting for her to choose their path before he accompanies her through the room, turning himself into a visual barrier between her and Tristan.

I stare after them, my lips parted. "Are they...?"

"True mates," Cody says, watching me carefully.

I guess I don't hide my surprise fast enough because he says, "You're shocked that my father has a protective bone in his body. You should be. He's an aggressive brute. He doesn't love anybody anymore. But he would die for my mother."

My heart sinks a little. The death of a true mate usually results in the death of the other. I'll be killing two shifters if I carry through with my mission tonight.

For the next hour, Cody and I make conversation. He gets me a drink—something strongly alcoholic—which I barely touch, before he whisks it away and gets me a water. He leads me to a small table in an alcove at the back of the room where we can sit without being disturbed. Like the rest of the room, the alcove is beautifully decorated with silver filigree across the walls and silver lights trailing across the table. I experience a pang when they remind me of the garden in Hidden House.

We start with small talk. The weather. The constant rain. Then we move on to music, favorite food, and movies, not that I've seen many. We've just moved on to hobbies when several young women venture over. They look my age, but they act young and are more than a little drunk. Judging by the fact that everyone else in this room is older, I suspect they've come over to this side of the house purely to see Cody.

He stands and greets each of them formally, another confirmation that he's transitioning to alpha. If he wasn't, he would have joined them already, possibly even taken me over there.

They eye me off with differing attitudes. One of them ignores me completely, another won't stop staring at me, and the third nearly sits in my lap trying to get Cody's attention.

I stop myself before I grab her arm and break it.

Cody takes one look at my face and rapidly dismisses them. They pout at him. "Come over to the fun side, Cody," they call as they leave. "We miss you."

"Boxing," I say, before the echo of their voices fades.

Cody's forehead creases. A quizzical smile breaks across his face. He lowers himself back into his chair, stretching his legs out in a deliberately relaxed pose. "Boxing is your hobby?"

I stare at the crowd. "Dad taught me. It was what we had in common."

I'd rather be fighting right now.

I seek Tristan across the room. By some miracle, he's in polite conversation with an older couple. Somehow, he's moving around the room, getting his bearings while I'm stuck in this alcove, making small talk, and getting nowhere.

Damn. My plan is unraveling. I didn't expect Cody to be so forthright with me. His honesty prevents me from using guile. I also didn't expect Baxter Griffin to have a true mate he would whisk out of the room. I'm sure he'll return at some point, but he hasn't yet. I need to get Baxter alone, but there's no hope of that right now. I need to think, revise my plan, and start again.

"May I use your bathroom?" I ask Cody.

"Of course," he says. His focus also shifts to Tristan, telling me he's as aware of Tristan's movements as I am. "It's back through the entrance, up the stairs, last door on the left."

He stands when I do and I'm not sure if he's going to follow me, but he remains where he is.

I take care maneuvering around the tables and groups of shifters, making sure I don't bump anyone. I consider whether or not to rejoin Tristan, but I think better of it. While we're split up, we appear placid and under control. Returning to his side could be seen as a hostile move.

I take a breath of fresh air when I emerge from the dining room, but I'm disappointed that the entrance isn't empty.

Two men stand at the bottom of the grand staircase, blocking it. Both are massive, although one is a full head taller than the other with piercing icy blue eyes and a shaved head. He's wearing black pants but no jacket, his white collared shirt unbuttoned at the top while the sleeves are rolled up over biceps that push at the seams.

The other man wears an eyepatch over his left eye. His long, dark brown hair is slicked back and his jacket conforms to his muscles. He smiles at me with a grin that makes me shudder.

They must both be supernaturals—my buzzing instincts tell me that they are—but I can't get a read on their exact species, which is even more unsettling. One of them must be blocking their supernatural status. If it were a magical barrier I could detect, then I might be able to break through it, but for now, I'll just have to accept that I don't know what they are.

"Excuse me," I say, trying a polite approach first. "I'd like to get past."

As I speak, another man emerges from the shadows at the side of the stairs.

It startles me that I didn't sense his presence sooner. In fact, even now that he's standing right in front of me, I can't get a reading on him.

"Don't mind my security guards," he says. "They're overzealous about my protection in situations like this."

His voice is rough, but also like honey, setting me on edge and relaxing me at the same time, an unnerving combination. He's tall, leaner than the other two men, wearing a suit of the darkest blue verging on black. His hair is light brown, but the more I stare at it, it could be dark blond, and his eyes are a shade of hazel green. Or maybe pale brown. While the details of his features are unsettlingly hard to determine, his jaw is shadowed with growth, his lips are perfectly curved, and high cheekbones round out his strong face.

I blink rapidly, my instincts screaming at me, but I'm not sure if they're telling me to run or stay.

"You're human," I say, drawing the only conclusion I can from the absence of any glow around him.

He leans on the balustrade at the foot of the stairs. "You've caused quite a stir, Tessa Dean," he replies, as if we're having an entirely different conversation.

I narrow my eyes at him in distrust. "What is a human doing here?"

The crease in his forehead disappears, a tension easing, but he doesn't extend his hand when he introduces himself. "My name is Ford Vanguard. Baxter Griffin is my business partner. We've made a number of profitable deals together."

"Sure." The hairs on the back of my neck have risen and my skin prickles all over my body. I rub my arms, disliking the tingling sensation. "Would you mind asking your men to step aside?" I say. "Cody directed me to go this way."

"Oh, he did?" Ford scratches his chin. "That's interesting."

The men continue to block my way and Ford continues to stare at me.

A growl threatens to erupt from my mouth. I take a swift step toward Ford, abandoning my polite approach.

"Tell your men to get the fuck out of my way or we're going to have a problem, do you understand?"

Ford breaks into a grin. "Ah, there's the woman I heard about."

He tips his head at his men, who promptly step aside.

Even so, the gap between them is narrow.

I turn on my side, make myself small, and angle between them while they watch me closely.

The big guy with the pale blue eyes glowers down at me while the guy with the eyepatch is impassive, weirdly distracted, as if his mind is elsewhere.

My arm brushes the big guy's bicep as I pass.

He's ice cold.

I jolt. My eyes fly wide.

I should have realized sooner. These two giant guys just happen to be at Baxter Griffin's party and they aren't shifters.

They're the ice jotunn and the warlock.

CHAPTER THIRTY-ONE

I fight every instinct in my body that tells me to defend myself against them.

Both men remain where they are, simply glowering at me. To strike out at them would start a battle I don't need right now.

Deftly slipping past them, I spin to keep the ice jotunn, the warlock—because that's who the eyepatch guy must be—and Ford Vanguard, the unsettling human, in my sights as I back up the stairs.

Some business deal this human has made.

Ford fixates on me, his focus unrelenting until I reach the top of the stairs and head to the left. I stop and press my back to the wall once I'm out of sight, expanding my senses and waiting to see what they do.

All three of them move on, and I exhale with relief when they don't follow me.

What I really need now is a place to catch my breath and figure out how I'm going to get Baxter Griffin alone. My time is running out. Tristan told Baxter and Cody that he wanted to negotiate a truce. If I haven't killed Baxter by midnight, then things will get ugly.

I hurry along the corridor, open the last door on the left, and stop.

This can't be right.

It's a bedroom, not a bathroom. Maybe Cody said to go right, not left.

I'm about to back out of the room when a photograph catches my eye. It's a familiar face I wasn't expecting to see.

Stepping into the room, I'm struck by the remnant scents inside the space. It's a distinctly feminine bedroom, beautifully laid out in pastels—a plush, pale blue armchair, a lavender bedspread, a large abstract painting on the opposite wall, a pair of heels set beside the armchair, one of them tipped on its side, as if its owner just stepped out of them and will return any moment.

I cross to the dressing table with the large mirror and the photograph tucked into the bottom of it.

My hands shake as I remove it.

Ella.

She's dressed in a strappy summer dress, smiling widely, her long, blonde hair falling across her face on one side, tucked behind her ear on the other, her brown eyes sparkling, her cheeks full of color.

Gripping the photo, I spin to the abstract painting hanging on the wall. My heart lurches into my throat. It depicts a forest by the ocean, the sun rising in the background.

The ocean is pink... the sunrise is violet... the forest yellow... and the grass... orange.

I sink into the chair in front of the dressing table. "Pink ocean... orange grass... violet sunrise... yellow forest..."

I need Ella's list more than ever, but it sticks in my throat now that I know where it came from—from her life before. Jemimah said that Jace looked outside of Tristan's pack for his mate, but I never dreamed he would look to Baxter Griffin's.

I'm too frozen to react when Cody appears in the open doorway behind me. He pauses there, filling the space with his big body before he steps inside and shuts the door behind him.

"Tristan didn't tell you about my sister, did he?"

Helen's voice whispers in my mind. *A little bit of knowledge can get you killed.*

Cody can't know that I've met Ella. Hidden House is hidden for a reason. It protects women whose safety depends on not being found. Cody wouldn't know that I've been there. He wouldn't know where it is. He might not even know that Ella is there. Probably doesn't even know that Hidden House exists.

I shake my head. "What's her name?"

"Ella," he says.

"She's beautiful."

"She's dead." Cody crosses to the painting and stands with his back to me. "Tristan got her killed. It's the source of the war between our packs."

I close my eyes, telling myself to breathe. I whisper the question that Helen taught me not to ask. "What happened?"

"She fell in love." Cody's shoulders are tense, his voice rough, but he remains where he is. "You've met Jace. He and Ella formed a true mate bond. Nobody wanted to get between them—not even my father—but Tristan's father was gaining a reputation for violence and bloodshed. We heard stories that would give anyone nightmares. My father tried to convince Jace to join our pack, but Jace refused to leave Tristan.

"So one night, Tristan himself shows up here. He tells us that he's going to challenge his father. He promises that Ella will be safe. He says it can be a new beginning between our packs, an end to any discord."

I remain silent while Cody turns to me, his fists clenched. "Ella went with him that night."

"What happened to her?" Again, the question sticks to my tongue like a betrayal of everything Helen taught me. But I need to know why the war between Tristan and Baxter began.

Cody shakes his head. "We heard nothing from her. Every attempt to contact Tristan or Jace failed and we went crazy with worry. A week later, we heard that Tristan's mother was dead. Stories finally started filtering through. Apparently, his father went on a rampage. He killed Tristan's mother and took Ella into the forest. We don't know what he did to her before he killed her."

Cody's lips form an angry line, the pain in his eyes making me shudder. "Tristan failed to keep her safe like he promised. He let his own mother die. It was another two years before he finally killed his father."

Ella's photo suddenly feels brittle in my hands. Tears burn at the back of my eyes. I want to tell Cody that she's alive, but I can't reveal where she is and I can't tell him how broken she is. It will only add fuel to his anger.

"You gave me the wrong directions to this room because you wanted me to know about her, didn't you?" I ask, unable to look up in case he sees my damp eyes.

"I wasn't sure how much Tristan told you about the history of the war between our packs," Cody says.

I give a shake of my head, biting at my bottom lip while I hunch over Ella's photo. "Tristan didn't tell me any of it."

Pieces are falling into place. The reason for the deep hatred between Baxter and Tristan is clear. The reasons for Tristan's frustration and rage, his inner turmoil are clear. His deep need not to lose another member of his pack, and his deeper need not to become like his father.

But what I still don't know is the role of the three-headed wolf in Tristan's past.

Swallowing, I raise my head. "What do you know about the three-headed wolf?"

Cody's forehead creases. "I don't know what that is."

The picture that was forming in my mind disintegrates again. Only Tristan and Jace have spoken about the three-headed wolf. Once between themselves, and then the other day Jace mentioned him to me. Jace said he hoped I would be strong enough to kill the beast. That Tristan was counting on me to do it.

Nobody in Tristan's pack has ever spoken about the white wolf and I don't believe Cody is lying to me now. But it seems strange that nobody else knows about him. Of course, I haven't exactly talked about meeting him, either.

When Tristan first spoke about the wolf, he said that the three-headed wolf was coming for him the same way it came for his father. The extent to which the three-headed wolf—the white wolf —is responsible for what happened to Ella is a frustrating unknown.

I shudder because I still only have pieces of the picture.

Now I'm here to kill Ella's father.

How can I do that when her family loves her and their hatred of Tristan is the result of incredible pain and distrust? Pain that Tristan shares?

I try to remind myself that Baxter Griffin's hatred might have been triggered by losing Ella, but since then, he has orchestrated brutal attacks on innocent wolf shifters. Even with that thought in mind, even though I scream at myself inside my head, I can't kill Ella's father.

One day, I hope that Ella will emerge, healed, from Hidden House and when that day comes, I need to be able to look her in the eyes.

"Tristan is not his father," I say to Cody as I rise to my feet. "You have to stop the systematic killing of his pack. They suffered at his father's hands. Now they're suffering at your hands. They don't deserve more pain."

Cody shakes his head, a slow side-to-side motion. "Tristan failed, Tessa—"

I snarl. "You've seen Tristan's strength and power! If he failed to protect Ella—if he failed to protect his own mother that night—then it's because *nobody* could have protected them! If it took him two years to kill his father, then he did it faster than anyone else could have."

I step up to Cody, inhaling the power that swirls around him, a power that allowed him to inhale my scent. I'm not afraid of him like I once was. I am calm. In control. But that doesn't mean I'm not angry.

"Destroying Tristan won't bring Ella back or heal your pain," I say.

"And yet you're here to kill my father for vengeance." Cody snarls, pointing out my hypocrisy.

"I came here to stop him," I say. "In any way I can. I see now that killing him isn't an option."

My plan was unraveling before, but now it's in ruins. I can't kill Ella's father tonight, but that won't stop me if he crosses into Tristan's territory intending to attack Tristan's pack.

Daring to grab Cody's hand, I push Ella's picture into his palm, trying to force him to listen to me. "Stop sending shifters across the border or I will kill them without mercy," I say. "Tristan's pack deserves a future."

I turn away from Cody, preparing to leave, but he catches my arm and spins me back to him, pulling me hard up against him. His head tilts down to mine as I catch my breath. One of his arms anchors around my waist; the other curves around my unmarked shoulder.

"Why do you smell different?" His voice is rough as he demands answers. Up until now, even when he spoke about Ella, he has been civil and in control.

Now I glimpse the animal he's keeping caged inside, the ferocity I experienced on the night of the Conclave. He wanted to claim me, even if he had to tear me apart to do it. He may have conquered his aggression since then, stepped off the path he was walking, but his animal's nature remains wild and wanting.

The sudden surge of strength in his hold tells me he's harnessing his wolf's ferocity and he won't let me go until I give him answers.

"Your scent made me crazy." He growls. "I was fucking savage toward you. And now I can't sense you at all."

I tip my head back with a whisper. "Because I'm more powerful now."

Despite my answer, his arms close tightly around me. His eyes narrow at me, and I sense him teetering on a precipice of choices. The desire in his eyes tells me he doesn't want to release me now that he's holding me.

"You're like a thorn I can't remove from my paw, Tessa," Cody says. "You're sharp. Painful. I've tried to rid myself of you. But you remain."

He fought me once and lost, but his appearance tells me he's spent the last two months making himself stronger and faster, the same way I have.

I've never used my magnified power to make someone do what I want. I'm not sure if I'll be able to accomplish it even now because I've never fully tested it, but manipulating Cody into letting me go is preferable to engaging him in a fight to free myself.

My hands slide beneath his jacket and up his sides, following the hard muscles of his back as I press myself closer to his chest, quickly leaning forward to nudge my cheek against his jaw.

I turn my lips toward the corner of his mouth as I allow my power to build inside me. It's a very different process to controlling my scent. When I control it, I must be calm, attain a level of peace and acceptance. But to magnify my power requires inviting its chaos, embracing the wild abandon that is not exactly out of my control but pulses with excitement.

My fingers tingle against Cody's muscles as I knead my palms against his back. My breathing increases and I arch a little. My lips are a breath away from his as my power flows through me.

All I need is for him to inhale.

"Is this better?" I whisper, preparing myself for a violent reaction. Even if he doesn't want to react aggressively, he might. I'm deliberately triggering his most basic instincts, forcing him to act without reason or logic.

He shivers as he inhales.

Whatever cages he was keeping on his animal disappear the moment his pupils dilate, a deep growl rumbling through his chest.

The civil, controlled mask he wore vanishes. Finally, I'm facing the wolf who tried to mark me at the Conclave.

"Fuck." He moves so swiftly that I'm still catching my breath as he pushes me back against the wall beside the dressing table, hooking my leg around his hips as he drives us into the solid surface.

His mouth descends to mine, a millisecond away from kissing me.

"Stop," I whisper.

He halts, his lips close to mine.

Relief fills me, but my power over him feels precarious, tipping between control and chaos.

I need to tell him to let me go now. I should do it quickly, but I suddenly wonder if I can plant a thought inside his mind, whether I can use this moment to influence the future.

It's a huge risk, but one I'm willing to take.

"You will be the alpha soon," I murmur. "When you are, you will have the power to change your pack's future. You must stop this feud with Tristan—"

Cody's arms clench around me. "My father won't give control to me until I prove I'm strong enough to challenge Tristan."

I shiver. "No, but you—" *Nobody is strong enough to challenge Tristan.*

"My father wants to destroy Tristan piece by fucking piece,"

Cody says. "Once Tristan's pack is torn apart, my father will send me to challenge Tristan, even if I end up dead. Revenge has consumed my father the same way bloodlust consumed Tristan's father."

Cody brushes the back of his hand across my cheek. "He doesn't realize that you're the one who can hurt us the most."

My feelings are in turmoil. Baxter's need for revenge is out of control. By coming here tonight, I've seen a side of Cody that I never thought existed. Maybe it didn't before the Conclave, but the memory that returns to me most sharply now is not when Cody fought me, but when his father backhanded him across the face.

Cody is caught in a different kind of cage. Facing down a future where he will fight Tristan—and he already knows how it will end.

I came here to control the future and now I feel it slipping through my fingers.

"Let me go," I whisper.

Cody's arms falls away from me. He steps back from me, shaking his head, trying to shake off my power over him. It won't be long before he's in control again.

I poise on the verge of hurrying away when his fists clench and I'm not sure whether it's his wolf speaking or him when he says, "I regret the past, Tessa. The fucker who attacked you is dead. I killed that part of myself. But now I'm caught between two ugly choices: Kill my father and take control of my pack by force. Or kill Tristan so that my father willingly steps aside."

He stares at the discarded picture of Ella that dropped to the floor when he grabbed me, and I know which choice Cody is going to make.

Oh, Ella.

I can't kill Baxter because of her and neither can Cody.

Unable to stay, I rush from her room.

I have to find Tristan. We need to leave. I can't go through with killing Baxter Griffin and the longer we stay here, the more danger we're in.

I won't breathe easily until we leave this place behind.

CHAPTER THIRTY-TWO

I race down the stairs, relieved that Ford Vanguard is nowhere to be seen. Ignoring the thumping music from the other side of the house, I hurry back into the dining room, scanning the crowd for Tristan.

Baxter Griffin has returned, standing at the bar, his sharp gaze boring into me as I hover in the doorway.

With a surge of relief, I spot Tristan standing in the alcove I left behind. He's leaning against the wall at the back corner, his shoulders hunched, setting down an empty shot glass onto the little table in front of him as I hurry toward him.

Trying not to cause a disturbance, I dart between guests to reach his side, grateful that the tables nearest to us are empty. "We need to leave—"

"No." Tristan's free hand clamps around my arm, shockingly tight, making me freeze.

His fierce eyes meet mine, his eyebrows drawn down, his mouth set in a hard line. A threatening growl hums in his throat. "We're not leaving."

I tug against his hold, suddenly wary of his anger. "Tristan, we need to go—"

I wince as he yanks me up against his chest, his hands gripping my waist so hard that it hurts.

He snarls. "Your emotions are wide open to me, Tessa. You

know what happened to Ella. You know I can't protect you or give you a future."

Forcing myself to breathe, to remain in control, I dare to slip my arms around his chest, my hands sliding up his back, slow and gentle, willing him to accept the embrace, even though he remains tense in my arms.

"We will have a future," I say. "We'll protect your pack. Together. We just need to find another way."

His chest rises and falls against mine, increasingly rapid, thrumming with growls.

"It's impossible," he says, grabbing both of my arms to push me away from himself. "Deceiver, coward, killer. As long as the three-headed wolf exists, you won't be safe. Nobody is. It has to end tonight. I can't ask you to kill him. I know that now."

"Tristan." My heart is a rapid hammer in my chest. "I don't understand what you're talking about."

Tristan said that his father was a deceiver, a coward, and a killer, but his father is already dead. I don't understand why he would reference his father in the same breath as the three-headed wolf, as if they are the same creature. "Please. Let's go."

"Please?" Tristan's voice is sharp. His gaze flicks past me—the quickest glance—to someone behind me. It's the same frighteningly clear assessment that he gave my father before my father was killed.

I shudder as I remember Helen's warning that Tristan has an unparalleled ability to perceive and neutralize threats. Cody also said Tristan is smarter than anyone knows.

Tristan inhales deeply, a moment of silence that feels like the second before thunder breaks. His mouth whispers across my forehead, the lightest kiss. Startlingly gentle.

"Don't ever beg, Tessa," he whispers. "Command. Order. Cajole. Rage. But never beg. My pack will need an alpha. They're your responsibility now."

My eyes widen. What is he saying—?

Before I can respond, he sets me aside so fast that I'm catching my breath as he strides from the alcove.

With a roar that echoes through the room, he lifts the nearest empty table and flips it, sending it spinning and crashing against the surrounding empty tables, knocking into them so hard that they slide across the room. Glasses shatter as they fall and silver table ornaments crash and roll across the floor.

The room freezes before it erupts. Shifters leap out of the way of the crashing tables. Some of them race toward Tristan. His fist darts out, knocking out the first man, sending the second sprawling, all while he rips off his jacket and tie and tears through his shirt.

While the shouting guests stream out, guards stream in, lining the room and pointing their guns at Tristan.

On the far side of the room, Charlotte suddenly appears in the doorway, along with Cody's brother, Cameron, but Baxter shouts for his guards. "Get my family the hell out of here!"

Charlotte struggles against the guards, kicking and scratching them, struggling wildly. She reaches toward the side of the room opposite Baxter and I follow her line of sight to Cody.

He stands against the back wall closest to me.

I suddenly know, without a doubt, that Cody was the one Tristan focused on before he started to rage because Cody must have been following right behind me.

Charlotte screams. "No! Cody! Don't fight Tristan. Don't do it!"

She struggles free of one of the guards, but another tackles her, lifting her off her feet and carrying her, still screaming, from the room. A third guard grabs Cameron, who struggles and shouts, but the guards succeed in hauling him away too.

In the center of the room, Tristan flips all of the tables that stand in his way until he's cleared a wide space in the middle.

I shudder.

It's a combat ring.

Cody meets his father's eyes across the room.

Baxter Griffin snarls and inclines his head sharply toward the combat ring.

Shadows grow in Cody's expression, his jaw clenching, his eyebrows drawing down. He vaults the nearest table to enter the ring, but he paces at the edge opposite Tristan.

"C'mon, Tristan," Cody calls. "Even if you win, the guards will gun you down. Is that what you want Tessa to see?"

Tristan levels his gaze with Cody's. "If you wanted her, you should have fought for her at the Conclave. You're a fucking coward."

Cody's jaw clenches as he smothers a growl. For a second, I think he's going to ignore the taunt. He must be smart enough to know that Tristan is goading him into a fight.

Cody tugs at his tie, slipping it from his neck before he slides off his jacket and unbuttons his shirt.

I smother my gasp.

Cody's tattoo is complete. A snarling wolf's head covers his muscled shoulder and the left side of his chest. The wolf is a glittering golden color—the same color as the golden flecks in his eyes—but it has a shadow, a second wolf snarling behind it that is insubstantial, made up of swirls of light.

The second wolf is cobalt blue.

I back up so fast that I bump into the wall behind me.

He had my wolf inked into his skin, a shadow of his own ferocity.

"Then consider this a fight for Tessa," Cody says.

My heart leaps into my throat as the two men stride forward without another pause. Their fists land on the first hit, thudding against each other's chests, their follow-up moves rapid and vicious. Within seconds, they're both bleeding from splits across their cheeks and chests, while claw marks cut across their biceps.

With a snarl of rage, Tristan leaps at Cody, shedding his pants and shifting midair from human to wolf so fast that it takes my breath away. I've seen Tristan at his full power when he fought Peter Nash for my life, but I smother my scream with my hands when Cody leaps and shifts just as fast.

My heart stops.

I suspected Cody was powerful, but I never thought he was as powerful as Tristan.

Their wolves meet midair, their claws ripping across each other's sides as they tumble and fall, tearing at each other. They are closely matched in size and strength. Tristan's wolf is as dark as coal, a savage beast, while Cody's is sleek and golden, his russet legs appearing as if they've been dipped in blood.

I bite my palm to stop myself from screaming at the sheer violence between them, my rising fear a sickening force inside me.

I don't want this.

I don't understand why Tristan chose this fight. He said that nobody is safe while the three-headed wolf exists, but he couldn't ask me to kill the wolf after all. He said that it has to end tonight. But all I can see is that he's trying to get himself killed.

One of the wolves yelps and it's too much.

I can't stand by and let them kill each other.

Vaulting the table that blocks my path, I run toward the snarling wolves as they separate, turn, and prepare to leap at each other again.

My power surges through me, out of control, panicked, cobalt blue power that gives me speed. I race between them, my arms outstretched on either side of me.

"Stop!" I scream as the wolves leap toward each other again.

Their wolves are like wrecking balls, unstoppable as they fly toward me, heavy, brutish, claws out. My hair flies around my face as I spin, my foot colliding with Cody's underbelly at the same time as my fist swings to thump Tristan's side.

But even with all my strength, I can't stop their momentum.

They veer off-course, one on either side of me, but their claws rake across me.

Cody's claws rip across my chest while Tristan's tear across my back. I need to arch and hunch at the same time, unable to protect either side of my body.

I drop to the floor, screaming with pain.

Both men tumble to the ground on either side of me. Within a blink, they shift back into their human forms.

"Fuck, no! Tessa!" Cody runs for me, but Tristan reaches me first, looming up over me, smashing his fist into Cody's face and driving him back, a harder hit than he used before.

Cody lands heavily on his side, but he leaps to his feet again, stepping toward me before Tristan's growl forces him to back off and pace around us.

Beyond the haze of pain, I'm aware of an extra disturbance at the side of the room, as if my scream drew even more attention. I catch a brief glimpse of Ford Vanguard with his two mercenaries looming in the doorway. Their hard stares burn into me before Tristan drops to his knees beside me, blocking them from my view.

"Tessa." He reaches out toward my back but doesn't touch me.

I can't see the damage there to know how bad it is. I'm hunched over my chest, nursing my wounds. The straps of my dress are holding on by threads. Blood slips down my chest and stomach, but it's a slow drip that tells me the wounds are rips across my skin, deep enough to cause me pain but not to kill me.

When Tristan reaches for my hands, trying to see my chest, I scream at him. "Tell me why you did this!"

Tristan flinches and his shoulders hunch. "Let me see the damage."

"No!" I snarl at him. "Don't fucking touch me until you tell me why you did this when we could have walked away alive?"

On the other side of the tables—on the side opposite where Ford Vanguard waits—Baxter Griffin leans forward, a gleam of anticipation in his eyes. I can read his thoughts as easily as if he speaks them. His gloating smile tells me he thinks he's witnessing the downfall of the most ruthless shifter, Tristan Masters brought down by a freak bitch.

Nearby, Cody wears a very different expression, the corners of his mouth turned down, the same as when he looked at the picture of Ella, a mix of deep regret and pain.

"The three-headed wolf is coming for me, Tessa," Tristan says, his voice rough. "It's better this way."

Better like this? How could this be better?

A sob tears out of me. I'm angry. I'm ready to rage. But I'm also hurting. Letting go of my chest, I spin to Tristan, allowing him to see all the damage, the cuts across my stomach and chest, my breasts barely concealed. Blood covers my hands and smears my clothing, dripping onto the tulle skirt.

"Then *I'll* kill him." I snarl, my voice rising again. "*I'll* fight him. I'm strong enough. You know that I'm strong enough to face any darkness."

"No." Tristan groans. His breathing is ragged.

Tears leak from his eyes, shocking me to my core.

"No, Tessa." He reaches out to grip my shoulders. "When I first inhaled your scent, I knew what you are. I know things about you, Tessa, but I need to take those secrets with me when I die. You need to live without the sins of your father weighing on your shoulders."

I jolt, fear striking through me, rising above my physical pain. I want to scream at Tristan to tell me what he knows. What does he know about my father? What does he know about me?

I remember all the way back to the night we first met. He leaned close to me, inhaled my scent, and told me that he had to be sure.

Clarity is sharp now.

"You knew my scent already," I whisper. "It was familiar to you." Somehow, he needed to be sure that my scent was what he thought it would be. "How did you know my scent?"

His expression hardens. "All that matters is that you have the strength to save my pack."

"I will!" My hands press to Tristan's cheeks, my blood smearing through his tears, trying to make him believe me. "Tell me where the wolf is. I'll go there. Right now. I'll end him."

Tristan closes his eyes. "He's right in front of you."

I shake my head. "Tristan... I don't understand..."

He opens his eyes.

As his gaze meets mine, his emotional walls crash down. His deepest impulses smash into me, a wave of darkness so pure that a scream builds in my throat. The darkness chokes me, a force so bloody, so full of hatred and malice and thirsting for pain that my scream fails and I can't breathe.

"He's part of me, Tessa," Tristan says. "The same way he was part of my father. And my grandfather, and his father before him."

The thirsty darkness rushes through me, growing, building, creeping toward my heart and curling around it, squeezing so hard that I fear my heart will stop beating.

"The deceiver. The coward. And finally, the killer," Tristan says. "They are the three personalities of Cerberus, my ancestor. The wolf whose three minds destroyed him. We can try to fight the impulse to lie. We can try to hide from our sins. We can rage against the need for blood, but eventually, our darker nature wins."

He strokes my hair from my face, nudges my lips with his, even though I'm drowning in his darkness and my screams can't escape.

"I am the three-headed wolf," Tristan says. "I will kill everyone I love. Just like my father did. Until someone is strong enough to end me."

CHAPTER THIRTY-THREE

*M*y scream rages through me, an incoherent wail that shrieks around the room. Tristan is tearing my heart apart. My wolf knows what needs to be done, but my human heart is breaking.

Tristan strokes my face before he draws back. "All you have to do is step aside, Tessa."

He rises quietly to his feet, pulling me with him.

I sense his physical pain where he allowed himself to be hit, where he didn't dodge blows, where he welcomed the wounds Cody inflicted. He could have really fought back—it looked like he was—but he could have *ended* the fight swiftly if he'd wanted to. The melding bond allows me to sense his heart hammering in his chest, a rapid beat.

His body is fighting to live while his mind has made its decision.

I don't know what he intends when he turns me toward Cody until he says, "Get Tessa out of here. Make sure she doesn't see anything."

There's a storm in Cody's eyes. The tattoo across his chest is smeared with blood, some his own, some Tristan's, possibly even some mine, but the ink isn't damaged. My wolf's silhouette is a perfect shadow to Cody's wolf within the tattoo.

His shoulders are squared, his incisors bared. I have no insight into his real feelings for me. When I tore away his inhibitions, he wanted me, but he also described me as a thorn in his paw, a pain he can't escape. I wonder now if his tattoo is a reminder that I am his enemy—the same way Tristan's tattoo is a depiction of self-destruction.

Now, Tristan is handing me over to Cody, willingly giving me to his enemy, requesting that Cody protect me.

I'm stunned as Tristan leaves my side and strides toward Baxter.

Tristan drops to his knees on the ground, bares his neck, and splays his arms out at his side, shouting at the same time. "Baxter Griffin! I want to make a deal."

It's a submissive pose, one wolves only make when they're surrendering.

Baxter shoves aside the tables that stand between himself and Tristan. His eyes are brighter than before, his smile cruel. "Name your terms."

"My life for my pack's," Tristan says.

Baxter folds his arms across his chest. His scars are hidden beneath his formal attire, but I remember them, curved and old, from the night I first saw him. "Repeat your offer so I understand you clearly."

"My pack isn't responsible for what happened to your daughter," Tristan says, keeping his neck bared. "I was prevented from killing my father that night. That's on me. My pack is innocent. They've paid a price they never should have paid. Take your revenge on me and let them live in peace."

Baxter's smile is triumphant. "I accept your terms. Prepare to breathe your last."

No. My objection chokes in my throat. I'm not bonded to Tristan, but I feel like my life is about to be ripped away from me, like it's my throat that is bared.

Baxter holds out his hand to the guard on his left, who gives him a dagger.

It's such an emotionless gesture that I want to scream. Every nerve in my body is on fire. Every beat of my heart thumps loudly. Every breath I take shrieks in my ears.

Tristan believes he's going to hurt and kill everyone he loves. He believes that his ancestor's curse will become his curse. He saw his father succumb to the darkness and now he thinks it will happen to him too. He chose me because he thought I'd be strong enough to kill him, like he had to kill his father. Jace tried to warn me; he told me I didn't know whose bed I was keeping warm, but I didn't understand his meaning. Helen tried to warn me too, when she told me that even the old magic of Hidden House couldn't control Tristan, that Tristan was more dangerous than I could imagine.

Tristan wanted me to hate him so that I would find killing him easy.

But there's a difference between him and his father.

His father didn't have me.

There has to be another way through this, a path that hasn't been walked before, a way to destroy the deceiver, the coward, and the killer before they take control.

I just need time to find it.

Right now, there's only one way I can buy that time, one choice I can make.

Just as I move toward Baxter and Tristan, Cody steps between me and them, blocking my path. His gaze flickers between my bloody chest and my angry eyes. "Come with me, Tessa."

"No!" My fist flies out.

Cody dodges the blow, but his evasive move allows me to duck around him.

Baxter prepares to grip Tristan's head with one hand so he can slash his throat with the other.

Tristan's emotional walls are back up, and now I'm getting nothing from him, no darkness, not even a shadow.

I slip between him and Baxter just as Baxter raises the knife.

My emotions are a volcano of anger and rage and fucking violent wrath, but I keep myself in check. My arm flies up in front of my chest, prepared to take the slash of the knife as I shout, "What will it take for you to leave Tristan and his pack in peace?"

"Tristan's death." Baxter snarls, gripping the dagger in his white-knuckled fist, ready to slash me with it.

My lip curls. "Don't lie to me. You lost your daughter—one of the few people you actually loved. You suffered without her. You're still hurting. So tell me again—what will it really take?"

Baxter's jaw clenches. "I want Tristan Masters to suffer what I've suffered."

My breathing is under control, more in control than I've ever been. "Then take me."

Tristan tenses behind me, his emotional walls suddenly slipping, revealing a fiery mess of anger and fear within him.

Baxter laughs. "You're his possession, Tessa. Tristan hasn't marked you. He has no love for you. Why would it cause him pain if you're taken away from him?"

My voice lowers, my speech careful, because I need Baxter to understand exactly what I mean. "It's the nature of my wolf that I can't bond," I say. "I will never have a true mate. But Tristan can."

"No." Tristan's whisper behind me is so furious that my gaze is pulled to him. His chest rises and falls rapidly as he shakes his head at me, growls rumbling in his chest. "Don't do this."

Only Tristan could make a plea sound like a threat.

Baxter's gaze narrows as he takes glances between us, a curious light entering his eyes. "What are you saying, Tessa?"

My human heart is in pieces. I saw the truth in Tristan's eyes when he nudged kisses all over my body, preparing me for his mark. I heard it in his voice when he told me that he couldn't ask me to kill the three-headed wolf. I felt it in his kiss when he told me never to beg. When he pulled down all of his walls and let me experience his true nature, the darkness that he allowed to rush through me nearly suffocated me—I felt it when we melded and I felt it again tonight—but his true nature also revealed the truth he's been hiding from me.

"I'm saying that Tristan Masters is bonded to me. I am his true mate. Even though he can never be mine." Tears burn in my eyes because even if my human heart loves Tristan, I will never feel what his wolf feels.

Tristan flinches, and then he becomes still, frozen as stone. His shoulders are hunched but it only serves to make him look more dangerous. He is the most powerful shifter I've ever met who is willing to give up everything for the safety of his pack but can't tell me what I mean to him.

I'm surrounded by enemies and my only ally is determined to end himself. But I won't let that happen.

The watching guards are a threatening force. Ford Vanguard

and his mercenaries are waiting in the shadows. Cody is pacing back and forth, and Tristan...

He snarls up at me. "You were meant to be my end, Tessa." His fists unfurl to reveal that his claws have raked across his palms and bloodied them. "You were meant to kill me and take control of my pack."

Our territory, he'd said. I remember the anger in his voice when he told Helen that he didn't have any heirs, no alpha-in-training, that *I* was the last hope for his pack. I never imagined he envisaged that I would lead them.

A tear slips down my cheek before I can stop it.

Tristan watches its path. His voice becomes a rasp. "You were meant to be *their* future, not mine."

Baxter is suddenly gleaming as he observes Tristan's reaction and the confirmation of my claim that Tristan has bonded with me.

I swipe the tear from my cheek. "Taking me away from Tristan will destroy him," I say to Baxter, my heart pounding in my chest. "Keep me here away from Tristan. In return, I ask that you leave him and his pack in peace. You will stop sending shifters across the bridges. You will let Tristan's pack deal with their alpha as they see fit."

A victorious smile grows on Baxter's face. I'm offering him the chance to rip Tristan's true mate away from him.

It's the truest revenge he could take.

It will hurt Tristan. Maybe tear him down.

But it will give me the time I need to find a way to keep Tristan from his father's fate.

"I accept your offer." Baxter drives the dagger into the nearest tabletop. "But you won't stay here."

What? My instincts reach screaming point when Baxter grabs my arm, his hand clawing around my bicep, scratching me as he yanks me away from Tristan.

Tristan jumps to his feet with a vicious snarl. He kept his rage in check when Cody patted me down, even when I flirted with his enemy, but his power rises now, telling me that he won't let Baxter take me away without a fight.

Sobs threaten to leave my lips. Tristan wouldn't fight for his own life, but he will fight for mine. I want to scream at him, hate him, loathe him, but I can't because I understand him. I understand his fear and his motives.

Baxter's descending incisors flash at me as he hauls me through the opening between the fallen tables and around the side of the room. He shouts at the guards, "Shoot Tristan dead if he tries to stop me. Wound Cody if he tries the same!"

Both Tristan and Cody growl behind me, snarling like caged beasts as Baxter drags me toward the door.

Baxter said he wouldn't let me stay here, so I assume he's going to throw me in a vehicle and take me somewhere else.

My heart jolts when he drags me toward Ford Vanguard, who peels himself off the wall, an expectant gleam in his eyes. Beside him, the ice jotunn glowers at me while a slow grin grows on the warlock's face.

There's a crash and Cody shouts from behind me. "Dad! No! You can't give her to that butcher!"

Two gunshots make me spin, my heart in my throat, but they were warning shots. One was at Cody's feet—I can see the chip in the marble—and the other at Tristan. A bullet hole smokes in the table that he vaulted.

Tristan halts only a few paces away from me. He's partially shifted, his teeth sharp and his claws descended, snarling at the guns pointed at him. His face is cut and bruised, his chest dripping with blood, and all of his rage washes over me, a final lifting of his walls.

I will fight my way to you.

"It has to be this way, Tessa." Baxter growls at me as he wrenches me forward so fast that I stumble. "You won't suffer if you stay here. My son would treat you too well."

With a final push, Baxter shoves me at Ford. "She's all yours."

I smack into Ford's chest. He catches me, his overly warm hands closing around my arms, strands of his not-quite brown hair falling across his not-quite hazel eyes.

He leans back to take in my torn dress, the welts across my chest, and the drip of blood slipping down my stomach and thighs. Reaching up to tug on my ruby red hair, he winds the strands around his fingers as dread rises inside me, a fear so deep that I fight my wolf's energy, fight to remain in control.

A pleased smile grows on Ford's face as he peers at me and, for a brief moment, his eyes settle on a single color.

Not hazel. Not brown.

Crimson red.

I'm frozen as he bends his head toward me and whispers into my ear. "You're mine now, little one."

Continue Tessa and Tristan's story in This Broken Wolf.

Then complete the series with This Caged Wolf.

THIS BROKEN WOLF: SOUL BITTEN SHIFTER #2

An urban fantasy romance.

This Broken Wolf.

I made a deal to save Tristan's life and instead, I fell into the hands of a monster.

The white wolf has me now and I am his to ruin. I thought I knew pain and fear, but nothing compares to this.

Tristan, the ruthless alpha whose destiny threatens to destroy him, has sworn to come for me. But if he does, he will put the lives of his entire pack at risk.

The white wolf wants me to start a war, but I'm strong enough to resist.

I will fight the pull of darkness that I sense growing inside me, my true nature that I'm only beginning to understand.

I will bite and tear and claw my way out of this.

This dark wolf will not break.

This is a full length urban fantasy romance, the second in the Soul Bitten Shifter series.

**Recommended reading age is 17+ due to sex scenes and language.

3. Assassin's Menace

4. Assassin's Maze

Assassin's Academy

5. Rebels

6. Revenge

The Monster Ball Year 2 Anthology

7. Assassin's Match - Novella

MORTALITY - COMPLETE

(Science-Fantasy Romance)

Mortality Complete Set: Books 1 to 4

1. Beyond the Ever Reach

2. Beneath the Guarding Stars

3. By the Icy Wild

4. Before the Raging Lion

Stand-alone fiction

The Crystal Prince (short story)

ABOUT THE AUTHOR

Everly Frost is the USA Today Bestselling and award-winning author of YA and New Adult urban fantasy and science-fiction romance novels. She spent her childhood dreaming of other worlds and scribbling stories on the leftover blank pages at the back of school notebooks. She lives in Brisbane, Australia with her husband and two children.

- amazon.com/author/everlyfrost
- facebook.com/everlyfrost
- twitter.com/everlyfrost
- instagram.com/everlyfrost
- bookbub.com/authors/everly-frost

CPSIA information can be obtained
at www.ICGtesting.com
Printed in the USA
BVHW070008140122
626141BV00003B/491